"You won't be able to tear yourself away as the story accelerates into a Tarantino-worthy climax and when you're left gasping in the wake of its gut-wrenching vigilante justice, you'll belatedly realize you learned a lot about a social travesty that gets far too little attention . . . *Livia Lone* is a harrowing tale with a conscience."

—Chicago Review of Books

"Everything you could want in a great thriller—a badass main character, an emotional and suspenseful plot, lots of high stakes, gritty murders and well-written action scenes."

—Night Owl Reviews

PRAISE FOR *LIVIA LONE*

AN AMAZON BEST BOOK OF 2016

A *KIRKUS REVIEWS* BEST FICTION OF 2016 SELECTION

AN AMAZON BEST BOOK OF THE MONTH: MYSTERY, THRILLER, & SUSPENSE CATEGORY

"An absolutely first-rate thriller . . . Emotionally true at each beat."
—*New York Times Book Review*

"An explosive thriller that plunges into the sewer of human smuggling . . . Filled with raw power, [*Livia Lone*] may be the darkest thriller of the year."
—*Kirkus Reviews*, starred review

"[An] exciting thriller . . . Eisler keeps a firm hand on the throttle of what could be the first of a rewarding series."
—*Publishers Weekly*

"Livia is a complex and sympathetic character . . . Readers of hard-boiled fiction, heavily tinted toward noir, may see in Livia something of Carol O'Connell's Kathy Mallory, also a cop with an abuse-filled past and an appetite for revenge."
—*Booklist*

THE
NIGHT
TRADE

ALSO BY BARRY EISLER

A Clean Kill in Tokyo (previously published as *Rain Fall*)
A Lonely Resurrection (previously published as *Hard Rain*)
Winner Take All (previously published as *Rain Storm*)
Redemption Games (previously published as *Killing Rain*)
Extremis (previously published as *The Last Assassin*)
The Killer Ascendant (previously published as *Requiem for an Assassin*)
Fault Line
Inside Out
The Detachment
Graveyard of Memories
The God's Eye View
Livia Lone
Zero Sum

SHORT WORKS

"The Lost Coast"
"Paris Is a Bitch"
"The Khmer Kill"
"London Twist"

ESSAYS

"The Ass Is a Poor Receptacle for the Head: Why Democrats Suck at
Communication, and How They Could Improve"
"Be the Monkey: A Conversation about the New World of Publishing"
(with J. A. Konrath)

THE
NIGHT
TRADE

BARRY
EISLER

THOMAS & MERCER

Text copyright © 2018 by Barry Eisler

Published by Thomas & Mercer, Seattle

www.apub.com

Amazon, the Amazon logo, and Thomas & Mercer are trademarks of Amazon.com, Inc., or its affiliates.

ISBN-13: 9781477820049 (hardcover)
ISBN-10: 1477820043 (hardcover)

ISBN-13: 9781477820032 (paperback)
ISBN-10: 1477820035 (paperback)

Cover design by Rex Bonomelli

Printed in the United States of America

First edition

For the memory of Major Douglas C. Patt (US Army, Retired), son of Arthur and Helen, father of Kara, Michael, and Gavin, loving partner of Vivian, who enjoyed these books and made them so much better.

1

Livia was warming up on the mats at Seattle Police Headquarters when her lieutenant, Donna Strangeland, came through the swinging doors at the far end of the gym. Alongside Strangeland was a big man in a gray suit, the jacket cut loosely—enough to conceal, say, a holster and a good-sized pistol. A visitor's badge was clipped to one of the man's lapels, but he strode in as confidently as though he owned the building. *Fed,* Livia thought. For one bad second, she flashed on what she had done to the senator and his men in that Bangkok hotel room.

But no, she was just being paranoid. If this had been about the senator, she'd be getting a visit from a platoon of FBI agents and the chief, not a single fed and the lieutenant. Besides, there was another possibility: a few weeks earlier, Strangeland had mentioned something about a Homeland Security joint anti-trafficking task force. Maybe that was what this was about.

Strangeland and the visitor walked past the group of men lifting weights in one corner and the two-on-two basketball game in the other, then stopped in the center of the cavernous space. Livia could see them conferring, but over the clank of the weightlifters' barbells and the squeak of the basketball players' sneakers and the reverberating dribble of their ball, she couldn't hear any of the conversation. Then Strangeland caught Livia's eye and motioned for her to come over. Whatever this guy was here for, it seemed they weren't supposed to discuss it in front of the class Livia was teaching.

Livia nodded an acknowledgment, then glanced at the six women cops limbering up around her. "Start from the guard," she said. "You know the drill. Protect the weapon and control the distance. Escape and create more distance. Draw and three-sixty. I'll be back in a minute."

She walked over to Strangeland and the man. He was black and completely bald, with a big pair of eyeglasses in green plastic frames. Mid-forties, maybe six-two and 220. She wondered if he'd played football in his younger days—he had the build for it, though it looked as though what had once been just muscle was now covered with a layer of fat. Maybe more time at a desk than in the field. He smiled as Livia approached—an exceptionally sunny smile she sensed he used to lull people.

"Sorry to interrupt," Strangeland said in her trademark Brooklyn-transplant accent, raising her voice over the sounds of the bouncing basketball and the music the weightlifters were playing. "Livia, this is Special Agent Little. Homeland Security Investigations."

Livia looked at him but said nothing. If he was expecting her to go first, he'd be waiting a long time. She'd known even before becoming a cop that people gave away a lot more talking than they did listening.

Little's smile broadened, maybe in recognition of Livia's composure. "Livia Lone," he said, conceding. He held out his hand. "I've been looking forward to meeting you."

They shook. He had big hands and a good grip, but he neither overdid nor underdid it the way some men would to demonstrate superior strength, or their views on equality, or whatever. She noticed that by saying her full name, he avoided having to choose between "Officer Lone," which might have seemed too deferential, and "Livia," which might have seemed too familiar. And maybe he was trying to build rapport, too, because a good interrogator knows there are no more beautiful words in the world than someone's own name. She'd read somewhere that if you walked up and said a person's full name three times, that person couldn't help but smile.

"What do I call you?" she asked, wanting to see how he would play that end of the introduction.

"Well, the full name is Benjamin Dixon Little, but most people call me B. D."

"B. D., then." She considered making a joke about a man of his size being named Little, but decided he'd probably been hearing cracks like that since he was a teenager.

Strangeland glanced at Little, then back to Livia. "Special Agent Little is here to talk to you about that joint task force I mentioned. I would have given you a heads-up, but I didn't get one myself."

Livia caught the deliberate rebuke, and so, apparently, did Little, because he said, "Apologies for that. Things are coming along a little faster than I'd expected."

It wasn't much of an explanation for a no-knock visit. Livia was familiar with the practice of dropping by for an interview without giving the person of interest a chance to prepare, and she didn't much appreciate being on the other end of it.

"I hope you won't mind," she said, "but for the next hour I have a class to teach. You're welcome to stick around and watch if you want. Or"—she glanced at Lieutenant Strangeland, suddenly inspired—"in fact, why don't you roll around with us? We usually have one of the big SWAT guys act as *uke*, but today it's just us girls. We could use your help."

Lieutenant Strangeland smiled ever so slightly. She knew Livia was messing with Little, and obviously didn't object. Maybe she'd even brought him down here with this outcome in mind.

Little glanced over at Livia's students, who were now drilling from the guard as she had instructed them—defenders on their backs, legs wrapped around their partners, protecting bright-green plastic training pistols while attacking the eyes, clearing the legs, scrambling free. The gym echoed with shouts of "Do not move!" as successive trainees escaped, cleared leather, gained distance, and pointed their weapons at their attackers, all the while doing a tactical visual sweep for danger at the periphery.

"This is a, what, a women's self-defense class?" Little asked, trying to buy time.

"Defensive tactics against a bigger, heavier attacker," Livia said. "What works on the street for someone like you isn't generally suitable for a small woman."

For an instant, Livia thought she saw something pass across Little's face. Wistfulness? Sadness? Disdain?

"You don't approve?" Livia said.

Whatever had opened up in Little's expression was suddenly gone. "I approve very much," he said.

"Livia's got a grappling background," Strangeland said.

Little chuckled. "Is that what you call Idaho state wrestling champion in high school and judo Olympic alternate in college?"

So Little had done his homework. And wanted them to know it, too.

"Have you had any training?" Livia said.

Little shook his head. "Not much."

She knew he was lying. *Not much* meant either none, or a lot. Probably the latter.

"Well?" Livia said.

Little glanced over at the basketball game. "I think that game over there would be safer."

Livia smiled. "But not nearly as much fun."

"Ha. Well, I'd plead the absence of a *gi*. But I expect you'd just offer to lend me one. And besides, I see you're all wearing street clothes."

Livia shrugged. "We try to keep it realistic."

There was a pause. Then Little laughed and loosened his tie. "All right," he said. "I guess I can't refuse. The honor of Homeland Security seems to be at stake."

"I'd like to stay," Strangeland said, "but I've got things to do." She nodded at Livia. The nod said, *I want to know what this is all about.* Livia returned the nod, and Strangeland turned and left.

Livia and Little walked over to the mats. "Good news," Livia said. The women disengaged and paused, watching them. "This is Special Agent B. D. Little, from Homeland Security Investigations. And he's volunteered to be our *uke* today."

Little gave the assembled women the sunny smile. "Well, *volunteered* might be a strong word, but yes, I'm happy to help if I can."

"Weapons against that wall," Livia said, pointing.

Little walked to the wall and did as she said, pulling off his jacket, setting it down, and then removing his belt, holstered gun, and spare mags. He set the gun belt down on top of the jacket, then took off his tie and glasses and added them, as well.

"Knife?" Livia called out to him, because it wasn't uncommon for cops to conceive of their firearms as weapons and their knives as tools. He shook his head. *Not a street operator,* she thought, confirming her initial impression. *Desk jockey.* Little added his wallet, keys, and watch to the pile by the wall, then walked back onto the mat.

"Okay," Little said, stopping a few feet from Livia. "I'm disarmed. How can I be of service?"

His overall friendliness seemed in line with his smile—something Livia sensed he would use to get people to underestimate him. She cautioned herself not to make that mistake.

"One problem we've seen again and again," Livia said, "is the blitz by a big attacker against a smaller cop—the kind that happens so suddenly the cop doesn't have time to get off line or access a weapon, and winds up falling to the ground or getting slammed into a wall, at which point the attacker presses his advantage. What we're doing is creating a kind of tactical pause within which—"

Without a word, Little lunged at her like a defensive lineman intent on sacking the quarterback. Somewhere far back in her mind, a voice was shouting, *This is exactly what he was setting you up for, what you should have expected . . .*

But the voice barely registered. Her body took over: dropping low as he plowed into her, her left leg coming up around his waist, her right heel planted in his crotch, her arms disrupting his grab and taking hold of his lapels as the two of them crashed to the mat. The impact was hard but was distributed all over her body—whereas Little absorbed it mostly through the foot jammed into his testicles. He grunted in pain but kept his weight on her, and she shifted her foot, kicked his leg back, and shot her leg up and around his neck in a triangle choke. She was right about the training, though, because he reacted immediately, planting a foot alongside her butt, dragging her closer, and bracing to come to his feet. Standing and then slamming was a common tactic for a larger, stronger opponent to employ when caught in the guard, and before he could manage it she released the choke, pivoted on her back, hooked one of his heels in a cupped palm, and kicked him onto his ass, using his backward momentum to pull herself forward and into a squat.

The tactical move at that point would have been to scoot back, create distance, and draw the practice pistol. But Little had been trying to make a point, and she was damn sure going to make one in return. So rather than scuttle away, she hopped forward and planted the sole of her right foot against the side of his face, rotating his head away and shoving it into the mat. He tried to roll with the pressure—exactly what she was looking for. She snared his left elbow, grabbed his wrist with her free hand, and dropped back to the mat, popping her hips up and straightening his arm to the limit. Little howled and tried to turn in to her, but between the foot planted against his face and the opposite leg across his chest, he was out of options. She cranked the arm bar harder.

"Okay, okay, uncle!" Little cried out, his voice distorted by the foot against his face.

Livia kept the arm extended, a millimeter from hyperextension. "You sure?" she said. "You don't want to keep going?"

"No, no, no, you've made your point."

"You going to be a good dance partner? Or are you going to try to trip me up again?"

"Hey, how stupid do you think I am? You win. I'll be good."

Livia released the arm and rolled away from him. She glanced around—the 360 perimeter check, a conditioned reflex. The women were all smiling. One of them, a senior sex-crimes detective named Suzanne Moore, called out, "That's what I'm talking about!" and started clapping. The other women followed suit.

Little sat up slowly, doubled forward from the pain of the ball shot and breathing heavily. He rubbed his elbow and nodded at the applause as though to say, *Yeah, okay, I deserved that.*

Livia held up a hand to the class, appreciative but also embarrassed. "Okay," she said. "Let's focus. What did I do wrong?"

"Not break his arm?" Moore offered. The rest of the women laughed.

Livia smiled. Moore was a good cop and one of the women who had taken Livia under their wings when Livia was a rookie.

"Seriously," Livia said. "What are our tactical goals?"

"Protect the weapon and control the distance. Escape and create more distance. Draw and three-sixty," the women said in unison.

"Correct. And when was my best opportunity to do that?"

"When you tripped him," Moore said.

"Correct again. A perfect opportunity. Now, I didn't take it because Special Agent Little here had a point he was trying to make, and I wanted to respond in a way I knew he'd understand."

There were some light chuckles, including from Little himself, and Livia continued. "But let's not confuse what sometimes happens on the mat with proper tactics on the street. Agent Little just did us all a favor—by showing how fast you can get body-slammed from the guard, especially by a bigger, stronger attacker. You know I love grappling, but the ground is not where you want to be, it's where you want to get up from. So today, let's drill the guard to the body-slam lift, to the heel hook, to the escape. Agent Little, you up for that?"

Little half smiled, half winced. "As long as it's the escape and not the arm bar, I'd be honored to be of continued assistance."

For the next hour, he was the perfect training partner, with a nice sense of how hard to push depending on the skill levels of his partners. And from the way he moved, Livia saw again that she'd been right in thinking he had some training—more, it seemed, than the standard hand-to-hand offered in military basic or to law-enforcement cadets. At one point, Moore tried to arm bar him, despite Livia's admonition that the point was escape, not further entanglement, but her technique was less refined than Livia's, and Little's counter had been sound, saving his arm from further injury.

When the hour was done, Little's stunt had been largely forgotten, replaced by a certain level of mutual respect and appreciation. The women collected their weapons, picked up bottles of water, and filed past him, shaking his hand and exchanging a few bluff courtesies. Moore was last. As she shook Little's hand, she nodded and said, "You're lucky my girl was in a good mood today."

Little smiled. "Yeah, that much I figured out on my own."

Moore returned the smile. "Okay. Now you know." She paused, then added, "Thanks for being a good training partner."

Little flexed his arm, which Livia knew would be sore for days. "My pleasure. Or at least it will be once I get some ice on this elbow."

Moore laughed and moved off, the squeak of her shoes on the polished wood floor echoing off the high ceiling. The basketball game was done and disbanded, the weightlifters departed, and once Moore had gone through the swinging doors, the only sound was the hum of an overhead air-conditioning unit.

Little flexed his arm again. His shirt was soaked. "She tried to finish what you'd started. I was lucky to get out of it."

Livia shrugged and handed him a bottled water. "One of my mentors. She's protective."

He nodded his thanks at the water, unscrewed the cap, and drained it, exhaling deeply when he was finished. "I don't think you need it."

"Anyway. It wasn't just luck. You've had some training."

"Not as much as I'd like. Mostly high-school wrestling. I should come by more often. Take your class."

"All the way from DC?"

"Why do you think I'm based in DC?"

"Just a guess. Homeland Security, right?"

"Other than the FBI, HSI is the largest criminal-investigative agency in the US government, with over four hundred domestic field offices and sixty overseas attaché offices. You know the work we do against human trafficking."

She certainly did. And Special Agent Little, it seemed, was too smart for her to play dumb with.

"Okay," she said. "Then where are you based?"

He smiled. "Oh, I move around a lot."

She didn't respond. Apparently he liked games, and there was no way to win this one. The best move was just not to play.

"I'm sorry about rushing you on the mat earlier," he said.

"Of course you are."

He laughed. "I mean, apart from you making me sorry. I've just heard so much about you, and I wanted to see for myself."

"I don't know what you heard. Or what you saw."

"What I've heard is, you can handle yourself and then some. And I saw that was true. I also hear you prefer to operate alone. Most of all, that you close cases."

"Who've you been talking to?"

"Lieutenant Strangeland, for one. She says you're the best sex-crimes detective she's ever seen. Of course, I wasn't supposed to quote her on that."

She knew from her own fitness reports how highly the lieutenant thought of her. So maybe Strangeland had praised her to Little. Or maybe he was bullshitting, to distract from other sources.

"What's your interest, Special Agent Little?"

"Please, call me B. D. And my interest is why I'm here. Is there someplace we could sit for a while?" He flexed the injured arm and smiled. "Hopefully with a nearby ice machine?"

2

Dox knew he needed to get the hell out of Phnom Penh. Probably out of Cambodia entirely. He'd told himself in the heat of the moment that Gant was nothing but a pissant, but he had to acknowledge now that he might have been rationalizing because he'd wanted to kill the man so damn much. With the benefit of hindsight, though, he was starting to realize that when word went out about Gant's head getting turned into a fine pink mist, and likely by the very guy Gant had hired to do the same to someone else, there might possibly be a bit of blowback.

So he walked south—skirting wide of the US embassy because said blowback would likely be coming from exactly there—and bought a cell phone for cash from a street vendor, then continued southwest toward the Olympic Market, armadas of *tuk-tuks* and motor scooters buzzing all around him.

It was eleven in the morning in Cambodia, so midnight in Langley, but he knew Kanezaki kept late hours. Hell, that boy worked harder than anyone Dox had ever known at the Agency—they ought to give him a damn medal. Though if they knew he was not above the occasional dispatch of a former marine sniper with considerable charm but a bit of a shady past, they'd as likely reward him with a prison cell.

He wandered, sweating in the tropical humidity even in his cargo shorts and loose tee shirt, periodically checking the phone's Wi-Fi settings for an unprotected Internet connection. When he found one, on the sidewalk in front of a dilapidated coffee shop, he paused to download the Signal app from Open Whisper Systems, then configured it for the call he wanted to make, looking up from time to time to check his surroundings. The Olympic Market was popular with tourists, and there were clots of foreigners among the crowds of locals, which made it a bit easier to blend. At near six feet and a solid 225, though, he would always draw a certain amount of attention—especially in Asia, where his sandy-colored hair and goatee were also conspicuous. Sometimes he liked to hide in plain sight by being ostentatiously loud and Texas friendly. But he also had the sniper's knack for retracting his energy, his presence, when he needed to, so that despite his size and whatever his surroundings, people tended not to take much notice of him.

When he was done with the configurations, he moved to the shade under a nearby palm tree and put the call through. The phone rang only once—either Kanezaki kept it by the bed or, more likely, he wasn't even sleeping. Then the familiar voice, crisp and professional: "Kanezaki here."

A second-generation Japanese American, Kanezaki's first name was Tomohisa, but he went by Tom. *"Buenas noches, amigo,"* Dox said. "It's fine to hear your voice."

There was a pause. "It's fine to hear yours, too."

"Read me the ID?"

At the outset of the encrypted call, Signal provided each user with a unique number. If the numbers didn't match, it meant someone was listening in. Kanezaki read the number aloud.

"All right," Dox told him. "We're good to go. Nice to know there are still a few means of privacy left in this brave new world of ours."

"Why do I get the sense you're not calling with good news?"

"Well, now you've gone and hurt my feelings. I thought just hearing from me was good news."

"Aside from that," he said, and Dox could imagine him smiling. "What can I do for you?"

"Okay, I'll get right to the point. Especially because you already have. I'm calling from Phnom Penh—"

"Oh, God."

That didn't sound promising. "What, you don't like Cambodia? The food is great and the women are beautiful."

"I should have known you'd be mixed up in this."

"Oh, hell. What have you heard?"

"We got a cable this morning from the embassy in Phnom Penh. Some guy got his head blown off at a restaurant alongside the Mekong River, and the UN official he was having dinner with says the guy claimed to be US intelligence. But according to this official, the guy never specified what agency, and there was no ID on his body. So the embassy cabled every member organization in the entire US intelligence community, asking if anyone could take ownership of the dead guy. So far, no one has."

"I think it's nice that y'all have your own community."

"You going to make jokes, or do you want to exchange some information here?"

"I don't see why it has to be one or the other."

"Okay, you've done the one. Now where's the other?"

For Kanezaki, intel was always the coin of the realm. And his greed for it was usually something exploitable. But only for something in return.

"All right, all right. I happen to know that the deceased called himself Gant. First name unknown."

"And you know this how?"

"Well, that's how he introduced himself when he hired me—he said to kill a guy named Sorm, Rithisak Sorm, who, he gave me to understand, is a notorious Cambodian child trafficker. But then I showed up and saw who this 'Sorm' really was—a guy I'd seen that very morning at the Raffles Hotel, surrounded by a bunch of foreign dignitaries, who looked like the damn Dalai Lama and I could tell was a decent man."

"You can tell that just by looking?"

A motorbike with high-output pipes went by, drowning out the background din of people and traffic. Dox waited until it had passed.

"Sometimes I can. Always had a good feeling about you, son, and I still do despite your suspect professional affiliations. Are you going to tell me I'm wrong?"

"Never."

"Anyway, once I saw the target I knew for sure there was something rotten in Denmark. Then old Gant came clean, told me actually the target wasn't Sorm, the target was a UN guy who was trying to prosecute Sorm for his crimes. And that Gant had to protect Sorm despite his shady dealings because he was some kind of US intelligence asset. I said fuck all that and sayonara, went back to my motorcycle ready for a clean getaway, and lo and behold, three Cambodian ne'er-do-wells are waiting for me in the darkness with knives. But luckily for me and unluckily for them, being a careful man, I took an unexpected route to the motorbike, so the element of surprise was mine. Plus there was the matter of I had night vision and they didn't. So our encounter ended happily for our hero and less happily for the villains of the story."

"Those were the bodies the police described? All shot with a high-powered rifle?"

"Barring a hell of a coincidence, I'd call it a match. There was a fourth, too—just a kid who they'd hired for five bucks as a lookout. I let him go."

"And then you went back and did Gant."

"Hell yes, I did. Fraudulent inducement I'm mature enough to just walk away from. I'll never do business with you again, but okay,

I'll figure nice try and we can just live and let live. Fixing to kill me on top of the fraud, though? Well, that kind of rudeness I cannot abide. Anyway, I just thought I'd check in and see what you might tell me. I'm hoping I haven't done something that could stir up undue animosity regarding the late and hopefully unlamented Mr. Gant."

"Understood. But like I said, as far as I know, no one's claimed him yet."

"Son, we've known each other long enough for me to recognize when you're trying to make something sound harder than it really is."

"Why would I do that?" Kanezaki said, and Dox could hear the smile behind it.

"Oh, I don't know. Maybe to extract concessions in return. So look, don't exhaust yourself or anything, but maybe you could do just a little discreet digging? This UN official—the Dalai Lama—Gant told me his name is Vannak Vann. Though I expect you already know that."

"Why do you expect that?" Kanezaki said, and again Dox could hear the smile.

"Because Vann's a material witness to a homicide, and the Cambodian police would have taken his name and shared it with the embassy. Look, I don't mean to be unkind, but I'm really not in the mood for too many games here."

There was a pause. Then Kanezaki said, "You're right. His name is Vann. He's the head of a UN task force called the Global Initiative to Fight Human Trafficking—GIFT. I know him."

"You know him how?"

"Come on, sources and methods. You know that."

Dox considered. If Vann were some kind of covert CIA asset, Kanezaki would never have let on anything at all. It must have been something more casual. An access agent, maybe. Or just a professional acquaintance.

"Fine. Well, I reckon Mr. Vann is still in danger, and I'd like to warn him."

"I'm not objecting, but . . . are you sure you want to get further involved in this, whatever it is?"

"Hell, how much further involved could I get than I already am? Besides, it wouldn't sit right with me to learn a week from now that someone finished the job and I could have done something about it and didn't. Think about it—the poor son of a bitch probably doesn't even realize he was the target, he probably thinks old Gant was. He won't think to watch his back, not even now. But look, it's not just what I have to tell him. Aren't you curious about what he might tell me? Don't you want to know more about what the US 'intelligence community'—of which you are a part—is up to with this? Not to mention what your tax dollars are funding."

He paused to let that sink in. Kanezaki was no greenhorn anymore, and part of his rise in the "community" was surely due to his knack for developing off-the-books sources of information like Dox—and sources of action, when action was called for. He was less able to resist a morsel of secret insight than Dox was able to resist a beautiful woman. Which was to say, not able at all.

"What are you trying to find out, exactly?" Kanezaki said.

"Who was behind Gant, for one thing. If I know that, maybe I can bury the hatchet."

"How do you mean? If you're going to bury the hatchet in someone's head, I can't help you."

"Where I bury it is up to them. Somebody made a dumb play that got old Gant killed. If they'll leave it at that, so will I. If not, they're going to have themselves a problem."

"But so will you."

"I'm assuming I already do. It's why I called you."

There was a pause. Then Kanezaki said, "It's interesting that this was about Sorm, or at least ostensibly about him. Because he used to be one of ours."

"What do you mean, 'ours'? And what do you mean, 'used to'? And you sure waited a long time to tell me the name *Sorm* meant something to you, if you don't mind my saying."

"Sorry about that. I just wanted a little more context first."

Dox let that go. He'd talked too much and elicited too little, and Kanezaki had taken temporary advantage, which was his training and probably his nature, too. You couldn't fairly blame a man for acting in accordance with his nature. You could only remember your own mistake so as not to repeat it next time.

He waited, and after a moment, Kanezaki continued. "Sorm is former Khmer Rouge. Started working with the Agency in 1979, right after Vietnam invaded Cambodia and the US started secretly arming the Khmer Rouge in response."

Gant had told Dox that Sorm was Khmer Rouge. The man sure seemed to have mixed in a lot of truth with his lies, which was generally the right way to go in these matters.

But as welcome as the confirmation was, he decided to act surprised. Kanezaki was a good man, but could sometimes be professionally slippery. "Khmer Rouge?" Dox said. "How old is this guy?"

"He was the nephew of Kang Kek Iew, nom de guerre Comrade Duch—the Khmer Rouge leader in charge of their prison and interrogation network."

"Interrogation . . . you mean torture."

"That's right. Sorm was only fifteen in 1975, when the Khmer Rouge took power. And nineteen when the Vietnamese invaded. He spoke fluent French—a lot of the Khmer Rouge leadership studied in Paris, and Sorm was born there. The Agency didn't have a lot of Khmer speakers at the time, and the Khmer Rouge promoted Sorm as the conduit for arms supplies, both because of his family ties to the leadership and because of his language skills."

"I thought the Khmer Rouge killed all the Cambodians who could speak other languages."

"They did. Apparently they weren't particularly attuned to irony."

"I'd call it hypocrisy, but yeah. So Sorm was your guy. But why 'used to be'?"

"We cut him loose after Vietnam withdrew its forces from the country."

"Why cut him loose? Didn't need him anymore?"

"More or less. We wanted to inflict some payback on the Vietnamese so badly after they beat us that we were willing to work with a genocidal regime to do it. But after they withdrew, that rationale was done. Simple cost-benefit."

"Come on, a guy like Sorm would still have lots of intel value, even after the Vietnamese withdrew. And yeah, sure, there's some public-relations risk in getting in bed with the Khmer Rouge, but you'd already done that for a whole decade, which is what I believe fancy economists call a 'sunk cost.' You're not telling me the whole story."

"You're not giving me a chance. You're right, it wasn't just the Khmer Rouge connection in general. I told you, Sorm was the nephew of Comrade Duch, who became the first Khmer Rouge leader to be tried by the UN-Cambodia tribunal on crimes against humanity and genocide for his role in administering the Khmer Rouge prison system. Sorm himself was in charge of the most notorious of those prisons—Tuol Sleng, where all but seven of twenty thousand prisoners were executed."

"That's the Genocide Museum today."

"Correct."

"This Comrade Douche, when they tried him, he implicated Sorm?"

"Correct again. It turned out Sorm was even worse than we knew. It wasn't just torture and murder. His specialty was sexual humiliation and rape—male, female, young, old. He would rape parents in front of their children. Children in front of their parents. Nothing was too grotesque for him."

"My lord."

"Yes. Imagine what it would take to distinguish yourself during five years of genocide on grounds of cruelty and sadism."

"But apparently he wasn't distinguished enough to frighten away the intelligence 'community.'"

"Listen, my friend, you're no choirboy yourself. You know that the best intel, maybe even the only truly worthwhile intel, comes from bad people. And Sorm definitely had a lot of intel goodies to offer. His contacts were extensive, he was a great access agent, and his knowledge of what was going on in various Southeast Asian separatist groups and insurgencies was invaluable. But still, there are limits. When we learned from Comrade Duch's testimony just how bad Sorm really was, we stopped using him."

Dox laughed. "You make it sound like principle, not public relations."

"I wasn't there at the time and it wasn't my call, but I don't see why it couldn't be both."

"I suppose. Call me a cynic if you like."

"Anyway. If the guy with Vann really was US intelligence, someone's going to claim him."

"Can you find out? I could contact the buddy who put me in touch with Gant in the first place, but I doubt he'd know anything himself. And besides, seeing how this whole op was supposed to end with me out of the picture, I'm not feeling especially trustful just now toward anyone who helped bring me into it."

"You think Rain could have set you up? I can't imagine him doing that."

Dox was horrified. "No, no, I'm talking about someone else, fellow marine from back in the day. Rain would never."

"Well, that was my sense, too, but you had me worried for a minute."

Dox snorted. If a man like Rain were after you, worrying would be nothing but a waste of time. Getting your affairs in order, and fast, would be more like it.

"Anyway," Dox said. "My marine buddy is a good man, but in the end a knuckle dragger without your remarkable access and keen insights."

"Now you're just trying to flatter me."

"Maybe, but that doesn't mean it's untrue. You're a division chief now, right? East Asia?"

"I am, though it took seventeen years to get here."

"Long enough to know where a few bodies are buried, I reckon. And where to go looking for the others."

He was expecting more protestations about how difficult and complicated it would be to find out more about Gant. So he was pleasantly surprised when Kanezaki said simply, "I've got a hunch. Let me follow up on it."

"A hunch?"

"Let's just say that not all the members of the US intelligence community have the same principles—or the same public-relations concerns—as CIA."

Dox smiled. "Well, I guess they don't call you Christians in Action for nothing. Or at least let's hope they don't."

3

Livia grabbed a cold pack for Little's elbow from the first-aid room, then led him to the tenth-floor cafeteria. It was late for lunch, and the room was mostly empty. Little bought coffee for himself and the mineral water Livia had requested, and they sat at a table overlooking Fifth Avenue, the outside traffic muted by the modern building's thick glass. In the distance, the waters of Elliott Bay sparkled under a clear blue sky. Livia was glad she'd ridden the Ducati that morning—a Streetfighter, and the fastest, best-balanced bike she'd ever owned. Maybe later she'd ride out to Alki Beach before heading home to her industrial loft in Georgetown. It had been a bad, wet winter, made bleaker by what she'd had to face from her past. But summer was here now, the darkness retreating, the days getting luxuriously longer, and she'd told herself the past was done. She'd faced it. And this time, buried it. Literally, in the case of poor Nason.

But watching Little as he carefully added cream and sugar to his coffee, slowly stirring it like a chef preparing a contest soufflé, she was suddenly uncertain. This couldn't be about Bangkok. But then why the surprise visit? Why the ostentatiously long devotions to his coffee, a show of relaxed confidence she knew was another attempt to draw her out with silence?

Maybe it was just habit. Well, she would have more information soon enough. In the meantime, the best move was to simply outwait him.

When Little was satisfied with his preparations, he lifted the cup and took a sip. "Damn, that is some fine coffee," he said, nodding in appreciation. "Seattle, where even police coffee is gourmet."

"You put enough cream and sugar in, I imagine you could be drinking anything," Livia said, though the truth was, she took her own coffee with a generous helping of milk and turbinado sugar. It tasted like her time with Rick, the adoptive uncle who had rescued her from horrors and who was one of the reasons she became a cop.

He smiled. "Well, I guess that's fair. Maybe I should have tasted it first, before sweetening it."

"Or maybe you just like to sugarcoat things."

That made him laugh. "I guess that depends on the topic."

That was a cue for her to ask what the topic was. But again she waited.

He took another sip of coffee. "You know, Livia, I don't want to show my cards until I'm sure you're in. But I guess you can't agree to be in until you've seen at least some of the cards I'm holding. So we're a bit stuck here."

"Really? I don't feel stuck at all."

He laughed again. "They said you'd be tough, and you're not disappointing me. How about this? Let me ask you a few preliminary questions. If you like my questions, and I like your answers, we'll take this a little further. If not, I'll thank you for the martial-arts lesson, you thank me for the mineral water, and life goes on."

"Works for me."

"Good. I hope you appreciate that I haven't been trying to hide how I've checked up on you. I've read your personnel file. Talked to your superiors. Read the results of your background check, your psych profile, everything. And same as for a good book, obviously I wouldn't have kept reading if I didn't like the story."

Having a federal agent dig into your past would be uncomfortable for anyone. For her it was worse. But for the moment, the only way she could respond would be with questions. And questions, she knew, could sometimes reveal as much as answers. So she said nothing.

"So here's the skinny," he went on. "If there's one thing everyone agrees on regarding Livia Lone, it's this: intensity. Straight-A student. State champion wrestler—and not in a girls' league, either, that was against boys."

For the second time, she thought she saw that odd look pass across his face. She didn't know what it meant.

"And then Olympic alternate with the judo team at San Jose State," he went on. "Top of your class at the academy. And your arrest-and-conviction record is off the charts."

Again she said nothing.

"But that's all just the what," he said. "The what is always right out in the open. I want to know why."

It seemed a harmless-enough inquiry. Which made her suspect it. "What do you mean?"

"I hope you're not going to tell me you just want to serve and protect. I'm sure that's part of it, and I'm sure it's noble. But I'm also sure it's not what gets you out of bed in the morning, or the middle of the night, for that matter, and makes you the great cop you are."

"You want to know what makes a great cop?"

"I want to know what makes you a great cop."

"The answer's the same. Compassion."

"All right. But where does all that compassion come from?"

She didn't like what he seemed to be implying. And what maybe he knew. "From being human."

"Human. Okay, I can see that. But people say you're like a warrior monk. A crusader. No interests, no hobbies, no life, beyond putting away rapists."

"You make it sound like putting away rapists is a bad thing."

"No, not at all. Like I said, just trying to figure out where it comes from."

"Got something to write with? Because it's complicated."

"Try me."

"I prefer rapists to be in prison. Is it not the same for you?"

Actually, she preferred them to be dead, but life was full of compromises.

"You're deflecting. I'm talking about what sounds like an obsession."

"You think I care too much?"

"Maybe."

"Maybe the problem is that people like you care too little."

She was getting tired of the dance. But she wasn't going to reveal more until he did. She knew she had more leverage. He was the one who had come all the way out here from DC or wherever. Who obviously had spent a lot of time evaluating her. He'd open up. All she had to do was outlast him.

"Oh, you'd be surprised at how much I care," he said, and for an instant she thought she detected genuine emotion in his tone. "And in fact, your singular focus is something I admire. But I still want to understand it."

In *admire*, she heard *want to use*. In *understand*, she heard *exploit*.

"Here's the thing," he went on. "Nobody seems to know about your past. It only goes as far back as your uncle—Rick Harris, in Portland, when you were finishing high school."

Only a lifetime of keeping secrets enabled her to conceal her discomfort at what she recognized as an interrogator's gambit—a direct probe into a likely sensitive area to elicit and evaluate a response.

The truth was, she knew SPD hadn't looked that deeply into her background. They'd talked to her professors and judo coach at San Jose State, of course, and received glowing recommendations. And they'd contacted Rick, who had told them how he'd taken in Livia after Rick's brother-in-law Fred Lone's heart attack. Rick was a hero with the Portland Police Bureau—a homicide detective with multiple decorations for valor—so his imprimatur was golden. Beyond which, SPD had wanted her badly: minority woman, straight-A student, collegiate judo star, and criminal-justice major made for an attractive combination. They didn't know that Livia had once been Labee.

"In fact," Little went on, "to the extent anyone is even aware of your past, there's a notion that you were some kind of boat person or other refugee, and the Lones adopted you. Not so unusual—Asian babies get adopted by white families all the time. Hell, some people think Lone is a Chinese name and you're not adopted at all, you're just Chinese American. The point is, no one really seems to know."

Was he threatening to tell people about her past? Why would he think—why would he *know*—this would make her uncomfortable? And did he know more than he was letting on—not just about her past, but maybe about her present, too?

But no, she was falling for another interrogator's trick, and a basic one: suggesting you knew more than you did, so the subject would feel he wasn't giving you anything you didn't already have. It helped to know the routine, though obviously knowing it wasn't a foolproof defense when you found yourself on the other end.

She gave him a long, bored look. "If they don't know," she said, "maybe it's because they don't care."

"Or it could be they don't care because they don't know. About your sister, I mean. About how you were both trafficked, and separated. How she wound up in a potter's field all the way in Maryland. I'm sorry for that, Livia. Truly sorry."

His use of Nason as some sort of elicitation tool was worse than offensive. It made her want to hurt him. A vestigial instinct, she knew. Nason was long since beyond protecting, but the instinct was inextinguishable, like the pain of a phantom limb. A limb Little was now deliberately prodding.

And he knew Nason had been buried in Maryland. It had taken Livia sixteen years and one dead rapist senator to learn that. Her initial, presumably paranoid suspicion that this visit was about Bangkok rekindled. Probably his next ploy would be to ask how she had learned what had happened to Nason and where she had been buried.

But instead, he said, "Is that where the intensity comes from? Childhood trauma?"

She took a sip of mineral water, deliberately casual. "If it makes you happy. I hate to think of the resources you spent on all this background. You could have just asked me."

"Well, that's the thing about the federal government. We have so many resources to waste."

"Look, it sounds like you already know everything about me. The what and the why. Or you think you do, anyway. While I still know virtually nothing about you. Is that the way you're going to play this? If so, you'll have to find someone else to psychoanalyze. I've got cases I need to get back to."

"You feel I've been trying to psychoanalyze you?"

She finished the mineral water and set down the bottle. "Reflecting the subject's words to encourage him to talk was one of the first things I learned about interviews. If I were stupid enough to fall for it, you probably wouldn't want to work with me. And if you're stupid enough to think I'd fall for it, I don't want to work with you."

He laughed and held up his hands, palms forward. "Okay, fair point. Enough fucking around, I guess. You're right, I think I know you. At least I hope I do. Like I said earlier, I just had to see for myself."

He cleared his throat and rubbed his hands together. "So here's the deal. HSI is trying to bust a trafficking ring in Thailand. We've had jack shit worth of success. I want your help."

So this wasn't about the senator. At least, probably it wasn't.

"What kind of trafficking ring?"

"The kind that's being protected by the Thai government."

Her heart started thudding in response to an adrenaline hit. Only two months earlier, she had finally learned the name of the leader of the group of men that had come to her childhood village in Thailand like monsters in a fairy tale and taken her and Nason: Chanchai Vivavapit. Chanchai Vivavapit, who, according to his *Bangkok Post* obituary, had been chief of the Central Investigation Bureau of the Royal Thai Police—the country's national police force. For sixteen years, she had fantasized about killing the man she had always thought of simply as Skull Face. But when she had finally done it, butchering him along with Senator Lone, who was both Skull Face's customer and his benefactor, it hadn't been enough. There were two other men in Skull Face's gang, men whose names she didn't yet know but who she still thought of as Square Head and Dirty Beard. And two others—the one who had been in the van, and the one who had whipped that little boy, Kai, in the field—men who had helped with the transit from their village in the mountainous northwest to the port in Bangkok.

And there was that girl. The little girl the senator had raped in his Bangkok hotel room. A girl about the same age Nason had been the last time Livia had seen her.

She would never be able to get that little girl's face out of her mind. She had beseeched Livia with her agonized eyes as Matthias Redcroft, Lone's "legislative aide," had led her, trembling and bleeding, away. And Livia, at gunpoint, had been helpless to do anything but watch.

If she were at all inclined to respond to Little's questions about her motivations, she knew, grappling with that demon of helplessness would be at the top of the list. Not that knowing the why ever had much impact on the what.

"May I take your silence as evidence of interest?" Little said.

She had been trying not to let it show, but she knew her excitement might have made it to the surface. Still, she said only, "You may take it as evidence that I'm listening."

He nodded. "Well, hopefully they're one and the same. So here it is. Over the last five years, HSI has sent three different agents to liaise with the Royal Thai Police. And yet our investigation has gone precisely nowhere. And this in spite of ample intelligence demonstrating that elements of the national police are intimately involved in every aspect of trafficking to, from, and within Thailand."

Her mind was screaming with questions, and she fought to push the urge away. This could be the chance she'd been hoping for. To finish the rest of the men who had helped Skull Face. To finally make every last one of them pay.

And even more than that: to find that little girl.

She focused on her breathing for a moment, the way she had always done before a match. When her excitement felt sufficiently in check, she said, "What do you think has been the problem?"

Little shrugged. "A lot of it is just burnout. Emotional exhaustion. The horror of trafficking . . . it's incomprehensible. It's natural for the mind to want to turn away from it, to rationalize that it's just a tragic aspect of a primitive foreign culture, something we Westerners of course disapprove of but are ultimately helpless to change."

Was he trying to play some kind of ethnic card with her? She said nothing.

"But you wouldn't do that, Livia, would you? You would never rationalize horror. Habituate to it. You're the kind of person who could stare horror in the face for the rest of your life and never once blink, isn't that right?"

"Is that your assessment?"

"Hell yes, it's my assessment. You want to disagree, go right ahead. But I doubt you'd be able to convince either of us. And look, obviously it's not just that you're the kind of cop who doesn't flinch or turn away. You're also ethnic Thai. You can blend. Do you still speak the language?"

Her native language was Lahu. She had learned Thai in school. And even that had been a long time before.

"I've forgotten most of it."

"Well, I'm sure it would come back quickly. And there's another advantage—you're a woman. They'll underestimate you."

She already knew she was going to say yes. But she also knew she had to continue to play it reluctant. The moment he sensed the answer was what he wanted would be the moment she lost her leverage.

"You don't have any Asian female federal agents?"

"We have a few, yes. But a federal agent would be wrong for this. We've tried that route and I told you, it's led nowhere."

"I don't understand."

"I want someone to liaise with the Royal Thai Police under the guise of learning more about international trafficking networks. A city cop, who combats trafficking at the street level. Someone who works the demand side, and could be even more effective via a closer understanding of the supply side. A holistic approach."

It sounded like jargon. Though to the people who approved the budget, she imagined it would sound cutting edge.

"You said 'under the guise.'"

"Correct. Not that there would be no independent value to the exercise— I expect there will be, otherwise the subterfuge would fail. But no, the ostensible purpose of your visit is intended to conceal the actual purpose."

She didn't like the way he had transitioned from "would" to "will." And from a generic "someone" to specifically her.

"And the actual purpose?"

"Well, to analogize for a moment to the war on drugs, we're doing street-level busts, we're getting points on the board, but cost is down, purity up, availability unaffected."

"You're saying the supply isn't being disrupted."

"Correct. Why are only street-level traffickers getting taken down? Because Thai officials are cooperating with, or complicit with, or protecting the higher-ups. Which is ultimately where the money flows. A street-level bust is like cutting off a tentacle. Hell, the tip of a tentacle. The animal will barely notice. We need to go after the head. So our actual purpose is, find out who's protecting whom, and how we can get around that protection. Or through it."

Now it was "our purpose," something she taught her women's self-defense students to recognize as "forced teaming," when a person suggests he has something in common with his intended victim to get her to drop her guard.

"How do you know so much about Thai government complicity?" she said.

"Well, obviously there's the fact that there are nothing but low-level trafficking busts. But beyond that, I'm afraid it's all classified."

She wasn't expecting him to show his cards. But the answer is always no if you don't ask.

"So you want me to go to Thailand," she said, her tone deliberately dubious.

"Bangkok, specifically. And only for six months. Maybe less, depending on how your investigation proceeds."

Six months to track Skull Face's men. To find that little girl. It was like a dream. But there was more she wanted, and she wouldn't get it if he sensed she was eager.

"Six months?" she said, recoiling as though shocked. "You know, despite your impression that I'm a monk or whatever, I have a life here. Cases to work. Classes I teach. People who need me. What makes you think I can just drop all that for your project?"

He leaned back in his seat and studied her. "In the end, it's a question of priorities. You can stay here in Seattle and fight the alligators. Or you can go to the source, and drain the damn swamp."

Well, he liked his animal metaphors. And actually, they weren't bad ones.

They sat in silence, regarding each other. She knew he wasn't going to speak first. That was okay. She didn't need him to go first to get what she wanted. She only needed to sweat him for a little while longer. So she let the silence spin out for almost a full minute before she said, "I want to see your files."

"Out of the question."

She sensed that was theater, intended to make a coming concession feel more valuable than it really was.

"I'm talking about the basis for the case you expect me to build."

"I understand that, but—"

"I'm not going to give you an answer until I have an idea of what I'd be getting into, who I'd be going after, and how much of a chance there would even be that I could succeed. If you're planning to send me off based on nothing but speculation, in six months I won't be able to accomplish anything. If you have solid leads and usable intel, then yeah, maybe there's a chance we could cut off the head, or drain the swamp, or however you want to put it. Otherwise, I'm not interested."

He looked away and drummed his fingers on the table. Rationally, she knew she had him. She was sure of it. But she was never going to have a better chance, or a better means, to go after Skull Face's men and find that little girl, and she wanted it all so badly she couldn't help feeling afraid he was going to say no.

After a minute, he looked at her and nodded. "The information is all classified. So just so you know, I'm breaking more than protocol here. I'm breaking the law. I'm showing you a lot of trust. I hope that's a two-way street."

"Show me your files," she said, relief and excitement washing through her. "And we'll see."

4

That afternoon, Dox was walking down a wide, dusty street west of the Bassac River and the Mekong just beyond it. He mopped his brow, taking in his surroundings, reflexively noting the places that would make for good sniper hides and ambush locations. Everything seemed copacetic. He was amazed at how, outside the city center, so much of Phnom Penh was practically rural. There were more bicycles than tuk-tuks, and so little engine din that as he walked he could hear insects buzzing in the trees. The buildings were smaller, too, the empty lots between them populated with scrawny chickens and lounging dogs. But there was a lot of construction, and he had a feeling that in just a few years, this district would be choked with fancy apartments and Starbucks signs. He was glad for the opportunity to see it before all that happened.

If Kanezaki came through and set up a meeting with Vann, Dox wanted to be familiar with the terrain, so he'd found the address of the Phnom Penh UN offices and decided to have a firsthand look. He strolled along, taking his time, and presently arrived at a four-story concrete building, one of the larger and sturdier-looking structures on the block. The blue sign in front said *Office of the High Commissioner for Human Rights* in both Khmer and English. An eight-foot perimeter wall, painted an incongruous gray-pink and topped with razor wire, surrounded the place, but compared with the US embassy, the security looked like not much more than an afterthought. There were several CCTV cameras affixed to the wall, which he didn't much care for. But no risk, no reward.

He kept on moseying along, casually taking in the terrain, imagining which way he'd run or attack back if this happened or that happened, making sure to feel like nothing but a tourist taking in the sights so anyone who noticed him would pick up a reassuring vibe.

When he was satisfied with his understanding of the neighborhood, he decided to head over to the Genocide Museum. He'd never visited it, feeling he was already sufficiently acquainted with the horrors of the world, but he had a little time to kill, and with what Kanezaki had told him about Sorm, he thought maybe he ought to have a look.

The museum was about two miles from the UN office, but the heat didn't bother him, and besides, in his experience, there was no better way to get to know a city than on foot. He headed north on Preah Monivong Boulevard, which at two lanes of traffic on either side was a touch noisier than he preferred for a stroll. So as soon as he could, he cut west and then headed north again on Oknha Nou Kan Street, a considerably sleepier little byway traveled mostly by a few tuk-tuks and bicycles, with small storefronts, dwellings, and abandoned lots to one side and a drainage canal to the other. There were few pedestrians, the locals being too smart to walk around in the heat, and he enjoyed the feeling of having the street mostly to himself.

About halfway to the museum, a blind beggar turned carefully onto the street and started heading toward him from about fifty feet away. The man wore big dark glasses and had one of those long canes that he was sweeping back and forth in front of him with his right hand, tapping the ground as he moved. In his left hand he held a cup, and Dox started to reach into a pocket so he could give the guy some money.

There was a pipe protruding from the crumbling foundation of the building to the guy's right. His previously straight path deviated left slightly and he avoided it, never having touched it with the cane.

Dox withdrew his hand from his pocket, irritated. A scam artist. They were everywhere.

They were about forty feet apart now, the guy still tap-tapping along. He was mostly bald, and what remained of his hair, shaved to stubble, was dark enough to be local. And the skin tone was nothing unusual. But though the dark glasses made it impossible to see his eyes, what bone structure Dox could make out seemed like . . . he wasn't sure. Not Cambodian, though.

A foreign scam-artist beggar?

Not impossible. Maybe one Khmer parent, one something else.

Then again, why would a blind guy, or even a fake blind guy, wear such big glasses? All he'd want would be concealment for his eyes—the rest would be deadweight on his nose and ears all day long.

Unless he also wanted to obscure his face.

Thirty feet.

Now that he was looking and they were closer, he noticed some other incongruities. Along with a pair of sneakers, the guy was wearing shorts and a tee shirt, and his arms and legs were ripped like those of a dancer or gymnast. Well, you didn't need sight to work out. But still it seemed odd, and doubly so if the guy wasn't in fact blind, because Dox had never seen a scam artist who was other than skinny and malnourished. This guy looked like he hadn't missed his daily whey-protein fruit smoothie in years.

And there were no scars on his knees and shins. A lifetime of getting around a city with nothing but a cane, you'd think you'd pick up a few dings along the way.

And there was one other thing. The most important and telling thing. The guy's vibe. It was getting more intense as they got closer. Like he was focused. Preparing himself to do something. Something big. Not many people could truly conceal that kind of intent. Rain could. So could Dox. But whatever was on this guy's mind, it was bleeding through on some level into his behavior—his posture, his pace, his gait. Not things anyone would ever really be able to articulate, maybe, but that your unconscious learned to read if you managed to survive the shit for long enough, and hoped to survive it longer.

But how could a hit be coming from that direction? You didn't even know you'd be going this way yourself.

His head was saying he must be wrong. But his gut wasn't having it.

Well, maybe there was a way to break the tie.

There was a demolished building to Dox's left. The curb in front had been reduced to a pile of rubble.

If he was wrong about the guy, he was going to have to put a major contribution into that cup. And he'd probably end up going to hell anyway.

Twenty feet.

He leaned down and with his left hand picked up a bunch of rocks, each about the size of a golf ball. Transferred the smallest to his right hand. And flung it directly at the blind man's face.

The rock sizzled in. At the last instant, Mr. Blind Man flinched. Then the rock landed, smacking him right below his glasses. He cried out and dropped the cup, which hit the ground with a metallic *clang*, and took a step back. He felt around his cheek for a moment, as though checking the extent of his injuries. Then his face contorted in rage. With his free hand, he gripped the shaft of the cane, pulled, and was suddenly holding a scabbard in one hand and a fucking sword in the other.

For one crazy second, Dox flashed on Zatōichi, the wandering blind swordsman from all those old Japanese movies. Then the guy tossed the scabbard aside, gripped the sword with both hands, and charged.

Dox felt a huge adrenaline dump. Sound faded out. Movement seemed to slow.

There was no time to deploy the Emerson Commander he had clipped to the front pocket of his shorts. Besides, bringing a knife to a sword fight was the kind of thing the Marines put on your tombstone as an object lesson to others.

Instead, he transferred another rock to his right hand and threw it like a fastball. He would have preferred another headshot, but he was more accustomed to a rifle than he was to rocks, so he aimed for center mass. Zatōichi stopped, turned to protect his right side, and took the rock hard in the left shoulder. Instantly Dox fed another rock to his throwing hand and launched again. He hit the same spot. This time the guy cried out. But then he rallied and started running forward again, albeit zigzagging now in an obvious attempt to make himself harder to hit.

Dox launched another rock. This one took Zatōichi in the neck and stopped him again. Dox launched another, hitting the guy in the chest as he twisted to try to avoid it and knocking him on his ass. It was obviously a lot of punishment, but then the guy got up and started zigzagging again.

Dox grabbed three more rocks and launched the first. They were only twelve feet apart now, and he was going for headshots. Zatōichi must have been hurting, because he stopped again, twisted, and tried to block the rock. But all that did was make him take the rock in the forearm, which was driven into his face, nearly causing him to cut himself with his own sword. Dox got off the second rock and it smashed the guy right in the glasses, which flew off his head. Yeah, some kind of mix, half-Khmer, half–something else.

The guy howled, and blood ran down his face. *Just run, you dumb son of a bitch,* Dox thought, chambering the third rock, which was almost the size of a fist. *Whatever they're paying you, it ain't worth being stoned to death.*

But the guy didn't run. Whether because he was exceptionally motivated, or exceptionally panicked, or exceptionally stupid, he looked at Dox, screamed a battle cry, and charged, holding the sword high over his head with two hands like he was some kind of damn samurai.

Except samurai wore armor. Zatōichi didn't. Dox gave himself an extra second to aim carefully, then launched the rock directly into the guy's face. It landed with a crunching *smack* and Dox could see the focus go out of the guy's eyes, but somehow he staggered forward, the sword wavering now but still held high. Dox took two big steps to his right, getting off the guy's path. His hand went to the Commander, but before he could clear it, the guy shuddered and did a weird half step that was straight out of the Ministry of Silly Walks. Then his knees buckled and he went down.

Which was fortunate, because Dox was out of rocks. Without giving the guy a second to recover, without even thinking at all, Dox stepped in, raised a foot, and smashed his heel down onto the guy's neck like someone trying to break a tree limb for firewood. Zatōichi's body convulsed. He managed to get an arm out in front of him as though to rise, and Dox stomped him again, and then a third time, and then yet again. By the fourth time, the guy was completely motionless.

He checked his perimeter. The few people around were staring, open-mouthed. He didn't see any phone cameras, but if there weren't any yet, there would be any second as witnesses emerged from their shock and confusion. So he put his head down, touched his fingertips to his forehead and his thumbs to his cheeks, kept his elbows in tight, and cut east down the nearest side street, back in the direction of Preah Monivong Boulevard.

It had all gone down so fast that he hadn't even had a chance to realize how scared he'd been. But two random tuk-tuk rides away from the scene, he got the shakes. He had the driver let him off and wandered into a temple complex—Wat Angk Portinhean. He walked in circles, keeping to the shade as best he could, feeling like the other visitors must have sensed his distress but unable to completely hide it. What the hell was that? Had it even happened?

The guy had clearly been there for him. Otherwise, what, he was just some random scam artist who happened to favor a cane sword, got pissed when Dox exposed him, and then attacked with such ferocity and determination that even if he'd prevailed, his rock-related injuries would have required six months to heal? No, thank you—the other available explanations didn't make a huge amount of sense, but that one made none. And besides, Dox had felt the vibe when the guy had seen him. It was like a missile acquiring a target.

But how could the guy have known where to look? Dox had turned off the phone after calling Kanezaki, storing it in a shielded case he traveled with precisely to ensure he wasn't tracked. He'd learned that lesson well, and nearly the hard way, a few years earlier in Bangkok.

And he hadn't discussed his plans with anyone. Hell, he didn't even have plans, mostly he was just wandering. The only thing he'd done that was even remotely operational was the walk past Vann's office.

Which, come to think of it, was something Kanezaki might have expected him to do, given that Dox had acknowledged he was hoping to warn the man.

All right, but still, he'd been careful the whole time to make sure he hadn't been followed, and anyway, Zatōichi had been coming from the opposite direction. And how could Kanezaki—even if he'd decided to betray Dox, which wasn't easy to believe—have put someone on him that fast?

Could it have been nothing more than bad luck? Someone deploying a contractor, or maybe more than one, throughout the city, hoping for a long shot?

No, that was about as likely as the enraged-legitimate-scam-artist hypothesis. Someone had sent this guy to take out Dox with at least some idea how to find him. And one way or the other, it had to be about Gant.

All right, he'd see what he could learn from Kanezaki. Watch his back extra carefully. And find a way to get a hold of a proper firearm, because the next time someone came at him with a sword, he was damn sure going to respond with more than a bunch of rocks.

He'd told Kanezaki that if Gant's people were willing to live and let live, so was he. Well, they'd sure gotten past that point in a hurry. On the one hand, it was troubling. But on the other hand, it provided some clarity about what he had to do next.

Which was: make whoever was coming after him understand it was going to take more than some Zatōichi wannabe.

Especially now. Because now he was pissed.

5

Late that evening, Livia rode the Ducati straight to her loft. The sun was still way above the horizon, the air cool and dry. Perfect riding weather, but she wouldn't take advantage of it this time. All day, as she'd worked her cases, interviewing witnesses, checking in with social workers, preparing to testify in an upcoming assault trial, she had thought about Little's files. She'd been badly tempted to log in to the secure site he had given her, but she knew once she started, she might not be able to stop. And besides, she wanted to log in from behind her own VPN rather than over the Headquarters network. No concrete reason, exactly; more a precaution. She knew what she was going to do to Dirty Beard and Square Head if she found them, and she didn't want to take a chance on anyone at Headquarters having a way to log her interest.

Of course, if his files had actionable information on two Thai cops who then died violently during her temporary duty there, it was possible Little might suspect. If anything went wrong, it might be worse than that. But she'd figure all that out. One thing at a time.

Her loft was in an industrial district—the top floor of a massive, hundred-year-old three-story building on a dead-end street badly misnamed South Garden. She loved it: isolated, empty at night when its machine-shop workers had gone home, the whole area nothing but brick and corrugated metal and razor wire, and not a fancy condo in sight. Investigating a burglary there when she had been a rookie had been one of her luckiest breaks ever. The owner was thrilled to have a cop living over the shop, and rented it to her cheap.

The sun was reflecting off the western windows as she dismounted, turning them into mirrors of the green Duwamish River and giving the façade the look of something both sentient and strangely stoic. She rolled the Ducati inside the first-floor corridor, locked the doors, and took the stairs to her loft. As much as she wanted to log in to Little's secure site right away, she had to shower first. It was a ritual—not just for her, she knew, but for other sex-crimes detectives as well—the hot scrub a way to wash away the filth, real and metaphorical, of daily contact with sadists and rapists and child abusers, people so vile it was hard to believe they were really human. No one who did what she did could deny the existence of evil, or avoid worrying, on some level, that by virtue of prolonged contact she might have been polluted by it.

She dried off, changed into jiu-jitsu gi pants and a sweatshirt, picked up her Glock, and glanced at the shrine in the corner—a small wooden Buddha she had carved as a teenager, an incense brazier, and a photograph of her and Nason from when they had been girls in the forest. For sixteen years after they had been separated but before Livia learned of Nason's death, she had spoken aloud to her sister every day, usually in front of the shrine. But since burying her little bird's remains in Chiang Rai, she had been trying not to. It was silly, really. Even when she didn't say anything out loud, the words were still in her mind. She no longer promised to never stop looking for Nason. Now she promised to never stop looking for the rest of the men who had hurt them.

You're being silly.

It's a ritual. There's nothing wrong with a ritual. Like your scalding showers. And it makes you feel better.

She sighed and walked over to the shrine. She set the Glock on the mat next to her, lit a candle and a stick of incense, and placed her palms together at her forehead in the traditional *wai*, closing her eyes and dipping her head forward as she did so.

"I'm sorry, little bird," she said. "Sorry I haven't been talking to you as much. But . . . I think have some new information now. Information that might lead me to the rest of the men. I'm going to find them. I won't stop looking. Ever. Not until every one of them is dead. Not until it's finally done. Until it's over."

She picked up the Glock, grabbed a protein shake and a jar of mixed vegetables from the refrigerator, then went to her desk, where she fired up the laptop. She punched in the URL for the secure site, and a moment later the screen was filled with an eagle-and-shield seal and the words *US Department of Homeland Security: Access Protected, Credentials Required.*

She smiled. Credentials she had. She typed in the first of two passphrases Little had provided, then navigated submenus until she came to an HSI page that said *Quis Custodiet.*

It was from the Latin aphorism *Quis custodiet ipsos custodes? Who guards the guardians?*

She felt the familiar surge of strength and determination and hate. The dragon.

I do, she thought, and punched in the second passphrase.

It was everything she could have hoped for: a cross-referenced database of key suspects among the Royal Thai Police, including photographs and all particulars. And though her eagerness made it painful, she spent a half hour querying and tracking down the connections of random names, to conceal her real interest in case anyone was logging her activity through the passphrases Little had given her.

Only when she was satisfied that she'd created a sufficiently thick fog for anyone watching did she allow herself to search for Chanchai Vivavapit—Skull Face. He was listed as deceased, which she already knew, having killed him with her own hands—but there was also an extensive bio that included every unit he had worked in, all the way back to 1995, when he had joined the RTP. All she had to do was query the cross-referenced members of those units and she found exactly who she was looking for. She would never forget their faces, or their smell, or the things they had made her do on the greasy deck of the ship from Bangkok when she had been only thirteen and such horrors had been literally unimaginable to her.

Square Head was Sarawut Sakda. Dirty Beard was Krit Juntasa. Along with Skull Face, they had been in a unit in the RTP Border Patrol, then Narcotics Suppression, and finally the Central Investigation Bureau. Dirty Beard—Juntasa—was still active duty, and still had the wisps of greasy whiskers she remembered, though now they were as much gray as black. But Sakda, the unusual contours of his head unchanged by the years, was listed as on medical leave. She wondered what that might mean.

She spent hours glued to the monitor, periodically going random to obscure her true interest, her keystrokes echoing in the silence of the cavernous loft, unused machining tools hulking all around like silent sentries in the dark. She paused repeatedly to take screenshots of key pages, for fear that Little might change his mind and revoke her access. She forgot about the protein shake and the vegetables. She lost track of time. And then, deep in the night, she had a cop epiphany, so clean, so elemental, that she was shocked she hadn't realized it sooner. She leaned back in her chair, eyes unfocused, mouth slightly agape as she tried to make sense of the outline of the new shape she could suddenly see.

All her life, she had believed that she and Nason had been taken randomly, just two unlucky girls sold by their impoverished parents from their village in the hills of Thailand, trafficked to America, repeatedly sexually assaulted in transit. When the ship transporting them had docked in Portland, they'd been separated. Livia had been put on another boat, a barge that continued inland all the way to Llewellyn,

Idaho, where she had been rescued in a police raid. A local industrialist, Fred Lone, feared and admired throughout the town, had taken her in, to public accolades for his and his wife's selflessness. And then Lone had begun systematically abusing her. This, too, she had attributed to bad luck, a hopeless karma. Even after she had killed him when she was seventeen, using a strangle she learned training in jiu-jitsu, she had never thought to question how someone's karma could have been as bad as hers. Maybe on some level she assumed her karma was punishment for having failed to protect Nason. Maybe she had just been too young to see things more clearly, too traumatized. But for whatever reason, she had never wondered whether maybe what had happened to Nason and her hadn't been karma at all.

Regardless, she had never stopped searching for Nason, never stopped waiting for the sole survivor of the police raid at Llewellyn, a white supremacist named Timothy "Weed" Tyler, to be released from prison. When he was, she squeezed new information out of him that made her realize she and her sister had not been abducted at random. Tyler's information led her in new directions, opened up trails she had thought grown over. As boys, Fred Lone and his brother, Ezra, who went on to become a US senator, had with their father relentlessly sexually abused their own sisters, killing one and driving the other nearly to madness. And then the brothers had become adults, and one day decided they wanted teen sisters again, sisters who loved and were devoted to each other as their own had been, who would do anything to protect each other, any sick thing the brothers could devise.

So two months earlier, Livia had tracked the senator to Bangkok. Before she killed him there, she learned that he had disposed of Nason years earlier. Nason, her little bird. She had recovered the body from a potter's field in Maryland, cremated the remains, and buried poor Nason in the emerald hills of Chiang Rai, where they had been girls together.

She leaned away from the monitor and blinked hard. Her tears fell to the floor. Then she blew out a long breath and started searching again.

She realized now that in the shock of learning the reality of their abduction, she had focused almost entirely on what had happened. Two sick brothers—one a wealthy businessman, the other a US senator with extensive contacts in Thailand because of his work on the Foreign Relations Committee and his focus on human trafficking. A craving to relive the depravity of their boyhood. A custom order to their contacts in Thailand for two sisters of the right age, the right appearance, the right level of mutual devotion.

Yes. Solving the imperative mystery of *what* had happened had distracted her from considering something secondary but also critical.

How.

How had the girls been procured? How was a custom order from the Lone brothers disseminated all the way from Washington and Llewellyn to the Lahu tribes in the jungles of Thailand's Golden Triangle? Who brokered such a far-ranging, specific, unusual sale?

Ezra Lone's contacts had been with the largest crime syndicate in Bangkok, a syndicate that had crushed its rivals in part due to Lone's patronage, a syndicate that filled orders more by quantity than type. Fifty Thai girls under age twenty, for brothels in Europe. A hundred Rohingya men for the fishing boats in the Gulf. The syndicate was about mass market, not bespoke. And she and Nason, she had belatedly learned, were an exceedingly unusual order, delivered to the specifications of two men with exceedingly detailed demands.

She remembered how Skull Face and the others had come to her village with a photograph of her and Nason—a photograph they had obtained from the girls' mother and transmitted to the Lones for their approval. Who could have had the reach to find two suitable Lahu sisters, and then get a photo of them to Washington and Llewellyn? And if the brothers had wanted to see the one photograph, they would have wanted others, as well, to ensure they were presented with a proper selection. Initially, she had thought the photo of her and Nason was just to confirm the men were taking the right girls. Now she realized the Lones must have wanted to compile a collection of prospects, so the brothers could have a variety to select from.

She continued with her queries, occasionally creating a screen grab, noting relationships, absorbing patterns, considering not just connections but also what might be missing.

The syndicate's relationship with the senator had been incredibly valuable to them. With his help, they had created a virtual monopoly on human trafficking in Thailand. He had provided them with an unusual order, something they knew would delight him if they could fulfill it properly.

Who? Who would they have gone to for something outside their core trafficking competency? Who was the spider at the center of that web?

By the time gray light was creeping into the sky outside the windows, she thought she knew. There seemed to be just one man who had been around long enough. Whose contacts were far-flung enough. Who spoke enough languages and knew enough border officials and invested in enough properties to keep all the local politicians in his employ.

His name was Rithisak Sorm.

6

Two hours following the first and hopefully only sword fight of his life, Dox was downing a lunch of *kuy teav* rice-noodle soup at a street stall alongside the Olympic Market. He was the only foreigner in sight—the Russian Market, so named for its popularity with Russian expats in the '80s, being the more popular tourist destination. He knew not everyone would want to know what went into Phnom Penh's take on *kuy teav*—pigs'-blood jelly, for one thing, and various chopped and ground internal organs, on top of it—but he had an imperturbable stomach, and anyway, when it came to food, he believed in doing as the Romans do. So after an epic surveillance-detection route to make extra sure he was clear, he'd found himself a plastic-covered table in the shade of a tattered green awning, and enjoyed his soup to the staticky sounds of Cambodian pop coming from a nearby AM/FM radio, the clamor of surrounding hagglers and passing motorbikes and tuk-tuks providing an orchestral accompaniment.

The phone was off and in the shielded case, he'd taken exceptional precautions in his movements, but still he was having trouble feeling as relaxed as he ordinarily would. It was just spooky the way Zatōichi had appeared out of nowhere. Dox couldn't figure out how the guy had found him. Meaning maybe someone else could find him the same way.

He lifted the bowl and drained the last of the broth, fired up the burner phone and logged on to the free Internet, and called Kanezaki. The thing with Zatōichi had spooked him, no doubt. And while he knew it was at least theoretically possible Kanezaki could have been behind it, he didn't really believe it. When Dox had first met him, Kanezaki had been nothing but an Agency newbie, albeit obviously a talented one. Since then, they'd been through so much together. Dox had been there for Kanezaki's first kill, and had talked him through it afterward. They'd worked on so many projects and accomplished a fair amount of good. Several times when the shit had hit the fan, they'd come through for each other, and in doing so had taken some serious personal risks. He just couldn't believe the man would turn on him.

Or at least he didn't want to believe it.

"I've been trying to reach you," Kanezaki said when the call had gone through.

"Yeah," Dox said, relieved despite himself to hear the familiar voice. "I've been keeping the phone off. You wouldn't believe the day I had."

He briefed him on Zatōichi. Maybe Kanezaki was a good actor, but he seemed genuinely surprised, concerned—and befuddled. He agreed that of course it had to be about Gant. And because it seemed hasty, improvised, and most of all, ineffective, they decided it was likely some sort of spasm, a last-ditch effort to eliminate Gant's cutout per the original plan.

"But let me tell you what I've found out," Kanezaki said. "Maybe that'll shed some light."

"That would be nice. I won't lie, if you've never been attacked by a guy who thinks he's a samurai, you might not be able to fully appreciate the way the experience stays with you."

"My hunch was right. Gant was DIA."

For whatever reason, Dox wasn't completely surprised. Though he wasn't exactly happy at the news, either. It really was beginning to look like Gant wasn't such a pissant after all.

He got up and started pacing, making sure not to stray beyond the limits of the Wi-Fi connection. "DIA?" he said. "You think the Pentagon would assassinate a UN official just to protect a damn asset?"

"Let's be careful to separate out what we know and what we think. We know Gant hired you to kill Vann, but told you he was Sorm. We think it was a DIA op, but it's possible Gant was freelancing, or fronting for another agency. And we think the op was about protecting Sorm, but so far, in that regard, we're relying entirely on Gant's claim. No corroborating sources."

"That's fair. But one thing I'm beginning to notice about old Gant was that he liked to mix a lot of truth with his lies. Remember, he wasn't expecting me to live a long, happy life after our conversation. So on the assumption that this op really was about protecting Sorm—"

"The question would be, what could Sorm have been giving the Defense Intelligence Agency that was so good they'd go to such lengths to protect him?"

Dox considered. "Maybe it's less a matter of what he gives them than it is of what he's got on them."

"Or both."

Dox paused and looked around. Beyond a riot of telephone and utility wires, the sky was a cloudy pastel gray. He tugged on the tail of his wet shirt and unstuck it from his back. The humidity, of course, and the aftereffects of his recent sword battle, but the news wasn't exactly cooling him off, either.

"Well," he said, "this does seem to be a bit of a pickle I'm in, I'll say that. I mean, if Gant's people think he told me anything about his affiliations, or revealed anything about Sorm and how the op was about protecting him, they're going to want to get that toothpaste back in the tube ASAP. Which is why they had those locals waiting by my motorbike in the dark after the hit. And maybe why I just had a damn sword fight. My lord, in the twenty-first century, too. Who could have imagined it?"

"The sword guy could have been exclusively Gant's man. Though I agree, it seems more likely he was sent in by Gant's people as a hasty Plan B when killing you right after the hit didn't pan out."

"Right, and you have to figure, since the plan was to kill me right after I killed Vann, they're looking for maximum closure here. If I'm rating the odds of Gant's people knowing about me at fifty-fifty, his people are likely giving similar odds about the chances of Gant having told me a little more than he ought to have. And why wouldn't he? He expected me to be dead myself five minutes later. You think these people are going to look at odds like those and just walk away? I mean, would you?"

There was a long pause. Then Kanezaki said, "No."

"Course you wouldn't. And neither would I. Which is why I have to assume the worst here. Gant's people likely know about me, and they're likely to figure I know more than I can be trusted with. Hell, for all they know, I killed old Gant because I had qualms about his op. Which wouldn't be so far from the truth, as it happens. This would be bad enough if it were just about retaliation. But it's not."

"You're right. It's also about protecting the integrity of their op."

"That's the way I see it. Because whatever the op is, it's important enough to kill a UN official over. There's going to be a lot of heartache for Gant's people if any of this comes out. Be a lot cheaper to just kill me and hire someone new to take out Vann."

"What are you going to do?"

Dox considered. His inclination was to kill a whole bunch of people, some of whom would have been direct threats, and others who would get the message: *Back the fuck off, or the next head converted to a fine pink mist from a half mile out in low-light conditions is likely to be yours.*

Barry Eisler

But Kanezaki had already claimed to be getting the vapors at the thought of Dox burying the hatchet in the wrong person's head. So he decided a little more subtlety would be the right way to go.

"I can't really know what I'm going to do until I know more about who. And why. And the place to start is with the UN guy. Mr. Vannak Vann himself. He's right here in Phnom Penh. If you really know him like you say, I want you to get me in to see him. And pronto, too. 'Cause I don't want to stick around here longer than I have to."

50

7

The morning after her late-night epiphany, Livia was sitting across from Donna Strangeland in the lieutenant's office. She had explained the opportunity with Homeland Security, and why she thought it would be good for the department and for her long-term effectiveness as a cop. But she hadn't made up her mind, she said, and to that end, she wanted to go out to Bangkok for a week or so right away to get the lay of the land and see if this was something she would be comfortable doing for the six months Little had mentioned.

Strangeland was a thorough listener—her posture, her expression, her nods and occasional grunts of agreement or acknowledgment conveying a sense of complete attentiveness to the speaker. It was a powerful approach for elicitation in interviews and interrogations, because there were few things people responded to more than the feeling of being listened to, really listened to. Livia realized it was having that effect on her, so she wrapped up her pitch and then waited.

A long moment went by while Strangeland nodded to herself as though carefully considering everything she had just heard. Then she said, "You want to tell me what this is really about?"

Livia looked at her, feeling wary. "I told you. Working the wholesale side of trafficking, the supply side. Learning how the networks operate from the other end. Bringing the knowledge back here and applying it at the demand side, the retail level."

Strangeland just looked at her, her brow slightly furrowed, her expression mildly skeptical, the overall impression that of a woman who already knew everything you knew, everything you were trying to hide.

"LT," Livia said, "I'm not really supposed to say more than that."

Strangeland shook her head. "I'm not talking about what Little wants from you. I'm sure there are levels to that, one for public consumption, others more need-to-know. I've worked with the feds. That's how they roll. But don't think for a minute that when Little told you the ostensible purpose of this joint operation and then shared the real purpose, he was actually leveling with you."

Not for the first time, Livia was in awe of the accuracy of Strangeland's instincts. "What do you mean?"

"I mean he's playing his own game, too. I could smell it on him. Why does he want you for this? You specifically. Yeah, you're a great cop, Livia, everyone knows that. But there are other great cops. Other cops doing outstanding work against trafficking. I'm sure he told you being Asian is a plus because you can blend, and they wanted a woman because blah blah blah, but I'm not buying it. What I can't tell yet is whether you are."

Livia didn't respond. The truth was, she hadn't sensed any additional angle. But was that because she hadn't wanted to?

"Why do you want to go out there early?" Strangeland continued. "It's not like you. You're smart. You never play it eager, even when you are. And this fed Little wants something from you, something you could bargain for. Instead, you're dropping everything to run out to Bangkok early, which tells him he's got you, he doesn't have to make concessions."

"You really think it seems that way?"

"I know it does. And so do you. So why?"

Livia considered. She didn't know how much the lieutenant knew about her past. They'd never talked about it. But maybe now was the time to open that door. Just a little. There was nothing like a layer of truth to conceal a lie.

"LT, do you know where I'm from?" The hesitancy in her tone wasn't feigned.

"You mean in the States? Or before that?"

"Then you do know."

"I know some. You were trafficked to America and rescued in a police raid. You think people don't know about that?"

"I don't know what people know."

Strangeland chuckled, not without compassion. "Livia, I gotta tell you, this is one of the things I like so much about you. It doesn't even occur to you how renowned you are."

"What do you mean?"

"It all happened in 2000, right? The articles are on the Internet. You went from trafficked girl to straight-A student and state wrestling champion in three years. People love a story like that. You're like the embodiment of the American dream."

Hearing that people knew even this much made Livia uncomfortable. It felt like a flashback to when she had been a girl in the Lones' house, struggling with English, and visitors would invariably tell her how "brave" she was and express sympathy for her "ordeal."

"I didn't think . . . I mean, who would want to look up those old articles?"

"Call it a paradox. When you offer so little, it makes you a mystery. Mysteries make people curious."

She realized she should have seen that herself. Maybe the problem was that she just hadn't wanted to.

"I guess I don't really like to talk about it."

"I think people sense that. And respect it."

"And you're one of those people. Thanks for that."

Strangeland shook her head as though it was nothing.

"You know I was trafficked," Livia said. "But do you know from where?"

Strangeland nodded. "Thailand, wasn't it?"

Livia realized she should have known. "Why do you even ask me questions? You already know everything."

"I know more than most, because I make it my business to know. And because I know more, I can't help but wonder why Little really wants you for this gig. Or why you want it for yourself."

There was a long pause. Livia said, "Do you have demons, LT?"

Strangeland shrugged. "Everybody does. Or at least, that's what I tell myself."

"Well, I have some. And I need . . . to see if I can face them. See if I can go back there."

"Are you sure this is even wise? If your demons are back there, why not just stay here?"

"They won't stay there. They never have."

Strangeland sighed. "What about Little? He's using you. I don't know for what, but he's using you."

"Maybe we're using each other."

"The one doesn't negate the other."

"No. But it offsets it. Give me a week. A week to figure things out and see how I feel about this opportunity. To make up my mind. Come on, I never take vacation. I'm due."

"I'd be a lot happier about a vacation than I am about this."

That sounded encouraging—like the prelude to reluctant acceptance. Livia said nothing. Her deception had been subtle, and she thought it would work. She didn't want the week to make up her mind about the task force. Not exactly. She wanted it to see how much she would be able to accomplish with Homeland Security's intel. Whether she would be able to finish Square Head and Dirty Beard. Whether she would be able to find that little girl. Whether she could find this man

Sorm, who she was now sure had been instrumental in her and Nason's abduction. Probably she couldn't do all that in a week, not even with the intel, but if she could, she might never need to go back.

Or maybe she'd need to go back for a long time. Or again and again. But none of that mattered. What mattered was being out there. Hunting those monsters. Protecting that girl. Finding the truth.

Strangeland sighed. "You know I'm not going to tell you no. What I'm going to tell you is to be careful. There are depths to this thing. I know that. I can't see them, but I feel them. And if I'm not seeing them, then neither are you."

"I'll be fine, LT. Really."

"Everybody always says that, Livia. But it isn't always true. This is personal for you. But personal and professional, they don't usually mix well. Not for anyone, and especially not for cops."

Livia nodded as though in understanding. On the one hand, she knew Strangeland was right. But on the other hand, Livia had indeed been mixing the personal and the professional since the moment she put on the uniform. Professionally, she'd secured hundreds of years of prison time for rapists. Personally, she had killed six of them. She'd won accolades for the prison sentences. No one knew about the others. But still, she'd been managing. Mixing the personal and the professional.

She didn't want to stop now. And even if she did, she wasn't sure she could.

8

Say what you would about Kanezaki, that boy got shit done. He'd contacted Vann's offices in Phnom Penh and arranged a meeting for that very day. "I told him you're an NGO worker," he'd explained to Dox over the phone. "With information vital to Vann's work with the UN Global Initiative to Fight Human Trafficking."

"Well, I am nongovernmental," Dox had said, "and my information does seem vital, so you didn't even have to tell a lie."

"I told him he could trust you. That'll count for a lot. But be careful about how much you say. I don't want this backing up on me."

"Roger that."

"And call me as soon as you're done. I want to know what you learn."

"Don't you ever sleep?"

"Power naps. And only when I need them."

He came to the office building he had passed before, again noting the cameras. He half expected another damn sword attack, but the street was utterly sleepy. He needed to get this done and get the hell out of Phnom Penh.

He walked up to a barred window adjacent to a metal door in the wall and presented the passport he'd been traveling with to the uniformed guard inside. "Adam Johnson here," he said. "I believe Mr. Vannak Vann is expecting me."

The guard examined the passport, then said a few words in Khmer into a landline telephone. A moment later, the door buzzed and Dox walked inside. Another guard appeared and led Dox into the building. He was taken through a metal detector, which was no problem because he'd hidden his knives and the burner under a cinderblock at a nearby construction site. Not having anything sharp on his person did leave him feeling a bit naked, especially following his recent close encounter of the pointy kind, but the type of cutlery he used for everyday carry would have been concerning to your average security guard, and memorable besides.

The inside of the building was warm. Whatever air-conditioning they had was obviously being fought to a standstill by the wet heat outside. Dox didn't mind it, though. He rarely used the air-conditioning in his own place on Bali.

They rode a cramped elevator to the fourth floor, then walked down a short corridor. In front of the office at the end of it stood the man himself—Vannak Vann, elegant despite the heat in a gray suit that matched a luxuriant head of hair.

The guard said a few words in Khmer—to which Vann offered a *sampeah* in thanks—and then left. Vann extended his hand. "Hello, Mr. Johnson," he said, his English lightly Khmer-accented, and his smile imbued with the outsized warmth Dox had first witnessed at the Raffles Hotel. And it was lucky he had, too. That warmth might not have shown up as well through an AN/PVS-14 night scope, in which case Dox might easily have just killed the man in reliance on Gant's bullshit information.

"Hello, Mr. Vann," Dox said, shaking his hand. "Anybody ever tell you you look a whole lot like the Dalai Lama?"

Vann laughed. "Sometimes. If I lose my hair, I'll probably be asked for autographs. Please, come in. Can I offer you something to drink? It's hot outside, I know, and not so much better in here."

"No, thank you," Dox said as they stepped inside the office. "I don't want to take too much of your time."

Vann closed the door behind them. The office was nice—much nicer than the building's exterior, with Khmer artifacts and artwork on a dark wooden desk and surrounding bookshelves. There was a lot of natural light—so much so that Vann hadn't bothered to turn on the overhead—and by reflex Dox scanned outside for the places a sniper would set up. Seeing nothing that alarmed him, he followed Vann's gesture to a wooden chair and sat. Vann took the chair across from it, without even a coffee table between them. It was a small thing, and maybe it was silly to think, but even the seating arrangement suggested this man preferred not to have barriers between people.

"It's a pleasure to meet you, Mr. Johnson," Vann said. "You come highly recommended by our mutual friend, Tomohisa Kanezaki."

"Well, sir, that's high praise, because Kanezaki's a good man. How do you two know each other, anyway?"

Vann smiled and the corners of his eyes creased into a series of delighted wrinkles. "Ah. I've known Tom since he was a young man. It's been most satisfying to see what he's made of himself."

It looked like Vann was going to be as circumspect as Kanezaki. You had to respect that kind of discretion.

"Yes, it has," Dox said. "And I'm glad he was able to put us in touch. You see, I have some information I think you might need regarding that man who was shot the other night."

Vann raised his eyebrows. "Yes?"

"The thing is, sir, that man wasn't the intended target. The intended target, I regret to say, was you."

Vann's brow furrowed, though seemingly more in confusion than alarm. "I'm sorry?"

"What I'm trying to tell you is that someone is fixing to kill you. And that man Gant was setting it up to happen. If my information is correct, you're out to prosecute a child trafficker named Rithisak Sorm. Gant was trying to protect him by removing you from the equation, so to speak."

There was the oddest sympathy in Vann's eyes. Damn, did the man not realize the danger he was in?

"How do you know this?" he asked.

Dox wasn't surprised at the question. "I apologize, sir, but I'm really not at liberty to say. I'm only here because I want to help you."

Vann nodded slowly. "That man Gant told me the same thing."

"He did?"

"Yes. He told me he had information relevant to my investigation. And he did. What he provided was useful. I assumed this was why he was killed."

"I don't doubt he gave you something real. That sort of thing seemed to be his stock in trade, as far as I can tell. But whatever he gave you was intended just as a kind of false bona fides, to convince you to trust him and let your guard down. So he could get you to a certain place at a certain time, where he'd have a man waiting in the dark."

Vann's brow furrowed again and he nodded as though to himself. This time, the expression looked like sadness. Dox didn't know what to make of it. He'd been expecting the man to at least be concerned, maybe even to freak out. Instead, he just seemed . . . well, sad.

A moment went by, and Vann said, "So you're telling me Mr. Gant was not trying to assist my work. Rather the opposite."

"Yes, sir, that's one way to put it, I guess."

"It's my own fault, I suppose. Even after all these years, it's hard for me to believe people would align themselves with such . . . evil. Don't they realize they have a choice?"

Dox had come intending to talk about intel and logistics. He hadn't been expecting the conversation to take a philosophical turn. "I expect they do realize," he said. "The choice they make is just the wrong one."

Vann looked at him and said gently, "And what about you?"

Damn, the compassion in the man's eyes . . . it really was like talking to the Dalai Lama. "Well, sir, I reckon I've done some questionable things along my merry way, but I've always tried to be one of the good guys. It's why I'm here today."

There was a pause. Then Vann said, "Was it you?"

Dox knew exactly what he meant. "Sir, I'd like to help you, but I can't answer that."

"It doesn't matter. Until they kill me, I'll continue my work."

"Well, sir, that's very brave and noble. But you have to understand, while you're going after Sorm with prosecution and all that—which I very much admire and respect, I should say—he's coming after you with something a whole lot worse. And you don't want to count on the next person they hire having my uncommon ability to recognize human goodness even from a distance."

He realized he probably shouldn't have said that, but hell, Vann already as much as knew.

"Is such a thing possible?"

"Hell yes, it is. Can't you sense it about me?"

"In fact, I think I can, even apart from the recommendation from our mutual friend. Though I'm afraid to count on it."

"Well, it would be foolish to just count on it. But luckily there are signs, even beyond that sterling recommendation. For example, have you noticed I haven't asked you a single question about where you live, or where you go, or when you go there? Nothing that would enable me to fix you in time and place."

"That's true."

"And I haven't asked for a cell-phone number, either. Here, do you know what this is?" He pulled out the shielded phone case.

"I'm sorry, I don't."

"It's called a Faraday bag. It blocks everything—Wi-Fi, Bluetooth, GPS, RFID, radio, and every kind of cell-phone signal. You turn off your phone, close it up inside, and no one can track you. You can get one in any electronics store. Or better yet, just lose your cell phone entirely. It's less convenient than having one, but it beats dying. I learned that from a friend of mine. Very smart man who's lived longer than most in a dangerous business in part because he eschews convenience in favor of security."

"What if you need to reach me?"

It was good the man was raising practical concerns. It showed he was listening. And it was encouraging that he seemed to be acknowledging, or at least contemplating, some kind of partnership here.

"If I need to contact you, I'll call you here at the office. If somebody comes out of the woodwork and says, 'Oh, I have important information for you, meet me at such and such a time and such and such a place,' or 'Give me your mobile number and I'll call you,' that person is not a friend, you understand? And you should vary your routes and times, too—when you come and go from work and where you live, and what time you do it, I mean. You need to watch your back until this thing is over."

"And when will that be?"

"I haven't figured all that out yet. But speaking of which, regarding the kind of information I'm not asking you about yourself, and that in fact I'm advising you not to share with anyone else, either—well, if you have any such information about Mr. Sorm, I'd be curious to hear it."

"And what would you do with such information?"

"Use it to protect you."

"How?"

"Look, Mr. Vann, we're from different worlds. But we both want the same thing."

"Which is?"

"Sorm neutralized, I'd say."

"I can't be part of something like that."

"I'm not asking you to be part of anything. I just want to know where to find him. And I won't lie to you, I'm not being entirely altruistic here. I think his people are after me now, too."

"I am genuinely sorry to hear that."

"I won't deny, it's been a bit distressing for me, too."

"But I don't know where he is. Up until a week ago, we had people watching him in Pailin Province here in Cambodia. But then we lost track. And he hasn't reappeared, not even in the usual places."

"What do you think is going on? He got wind of your investigation?"

"This is what I'm beginning to think. So many people seem to know of it—even you."

"I heard about it from Gant. Though I don't suppose that should count as a comfort."

"You already know a great deal, it seems, and Kanezaki said I should trust you. So I will tell you this: recently, a grand jury voted to indict Sorm in New York. The indictment is sealed. That is, secret."

"But Sorm got wind of it somehow."

Vann nodded, that sadness in his eyes. "I've worked for so many years to bring this man to justice. It seems he's finally won."

"What do you mean? What about your indictment?"

"The indictment is worthless if Sorm can't be brought to trial. I won't be the head of GIFT forever. And when I'm replaced, there will be a new head. With new priorities. Perhaps someone more amenable to the sorts of . . . inducements Sorm and his benefactors wield against justice."

"Maybe I can find him for you. So you could bring him in." He said it without really considering. Because he had no interest in just finding Sorm. The point was also to fix and finish him.

Vann shook his head sadly. "He has so many protectors. Even on the grand jury, there were jurors who were being pressured to vote not to indict. Ironically, this was something Gant claimed he could help with."

"Well, Gant's not protecting him anymore, if I may be permitted a moment of characteristic immodesty."

"Yes, but who is behind Gant? He told me only that he was part of US intelligence."

"Now you're asking the right questions. Kanezaki might be able to help with that." He didn't want to let on that Kanezaki could definitely help. He'd leave that to Kanezaki.

"Yes, I suppose that's true."

"Come on, don't look so glum. It might be the fourth quarter, but the game's not over yet. You told me yourself, Sorm's movements just now are unusual. You're talking about him like he's got it all dialed in, but it sounds to me like you've got him spooked and on the run. When people run, they have to break with the familiar. They make mistakes and they get spotted."

"Perhaps."

"Well, let's put our heads together. A little while ago, you mentioned his usual haunts."

"Yes."

"You've got eyes and ears in these places, but nobody's seen him?"

"That's right."

"Okay. You've been tracking this guy for years. I doubt there's anyone who knows him the way you do. Put yourself in his shoes. Where do you go if the usual places are too hot?"

"I don't know."

"Do you stay in Cambodia?"

"No."

"Then where?"

There was a pause while Vann considered. Then he said, "His most extensive protection, maybe even more extensive than here in Cambodia, is in Thailand."

"Are there any usual places in Thailand?"

"He has an interest in various establishments in Bangkok. And Phuket."

"But you've said he hasn't been spotted there. That you're pretty sure he's somewhere else. Where would that be?"

Vann nodded slowly. "I have an idea. But . . . I can't share it with you. I can't countenance what you would do with it. I'll go through the usual channels."

"You just got done telling me that somebody in your usual channels warned Sorm about this grand-jury indictment, which is the very reason he's now in the wind."

Vann didn't answer.

"Plus," he went on, "I told you, in addition to everything else, this guy is a danger to you."

"I want him to face justice," Vann said. "But my justice. Not yours."

"For a guy like Sorm, I'd say justice is justice."

"No. He is a terrible man. But still, a man. A person. My own judgment of him is not an excuse to go around the law. To subvert the proper order of things."

Dox had his own well-settled views about what constituted "the proper order of things." But damn it, the look on the man's face was so earnest it was practically irresistible.

"I'll try to find him," Dox said. "But I can't promise—"

"But you see, that is precisely what I need. I need you to promise. Or I won't tell you where I think he can be found."

Dox would have thought the man drove a hard bargain, but the truth was there was nothing hard about him. He was determined, obviously, but more than anything else, what came through in his eyes and expression was that damn compassion.

Maybe he really was the Dalai Lama, albeit with more hair. Because there was a power about him, a gentle power that made Dox feel almost . . . ashamed.

"All right," he said. "I promise if I find him, I won't give him my justice. I'll give him yours. I'll find a way to bring him in."

Vann looked deeply into Dox's eyes. It felt like the man was seeing into his soul.

"I hope this won't come out the wrong way," Vann said. "But . . . I'm proud of you. I was right about you being a good man."

Dox felt himself blush with confusion and embarrassment. "Well, let's not go too far here. I'm going to regret the hell out of that promise if Sorm winds up slipping away as a result. Or worse, killing you. Not to mention me."

"In the scope of the universe, and the arc of justice, my life is of little consequence."

"I don't know if I can agree with that."

Vann smiled. "Nor should you. It's something a person should only conclude about himself. All other lives are precious."

Dox shook his head in reluctant admiration. "When this is over, sir, I'd fancy a long conversation with you, maybe over a beer if that's your thing. You seem to have an interesting and admirable philosophy. But for now, I have a job to do, and I need your information to do it."

Vann put his hands together in a *sampeah*. "I would very much enjoy that conversation. As for my information, in talking with you just now about the usual places, the expected places . . . well, now that I'm about to tell you, I almost feel silly. Because I realize it's really just a hunch."

"No, no, believe me, I learned something valuable from someone just recently that started with nothing but a hunch. Don't think about it. Just say it."

"All right. About six months ago, a consortium of developers built a five-star hotel in Pattaya called Ruby, with a massive nightclub called Les Nuits. This is part of an ongoing effort to re-rebrand Pattaya—first there was sleaze, then there was the attempt to brand the area as something for a 'wholesome family vacation,' and now there's an attempt to combine the two with upscale clubs like Les Nuits."

Pattaya was a beach town about a two-hour drive southeast of Bangkok, known for its profusion of beer bars and go-go clubs, and though he hadn't been there in years, Dox had gotten to know it well enough back in the day. "Sure," he said, "a little like the evolution of Las Vegas."

"Yes, the American sin city is in fact a model for the Pattaya town fathers. At any rate, there were some indications at the time that one of Sorm's front companies had invested in the project, as a money-laundering scheme, but we were never able to uncover anything concrete. And I decided that our information was faulty, because Sorm's practice was to invest in smaller, lower-profile, and more . . . déclassé establishments, and mostly in Bangkok and Phuket. But now . . ."

"Now?"

"Now I'm wondering. If Sorm is in hiding, Ruby would be the kind of place I wouldn't expect. Certainly we made no mention of it in the indictment. He would have protection there—probably a lot of it. It would be comfortable. It would be . . . well, as I said, it's just a hunch. I doubt there's anything that could be done with it."

"Hell, Mr. Vann, I know low people in high places and high people in low places. You'd be surprised what I can do with a hunch like yours."

9

Three mornings after her conversation with Lieutenant Strangeland, Livia was in a cab en route to Saint Clare Hospice northeast of Bangkok, part of the Franciscan Foundation of Thailand, a haven for indigents gripped by the final ravages of AIDS. One of whom, it seemed, was Square Head.

Her decision to approach Square Head first was based on the simple fact that the Homeland Security database didn't list a mobile-phone number for Dirty Beard. But Square Head's mobile was known. And Livia still had the Gossamer cell-phone tracker she had permanently borrowed from SPD inventory. She had checked out one of the units, then returned the machine-press-crushed remains of a replica, claiming to have dropped it on the tracks at a Seattle Link Light Rail station just as a train was pulling in. The department had six of them, purchased with a grant from Homeland Security, as it happened, the formidable units all tightly controlled pursuant to a contract with the manufacturer. Alvin, the head of police inventory, had a crush on her and was happy to fill out the paperwork explaining the accident and requisitioning a replacement.

Which meant Livia had her own handheld cell-phone tracker, sensitive enough to place a phone to within a yard of its actual location and to listen in on calls. She had used it to track Senator Lone to his hotel room in Bangkok. And as soon as she'd checked in to a business hotel in Sathorn after arriving from Seattle, she had used it to locate Square Head. The thought of him slowly eaten alive by disease was enormously pleasing. Because he deserved it, of course. But also because, with just a little luck, it would make him more vulnerable. If she couldn't manipulate him, she didn't know how she would get to Dirty Beard. Or Sorm.

Or find that little girl.

Once they were clear of metropolitan Bangkok, the landscape changed dramatically, the cluttered canyons of concrete, the congestion of untold thousands of cars and tuk-tuks and motorcycles, the metastasized tangles of electric wires, all suddenly leveling off almost with a sigh, replaced by a far-reaching flat landscape of green rice paddies and a vast pale-blue sky. The windows of the cab were open, and for the second time in as many months, the smell of the air, the colors of the earth and sky . . . it all stirred powerful feelings of her childhood. Nostalgia. Sadness. Grief. Regret. She had spent her adulthood convinced the girl she had been was gone, the child cut off, the amputation site cauterized. It seemed this country insisted on proving her wrong.

About an hour outside Bangkok, they came to a modest road sign, so small as to be deliberately humble, with a message in Thai and English saying *Garden of Gospel Peace: Franciscan Friars 4 km.* The anxiety Livia had been keeping at the periphery pushed in harder, and she felt her heart begin to kick from an adrenaline hit. She closed her eyes and breathed slowly and deeply, the way she had learned to do before judo matches, the way she always did while hunting a rapist. This time, though, it barely helped. She was about to face a monster from her childhood. And everything else she needed to accomplish depended on success with him.

They turned off the two-lane blacktop and followed an older, rutted road, bleached gray by the sun. Other than two cars and a single motor scooter, they passed nothing but grass and swaying palm trees. It was a bucolic setting, detached, dreamy, and peaceful, and it was easy to see why the Franciscans would have chosen it. But the incongruity between the ambiance and what Livia was here for made her anxiety worse.

Come on, girl. It's a good plan. You've done this before. You've always made it work. Just breathe. Breathe.

After a few minutes along the rutted road, they came to another sign, again in Thai and English: *Friary, Retreat House, St. Clare Hospice.* Arrows indicated that the friary was one way, the retreat house and hospice the other.

The cab followed the sign to the retreat house. They passed a *sala*, the small Thai pavilion, under which stood a life-sized statue of Saint Francis, one hand open in welcome, the other holding a dove. Beyond it was a simple white building with a red-tiled roof. A sign read *Retreat House.*

She paid the driver, shouldered her backpack, discreetly used a bandana to pull the door handle, and got out of the cab, her damp shirt clinging to her back. She waited under the portico of the building for a minute, watching the cab head off, getting into character. She was a backpacker, visiting Thailand from San Francisco. In reality she was thirty-one, but she could pass for considerably younger, and right now, in her cargo shorts, tee shirt, light hiking boots, and boonie hat, she knew she looked like someone recently out of grad school, traveling on the cheap for a while before figuring out her next move. The clothes and backpack were all new, purchased in Bangkok just the day before, in fact, but she'd been sure to scuff the shoes and rub dirt into the pack and otherwise give everything a lived-in look that would pass anything less than a careful inspection. And the nonprescription horn-rimmed glasses she had on did a lot to alter her appearance generally.

When the cab had disappeared around a bend in the road and she felt like who she was supposed to be, she walked inside, finding a long room stretching left and right, empty but for dozens of chairs lining the walls. There was nothing remotely fancy about the facility, but it was clean and looked well cared for. In contrast to the heat and glare outside, the air was pleasantly cool and dry, the walls and floor illuminated only by rays of light coming softly through the windows. A ceiling fan spun lazily overhead. The space felt like a sanctuary.

A young Thai man in a brown habit was sitting behind a plain wooden desk facing the entrance. He stood when he saw her, pressed his palms together in a *wai*, and said in Thai-accented English, "Welcome to the Garden of Gospel Peace."

Livia used a heel to close the door, then returned the *wai* and approached the desk, her footfalls echoing off the tile floor. "My name is Andrea," she said. "Andrea Brown. I made a reservation online . . . ?"

"Oh, yes, Ms. Brown. I am Brother Panit. I have your reservation right here. For two nights, one person, one of the small rooms with air-conditioning, is that correct?"

"Yes, that's correct."

"Half the payment is due upon check-in, the other half one day before checkout—so tomorrow."

"Of course. Why don't I just pay it all right now?" She was carrying thousands of dollars worth of greenbacks and baht. She expected there was a lot she would have to buy during the week and wanted to be able to do so anonymously. Now she took fifteen hundred baht from one of the pockets in her shorts and placed it on the desk. About twenty-two dollars a night. A bargain, for an opportunity to indulge in a little solitude and quiet contemplation.

Or to interrogate and kill one of the men who raped you and your sister when you were children.

"Thank you, Ms. Andrea," the man said, placing the baht in one of the desk drawers. It was a small thing, but still bewildering—in a good way—to be a Seattle cop suddenly in a world where without a second thought people left cash in unsecured drawers.

Brother Panit escorted her across a pedestrian bridge spanning a fish-pond, through a garden filled with chirping birds, and along a stone path to a small, solitary bungalow. The door was unlocked, and Livia was careful to touch nothing as they went inside, just as she had been at the reception center. The space was Spartan: plaster walls, two single cots, a writing desk, a plain wooden chair. The bathroom was just big enough to contain a stall shower and a toilet. Brother Panit closed the door behind them, and suddenly the world was noiseless, even the buzzing of insects gone.

"Everything is so . . . quiet," Livia said.

Brother Panit smiled. "Always, but especially now, because hot season in Thailand not as popular to visitors. But all times the retreat is for meditative stroll. And meditative sitting in gardens. You can pass hours being with tropical tree and nature flower beauty. So yes, very quiet place. Peaceful."

And no security cameras, Livia thought. *Why would there be, in a place where they leave doors unlocked and cash in unattended desk drawers?*

She noted that his syntax, which had been natural—presumably because their initial exchange about the room was rote—had grown strained as their interaction progressed.

"Thank you," Livia said. "And . . . you have a hospice here, too, don't you?"

"Oh, yes. Saint Clare, named for Clare of Assisi, one of Saint Francis's first followers."

"Who are your patients?"

"The poor who are in the final stages of AIDS. Saint Francis's path to God lay in his compassion for lepers. Today we embrace our patients with that same love and happiness."

The syntax was natural again, so apparently they were back on familiar ground. He was accustomed to discussing the hospice with visitors to the retreat. Meaning her inquiries wouldn't feel unusual to him. Or memorable.

"I had a friend who died of AIDS," Livia said. This wasn't technically true, but she'd worked with victims forced to live with AIDS transmitted by the men who raped them. "Thank you for what you do here. I think you must ease a lot of suffering." The initial statement might have been untrue, but the accompanying sentiment was heartfelt.

Brother Panit offered a *wai* of acknowledgment. "I'm sorry for your friend. If you would like, you are free to visit the hospice. Only a few of our patients receive visitors. Mostly, the world shuns them, as it once did lepers. For such people, just to have a conversation can be a great comfort. And many of our guests find a visit to the hospice to be the most rewarding part of their stay. As we like to say: 'Work is love made visible.'"

Again, the natural syntax, like something memorized from a brochure, for frequent use. "Of course," Livia said. "Thank you for suggesting it."

Once Brother Panit had taken his leave, Livia inventoried the contents of the pack. Mostly it was just spare clothes and a few toiletries. The relevant items were even fewer, and all sealed in individual plastic bags: A long-sleeved sweatshirt. Two back issues of *Rider* magazine—"Motorcycling at Its Best." A roll of duct tape. And a pair of motocross gloves with wrist protection and carbon-fiber finger and knuckle inserts. None of it would be incriminating if anyone were to see it, and all of it was explainable by virtue of her enthusiasm for riding and plans to rent a bike sometime on her trip. Still, after changing into the sweatshirt, she took the pack with her. If things developed quickly, she wanted to be in a position to improvise and not have to run back to the bungalow for her gear. And if things went sideways, she wanted to be able to leave just as quickly.

She checked the Gossamer and confirmed that Square Head's phone was at the hospice—less than a hundred yards from where she stood. She wanted to go straight there, but that might seem strange. So she forced herself to eat a light buffet lunch, included in the room charge. She kept on the boonie hat—not much of a disguise, but along with the eyeglasses, not useless, either. Sunglasses would have been better, but there was a fine line between obscuring your features naturally and drawing attention by overdoing it.

Like the reception area, the dining room was illuminated only by the natural light coming through its windows. There were three other people inside—two women sitting together, and a man by himself, all young, probably Aussies or Kiwis, all looking like trekkers. Livia nodded an acknowledgment and sat alone with a plate of rice and vegetables and a bottled water. She had a cover story prepared in case she had to engage anyone, but it was better to make as few contacts as possible. And in a place built for solitude and quiet meditation, a little aloofness was natural enough.

After lunch, she spent some time strolling the gardens. They really were startlingly peaceful: devoid of the sounds of traffic, construction, conversation, or any other human activity, noiseless beyond the buzz of insects and the chirping of birds. Birdsong would forever remind her of Nason, who had been such an uncanny mimic as a girl, and though she knew it was silly, the feeling that Nason was somehow with her, keeping faith with her, still needing her, was always a comfort. And especially now.

She imagined how she would appear to a casual observer: nothing more than a visitor to the retreat, strolling and lost in thought. Satisfied, she started reviewing her plan, imagining every way it could be interrupted or otherwise go wrong, devising improvisations. She had already done all of this, of course, but planning based on a map or its equivalent was one thing. Everything always needed to be refined after contact with the actual terrain.

The sun was well past its zenith when she emerged from the shade of the garden trees and followed a series of signs along snaking gravel paths to Saint Clare Hospice. To Square Head.

I've found him, she thought, using the long-ago pet name for Nason. *And I'll use him to find the others.*

If anything, the hospice was even greener and more peaceful than the retreat. It consisted of a series of white buildings with red tiled roofs, all connected by walking paths lined with potted flowers and interspersed with shimmering ponds and copses of palm trees. She passed patients in hospital gowns playing board games, listening to a sermon from a friar in brown habit who looked Indian or Sri Lankan, receiving physical therapy from attendants in blue scrubs. Some of the patients, hunched and emaciated, were being pushed in wheelchairs by their healthier-looking peers. A few people nodded or waved, but no one paid her undue attention. It seemed Brother Panit was right—it wasn't unusual for guests of the retreat to also visit the hospice.

In one of the gardens, a Thai man who was probably her age but looked at least twice that, with shrunken features and overbright eyes, gave her a weary wave and a wan smile. "Hello," he called out in Thai-accented English. "Hello. Where you from?"

Even debilitated as he was, he'd made her instantly as a foreigner. Her features were local, but her posture, her gait, her overall presence . . . it all gave her away. It wasn't as bad as if she'd been a statuesque blonde, of course, but still, she would need local exposure and practice if she really wanted to blend.

She walked over and shared her cover story with the man—visiting from San Francisco after grad school. His English was poor, and she sensed he understood little of what she said. But having her engage him in pleasantries seemed to make him happy, as Brother Panit had said would be the case, and for a moment his reaction eased her anxiety about facing Square Head. Besides, it never did any harm to practice a cover story, especially with someone unlikely to understand, or to remember, the details.

After a while she excused herself and found a bathroom, where she removed the sweatshirt, took the magazines from her pack, duct-taped them around her bare forearms, and pulled the sweatshirt back on. Then she re-shouldered the pack and made her way to one of the white buildings. None of the doors was closed, let alone locked, and in fact there were no signs of any security whatsoever. And why would there be? What kind of security was required at a leper colony?

The building contained a single rectangular room, three hospital cots along either side. Despite the open doors, the air smelled strongly of soap and disinfectant, none of it quite enough to conceal the odors of urine and disease beneath.

All the beds were empty save two adjacent at the far end on her left. She walked slowly up the center, her heart pounding. In the near bed was a woman, a blue gown loose as a sheet over her wasted body. Her eyes were closed and she was twitching slightly, whether from a dream or disease, Livia didn't know.

In the bed beyond that was Square Head.

He lay on his back, slightly twisted away from her, both legs bent sharply, one against the bed, the other vertical. His body was skeletal beneath a formless blue gown, emaciation rendering his overlarge head more prominent than ever. His nose was hollowed out above a taped-on oxygen tube, his eyes enormous in their sockets, his knees and ankles giant bulbs connected by calfless shins. Beneath his gown, she could make out the outline of a diaper. Too far gone, it seemed, even for a bedpan.

For a surprising instant, she felt . . . sympathy. Compassion. And then she felt the memory of Nason, shoved back into the shipping container where they were held, bleeding and catatonic from the rape, and she felt a hot surge of satisfaction, a sweet, cruel joy, at his misery.

She forced herself to wall off the emotion. To get what she needed from this man, she had to be her cop self. She was here for information. She was interrogating a suspect. To that end, she would use all her skill, and exploit all his weaknesses. And allow herself to feel nothing about his crimes until she'd extracted what she needed from him.

At that point, she wouldn't need to be a cop anymore. She could be something else. The other thing. The dragon.

She approached the bed, the soles of her hiking boots squeaking slightly on the linoleum floor, the room silent but for the hum of a few medical machines and the whoosh of a fan by one of the doors.

When she reached the bed, she stopped. He turned his head slowly and looked at her. A long, sibilant exhalation escaped him, and his wasted body seemed to slacken and settle farther into the bed. He groaned something in Thai.

"English," Livia said. "I know you speak it. You dealt with Hammerhead getting me and Nason to Portland."

There was a pause. Then he took a breath and whispered in English, "I knew you would come. I knew."

Even aged and wasted and deformed as he was, there was enough of the face she remembered to take her back to the cold and the wind of the deck on that boat, the artificial turf biting into her knees, and the stink of curry on all of them as, one after the other, they made her do the disgusting thing. Making her believe if she did it she could save Nason.

She felt the dragon struggling, trying to get to the surface, to take back everything they had stolen from her.

Not yet. Not yet. NOT YET.

She forced herself back into cop mode. This man was about to incriminate himself. Maybe even to confess. There was nothing more critical in an interview than properly documenting a confession. She realized there might be a use to which she could put his.

She pulled the burner phone she'd purchased in Bangkok from her cargo shorts, switched it to video, and held it unobtrusively alongside the cot. "What do you mean?" she said.

He shook his head feebly. "It was wrong. I'm sorry. All I've done. Terrible things. I'm sorry."

Even beyond her personal connection, she was sufficiently familiar with jailhouse conversions, and particularly death-row conversions, to remain unmoved.

On the other hand, how long did Square Head have? Days? Weeks, if that? What did he have to gain by pretending?

All right. Assume he's sincere. Exploit that.

"If it was all so terrible," she said, "why did you do it?"

"Chanchai. It was Chanchai. So afraid of him. All of us."

Chanchai Vivavapit. The man she would forever think of as Skull Face.

"Are you really going to blame what you did on someone else?" she asked, feeling in control again. Feeling like a cop. "Is that what you mean when you say you're sorry?"

"After you cut his eye, he . . . crazy. We should have stopped. Shouldn't have done. I'm sorry. I wish . . ." His head rolled for a moment as though he was lost, and then he recovered himself. "I wish I could do again. Everything. I wish I could be better. The boy I was. The boy my parents . . ."

He didn't go on, but she sensed an opening. "Where are your parents now? Don't they visit you?"

He groaned. "Don't want them to see me like this. To see my karma."

She logged that for later use. "Why did you take me and my sister? Why us?"

"Chanchai knew. Chanchai told us."

"Told you what?"

"We . . . supposed to. Senator wanted you."

That tracked with what she knew. "But how? How did you find us? You had a photograph of my sister and me. How did you get it? Who told you the senator wanted us?"

"I don't know. Chanchai told us. Chanchai."

Damn it. It was maddening—to be this close, and yet still unable to get the pieces she needed.

"What about Sorm? Where can I find him?"

At this, his eyes seemed to brighten with fear. "I never know Sorm. Even Chanchai never know. Sorm is . . . devil."

"Was he involved? Did he tell you to find my sister and me?"

"I don't know. I never see Sorm. Bad man. Devil."

She wanted to scream. "You said you knew I would come. How?"

"Chanchai. And senator. And senator's . . . helper. The hotel room. Juntasa . . . he told me. He told me it was you."

Dirty Beard. "He was there?"

"Yes."

"How do you know?"

"He . . . bring . . . a girl. For the senator. And then you come. Chanchai told him. Told him to come for girl."

It tracked with what she remembered. The senator told Skull Face to get rid of the girl. Skull Face placed a call. Matthias Redcroft, the senator's aide, escorted the girl into the adjacent suite. Someone came to the door, beyond Livia's field of vision. It must have been Dirty Beard. And then Redcroft came back, and the girl was gone.

"Where?" she said, struggling with her excitement. "Where did Dirty Beard—where did Juntasa get that girl?"

"I don't know."

"You must have some idea. Where?"

"Juntasa know. So many place. So many girl. I'm sorry. I'm sorry."

She forced herself to think. Was she in danger? Square Head said he knew she would come. Did that mean the others did, too?

No. Because they aren't plagued by mortal guilt and its unwelcome insights.

Still, she said, "Did you tell Juntasa you knew I was coming?"

"Yes."

Shit, she'd been wrong. "When? When did you tell him I would come?"

"For all of us. That you would come for all of us. You are . . . our karma."

Okay, then, she'd been right the first time—it wasn't a prediction about where and when, more a prophecy of doom. General guilt, not specific insight. Of course Dirty Beard would be afraid she would come—how could he not be, after she'd left that hotel room an abattoir? But he'd have no way to know how she would track them. Or the order in which she'd move against them. She doubted he would waste resources in this godforsaken place, waiting for days or weeks or months on the off chance that she might show up.

Still, the possibility that she could have been anticipated was sobering. She was accustomed to hunting unseen. This time, she was expected. Meaning the hunting might be going both ways. She had to keep that in mind. And adjust her tactics accordingly.

She glanced at the woman in the adjacent bed. Her eyes were still closed, her body still trembling.

"Where can I find Juntasa?"

"Please. I accept my karma. I know why you come. I am ready. Please."

"Where can I find Juntasa?"

"My karma. Please. I can't anymore. Please."

It was horrible. She had thought to threaten to kill him. Now he was begging for it. It was like entering for a judo throw, only to have your opponent turn your entry into a throw of his own.

She fought to regain the initiative. "I'll be your karma. But tell me first how to find Juntasa."

"I don't know. At work. Headquarters."

She already knew that and she wasn't going to be able to touch him there.

"Juntasa," she said. "You said he told you about Chanchai and the senator. How? How did he tell you?"

"He call me."

The thought of Dirty Beard warning Square Head, and maybe being warned in return, was unsettling.

"When?"

"No one talks to me now. Look at me. Look at my karma."

"Does Juntasa have a phone? A mobile phone. Do you know that number?"

Square Head groaned and his eyes went to a small shelf alongside the cot. There were a few books in it, some clothes. An old photograph of himself when he was younger and healthy, with a small girl in his arms and an older couple alongside them. A daughter, she thought, and his parents. She should have noticed it earlier. If this all hadn't been so personal to her, she would have.

And there, alongside the books, an older-model iPhone. She set down the pack, then reached across the bed and grabbed the phone. She pressed the power button, and the screen lit up with a message. It was in Thai, but she could see what it meant.

"The passcode," she said. "Tell me."

He shook his head. "I can't. Please. I can only be responsible for my own karma. Please."

She glanced at the photograph on the shelf, then back to him. "Tell me, or I'll tell your parents what you did to my sister and me. And your daughter, unless she already knows because you did the same to her. I'll tell them what you are."

He licked his lips and shook his head spastically. "Please, no."

"Yes. Unless you tell me the passcode. And show me which mobile number is Juntasa's."

He shook his head again. "They won't believe you. No."

"You won't be around much longer to contradict my story. They'll wonder why I would invent something so horrible. They'll live the rest of their lives with doubts. Their memories of you poisoned. Their peace of mind destroyed."

His staring eyes filled, and the tears slipped down his face. It didn't make her feel sorry. It made her feel triumphant.

He croaked out four numbers in Thai. She pressed them on the keypad—and was in. But the interface was in Thai.

"Show me," she said. "Show me his mobile number. And if I find you've lied to me, you know what I'll do."

Tears leaked from his eyes. "Please don't tell them. Please."

"Which is his?"

He reached for the phone. She handed it to him. He tapped the screen several times, then pointed to a name and number. She took the phone and looked. Yes, Krit Juntasa. Her Thai was rusty, but properly cued, she could read it. With an entry for a mobile number.

She used the burner to snap a photograph of Dirty Beard's information, then did the same for the "Recent Calls" screen and the address book. There weren't many entries. The iPhone might have had other valuable information, and she wished she could have just taken it. But someone might notice it missing. She judged the risk not worth it. Besides, she had the photos.

She pulled a sleeve down over her hand and wiped down the iPhone on the sweatshirt. She passed it back to him to ensure his prints would be on it. Not that anyone would look, but if they did, no prints at all would have seemed odd. He took it in his right hand, transferred it to his left, and placed it back on the shelf.

She switched the burner to video again. "Tell me what you did," she said.

He shook his head. "Please. No more."

"You need to confess. You know that. You can feel that. Don't tell me you're sorry if you won't even confess."

"Please."

"You kidnapped and raped little girls, didn't you?"

Tears streamed from his eyes. "Yes."

"And your accomplices were Chanchai Vivavapit and Krit Juntasa?"

"Yes."

"Stop hiding from it. Own it. Say what you did."

"I kidnapped and raped little girls. With Chanchai Vivavapit and Krit Juntasa. I'm sorry. I'm sorry."

"Now in Thai. Say it in Thai."

He did. She recognized enough of the words to know it was accurate. Besides, he was obviously beyond dissembling.

She clicked off the burner, dropped it back in one of her shorts pockets, and glanced around. Everything was still silent but for the hum of the machines and the whoosh of the fan. The woman remained insensible. No one else was about.

She reached into the pack and pulled on the motocross gloves. She glanced around again. Still no one.

Alongside Square Head's torso lay a spare pillow and an unused blanket. She took hold of the top of the pillow with one gloved hand and slipped the blanket over it so that her hand was sandwiched between pillow and blanket. With the other hand, she pulled free the oxygen tube taped under his nose. Despite all he'd said of karma, his eyes popped panic-wide and he fumbled for the tube.

Too late. She swept one hand down and pressed his arms to his abdomen. With her other hand, she pushed the pillow over his face.

His bony legs kicked feebly. She released his arms and used both hands to compress the pillow against his face. He scratched at her, but his nails danced harmlessly over the blanket, beneath which was the carbon fiber of the gloves. His body began to shake, and he gripped her forearms and tried to push her away. Despite his decrepitude, in extremis he was able to squeeze hard enough for her to feel the pressure even through the magazines taped over her forearms. But a little pressure through the magazines, even a lot, wouldn't matter. There would be no bruises on her, and no DNA on him. She doubted there would be any fibers from the sweatshirt to be found, either, or that anyone would look for them, but even if she were wrong, she had purchased the garment just yesterday, kept it in plastic separate from her other belongings, and would quickly dispose of it.

Square Head's struggles lasted only a few seconds. Then his body relaxed and his hands collapsed to his sides. His knees, which had been pointing toward the ceiling, fell open in a spread eagle, creating a gap in the diaper through which Livia could smell that he had fouled himself.

She kept one hand pressed firmly on the pillow. With the other, she moved the blanket back alongside him. She used her teeth to pull off one glove, then the other, slipping each back into the pack with one hand while maintaining the pressure on the pillow with the other.

When she was sure he was past any possibility of revival, she moved the pillow alongside the blanket. Doubtless there would be some drool on it, but that would mean nothing.

Square Head's head was tilted back, his mouth agape in a pantomime of a desperate gulp for air, his eyes frozen wide in terror and despair. Maybe in his final moments he'd realized there was something worse than karma in this world. Maybe he'd seen a vision of hell in the next one.

She glanced around one last time. The woman in the adjacent bed hadn't stirred. A breeze drifted in through the open door at the far end, but beyond that everything was still. She replaced the oxygen tube, wiped the spot she had touched with a sheet, shouldered the pack, and walked out the way she had come.

She felt strangely empty. Seeing his face again had made her want to tear him apart, the way she had Skull Face. But in the end, she'd dispatched him with not much more than euthanasia.

It was the right call. It couldn't look like murder. You'd be a suspect. Dirty Beard would know you're coming. You wouldn't get to Sorm, the brains behind what happened to you and Nason. And you'd never find that little girl. You killed him. After all these years, you killed him. Let that be enough.

But what if it isn't enough?

She'd spent sixteen years—almost half her life—craving revenge. And killing the senator, and his aide, and most of all Skull Face, was sweet. It was.

But all that had been only two months earlier, and now she was back. And . . . it wasn't helping the way it had before.

What if it's never enough?

It has to be. It has to be.

But all at once, she didn't really believe that. And she had no idea what that meant. Or what to do about it.

10

Dox woke at first light in the small room he'd taken at the Blue Bat Hotel in Battambang. At the riel equivalent of about twenty dollars a night, the place was cheap enough to take cash and accept a story about a lost passport, but decent enough to have solid doors and locks. And overall it was more than comfortable. The bed was nice and soft, the way he liked it—he'd spent enough nights in cramped sniper hides to appreciate a good mattress and feather pillow. But despite the furnishings, he hadn't slept well. It was the feeling that he should get the hell out of Cambodia. If Rain knew he'd stuck around after a job, he would have told Dox he ought to have his head examined, and Dox knew he wouldn't be able to argue. And job, hell, it was more than that. He'd killed the guy who hired him, a guy who'd turned out to be—*oops!*— a DIA officer up to his neck in unspecified skullduggery. And three accomplices right after. And now there was the damn sword guy on top of it.

The problem was, there was at least some chance Sorm would turn up in Cambodia, and Dox didn't want to cross a border only to learn that he had to go back right afterward. On the other hand, according to Vann's hunch, which Dox had relayed to Kanezaki, Sorm was likely in

Pattaya. So he'd compromised, taking a late bus to Battambang, a city northwest of Phnom Penh with a laid-back vibe, some remarkably well-preserved French-colonial architecture, and a name Dox had always secretly loved. Battambang would give him reasonably good access to Pailin, Sorm's home province, as well as to various border crossings into Thailand, where he'd be within shooting distance of Pattaya, figuratively speaking, if Kanezaki wound up confirming Vann's hunch.

He headed down to the hotel restaurant. It was far too early for the hotel's trekker clientele to be up, and he enjoyed having the pastel-colored room to himself for a meal of scrambled eggs, tropical fruit, and black coffee. When he was done, he used another burner to call Kanezaki.

"New phone?" Kanezaki asked.

"Just trying to avoid any more unpleasant surprises."

They quickly confirmed the Signal ID was a match. "Well, how'd old Vann's hunch work out?" Dox said. "As well as yours?"

"Maybe better."

It was hard not to smile at that. "You don't say."

"I don't want to give him too much credit. But he got me looking in the right direction. Helped me eliminate some false positives and probably saved us a lot of time overall."

"That's good. I'd certainly like to resolve this unpleasantness sooner rather than later."

"Don't get me wrong. This wasn't easy. At all."

Dox laughed. Kanezaki couldn't stop himself—he always had to remind you of how difficult a task was so he could exact some greater concession in return.

"When this is over, I'm going to send you a bouquet of roses and give you a big wet sloppy kiss. But for now, could you just tell me what you found out?"

"All right. Vann's sense that a Sorm front company was investing in that deluxe hotel in Pattaya was key. I pointed some financial-forensics people in that direction, and they uncovered connections Vann hadn't managed to."

"And then?"

"This is the good part. In the last week—the same period Vann told you Sorm has been in the wind—a dozen calls have been made from a dozen burner phones, all from the nightclub in that hotel, all to known Sorm associates."

"Son? I don't just appreciate you. I think I love you."

"Wait, that was only the good part. Here's the best part. The mobile phone of one of said associates has shown up in the club three times in the same week. Not proof positive, but about as solid a trail as we ever get in this business. Sorm is there. And he's meeting people."

Dox took a sip of coffee, suddenly suspicious. "Yeah, it sounds solid, all right. A little too solid, you think?"

"I had the same thought. But I really did have to work a lot of angles to get this intel. Sorm doesn't know all our capabilities. You wouldn't believe how many bad guys out there are careful about their own phones but don't think about the patterns created by the phones of known associates. And sure, Sorm is being careful, but he also knows he's being protected. Maybe that's making him more complacent than he should be."

That did sound about right. It just always made him twitchy when a trail seemed a little too easy to follow. "All right," he said. "You've convinced me."

"Now listen," Kanezaki said. "The intel is good, but you need to be careful. Sorm's not just a monster. He's a survivor. He'll have heard about Gant. I doubt he'll be out in the open. And I expect he'll have bodyguards."

"I expect the same," Dox said. "Speaking of which, sadly, I had to ditch the SR-25 Gant had procured for me after I sent him to his reward with it. So other than my usual collection of exotic sharp and pointy things, I'm feeling a little light on tools at the moment."

"No. I can't help with that. Whatever else is going on, Sorm is a DIA asset. You can't kill him. I can't be part of that. It's a bridge too far."

"Look, I already promised Vann I wouldn't kill the man. But I do at least need to have a word with him. And I'd prefer that word to be *Glock*, say, or *SIG*, or, ideally, *Wilson Combat*, which yes I know is two words, not one. Just to establish the right conversational tone. You want him to open up to me, don't you?"

There was a pause. Then Kanezaki sighed. "All right. I'll have something for you in Pattaya. I need to reach out to a contact in the area, and then I'll let you know where and how."

"Good. And while we're on the subject, I favor the Tactical Supergrade in .45 ACP."

"What do you think I am, Santa Claus?"

"Well, you're both miracle workers, right? Oh, and a bellyband holster wouldn't offend me, either."

Kanezaki laughed. "I swear, one day you're going to get me into real trouble."

"Maybe, but you know I'll always be there to help you get out of it, too."

"Yeah, I do know that. And no bullshit—thank you."

Dox hadn't been expecting that, and was surprised to find himself touched. "Well, same to you, amigo. Lot of water under the bridge between us. I'm glad you know I've got your back. And it feels good to know you've got mine. The only way to make sense of this crazy world of ours is to know who your real friends are."

Kanezaki laughed again, and the unfamiliar emotional moment was gone. "Remember, I want to know what Sorm has been feeding DIA. The basis for that relationship. And why they tried to kill Vann."

"I know, I know."

"And don't kill him, damn it."

"I won't. Can't promise I won't hurt his feelings, though."

He clicked off, powered down the phone, and slipped it into the Faraday case.

Yeah, he wouldn't kill Sorm. Not unless he had to. For the moment, Sorm wasn't the real threat. That was the people behind Sorm. So as much as he might enjoy it on a personal level, there wouldn't be much point to killing Sorm without first learning who at DIA was backing him.

But he hadn't said anything about killing bodyguards, had he? No, he sure hadn't. Must have slipped his mind.

11

Livia spent the next two nights at the retreat. Remaining at the scene was contrary to all her instincts, but she'd reserved for two nights, and leaving abruptly would draw attention.

It wasn't logical, but she half expected police to show up. They didn't. Instead, there was a small and dignified ceremony in the chapel for a recently deceased patient. The body was wrapped in red cloth, incense was burned, and one of the friars said a few words. The only mourners, so far as Livia could see, were hospice staff and other patients. Everything about the simple send-off seemed familiar and routine. And why not? This was a hospice for the indigent dying of AIDS. What could be more unlikely here than murder? And what could be more common than another ravaged patient succumbing to the disease?

At least she was able to use the time well. With the Gossamer, she plotted Dirty Beard's movements. Over the course of just under forty-eight hours, his primary points of contact were Royal Thai Police Headquarters in Pathum Wan, and a building in a nearby neighborhood called Ekamai, which she learned online was known for its pricey condos. Not the kind of place a Thai cop could ever hope to afford on his salary alone. She wondered whether it was his primary residence, or whether he owned it through some sort of cutout. A cop living ostenta-tiously beyond his means would be a huge red flag in the States. Maybe here, the brass was content to ignore it.

As long as they got their piece, too.

She edited the confession video down to its most salient aspects right on the burner, then transferred the photos and video using the Tails operating system and an encrypted thumb drive to keep her laptop uncontaminated. After that, she roamed the Internet behind a VPN, scouting locations, acquainting herself with routes and distances, judg-ing potential risks and rewards. She didn't see anywhere she might have a shot at taking Dirty Beard by surprise. And she didn't have time to wait for a lucky break. She would have to force him to come to her. The problem was, it wasn't like Seattle, which she knew intimately as a cop and from innumerable weekend rides. In Bangkok, it was the other cops who had the advantage. She could mitigate that through meticulous preparation. Find ways to keep them moving, reactive, off balance, the way she would on the mat against a bigger, stronger opponent. If she could take away their base, their footing, all their natural advantages would be neutralized.

If.

On her second night at the retreat, she tracked Dirty Beard's phone to the Srinakarin Rot Fai Night Market, east of the city center. She checked online and saw a dense, labyrinthine network of thousands of stalls and pop-up restaurants selling every manner of books, food, clothing, electronics, and assorted arcana. From the Night Market, he headed south all the way to Pattaya, a beach town on the east coast of the Gulf of Thailand, arriving at a new hotel called Ruby. It was nearly a two-hour drive from Bangkok, and whatever he was doing there, she expected he would stay the night. But when she checked upon wak-ing the next morning, she saw that he had turned around after only about an hour. She didn't know what any of it meant, but it would likely be useful to have two known points of contact about which to interrogate him.

She left later that morning, thanking Brother Panit for a wonderful experience that had allowed her to at least temporarily clear her mind of her everyday concerns.

"You must come again," he said as they waited for the cab he had called her. "Two days is good for the spirit. Two weeks is better. Or longer. Many people have stayed with us as volunteers, caring for the dying. Like Saint Francis, most of them have found the experience transformative."

She smiled, recognizing from the natural diction that the speech was practiced. Not that she doubted its sincerity.

"I can imagine," she said. "And by the way, was that a funeral I saw yesterday?"

"Oh, yes, Mr. Sakda. He came to us three months ago. He speaked very little and I think had so much sadness. But he is at peace now."

I hope not, Livia thought. She wanted to ask more, about Mr. Sakda's visitors especially, but knew too much interest would look strange and would be too memorable.

Two hours later, she was back in Bangkok. She'd kept the room she took in the Sathorn business hotel after arriving from Seattle. She was in town practically on official business, after all, so she was using genuine ID at check in and credit cards to pay. Anything else would have looked odd. For the same reason, keeping the room made sense. For anyone looking, it would seem as though she'd been in Bangkok continuously, and she wouldn't have to account for the two nights she'd spent at the Franciscan retreat.

She'd left her personal cell phone powered down at the hotel. If someone were tracking it, it would look odd that it had been off for two days. But that was better than someone using it to follow her to the scene of Square Head's demise.

There were a few work messages. And one from B. D. Little, left the previous evening, asking that she call him back.

Before leaving, she'd signed up for an international plan—call anywhere from anywhere for thirty cents a minute. She didn't know where she'd be reaching him, but if he were in the States, it would be the middle of the night. She didn't care. She pressed "Call Back."

She waited while the call went through. Then: "B. D. here."

She'd been expecting something like *Hello, Livia.* He didn't recognize her number? She wasn't buying it. "You called?"

"I did. You're a hard person to reach."

She didn't like the sound of that. "What do you mean?"

"I guess your phone's been off."

She'd interrogated enough suspects to recognize when a cop was fishing. And to know better than to respond with anything the cop could then use.

"I'm in a new place. Lots to see." Neither confirming nor denying that the phone had been off. Essentially saying nothing.

"Oh, I get that. I can be the same way when I travel. But I'm glad we're talking now."

She didn't respond. The less you said, the less you had to explain.

"Anyway," he went on after a moment. "How's it coming out there? You feeling like maybe you want to be on the team?"

"I'm not sure yet. I've only been here two full days."

"Of course, of course. But I'd love to hear your preliminary impressions."

"I'd rather absorb a little more and then issue a final report. I don't want to get your hopes up prematurely."

He laughed. "Okay, fair enough. Just don't forget to check in from time to time, okay? I like to be able to reach the people I'm working with."

"You're not working with me. At least, not yet."

He laughed again. He put up with a lot of pushback. Either he was an exceptionally affable person, or he really wanted her. For what, though?

"You are tough. But okay, fair point. Thanks for calling, and I hope the trip goes well." He clicked off.

There had been a slightly false note to that *I like to be able to reach the people I'm working with* line. If she didn't know better, she might have thought he was trying to get her to think that phone calls were his only way of being in touch with her.

But if he had a Gossamer himself, and of course he would, he'd be able to monitor her cell phone's movements. Gossamer, hell, he probably had people who could hack the mobile-phone company's own database. Or who were receiving the data with the mobile company's full knowledge and cooperation.

Well, no problem so far, because she'd left the phone in the hotel room as a precaution.

Yeah, but then he knows what hotel you're staying at.

She realized she should have powered down the phone before arriving at the hotel.

Something else occurred to her. Had he called the hotel in the middle of the night, and told someone to put the call through to the room? *I'm sorry, sir, your party isn't answering.*

Explainable, of course. *I was wearing earplugs. Didn't hear the phone.*

But Little wouldn't ask for an explanation. He'd assemble the pieces quietly and draw his own conclusions.

She remembered Lieutenant Strangeland's admonition: *There are depths to this thing. I know that. I can't see them, but I feel them. And if I'm not seeing them, then neither are you.*

Shit, she'd been complacent. She considered what else she might have overlooked.

Could you be under physical surveillance?

That was a sobering thought. On the one hand, probably not. On the other hand . . . how had Little put it? *We have so many resources to waste.*

She hadn't been followed to the Franciscan retreat. She was sure of that. There had been long stretches on those secondary roads where there wasn't another car in sight.

But she had to be more careful. She had to assume she was being watched.

She went out, leaving her cell phone behind again. After an hour of tuk-tuk rides, BTS Skytrain station changes, and two river crossings, she was sure she didn't have a tail. Maybe she was being paranoid. Still, it would be smart to get a room at another hotel. Keep the first one, crash at the second. Just in case.

She found a mobile-phone vendor and bought a new burner. At a place called Rocket Coffeebar, she uploaded the photo of Square Head's mobile-phone contacts and the video of his confession from the old burner to the new one, purging and then tossing the old one in a sewer after heading out again. She'd connect the new one to the cellular network and the Internet later, far in time and distance from where the old one had been permanently switched off.

She paused to check the Gossamer. Dirty Beard was at headquarters. From where she stood, he was only a couple of kilometers away. She wondered if he'd heard that Square Head had died. And if so, whether he suspected her.

She realized he could find out. A cop, calling the retreat center, speaking with Brother Panit, asking whether an American woman of Thai ethnicity had visited recently.

It doesn't matter. You're going to tell him yourself.

There was a motor-scooter dealer right next to the hotel, and she rented a Suzuki Nex—a toy compared to the Streetfighter, but perfect for getting past, through, and around Bangkok's legendary traffic. She spent the afternoon reconnoitering. And as the sun was setting through the polluted haze in the western sky, she rode out to the Rot Fai Night Market, the evening breeze a mercy on her damp tee shirt. She was curious, of course, because Dirty Beard seemed to have business at the market. But her primary purpose was a vehicle.

The market had opened only an hour or so earlier, and the parking lot wasn't yet crowded. She left the scooter and went inside. The density of the place was staggering. There must have been two thousand colorful tents, all crowded together over several acres at least, surrounded by shipping containers and trucks and brick-and-corrugated-metal buildings. She wandered for over an hour, the smells of fried rice and braised pork surreal on the night air, like a memory from her childhood calling from a reanimated past.

When she felt she'd seen enough, she went back to the lot. There were numerous small delivery trucks parked along the curb. She came across several possibilities, but she was looking for something just right, and took her time before she found it. And there it was, double parked, this one old and dilapidated, two seats up front, windows rolled down, windowless cargo area behind. The hatch was open, and though the dome light seemed not to be working, she could see the cargo area was half-filled with crates of vegetables. A shirtless Thai man with long, stringy arms was hustling back and forth between the truck and the Night Market entrance, where he would disappear around the corner and then return a few seconds later, moving fast and breathing heavily, beads of sweat running down his back and chest. Obviously, he was making deliveries to some of the food stalls. Livia glanced inside the truck as she passed, and saw what she'd been hoping for: the key in the ignition.

Based on what she'd seen in the cargo area, she estimated the man had another dozen trips. He was already winded. His pace would likely slacken.

It did. She watched from the shadows beyond a streetlight, obscured by passing crowds, as the man went back and forth again and again, huffing harder and sweating more profusely with each trip. She didn't need a stopwatch to recognize the intervals were getting longer. And as he turned the corner for the eighth time, she slipped out of the shadows, closed the rear hatch, opened the driver's door, eased inside, and turned the key.

The starter coughed fitfully and died.

Fuck.

She turned the key again. The starter groaned a little more gamely, but still sputtered out. *Shit.*

But the guy had driven the damn thing here. And if the starter were that crapped out, he would have left the engine running. Probably it was just a faulty relay. She turned the key again. Again the starter coughed and died.

She adjusted the side-view mirror. No sign of the guy, but she couldn't have more than a few more seconds.

Abort. Get out. Find another.

Instead, she turned the key again. The starter coughed, faltered, caught . . . and the engine growled awake.

She popped it into reverse, fought the impulse to hit the gas, and backed up smoothly to create room between her and the car double parked in front of her. She glanced in the side-view and saw the guy coming around the corner. He cried out something in Thai and started running.

Livia cut the wheel right and cleared the car in front of her. The guy must have gotten an adrenaline burst, because as winded as he'd looked, he was able to reach her faster than she'd anticipated. He pulled abreast and got a hand on the door, his eyes desperate, almost terrified. He yelled, *"Mai! Mai!"* No! No! But it was already too late. She shot ahead and the man fell back. She cut around two cars in front of her and almost turned the wrong way on the street before remembering that in Thailand she had to drive on the left side. She swung left, swerved around more traffic, and was out, just another vehicle among thousands, tens of thousands, like it.

For a full second, she felt triumphant. She'd done it! It had been risky, and close, and crazy with that faulty starter, but she'd done it. She had the vehicle she needed. Her plan was good. It was going to work. She was going to get Dirty Beard, and then, and then . . .

An image cut through her exultation: that man's eyes. His desperation. His terror.

She realized he'd been no delivery-truck driver, paid a wage by a company that would be insured against loss. That man worked for himself. And that truck was probably everything he owned. Everything his family depended on. If he couldn't afford to replace a faulty starter relay, what were the chances that he had any kind of insurance?

Not your problem. Keep going. Drive. Dirty Beard. That's what matters.

She tried to listen to that part of her mind. To ignore the image of those wide, terrified eyes.

She couldn't.

She circled the Night Market and double parked about fifty yards back from where she'd taken the truck. She got out, took the key, and walked forward, looking for the man. If she saw him, she would toss him the key and take off running. She was in shape, while he was winded. She had no doubt he'd settle for the key and find his truck, and probably not even try to chase her. She'd figure out another way to get the vehicle she needed.

Ten yards ahead, she spotted him. It wasn't hard. He was sitting on the curb, his face in his hands, sobbing. Scores of people glanced at him as they passed, but no one stopped to help or even inquire.

Her resolution faltered. Without thinking, she kept walking, stopping just in front of him and holding out the key to the truck. *"Khor thot ka,"* she said, using some of the Thai she remembered. *"Khor thot ka."* I'm sorry. I'm sorry.

The man looked up. He saw her. He recognized her. She expected him to fly into a rage, and she was ready to toss him the key and take off. But he didn't. He came shakily to his feet and just looked at her, crying harder.

It was unbearable. "I'm sorry," she said again in Thai. "I'm sorry." She held out the key.

He shook his head and wiped his face. "Why?" he said in Thai. "Why did you do that?"

She struggled for a moment. It was hard because she understood more Thai than she could speak. "Come. Please. I'm sorry."

The man shook his head, plainly at a loss.

"Please," she said again, motioning in the direction of the truck. "Please."

Still shaking his head and slack jawed with apparent shock and relief, the man took the key and followed her to the truck. She motioned that he should open the hood. He reached inside and did so.

It was an older engine—everything visible and accessible. She pointed to the starter.

"Broken," she said. "Broken." She pointed to herself. "I fix."

The man said nothing. He seemed stupefied.

It took her less than three minutes to locate the corroded wires that were causing the problem, scrape them clean with the knife she was carrying, a Benchmade 3300 Infidel with a four-inch tactical-black blade, and reattach them properly. "Go," she said, pointing to the driver's seat. "Go. Start. You try."

His expression poised uneasily between suspicious and bewildered, the man did as she asked. He turned the key and immediately the engine came smoothly to life.

The man laughed delightedly and looked at her. She smiled at him. He cut the engine and got out of the truck.

"I'm sorry," she said again.

He smiled and shook his head. He must have been so relieved to have his truck back, and so confused, that he didn't care about anything else.

She was still horrified that she could have been so blinded by her lust for revenge that she would have ruined this man's life pursuing it. That for a moment, she had forgotten who she was.

Or who she thought she was.

Something occurred to her. Maybe it would have worked sooner. But maybe not. Because before, weirdly, they didn't know each other. Or trust each other.

She gestured to the truck. "How much?"

He shook his head. "How much what?"

"Money. You sell. I buy."

The man laughed. "Now you want to buy it?"

"Yes. I'm sorry. How much?"

"I can't sell it. I need it. It's why I was so angry."

He hadn't looked angry. He'd looked bereft. But that was a harder thing for a man to admit to.

"I give . . . two thousand dollar. American dollar. Okay?"

The man's eyes widened. "What? No, I can't—"

"Two thousand. American dollars. Right now. Okay?"

The man shook his head, stupefied again.

She reached into a cargo-pants pocket and pulled out a roll of bills. She counted out twenty hundreds, making sure he could see each one.

She extended the cash to him. "Okay? I give money. You give truck."

"Why?"

"I want truck."

"You don't have to. It's okay."

"I want to. Please."

He stared at the money for another moment. Then his face broke out in a huge smile and he nodded. "Okay. Okay, thank you. Okay." He took the bills and handed her the key, then just stood there, beaming as though he'd won the lottery after an incredible reversal of fortune. Which, she supposed, was pretty much what had happened.

She pointed to the back and paused, trying to remember the Thai word. "Vegetable," she said, after a moment. "Your vegetable."

The man laughed, retrieved the remaining crates, and set them on the sidewalk. "Thank you," he said in English, pressing his palms together in a high *wai*.

She shook her head and returned the *wai*. "Thank you."

She got in the truck. It started up easily and she drove off, waving a last time to the man before pulling out into traffic.

She was happy. Relieved. It had all worked out. She had everything she needed now. The fuel was gathered. All she needed to do was arrange it. And light the match.

But she was also uneasy. She remembered when she'd been in college and had come across the Nietzsche quote: *Beware that, when fighting monsters, you yourself do not become a monster.* It had felt like he was speaking to her, warning her, her specifically.

She had always promised herself she would never cross that line. But she realized now the line might be harder to see than she'd thought.

She shook off the feeling. She would think about it later. Now she had to focus.

She found herself thinking about a place she'd come across online. An airplane graveyard, in Bang Kapi, a suburban Bangkok neighborhood about twenty kilometers east of the city center. It sounded unusual. Not well known, even among locals. And isolated.

She decided to take a look for herself. A graveyard felt right for what was coming.

12

The next day, Livia visited all the places she needed to see, but particularly the airplane graveyard. She rode out on the Nex and instantly
liked what she found: an empty, overgrown rectangular field, maybe
four acres total, enclosed by a concrete wall on one long side; trees,
underbrush, and a drainage canal on the other; a six-lane divided road
in front; and another canal at the far end. Within, for reasons no one
seemed entirely clear about, were the enormous, scavenged remains of
a pair of huge commercial passenger jets.

She circled the area a few times, getting familiar with its layout and
rhythms. She was still in the city, no doubt, but it was nowhere near
as dense or noisy as the Central Business District. The buildings were
lower, with a few high-rise condominiums that stood out by contrast.
The roads weren't terribly congested. And though there was still plenty
of urban background noise, it was nothing like the din of construction
and traffic and commerce of central Bangkok.

A long driveway ran adjacent to the site's western wall, and she
followed it to a restaurant called Green View Chill Cuisine. A sign said
they would open at five for dinner. That was fine. She parked the Nex
at the far end of the driveway, almost at the edge of the canal.

There was a break in the wall here, she saw. And though the far end of the graveyard was thick with trees, there was a dirt road snaking through them. She followed the road. It was narrow and rutted and disused, but she thought her newly acquired delivery truck could handle it.

The field itself looked like a crash site—as though a pair of white planes had collided at low altitude and plummeted into a green field, scattering their innards on impact. Here was an enormous, skeletal fuselage. There, a giant, amputated wing. And there, a dismembered tail. Everywhere was the detritus of commercial air travel: seats and oxygen masks. Overhead luggage racks, one side closed and locked, the other open to the sky. A flight-instrument panel, the pilot's seat still attached to the flooring connected to it. And all of it gradually disappearing beneath weeds and dead leaves and vines.

She walked along, part of her observing the terrain tactically and calculating how to exploit it, part of her marveling at the sheer strangeness of the place. Six-lane Ramkhamhaeng Road was only a few hundred feet away, but the noise of traffic was muted, the field filled with birdsong instead. The whole place was an improbable, incongruous urban memento mori.

A dusty strip of dirt ran the length of the site. She watched a lean dog trotting along it, coming toward her. It stopped a few yards away and stared. Her hand dropped to the Infidel, clipped to a shorts pocket, and she bared her teeth. The dog decided it had no interest, and moved on.

She imagined how it would all look at night. Well, she'd be back soon enough, she wouldn't have to imagine. She thought about night-vision goggles. You could buy them commercially in the States. Maybe there was a store in Bangkok, though she hadn't seen any in the surplus place where she'd bought her other gear.

What if you can't get it, and Dirty Beard can?

That was a disquieting thought, and she was suddenly furious at herself for not having thought of it sooner.

It's okay. You're overloaded. The unfamiliar terrain. Everything dredging up the past. It was late, not never. And no harm, no foul.

That was true. The main thing was that she had spotted the potential problem while there was still time to mitigate. Besides, she had an idea about how.

When she had thoroughly finished exploring the interiors of the wrecked fuselages and everything about the site itself, she walked the perimeter, assessing the likely approaches, determining the best tactical hiding spot. She decided on the eastern boundary of the field, a thick line of trees and ferns and underbrush dropping down an embankment to the drainage canal. There was a particularly dense tangle of ground foliage about forty feet from the back of the fuselage. The soil beneath was loose, and she used the Infidel to carve a trench in the sloped ground about the length of her body. A crime to use such a fine blade to hack a hole in the dirt, but she hadn't thought to bring a shovel and she could sharpen and oil the knife later.

By the time she was done preparing the spot, she was covered with dirt and soaked with sweat. She didn't care. It felt great. Deliberate. Methodical. Effective. She wiped her face with a shirtsleeve and walked back and forth to the fuselage, clearing the few pieces of debris in between so she'd be able to sprint across in the dark without having to worry about her footing.

She wiped her face again and took one last look around. Everything felt right. The plan. The preparations. The purpose.

It's going to work, little bird. I'm going to get him. I'm going to make him pay.

She went back to the Nex and left. On the way into central Bangkok, she stopped to buy some items she would need. At a hardware store, a propane torch, a set of metal files, a multibit screwdriver, duct tape, and a Zippo windproof lighter. At a mobile kiosk, a second iPhone burner. At a photography store, two 600-watt strobe lights and a wireless activator, along with a pair of tripods to support them, and a FLIR—forward-looking infrared—attachment for the iPhone. At a sporting-goods store, a daypack, talcum powder, a microfiber towel, a box of chemical heat packs, a pair of running gloves with touchscreen index-finger tips, and a single-piece, five-millimeter-thick cold-water wetsuit along with matching boots and gloves. And at a surplus-and-police-gear store, a twenty-four-inch ASP expanding steel baton and a pair of Smith & Wesson handcuffs, both the genuine article, both exorbitantly expensive compared to in the States, both well worth it.

Her last stop was a car park. After checking for video cameras and seeing none, she used the screwdriver to remove the license plates from a van, pushed them into the backpack, and headed to the hotel. She tried to sleep, but didn't even come close. Too much riding on what would happen that night.

When it was dark, she went out again. She paid cash to check in to a new hotel, a trekker place about a half mile away. If Little was watching, tonight would be a bad night to be seen. She left the new gear in the room and went out to the truck with the propane torch and the metal-file set. She drove around until she found a suitably lightless alley, where she used the files to remove the vehicle identification number from the front of the engine block, softening the metal a few times with the torch to make sure all traces were obliterated. She checked the other places a VIN might be hiding—front of the frame, under the rear wheel well—and found nothing. The one on the driver's-side interior dash was aluminum, and the one on the driver's door frame was just a sticker. Neither of those would matter.

When she was satisfied about the VINs, she stopped at a gas stand, where she filled the tank and bought two ten-liter containers, filling them, too, and putting them in back. She picked up an order of *som tam* green papaya salad and a bottled water at a stall, then went back to the trekker hotel and ate, checking the Gossamer every hour, irrationally afraid that Dirty Beard would somehow disappear—get on an airplane, or turn off his mobile phone, or something else that would ruin her opportunity. But he didn't. He was at work. She needed to stay calm. To wait for the right moment. To make him come to her and not give him time to prepare.

At nine o'clock, she checked the Gossamer again. *Shit*—in the twenty minutes since she'd last checked, he'd left work. But he was traveling his usual route toward the condo in Ekamai. No, wait, he wasn't. He was heading farther east. Toward the Night Market.

If he continued south to Pattaya again, it would spoil everything. She breathed slowly and deeply, calming herself.

Not spoil. Just delay. Wait.

She did. And watched him head west again, back toward Ekamai, after another brief visit to the market.

Something was going on there. And she was going to find out what.

She grabbed the backpack, already loaded with the gear she would need, and went out to the alley where she had parked the truck. She swapped the plates, keeping the legit ones in case things didn't work out the way she had planned and she needed the truck again.

The worst of the evening traffic was past, and it took her only forty minutes to get to the airplane graveyard. She headed up the driveway she'd used earlier, past Green View Chill Cuisine. It was lively now, apparently with a wedding party, a dance floor set up outside with a band alongside it. The parking area was full—beyond full, with several cars perched on the grass. She left the truck at the far end, between a pair of trees, then walked into the field, carrying her gear.

The walled interior was devoid of any illumination of its own, but was suffused with a gray glow from the surrounding ambient light. She paused amid the trees and waited for her night vision to adjust, then continued on toward the wreckage of the planes at the opposite end. A dog barked from somewhere inside, maybe the one she had seen earlier. She continued on. The dog barked again. The sounds of traffic faded quickly, and soon the field was eerily quiet.

She came to the gaping, circular mouth of the fuselage closest to Ramkhamhaeng Road and looked inside. It was too dark to see, even with her eyes fully adjusted to the dim light of the field. *Good.*

She pulled on the running gloves and used a SureFire mini light, her everyday carry, to look inside the wreck. Everything was exactly as it had been just a few hours earlier.

She carried the pack inside and sat on the floor for a moment, the SureFire extinguished. She checked the Gossamer again. Dirty Beard was in Ekamai, probably thinking he was in for the night. Thinking wrong.

The feeling of being *this close* to killing another of the men who had hurt her and Nason, and who had doubtless spent decades doing the same to countless others, was making the dragon breathe fire. She couldn't let it. Not yet.

Her heart pounding, she attached Square Head's confession to a text in the burner, wrote a message that included the names and mobile numbers of several of Dirty Beard's superiors, all gleaned from Little's file, and input Dirty Beard's number. She paused for a moment, looking at the text.

Enough thinking. It's a good plan. You're ready. You can do this. For Nason. For that little girl.

She took a deep breath and hit "Send."

13

Livia sat in the dark, her eyes readjusting, breathing steadily, focusing on slowing her galloping heartbeat.

It worked. A little.

Dirty Beard was a cop, and a corrupt one at that. She didn't have to worry—she knew his phone would always be on. Still, her mind was insisting on playing *what if* games. She reminded herself of who she was. A cop, not a little girl. A warrior, not a victim. She didn't think *what if*. She thought *when/then*.

It felt like longer, but according to the phone clock less than three minutes had passed when the reply came. It was Thai, but simple enough for her to read. *What is this?*

She called him. She continued to focus on breathing slowly and deeply, but her lungs felt hot. The dragon's breath.

He picked up instantly. "You," he said in English.

Hearing that voice—the voice from the deck of the boat sixteen years earlier—caused her heart to start pounding again. "Give me a good reason I shouldn't upload that video to everyone named in my text," she said.

"I pay you."

She thought he might say that. "You're damn right you'll pay me. Because you know as well as I do those people will never let you be prosecuted for your crimes. They'll kill you first."

"One million baht," he said.

She laughed harshly. "Thirty thousand dollars? That'll barely get me a first-class ticket home. Ten million."

"Okay. Ten million."

"Right now," she said. "Cash, in a bag, per my instructions."

"You tell where."

Even as corrupt as he obviously was, she doubted he had the baht equivalent of three hundred thousand dollars just lying around. She might have believed he was panicked. But she didn't. His response felt planned. And why not? He knew she'd killed Skull Face. And the senator. He'd even warned Square Head. He knew she was coming for him. What he didn't know was how.

"The airplane graveyard."

"What?"

"In Bang Kapi."

"I don't know this place."

"You don't know Bang Kapi?"

"I know Bang Kapi. I don't know airplane graveyard."

She smiled. It might have been true. What occasion would he have to come here? And from what she'd managed to find online, the graveyard was an oddity even locals had never heard of.

"It's on Ramkhamhaeng Road Soi 101. Next to the Thanombutra School."

"Okay."

"Meet me at the back of the plane closest to Ramkhamhaeng Road."

"Okay."

"If you're not here in under an hour, with the money, I upload the video."

"I be there. With money."

"If you're not alone, I upload the video."

"I come alone."

Bullshit, she thought, and clicked off.

It took her less than ten minutes to rig the strobe lights and tripods inside the fuselage. She tested them with the wireless remote, turning her back to preserve her night vision. They worked perfectly, like a flash of indoor lightning. She checked the rest of her gear. Everything she needed, all where she wanted it.

She left the burner powered on, under a ripped-out seat just inside the fuselage. It was possible Dirty Beard had a Gossamer of his own. If so, the phone would act as a decoy. Alongside it, she left the duct tape and the handcuffs.

At the back of the fuselage, she opened the box of hot packs and squeezed each of them, mixing the chemicals inside and activating the heat. Then she arranged them behind the innards of a ripped-out seat. Back at the opening of the fuselage, she checked with the FLIR-equipped second burner. The image was perfect. If she hadn't known better, she would think she was looking at the heat bleed of a person hiding behind the seat.

She checked the Gossamer. Dirty Beard was heading toward her. A hot rush of adrenaline snaked out from her gut and into her limbs.

Easy. Easy. Still plenty of time.

She shouldered the pack and exited the fuselage, then made her way to the spot she had prepared. Along the way, she double checked the route. Everything was still clear.

The density of the foliage made the eastern side an unlikely route into the field, and she expected Dirty Beard and whomever he might show up with to enter at the front end, or perhaps at the back, as she had. But if she were wrong, the undergrowth would offer concealment, even against night vision. Thermal imaging, which would identify her by her own body heat, would be a different problem. Hence the wetsuit.

It was far from a perfect solution. Because over time, her body heat would make its way through the neoprene insulation and warm the exterior of the suit. Meaning the longer she wore it, the less invisible she would be. But for a short time, in this environment, and if Dirty Beard entered at the opposite end and focused on the fuselage, as she expected . . . it would be enough.

She checked the Gossamer again. Assuming he made no stops, she estimated she had thirty minutes before Dirty Beard arrived.

She pulled off her boots and clothes, spreading them out so their temperature would more quickly equalize with the ground. The clothes were cotton, which lost heat quickly. The insides of the boots would be hotter and would take longer, but buried in the pack it wouldn't be a problem.

She stood and closed her eyes for a moment. The night air was still sultry, but there was a slight breeze, palpable now against her naked skin. It wouldn't cool her much, but every little bit would help.

Keeping one eye closed to protect her night vision, she pressed the wireless remote for the strobe lights again, even though she'd already confirmed at the hotel that the setup would work at this distance. The lights popped lightning-stark inside the fuselage. She adjusted the setting to a three-second burst—more than enough time to reach their position.

From the pack, she removed the wetsuit and set it on the ground. It was too soon to get into it. Besides, she wanted the neoprene to be the same temperature as the ground, not the air. Probably overkill, but again, every little bit would help.

She scoped the field through the FLIR. There were no people anywhere, just the heat of traffic on the street off to her left and, alongside some distant debris, a small signature she suspected was the dog. She checked the Gossamer. Ten minutes now, maybe less. She took a deep breath and nodded to herself. It was a good plan. A good setup. She could do this.

She closed down the FLIR. The unit threw its own heat signature, and if she was using it when Dirty Beard showed up, it could give away her position. She set it down in an indentation in the earth. With her body over it, it would be invisible to thermal even before it had cooled.

She was sweating, so she toweled off and doused herself with talcum powder. Even so, it took longer to get into the wetsuit than when she'd tried it on in the air-conditioned store. When she was done, she pin-wheeled her arms, rotated her torso left and right, and did a quick pair of drop steps. For five millimeters of neoprene, the thing was incredibly flexible. But in the Bangkok heat, it was oppressive the instant she got into it. She pulled on the integrated balaclava hood and drew the drawstring tight. Then the neoprene boots and gloves. The ASP steel baton, retracted, fit nicely in a zippered stomach compartment, along with the wireless remote.

She checked the Gossamer again. Less than five minutes. Time to get in position.

She proned out and burrowed into the ditch she'd dug earlier, making sure she was well covered with leaves and vines, the FLIR concealed beneath her stomach, her head protruding just enough to maintain a view of the fuselage and the likely routes into the field. She closed her eyes and listened. The thick balaclava impeded her hearing. She'd considered cutting small earholes, but didn't know how much heat might bleed through and decided the thermal-imaging protection was more important.

After a few minutes, she thought she had a reasonably good notion for the baseline sounds of the area. An intruder would disrupt that baseline.

Another few minutes passed. She thought he should have arrived by now. She wasn't worried about waiting—she'd waited sixteen years—but the interior of the suit was already sauna-hot. Even five millimeters of neoprene wouldn't conceal that heat for much longer.

You're okay. Half-buried in dirt and covered with underbrush. And it's nearly ninety degrees out here. The contrast will be minimal. And it's humid as a steam room, especially alongside that drainage canal. That'll cut the contrast, too. You're okay.

The dog barked. She glanced around, moving only her eyes. She saw nothing. The dog barked again.

The way it had when she arrived. And hadn't since.

Someone was coming in. But where?

She resisted the urge to take out the FLIR. Instead, she closed her eyes again and listened intently. It was maddening to have the sound dulled by the neoprene. For a moment, she regretted her decision not to cut earholes and was tempted to pull off the balaclava.

She heard a branch snap behind her and to her left. She froze.

Footsteps, moving slowly, crunching the underbrush, more than one pair. The sound couldn't have been ten feet away. They were practically on top of her.

14

If they had thermal, the part of her that would show most clearly would be the exposed area around her eyes. From this close, that would be enough.

Slowly, she lowered her face and pressed it to the earth, breathing shallowly to minimize any heat signature from her own exhalations. She kept absolutely still, withdrawing all her energy, feeling as though she wasn't even there, that she had ceased to exist. If they saw her, she was dead.

The footsteps came closer. They slowed. Stopped.

She felt nothing. She thought nothing. She was. Nothing.

The footsteps continued past her. It took her a moment to realize it, as though she was rebooting from some suspended state. She waited, and when she couldn't hear them anymore, she raised her head and glanced right.

There they were, three of them. All holding pistols. In the dim light, she could make out gear protruding from their faces. Night vision, as she'd feared.

Feared, yes. But prepared for.

She wondered what level. It might have been anything. Cheap surplus. Or state of the art, provided under an export license by the US government, maybe Gen 3 dual sensor—image intensifier and infrared combined. The anti-gang unit had that gear. These guys might, too. And what else? Vests, probably. Something else to work around.

She watched them creep out from the tree line and toward the back of the plane, their heads and torsos sweeping back and forth as they moved, their pistols tracking their gaze. She was in luck: they were all right-handed. She'd be approaching from behind and to their right, meaning they'd be forced to turn clockwise to face her, biomechanically an awkward angle of defense for someone right-handed, and one that offered scant opportunity to engage with the left hand while shooting with the right.

When they reached the back of the fuselage, they did one last 360-degree sweep. She knew that would be it—now they would turn and focus on the interior.

They did. As soon as their backs were to her, she pulled off the neoprene gloves and slid the FLIR from underneath her. Keeping one eye closed to preserve her night vision, she quickly confirmed no other human heat signatures anywhere in the field—just the three of them. The closest and the one in the middle were big. The farthest was small. That was Dirty Beard. He must have felt safer with muscle.

Dirty Beard held up a hand to the other two, then gestured inside the fuselage. He'd seen the heat signature from the chemical packs. They thought they'd spotted her.

She placed the FLIR next to the backpack, brought her knees in, and came smoothly to a sprinter's starting crouch. With her left hand, she took the wireless strobe remote from the stomach compartment, and with her right eased out the ASP. The pound and a half of steel in her hand felt reassuringly deadly.

She took a deep breath. Blew it out. Inhaled again. Tensed. And pressed the wireless trigger.

The inside of the fuselage was instantly turned into a lightning storm, the hot white light staccato-silhouetting the three men and over-whelming any auto-gating bright-light cutoff their equipment might have had. She burst from her crouch and flew across the distance, her arms pumping, one eye closed to avoid the blinding strobe. All three of them had been jolted back by the flashing bulbs. Their free hands were up to protect their eyes, and they were sweeping the muzzles of their pistols back and forth across the opening of the fuselage interior, trying to acquire a target that they couldn't see and wasn't there.

She snapped the ASP to her right as she approached the nearest man, extending it to its full twenty-four inches, planting her left foot just short of his position and whipping the baton around as though she was swinging a war hammer. The strobe cut out and suddenly everything was dark again, but with the eye she'd kept closed she could still see well enough. The man must have sensed movement, because he flinched and began to turn toward her. A mistake. The steel bar caught him just above the teeth and shattered his maxilla. Somehow his night-vision goggles stayed secure even as a shock went through his body and his gun flew from his hand. Then his knees went out and he started to slide downward.

Before he had even hit the ground, she was on to the second. Like the first, he was turning clockwise, at least partially blinded and trying to orient his pistol on whatever the danger was. The ASP was across her body now, not yet retracted from the first strike, and she backhanded it into his forearm, snapping his ulna in two. The gun dropped and he howled, a howl she cut off by bringing the baton around and blasting it into his trachea. His arms flew up and his chin came in so hard she had to jerk the baton to clear it, and she slipped past him, closing on Dirty Beard, closing as he spun clockwise to face her, his feet scrabbling back to create distance and buy time, the gun coming around, the muzzle sweeping in, closer, closer—

The ASP was out of position from the way it had buried itself in the second guy's neck—it was trailing her body now, and hitting Dirty Beard's gun arm from this angle would bring the muzzle across her body, not clear of it. Without thinking, she dropped the baton, angled in, and slammed her left shoulder into his right, staying just outside the ambit of the muzzle. Before he could ricochet off her, she caught his gun wrist in her right hand, grabbed the straps of his night-vision gear and a fistful of hair with her left, and took out his right leg with her left in an unorthodox *de ashi barai*—a judo foot sweep. His legs flew right, his head and torso went left, and as she took him to his back she kept the gun hand, got her legs across his chest and face, and ripped his arm back with a classic *juji gatame*—the cross-body armlock. He shrieked as his elbow snapped, and she snatched away the gun, donkey-kicked his face, scrambled to her feet, and dove to her left just as the first guy's gun went off. Between the neoprene balaclava and the adrenaline, it sounded like not much more than a pop, but she saw the muzzle flash and felt the round sizzle past her shoulder. She rolled, brought up Dirty Beard's pistol, and sighted in the direction the shot had come from. In the dim light she could see him, shaking from his injuries, trying to reacquire her through the goggles—

She pressed the trigger. The gun was a .45, bigger than she was accustomed to, and the round went high. The guy shot again. The bullet blew past her to the left. She adjusted, sighted in, squeezed the grip, and shot three times. His body jerked as the rounds hit home—two in the stomach, one in the chest. He might have been wearing a vest. It didn't matter. She paused, sighted carefully, and put a fourth round in his face. His head snapped back and his body shuddered and she knew he was done.

She rolled to her feet and quickly closed the distance to the second guy. He was writhing and twitching, his hands clutching at his throat, trying to draw air through his ruined windpipe, the night-vision goggles flopping around his mouth. She shot him twice in the head.

She looked back at Dirty Beard. He had gotten to his knees. His right arm dangled uselessly, but he was trying to access something in his right pants pocket with his other hand. Probably a knife. She strode forward and kicked him in the balls, the impact hard enough to almost lift him from the ground. He made a retching sound and fell to his side.

She undid the drawstring and peeled the balaclava back off her head. The feel of the night air on her wet neck was delicious. Then she circled behind Dirty Beard, ripped the goggles off his face, and secured them over her own. The tubes were functioning, apparently undamaged by the strobe. And the unit was indeed top quality—dual night vision and infrared. But now the advantage was hers.

She scanned the ground, every detail clear now and beautifully illuminated, and immediately saw where the first two guns had fallen. Too far for Dirty Beard to access, even if he'd been uninjured. The other men lay still, the ground around them glowing with white pools of hot blood.

She retrieved the guns and placed them inside the fuselage, then turned to Dirty Beard. It took her only a moment to reach into the right pocket of his cargo pants and retrieve the folding knife he'd been trying to access. She placed it alongside the guns and grabbed the handcuffs and duct tape. He'd managed to squirm to his knees again. She kicked him onto his stomach, knelt on his back, and cuffed him the way she had scores of suspects when she'd been a patrol officer. He screamed at the manipulation of his broken elbow, and though she was focused on the plan and was trying to be as tactical and dispassionate as possible, she couldn't help but find the sound profoundly satisfying.

As soon as he was cuffed, she wrapped his mouth with duct tape, taking care not to close off his nostrils in the process. Then she wrapped tape around the cuffs. She didn't have time to search him for a handcuff key, and even if he had one, the chances he'd be able to manipulate it with a broken arm were slim. But now the chances were none. And then, though it was almost certainly unnecessary, she taped his ankles together, too.

She ran back to her hiding spot and retrieved the pack, the gloves, and the FLIR, then returned to the fuselage, where she gathered the hot packs, the spare burner, the strobe assembly, and the knife and guns. She realized the dog was barking. She scanned the field and saw no one. The animal must have been reacting to the noise, the violence. Maybe the smell of blood.

She was desperate to get out of the neoprene, but couldn't risk the time. She sprinted back to the truck, threw the pack in the passenger's seat, fired up the engine, and drove down the narrow dirt road, leaving the headlights off and using the goggles to navigate. The ride was bouncy and the suspension bottomed out repeatedly over the deep ruts. It didn't matter. If all went well, tonight would be the truck's last ride.

She pulled up next to the fuselage. The inside of the wetsuit was sloshing with sweat, and she felt light-headed.

Almost there, girl. Almost there.

She left the engine running—the starter relay was sound now, but she wasn't going to take a chance, either. She popped the hatch, yanked Dirty Beard to his feet, and shoved him sprawling inside. Then she dragged in the two bodies. They were heavy, as bodies always are, but the hatch was low to the ground and she managed. She scanned the field and saw two people looking in from Ramkhamhaeng Road. They must have heard the gunshots, or the screams. Or maybe they saw the strobe lights. But they wouldn't be able to make out anything.

She slammed the hatch and took one last look around, ensuring she hadn't overlooked anything. She could see some of the spent casings from the gunfight, still hot, but even if they were found, they'd be irrelevant. Other than the cooling blood soaking into the earth, she saw no evidence that anything at all had happened here, nothing important left behind.

She drove out along the dirt road again, using only the goggles to navigate, smiling grimly at the sound of Dirty Beard screaming behind the duct tape as the suspension repeatedly bottomed out in the deep ruts. The wedding party was going full force—a young Thai woman in a white gown dancing on the stage, surrounded by merrymakers. If they'd heard anything, they hadn't been inclined to investigate. It was easy to rationalize away the sound of gunshots. People did it all the time in Seattle.

When she hit the street, she turned on the headlights and pulled off the goggles. Traffic was moderate, and she made no attempts to get around it lest she draw attention from a passing patrol. Besides, she was in no hurry now. She could take all night, if she wanted to. And she thought maybe she did.

She uncapped a liter bottle of water and took two big swallows, then forced herself to set it aside. She'd learned in competition that small sips were better.

I have him, little bird. I have him. He's finally going to pay.

In the lightless corner of an after-hours shopping-mall parking lot, she peeled off the neoprene. She'd gotten somewhat used to the feel of it, but the moment it was off, it was like being able to breathe again. God, she was drenched. She should have thought to bring a towel. She threw the wetsuit in the passenger's footwell and got back into her street clothes. While she changed, she heard Dirty Beard, trying to talk through the duct tape, the cadences of the muffled words urgent and terrified. She nodded in satisfaction.

Oh, you're going to talk, she thought. *I promise you that.*

15

About five miles west of the airplane graveyard, she turned onto a dirt road, cut the truck lights, and pulled on the goggles. A half mile up the road was a small quarry she had scouted out earlier. It was empty now, as she'd expected, some perimeter security lights illuminating the machinery on the other side of a chain-link fence, but otherwise devoid of signs of life.

Opposite the main plant, on the other side of the dirt road, was an empty gravel field, fenced in on all sides by barbed wire. Maybe overflow parking for the plant. Maybe a future excavation site. Maybe both. The field was deserted, just as it had been during the day.

She turned right and gave the truck a little gas. There was a moment of resistance from the barbed wire, and then it snapped and she was through. She drove to the middle of the field, parked so the hatch was facing the tree line rather than the road, cut the engine, grabbed the daypack, and got out. There was a slightly acrid smell carried on the night breeze—stone dust and metal filings and machine oil. She heard insects buzzing and the muted sounds of distant traffic. Other than that, silence. She finished her water, tossed the plastic bottle back onto the seat, took off the goggles, put them in the daypack, and waited while her eyes adjusted to the dark. Then she went around to the back of the truck and popped the hatch.

Dirty Beard was lying on his stomach to one side, the bodies of his partners jammed against him. He was still trying to talk from behind the duct tape, but the tone was past panic now, tinged more with exhaustion than terror. The interior, which earlier had smelled faintly and pleasantly of produce, now reeked of blood and piss and sweat.

She dialed the SureFire down to fifteen lumens and placed it on the truck bed. Reflected off the roof and walls, it provided enough light to see by, but would only be minimally noticeable from a distance through the open hatch. Although she doubted anyone would be able to see anything at all through the faraway tree line.

She picked up the daypack and checked the guns. They were Glock 21s—the .45 ACP. She'd keep all the magazines and chambered rounds, but would keep only one of the weapons. She could clean it with oxygen bleach later to at least make sure no blood was on it, though if things got to the point where she was explaining how she came into possession of a murdered cop's gun, some blood traces would be the least of her worries. She'd buy a change of clothes and shoes, too, and lose the ones she was wearing. Probably they were fine—the wetsuit would have shielded her from any blood that sprayed when she hit the first guy in the face with the baton, and any she might have picked up while moving the bodies. But it was better to be sure.

She unclipped the Infidel, popped the blade, and knelt alongside Dirty Beard. "Don't move," she said, showing him the knife. "I'm going to cut the tape, and I wouldn't want to miss and slice the wrong thing."

She cut through the tape under one of his ears. He held very still, and she managed not to slip. He whimpered as she tore the tape loose. She saw his skin color was bad—green, as though he'd been fighting the urge to vomit. She realized she should have thought of that. If he'd puked behind the duct tape and she hadn't been able to get to him in time, he would have aspirated it and died. Well, sometimes you just get lucky.

"I can get you money," he said, panting. "I . . ."

Before he could finish, he turned his head and threw up. She felt a weirdly detached satisfaction at the poetic justice of it. She had repeatedly thrown up on the deck of the ship after finishing what he and the other two made her do to them.

"My arm," he moaned. "My arm."

"You were supposed to bring the money. Did you forget it?"

"I can get money."

"It's not that I wouldn't like the money. I would have given it to Saint Clare Hospice."

His sickly color worsened.

"I didn't make him suffer," she said, feeling the dragon stir. "He gave you up without that. But if you don't tell me what I want to know, and if what you tell me doesn't track with what I already know, you're going to think what I did to your partner Vivavapit and the senator was *nothing*." She pressed the tip of the Infidel against the skin just under his left eye. He yelped and tried to jerk away, but his head was pressed against the wheel well and there was nowhere for him to go.

"I tell you," he said, panting now. "Whatever you want. Just . . . please. My arm. I cannot think right. Because of pain."

He had a point. The broken elbow, exacerbated by the handcuffs and the bumps in the ride, must have been excruciating. And severe pain didn't just cause people to pretend things. It caused them to imagine them, too. And yet.

"But that's the thing," she said. "I *want* you to be in pain. Because no matter what I do to you, it'll be nothing to what you did to me. What you did to my sister, Nason."

"I'm sorry."

No you're not, she thought. *But you will be.*

"I have three questions. All very simple. And I already know most of the answers. So if you lie, I'll know it. Do you understand?"

"I tell the truth. And you let me go."

She wondered how he could believe an exchange like that was remotely possible. Desperation, she supposed. Whatever. What mattered was that she would exploit it.

"If you tell the truth," she said, trying to let a little reluctance creep into her tone.

He shook his head, as though knowing she didn't mean it. "Think," he said. "I can't tell anyone. You have Sakda confession. How could I explain, explain any of this?"

"All I want is information."

He shook his head again, obviously not buying it. "I'm sorry," he said. "For what we did. It was Vivavapit. We all afraid of him."

Square Head had claimed the same. And who could say? It might even have been true.

"Who told you to take Nason and me?" she said. "Who gave you the photograph? Who told you where to find us? Where to take us? Who?"

"Vivavapit," he said quickly.

"Bullshit," she said, feeling the dragon unfold inside her, hot and impatient and enraged. "You're not going to blame it all on the dead. Maybe the order went through Vivavapit, but don't even try to tell me you didn't know where it came from. The two of you went all the way back to the RTP Border Patrol, then Narcotics Suppression, then the Central Investigation Bureau. You shared secrets. You shared sisters. You shared *everything*. Don't you fucking tell me you didn't know where the information came from."

She breathed deeply, trying to calm herself. Part of what made her such an effective interrogator, she knew, was her ability to wall off her feelings and approach the subject dispassionately. But finally having Dirty Beard in her power, after so many years of fantasizing about what she would do to him if this moment ever came . . . it was too much. It was distorting her perspective, eroding her tactics.

At least she'd mentioned his history with Skull Face. Implying she knew much more and would catch him in any lies. At least she'd done that.

A moment went by, punctuated by nothing but the smell of his sweat and the sound of his breathing. Then he whispered, "Sorm."

Yes.

"Rithisak Sorm?"

His eyes widened at the mention of the name. She nodded, in confirmation to him and satisfaction to herself. Her tactics were coming back to her.

"Sorm told you to take Nason and me."

"Yes."

"And how did he know where to find us?"

"He . . . just know. Everything he know. Everyone."

His English was degenerating, she noted, from fear and pain and exhaustion. She had to be careful to manage that. Not to let him get to the point where he would invent or imagine whatever he thought would please her and alleviate his suffering.

"Who was Sorm working for?"

"Sorm . . . work for everyone. And everyone work for Sorm."

His mind was starting to drift, his answers to fragment. She had to keep him focused.

"Who gave him the order? Was it the senator?"

He shook his head. "I don't know. Maybe senator. Maybe Thai bosses. Senator . . . he know everyone, too."

All right, maybe it didn't matter that much. Ultimately, it was the senator, whether directly to Sorm or through intermediaries.

"Second question. Pay attention. The night I killed Vivavapit and Redcroft and the senator. The night I butchered them, yes? There was a girl at the hotel. A girl you brought to the senator so he could rape her. Where did you get her?"

"I didn't want. Senator, he—"

She jammed the point of the Infidel against the skin under his eye again. Again he yelped and tried without success to pull away.

"Where. Did you get. That girl."

"Sorm. I get from Sorm."

"Sorm gave you the girl?"

"Yes. He always can get. Anything. Everything you ask."

"No. I told you, we're not going to play that game where everything is someone else's doing. Maybe Sorm provided her, but don't tell me he handed her off personally. You took care of that. You brought her to the room, and you picked her up at the door from Redcroft when the senator was done with her."

She didn't know for sure it had been Dirty Beard, but she was confident enough to accuse him outright. A gambit she'd used countless times while interrogating suspects. And now, if she was lucky, he'd feel that if she knew this much, there was no harm in confirming the rest.

His eyes widened, and she knew she'd been right. He shook his head, but too late—the eyes were the tell, and she'd already seen it.

"No!" he sputtered. "I didn't, I wouldn't—"

She pressed the Infidel hard. The point broke the skin under his eye and he howled.

"You want me to think she appeared and disappeared by magic?" she said, her voice rising. "Is that what you're fucking telling me?"

He vibrated his head—plainly too afraid to shake it.

"Then where did you get her?" she shouted, flecks of spit hitting him in the face. "Where did you take her? Where? Where?"

The dragon had her. She couldn't hold it back anymore. She tightened her grip on the Infidel, took him by the hair with her free hand—

"Night Market," he bleated. "Srinakarin. Night Market."

Her heart kicked hard. It tracked with what she'd seen on the Gossamer. The dragon didn't care. It offered up an image of his skewered eye.

Back off back off BACK OFF

"Where you went two nights ago?"

He glanced at her, his expression one she had seen many times before in reaction to a successful probe: a mix of horror at the scope of her knowledge, and resignation that the escape routes he was hoping for were all walled off.

He nodded. "Yes."

"And where you went tonight, too?"

He didn't respond. He didn't need to. His face said everything she needed to know.

"Who did you meet there?"

"Leekpai. I meet Leekpai."

"Say his full name."

"Udom Leekpai."

"Keep going."

"Leekpai . . . he the one. Who give me girl for senator."

She struggled with the dragon. "Where does Leekpai get the girls?"

"I don't know. Maybe villages. I don't know. When senator want girl, I go to Leekpai."

"Why did you meet him two nights ago, and then again tonight? Were you picking up more children to deliver?"

"No. He give me money."

"Money for what?"

"Because . . . I police."

"Your cut of the profits. From selling children to be raped."

He didn't answer. He didn't need to.

"Why two nights, then? Don't tell me you pick up your bribes every day."

"Leekpai not have all money first time. Sometimes he not have. So I go back."

It might have been true. She didn't have enough information to know.

"Where at the Night Market? And before you answer, the way I've been tracking you is accurate to within about three feet. Whatever you tell me, I'm going to check."

"He have stall. Many stall. He tell me where to meet."

"He's not holding slaves in a stall. Where does he keep the children?"

"Container. Shipping container. Stalls pack up in container when market closed. When I need girl, he take me to container."

She struggled to push back the excitement again, and the rage. "Where is his container?"

"It . . . outside. Outside stalls. But so many container. He take me."

She didn't know whether he wouldn't be more detailed, or couldn't. And hurting him wouldn't clarify anything. He'd start screaming east, or west, or the blue one, or the striped one, or container number thirty-three, or whatever.

But she thought she might have another way.

She wiped the Infidel across the sleeve of his shirt, cleaning the bit of blood on it, then closed it and clipped it back in her pants. She searched his pockets. It took her only a moment to find his cell phone. She pressed the "On" button and was unsurprised to see a passcode lock.

"What's the passcode?" she said.

"I tell you, you let me go?"

"You're going to have to tell me more than just that. But it'll be a step in the right direction."

He nodded and spoke four digits. She input them and the phone unlocked. Naturally, it was all in Thai. But the interface was easy enough, and she went to the address book. She held it so he could see.

"I'm going to scroll through. When I get to Leekpai, you tell me."

He did. She checked and saw a one-name entry she recognized from the spelling as *Udom*. The other entries were two names. So for this one, it seemed, he preferred not to include a last name. That was promising. She used her phone to snap a photo of the entry.

"Now Sorm," she said.

It was the same for Sorm—a first-name-only entry for *Rithisak*. She snapped another photo.

She scrolled through the list of recent calls, and saw calls to and from "Udom" for both nights Dirty Beard had been at the Night Market. All right. It seemed he was telling the truth. About Leekpai, anyway. But there were no calls to or from "Rithisak." She would come back to that.

"Now," she said, "tell me what you were doing in Pattaya two nights ago."

This time, there was no horror in his eyes at the extent of her information. Just the resignation.

"Sorm call me. He say he need money. That why I go to Night Market. Money from Leekpai. And I give to Sorm."

"Why does Sorm need money? He doesn't have an ATM card?"

"He not say. I give him what Leekpai give me. And go back when Leekpai has more. My . . . my part."

"You mean Leekpai was short, but you gave whatever he had to Sorm. And came back for your own cut after."

"Yes. That."

She wondered if it was true. If it were, why would someone like Sorm be so desperate for cash?

She held up his phone. "There are no calls to or from 'Rithisak,'" she said.

"Sorm not call from his phone. Call from new phone."

She looked and saw calls to and from a number with no name associated with it, meaning not one in his contacts list.

"Why is he using a new phone?"

"I don't know. I don't ask."

"Does he ordinarily call from his own phone?"

"Yes."

If it was true, it was interesting. Sorm needed quick cash. And seemed suddenly afraid to use his own phone. Something was going on with him. But she didn't know what.

"But you met Sorm in Pattaya. To give him money."

"Yes."

"Where in Pattaya?"

"His club. Les Nuits. Hotel Ruby."

That tracked with what she'd observed with the Gossamer. It seemed he was telling the truth. At least about the most important things.

Where to get to Sorm.

And where—maybe—to find that little girl.

"Okay?" he said, looking up at her. "I tell you everything. Okay?"

She squatted alongside him and looked at his face, still sickly green in the reflected glow cast by the SureFire, his eyes wide with hope and fear.

"Remember what you made me do?" she said quietly, after a moment. "On the deck of that ship. When I was thirteen."

"Please. Chanchai. We were afraid."

"You didn't look afraid. Not even a little. You looked like you were doing exactly what you wanted to. Night after night after night."

"Please."

"And do you remember what you did to my sister?"

"Please."

"I do. Because for me, anything you did to her was worse than everything you did to me."

"I'm sorry. Please."

"And then I spent sixteen years not even knowing what had happened to her. Whether she was alive. Whether she was dead. Whether some sick, degenerate, sadistic monster like you was raping her night after night after night."

"Please. Please."

"You know, your partner Sakda talked a lot about karma right before I killed him. Do you believe in karma?"

"Yes. But also I believe . . . mercy."

"I'm not sure I believe in karma. Sometimes I guess I do. The things you absorb when you're a child . . . they stay with you."

"Please."

"But after you and Sakda and Vivavapit stole Nason and me, and raped us, and sold us, I grew up in the West. And they don't really believe in karma in the West. In the West, they believe in hell."

"No. Please."

"You're lucky," she said. "For you, it'll be over in minutes. For me, it's been my whole life. And it'll never go away. I'm beginning to realize that, more and more. There are things I do that dull the pain. But only for a while. And then there's always just . . . more pain. Forever."

"Please."

"Unless there really is a hell," she went on. "In which case, the next few minutes will be just a preview for you. I don't know. You won't be able to tell me. Unless one day I see you in hell myself."

She stood, picked up the gasoline canisters, and moved them to the hatch. Then she stepped out, leaned inside, and unscrewed each one. The smell of gasoline was overpowering in the small space.

He struggled against the handcuffs and the duct tape. "No!" he shouted. "No, I told you, no, I sorry, I sorry, no, please, please!"

She picked up one of the canisters and circled the truck, dumping it out on the hood and the roof as she walked. When it was empty, she threw it in back again.

"No!" he kept on shouting. "Please, stop, no!"

She reached in and picked up the Surefire. Then she kicked over the second canister. The gasoline poured out of it, flowing over the floor, soaking into Dirty Beard's clothes.

"Mai!" he screamed in Thai, his voice high and hysterical now, his body thrashing in the gasoline. *"Mai, mai, mai, mai, mai!"*

Then his voice cracked and he stopped. The interior of the truck was suddenly, strangely silent. She pointed the flashlight at his face, and watched for a moment as he stared at her, hyperventilating with terror, his teeth bared, his eyes bulging.

"That's funny," she said. "I used to beg you, too. Remember?"

This time, he didn't speak. He threw back his head and wailed.

She moved back, took out the Zippo, flicked it to life, and tossed it into the truck. Instantly the interior erupted in a ball of orange fire. She stepped farther from the inferno, and then farther still as the heat became increasingly intense. From inside, she could just make out Dirty Beard, bucking and twisting and thrashing. Even the roar of flames wasn't enough to drown out the peals of his agonized shrieks.

In seconds, the vehicle was a fireball—the wheels, the paint, everything ablaze. She continued to back off as the heat grew increasingly intense. At twenty feet away, she could no longer hear Dirty Beard, whether because of the roar of flames or because he was past screaming.

She imagined they'd identify the bodies from dental records. But whatever evidence of her presence might have been in the truck would be incinerated now. And though she doubted the previous owner would be a useful lead to her, they wouldn't find him, either. The VIN on the aluminum plate below the windshield would melt. The one on the sticker on the driver's door frame would be gone entirely. And the others she had filed off. The truck would be useless to anyone investigating. It was nothing but a funeral pyre now.

She turned, pulled on the goggles, and started walking toward the tree line. There was a road beyond it. Tomorrow she would get rid of the extra guns and the contaminated clothes. But for now, she'd just find a tuk-tuk, or a cab. Get something to eat. Drink another bottle of water. Go back to the hotel. Take a scalding-hot shower. Get in bed. Replay all of what had just happened. She knew she wouldn't be able to sleep, at least not for a long time.

It didn't matter. Tomorrow she would go to Pattaya to deal with Sorm. She had an idea about how. She thought it would work. But she still didn't like it.

16

Dox strolled along Beach Road in Pattaya, the beach in question to his left, a long string of cheap restaurants and stores and bars to his right. The palm trees were swaying by the water and the noonday sun was partially hidden by clouds, but still it was like walking through an open-air steam room, with even the stray dogs of the area taking a break from begging and foraging to lie motionless in whatever pavement shade they could find instead. He didn't mind the climate, though. Heat and humidity had always suited him. Cold, on the other hand, he didn't much care for. Back in the day, he'd trained with SEALs on Kodiak Island in Alaska, at the Naval Special Warfare Cold Weather Detachment, and calling conditions on Kodiak Island "cold weather" was like calling bubonic plague a damn runny nose. And then there was the Mountain Warfare Training Center in Bridgeport, California, and a deployment in Norway, for God's sake, practically the North Pole. If he never saw snow again—hell, if he never saw his breath fog up again—he would die a contented man.

He'd rented a motorcycle—a Kawasaki Z800 because the shop was out of anything smaller, not that he minded a big bike, but it didn't blend quite as well here in Pattaya. He'd thought it best to park a little ways off and walk to meet Kanezaki's contact. He was sure Kanezaki was all right. But still, that sword guy in Phnom Penh hadn't just materialized out of the ether.

There was some motorcycle traffic—Pattaya wouldn't be Pattaya without the incessant background buzz of two-stroke engines—but this was a relatively quiet time of day. The partygoers were still sleeping it off, the clubs wouldn't open for at least another six hours, and anyway, who in his right mind wanted to be out and about when the afternoon was at its most sultry?

Well, a few people, at least. The expats who made the beach town their retirement homes, for example. They were mostly Australian and British, sixties on up, with stick arms and beer bellies, divorced, rheumy-eyed old men subsisting on their pensions and trying to persuade themselves that Pattaya was a paradise, where you could sip from dewy bottles of sixty-baht Singha beer al fresco all day and get chased by pretty brown prostitutes outside the go-go bars all night. Where your money, such as it was, made you matter. Not like at home, where leveling things off every afternoon at the local pub with a pint, or three or four, would be prohibitive and, worse, make you feel pathetic, like the old men you'd seen doing the same when you were younger. No, that wasn't you. That was someone else. Pattaya was paradise, and don't you forget it.

He kept moving along, wondering why he was feeling so cynical. It wasn't really like him. He tried to shake it off.

Kanezaki had told him the lab boys had schematics for the Les Nuits nightclub, and in fact for the entire Ruby Hotel. And they'd used their phone-tracking "national technical means" to track the burners Sorm was using to a VIP room at the back of the club. Apparently the VIP room doubled as a safe room, because it had reinforced doors front and back, one attached to the club and the other opening onto a riser of stairs that led to a fire exit at the rear of the building. And though Dox would have preferred something classic and simple, like bursting in, dropping the guy with two in the chest and one in the head, and getting the hell out of Dodge, Kanezaki was insistent about the indictment and Sorm being taken alive. So Dox's role was somewhat unaccustomed: drop any bodyguards, toss in a multibang flashbang to disorient Sorm and anyone else inside, and drag or chase Sorm down the stairs and out the back, where a detachment of contractors would grab him, bag him, and render his ass to New York for trial.

The tricky part was, apparently the club entrance was staffed by a bunch of former Royal Thai marines, with metal-detector wands, sidearms, and a no-nonsense attitude. They'd be focused on what was coming in through the club entrance, not on people running down the stairs on the other end, so the getaway wouldn't be a problem. No, the problem wouldn't be getting out, it would be getting firearms and flashbangs in, as such items had a tendency to set off metal detectors and upset former Royal Thai marine guards. Meaning he needed a way to get in there after hours so he could have the gear already in place when the club opened. The good news in that regard was that the hotel and club had state-of-the-art security, which against your average intruder offered a lot of advantages, but which against the Kanezaki geek squad meant a hacked hotel server and the doors being opened and closed remotely whenever Dox gave the word.

"Can you get me some of them Asian-midget-porn channels for free?" Dox had asked, upon hearing the news about the club's vulnerabilities.

"Absolutely," Kanezaki had replied, dry as ever. "And we'll erase any minibar charges, too."

"Oo-rah, I knew there was a reason I agreed to do this job."

Kanezaki laughed. "Look, we know from the server log when the locks are activated and deactivated. There are workers in Les Nuits getting the club ready for business from six o'clock every evening. Then the club opens at nine and closes at four in the morning, at which point cleaning crews are there until eight. So I can pop the locks and get you close to a ten-hour window with the club all to yourself. But you also have security cameras everywhere."

"If you can open the doors for me, can't you take out the cameras?"

"We can, but we can't guarantee a security guard won't be watching the feed. Probably there won't be—it's just an empty club, after all, not a bank or a military installation—but we don't know. Sorm's presence might have changed their security posture."

"Call me old fashioned, but I have to respectfully tell you once again that I think it would be a whole lot less trouble for me to just shoot this sumbitch and be on my way. Fewer moving parts and all that. Though damn it, I did promise Mr. Vann I wouldn't."

"Also, if you killed him, my guys wouldn't get a chance to interrogate him en route to New York."

"My God, the lengths you will go to, just to satisfy a little curiosity."

Kanezaki laughed. "It's more than that. Sorm has been around forever, first with CIA, and now DIA. He's always been dirty, as dirty as it gets. Which makes him a poison pill for everyone. I mean, if he were ever to testify, shit, how would we explain working with, protecting a guy like that? Former Khmer Rouge? Human trafficking?"

"You want to know why DIA would take that risk. Especially with Sorm under indictment."

"Yes. What are they getting from him?"

"And how do you get it for yourself?"

"Maybe. Depending on the risk-reward ratio. But look, from your perspective, once Sorm is at trial and then in a cell, no one will be motivated to kill Vann anymore. Vann said killing him was about slowing down his Sorm investigation, dragging things out until the next GIFT person takes over and the whole thing can be deep-sixed. But once the trial starts, there's nothing to slow down anymore. There's no longer an advantage to killing Vann."

"Well, I'm fond of Mr. Vann, seeing as how he reminds me of the Dalai Lama and all. But remind me of how all that helps me?"

"Once we interrogate Sorm and figure out who at DIA is behind him, we shouldn't have much trouble mending fences. Maybe what you did to Gant feels a little personal to them, but not unduly so. After all, you only killed Gant when you found out he was trying to do the same to you. Right?"

"That's right."

"I think they should understand that. And Gant's accomplices and the sword guy, too. You never behaved other than professionally. Anyway, maybe right now they're worried about you. But when Sorm is in custody, they'll be worried about him. He'll want to cut a deal, for immunity or at least a reduced sentence. He'll threaten to spill everything. At that point, you'll no longer be a focus."

"I don't mean to sound as though I'm not reassured, but I'm looking for something a little longer term than 'at that point.'"

"At that point—and after—we ought to have plenty of opportunities to ameliorate tensions. There are only two ways this thing ends. Either Sorm will spill the beans about what he's been up to for all these years while on the Uncle Sam payroll, and what DIA tried to do to Vann to protect him, in which case your knowledge of how they tried to kill Vann is superseded. Or—"

"Or Sorm hangs himself in his jail cell."

"In which case I make sure to explain to whoever that if you were going to be indiscreet, you would have done so already. But you haven't been, because overall you're a live-and-let-live kind of guy."

Dox would have preferred the first scenario, with Sorm testifying, but the safe bet seemed like the second. And he knew Kanezaki was stringing him along at least a little, but he'd also learned that when Kanezaki played the game, there was always some kind of secret side bet. So far, there had never been a conflict between that side bet and the primary action.

So far.

And that's where they'd left it. Not a perfect plan or a complete solution, but it was also true that when you wound up blowing a DIA officer's brains out, the road back to whatever you called *normal* was apt to be somewhat serpentine.

He kept strolling along, passing more bar patios and more rheumy-eyed old white men. Seeing them everywhere made the town feel like a damn hospice or something. He wondered about his mood. He'd liked Pattaya well enough back in the day. Maybe it was different when you got older. Maybe seeing all those pensioners made you start thinking about how you could become one of them, about how maybe that process was already stealthily under way. After all, they'd never expected it to happen to them, had they? And then, one day, you'd find yourself nursing a hangover and your fourth noontime beer on the patio of your local bar, trying to make sense of it all, how'd you'd fallen so far and never even noticed, how all the goodness you'd always expected from life had gone and evaporated and you'd never even realized until it was too late.

Jesus, man, what's wrong with you?

He shook it off. There was a place for philosophizing, and okay, maybe he ought to make a little more time for it. But right now, he was operational. Best to do things in their proper order.

He came to what Kanezaki had told him to look for—an alley between a tiny store called Siam Silver and an open-air restaurant called Best Foods. He made a right and immediately came to a dilapidated place called Best Friend Bar 10, with vinyl-covered stools lined up under a corrugated awning. It seemed there was only one patron, a white guy of about sixty in tan cargo shorts and a plain blue tee shirt, sitting on one of the stools and angled in such a way that he had a view of the alley and the street beyond it, a half-empty bottle of Singha in front of him. The guy was wearing gray aviator shades, but even so, Dox could tell the guy had clocked him immediately, not that he'd made any show of it, his head turning slightly past like he'd been taking in the sights and not focusing on anything in particular. Unlike the area's typical retirees, this guy looked solid—not a gym rat, exactly, but not someone whose only exercise was lifting a beer up and down all day, either. Plus the guy was wearing hiking sandals—the same as Dox, in fact, light enough not to be out of place in the area, but a hell of a lot sturdier, more protective, and more reliable than the flip-flops more commonly favored by Pattaya expats. His toes were on the ground, too, where they could do some good in a hurry if there were a problem, not wrapped around the back of the bar stool. A khaki mailbag rested by his feet, the strap looped over one of his knees.

Dox made sure the guy could see his hands were empty and moved slowly past. He stopped a little ways down and plonked himself onto a stool, the guy to his left and well within his peripheral vision. The guy was facing forward now, keeping an eye on Dox just like Dox was keeping one on him, his hands on the bar like a good professional letting a contact know he wasn't a threat. Or at least not an immediate one.

A young Thai guy was sitting behind the bar, reading a magazine and getting hot air blown onto his back by a fan perched alongside the bottles lined up behind him. "Hey there," Dox called out to him. "What's a man gotta do around here to get an ice-cold beer?"

The bartender stood. "Singha sixty baht."

"I favor Chang. Got any of that?"

"Chang sixty-five baht."

"Well worth the premium, in my opinion. I'll have one, thank you. And it can't be cold enough."

Dox pulled out a crumpled hundred-baht note and smoothed it out on the bar. A moment later, the bartender placed a frosty bottle of Chang in front of him, popped the cap, and went back to his reading.

Dox glanced at the guy to his left, lifted the bottle, took a long, tasty pull, and belched. "How's your day going?"

"Can't complain."

The guy had a gravelly voice. Maybe a smoker. For some reason, Dox had the sense he was a former marine. It would have been hard to say why—it was just one of those things you could tell, like when a beautiful woman was actually a lady-boy. Well, scratch that, there'd been that one time in Bangkok when he *hadn't* known, and was about to go back to his hotel with a gorgeous creature named Tiara when Rain had belatedly—and way too reluctantly—interceded. The man still liked to give Dox grief about the incident, or near incident, and it was true Dox had been mortified at the time. But he'd come to figure, hell, if it had happened with Tiara, the world would have kept on spinning and it would have been just one more strange thing that had happened to him on this crazy ride of life.

"I'm guessing you're from around here," Dox said, departing somewhat from the bona fides Kanezaki had provided him. Just walking up and saying *The moon is blue* or whatever always felt so artificial to him. "You mind if I ask you a question?"

The guy took a sip of beer. "Go ahead."

"What do you reckon is the best go-go bar in all of Pattaya?"

"Pattaya go-go bars are overrated. Try Phuket. Better yet, Soi Cowboy in Bangkok."

Bingo.

The script now called for the guy to exit stage right, leaving behind the mailbag. But for whatever reason, that scenario was suddenly making Dox's teeth itch. He got up and sat next to the guy. The guy watched him, scowling a little as though perplexed or irritated at the departure from the script, and from sound tradecraft, as well. But the way Dox saw it, scripts and tradecraft and all that were more a guideline than a rule. Marines were encouraged to adapt and improvise. And besides, his whole nom de guerre was short for "unorthodox." It would be a pity not to live up to the name.

"I like your bag," Dox said, gesturing with a finger and thereby drawing attention to the very thing that was supposed to be most unobtrusive in their interaction. "Had one just like it I bought from a J. Peterman catalogue back in the day, but a light-fingered lady made off with it in the dead of night, along with my heart."

"That's a sad story," the guy said, appealingly unfazed.

Dox raised his beer in agreement, took a sip, and set it down. "It is, it is. Though in the strangest way, I realize now the bag is somehow associated with her in my mind. Would you do me the kindness of allowing me to have a look at yours? For me, it would be a little trip down memory lane, and I'd be grateful."

The guy took a casual glance around. It didn't feel like a witness check, more an *Are we being watched?* kind of thing.

He pulled the strap from his knee and handed it to Dox. "Be my guest."

Dox set the bag on his lap. If there was a bomb in it, it would blow his balls off, but the rest of him would be gone, too, so he wouldn't have to miss them. He didn't really think there was a bomb—Kanezaki was solid, he knew that—but the shit with Gant and then the sword guy had rattled him a little, and he didn't like the idea of a stranger handing him a package and walking off to some minimum safe distance, at which point the package could easily go *boom*. Better to confirm. And the fact that Mr. Gravelly Voice seemed unperturbed to have Dox handling the bag right alongside him, while perhaps not confirmation itself, was at least reassuring.

He opened the flap and took a peek inside. Immediately visible was the very Wilson Combat Tactical Supergrade he'd requested, along with two spare magazines. There was also a fist-sized metal canister labeled *CTS MODEL 7290-9 FLASH BANG. 1.5 SECOND DELAY.*

He might have reached inside, but that could have made his new friend understandably nervous. In his experience, these encounters tended to go better when everyone tried to keep everyone else relaxed. So instead, he gave the bag a good shake. The guy just frowned a little, as though perplexed or impatient. Well, perplexed and impatient were fine, as they weren't the typical reactions of a man sitting alongside someone shaking a bag with a bomb inside it.

He supposed it was possible the guy himself had been duped and didn't know that what he thought was a flashbang was in fact an IED. But these what-if scenarios were getting increasingly unlikely. Probably Rain would have brought along an X-ray machine, or explosive-detection wipes, or a bomb-disposal robot, or whatever, before signing for the package, but Dox himself felt satisfied.

He took another swallow of the cold Chang, glanced around, shouldered the bag, and stood. "Well, sir, I'd like to stay and chat, but I've got places to go and people to meet. If you don't mind my saying, I do like your style, and I'm not talking only about your taste in mailbags."

"Yours is interesting, too." The guy seemed to be struggling not to smile.

"Well, thank you. People say it's an acquired taste, but I like to think your more discerning types can appreciate it right away. I hope our paths will cross again sometime."

The guy looked at him as though trying to decide something. Then he reached into a pocket and produced a card. Dox took it. *Mark Fallon*, the card said. *Tips Tours & Trips*. With an address, email, and phone number. On the opposite side was the same information in Thai.

"You speak Thai?" Dox asked, pocketing the card.

"I've been out here for a while. You think you're the only one with a sad story about a stolen heart?"

Dox chuckled. "No, sadly, life's hardships are more widely distributed than just that." He held out his hand. "Call me Dox."

They shook. "Fallon."

"I'm glad to make your acquaintance, sir."

Fallon lifted his beer. "Good luck to you."

"And to you. Semper fi."

Fallon smiled at that, and Dox knew he'd been right about his being a fellow jarhead. He gave a nod, headed back to the street, and caught a tuk-tuk. It was time to get to know the world-famous Ruby Hotel.

17

Livia tossed and turned for a long time, juiced on adrenaline, replaying over and over in her mind everything that had happened at the airplane graveyard and the quarry. Killing Dirty Beard, knowing he was dead, remembering his terror and helplessness and shrieks of agony . . . it suffused her with something. Peace. Fulfillment. A measure of satisfaction, she supposed, at the feeling that maybe there could be a tiny bit of justice amid so much horror and cruelty.

But at the same time, she was worried again the feeling wouldn't last. She didn't sense that emptiness, the way she had after killing Square Head. But she could tell she would. She didn't understand how that could be. She was making them pay. All of them, one by one. What she'd longed for, dreamed of, fantasized about, obsessed over, for sixteen fucking years. It wasn't right that killing them wouldn't offer more than a palliative. It wasn't fair.

She tried thinking of something else. How to get to Sorm. Yes. That seemed to help. She needed a way that didn't involve Little. But she couldn't find one. The best she could devise was something that might mitigate her risk, not eliminate it.

But no risk, no reward.

She called him. It was the middle of the night in Thailand, so afternoon the next day in the States.

"Livia," he said when she put the call through. "This is a nice surprise."

"Or a surprise, anyway."

"Is there a problem?"

"More an opportunity."

"What can I do?"

"Do you know someone named Sorm? Rithisak Sorm."

There was a pause. "You know I do," he said. "His name is in the files I shared with you."

"And do you know where he's located?"

"If you read those files, you know I don't."

"Well, I think I do."

There was another pause. "I don't mean to sound doubtful," he said. "But . . . I've had people looking for Rithisak Sorm for a long time. The man's a ghost. Are you sure you've located him?"

"No. But it's a solid lead."

"What kind of lead?"

"Just a lead. But to follow up on it, I'm going to need your help."

"And you don't like asking for help, do you?"

"Do you want to keep trying to psychoanalyze me? Or do you want to get Sorm?"

"Can't I do both?"

She ignored that, having made her point. "I think he's at a club in Pattaya. Les Nuits. In the Ruby Hotel."

"Okay."

"I think he's using the club as a trafficking conduit." That wasn't exactly true, but it wasn't untrue, either—she didn't know that Sorm *wasn't* using the club that way, and the elision would obscure her reasons for asking Little for help. "I want to get a closer look."

"Why do you need me for that?"

"Because I want to get into areas not ordinarily accessible to guests."

"Livia, I like your style."

"But I don't know your capabilities," she went on. "You said you have resources to waste. Well, can you get schematics for the club? Identify security vulnerabilities? Exploit them?"

"Yes, yes, and maybe."

"I need three yeses if this is going to work."

"Give me a few hours."

She clicked off and tried without much success to sleep. And then, when the sun was just coming up and she was finally beginning to drift off, her phone buzzed. Little.

"Good news," he said. "Three yeses."

"Tell me."

"The hotel and club are brand new. State-of-the-art systems, with everything centrally controlled—lighting, door locks, HVAC, alarm system, everything. And I have people who can gain control of all of it."

It was what she'd been hoping for, and at the same time trying not to. She pushed away her excitement and focused on the plan. "Does that mean you can get me into the club during the day, when it's empty?"

"That's exactly what it means."

The next part would require a little more . . . explanation. "What about while it's operating? Could you cut the lights?"

There was a pause. "Everything but maybe the bathrooms, which apparently are manual. Why would you want me to do that?"

"I want to check it out when it's closed. Learn whatever I can learn. But I'm guessing what I'm looking for won't be there during the day. So I'll need to go back at night."

"But the club will be open at night."

"The club will be open. The parts I want to get into will be closed. I want you to unlock them. And at the same time, cut the lights. Just for a minute. Long enough for me to slip inside places I'm not supposed to be."

"I think I get it. But if the lights are cut, how are you going to see?"

She was ready for the question. She might have told him she'd have a flashlight handy. But he would have called bullshit, because in the dark, people would see the flashlight. So she told him the truth. Or part of it, anyway. "I have night vision."

"Night vision? How the hell did you get night vision in Bangkok?"

"Are you going to keep asking me how I do things, or are you going to help me get them done?"

"I'm just impressed, that's all."

"I'll bring in the night-vision gear during the day, when you pop the locks. Find a place to hide it. Have a good look around, then come back at night, get the goggles, and, when I'm ready, give you the sign. At which point you kill the lights and pop the locks, and I have a good look in places I'm not supposed to go. Sound like a plan?"

"I knew this was going to be a beautiful friendship."

"Don't get ahead of yourself. And brew some coffee. When I go in the first time, off-hours, it'll be the middle of the night for you, assuming you're in the States."

"Don't you worry about me. I'll be too excited to sleep."

She imagined herself in the club, hiding not just the goggles, but the Glock she'd taken from Dirty Beard.

Yeah, she thought. *Me, too.*

18

Dox rode the Kawasaki to Bali Hai Pier—the southern side of the city, and the western end of Pattaya's famous Walking Street. This was the jumping-off point to surrounding islands in the Gulf of Thailand, a place busy throughout the day with ferries, speedboats, fishing charters, and scuba outfitters. Hundreds of people were coming and going when Dox got there. No one would notice, much less remember, yet another tourist taking in the sights.

He parked the bike, locked the helmet to it, adjusted the mailbag, and started strolling along, sticking to the shade when he could, just picking up the vibe, getting a feel for the place. It was more crowded than he remembered, and definitely more frenetic. But the overall feel of it was the same—an overbuilt Southeast Asian beach town selling sun and surf and sex. The big orange Pattaya City sign was still there, perched on a green hillside, the city's answer to the Hollywood sign across the Pacific. The biggest change was just to the left of the sign: a massive gray building, fifty stories tall and shaped like a backward lowercase *h*. The Hotel Ruby. With Club Les Nuits, according to the hotel website, occupying the entire fifteenth floor all the way across the horizontal line of the *h*.

He spent an hour just moseying around, moving with the crowds, making sure he knew his best routes out if the shit went sideways. When he was satisfied with his recon, he headed over to the hotel. The building was visible from half of Pattaya, but the main entrance revealed itself only after a walk along a curving, bamboo-lined flagstone path. And what an entrance it was: fifty feet of soaring glass and steel, with three giant granite fountains in front shooting synchronized arcs of water from one to the other. Dozens of people were lined up to watch the show, the sounds of their laughter and conversation periodically drowned out by the splash of the jetted water landing in the fountains. Most of the people were holding up cell phones and taking pictures, maybe video. Dox was glad to be wearing shades and a baseball cap—not the best disguise in the world, but a whole lot better than nothing.

He headed past a line of fancy cars and hustling valets, then a platoon of bellboys in vests and ties, and went inside. The place was impressive, no doubt. All that glass, and trees in the lobby growing right up to the soaring ceilings. There must have been a hundred people, sipping coffee in the lounge, checking in at reception, gawking at the sights, and the sounds of all their comings and goings echoed in the vast space. He tended not to care for places that practically tried to make you cry uncle with their own opulence, and this was clearly one of them.

There was free Wi-Fi in the lobby, and he called Kanezaki using Signal. "Hey, amigo. You ready to get me into places I'm not supposed to be?"

"On your mark."

"Okay. Exactly five minutes from when we click off, kill the camera feeds and open the club locks. I'm about to get into the elevator and might lose the Wi-Fi reception. Though from the look of this place, I'm guessing they have Wi-Fi everywhere, probably even in the swimming pools."

"They do. Not the pools, but yeah."

"Okay, good to know. If there's a problem, I'll holler. If not, I'll check in when the equipment is in place. If you don't hear from me, call the president."

"He's standing by."

Dox chuckled and clicked off. He checked his watch, then headed up to the fifteenth floor, shedding the operational feeling, getting into character.

The elevator was wood-and-leather lined, and fast enough to pop his ears. He got out on the fifteenth floor. Just a long and satisfyingly empty corridor, floor-to-ceiling glass on both sides with views of the harbor. At the end of the corridor stood a pair of massive, black-lacquered doors, each emblazoned with a bold sign reading *Les Nuits* in gold script.

Above the door was a camera—no surprise, and not a problem, either. He gawked out the windows like a tourist until his watch said the five minutes was nearly up. Then he continued slowly down the corridor, just a visitor awed by the sights and with no particular purpose. He paused before the massive black doors and stared up at them for a moment as though in wonder, in case there had been a problem and Kanezaki hadn't managed to cut the camera feed. Then he reached out, gripped an oversized bronze handle, and pulled. For a second, he thought it was locked—but no, it was just that the door was heavy as a damn mountain. He pulled harder and it opened right up. He smiled and headed in, letting the door swing slowly shut behind him.

The inside was completely crazy—like the designers had studied the glitziest Las Vegas clubs and decided to merge them all in a parody. In the light coming through the partially draped windows, he saw giant blown-glass chandeliers, and gilt-framed Renaissance-looking paintings, and high ceilings all done up like the Sistine Chapel. The walls were papered in gold lamé, the carpet was deep green and plush enough to sleep on, and the chairs and tables were all mahogany with gilded edges. He stood for a moment, taking it all in, marveling that people thought hillbillies like him were the ones with the bad taste.

He figured his best place to hide the gun and the flashbang would be a bathroom, so he found one, went in, and flipped on the lights. But rather than the expected porcelain, behind or inside of which he could easily tape the hardware, he was confronted by the most minimalist nonsense he'd ever seen. Instead of urinals, there were just short metal shelves protruding from the mirrored walls. Hell, did they really expect a drunk to be able to direct a urine flow with that kind of precision? He was a damn marine sniper, and he wasn't sure, three Bombay Sapphire martinis in, he'd be able to manage it himself. And the stall toilets were worse—just the crapper, set against the wall with nowhere to tape a package out of sight, and not even a tank you could put something inside. Damn, back in the day, Rain had once hidden himself underneath a bathroom vanity using a mountaineering rig. Here, you couldn't hide a baby hamster.

All right, time to improvise. He killed the lights and went back out to the club. He imagined it later on—noisy, crowded, darker. With people around, he'd need his back to a wall so he'd only have to worry about being seen from one direction.

He moved along briskly, not seeing quite what he wanted, mindful that if a security guard had noticed anything weird with the camera feeds, he might have only another couple of minutes. The rooms seemed to be done up in different themes—some kind of Greek or Roman thing going on in one, Michelangelo on acid in another, priapic Louis XIV in a third . . . and wait, what was this, a set of karaoke rooms. No locks on the doors, either—they swung right open.

Inside it was dark. He didn't want to try the lights, in case a guard were to come along, so he pulled a duct-tape-wrapped mini light from his cargo shorts and used that instead. The room was done up in gold and black velour, with a giant flat-panel screen, a long cushioned built-in bench, various leather chairs, and—*bingo*—one giant leather ottoman.

He held the flashlight between his teeth, flipped the ottoman up on its side, and ran his fingers along the lining at the bottom. It felt like plywood underneath. He rapped it with a knuckle, and yeah, just thin wood to keep the batting in place. Okay, good to go.

He opened his trusty Emerson Commander and started hacking into the plywood near one of the legs. After a minute, the floor had a bunch of plywood chunks on it, and there was about a six-inch-square hole in the underside of the ottoman. He reached inside and felt around. Nothing but batting. Good. He pulled the gun, spare magazines, and flashbang from the mailbag and slid them all inside. After a moment's thought, he slid in the Emerson, too. He doubted he'd miss it in the short term—his backup, a Fred Perrin La Griffe, was dangling from a lanyard around his neck as always, and this way he'd only be unarmed briefly, on his way back into the club and before retrieving his gear.

He pushed in the plywood chunks and returned the ottoman to its place, making sure to line up the legs with the indents they'd worn into the carpet. He took the flashlight from his teeth and swept it over the area. *Perfect.* Even if he'd missed a few wood splinters or sawdust, it would be concealed under the bulk of the ottoman itself.

He straightened, cracked his neck, put away the flashlight, and walked out through the swinging door. Those crazy toilets had thrown him for a minute, but he'd found something even better. He moved quickly back through the club. The entrance doors were just twenty feet away now. No guards in sight and mission accomp—

One of the entrance doors swung open. Not a security guard, though— a pretty woman with a Thai face but a stride he made as American. Had she just wandered up here and randomly tried the doors, only to find them unlocked? He realized he should have thought of a way for Kanezaki to lock up while he was inside. But he'd expected to be only a few minutes.

For one bad second, he flashed on the sword guy. Was it possible this was another damn setup? If so, the only possible explanation would be Kanezaki.

But whether she was good news or bad, the approach was the same. He continued right on toward her and switched reflexively into character, calling out, "Well, hello there. I had a feeling I was early, but it looks like we can get this party started after all."

She watched him, casual in shorts, a tee shirt, and hiking sandals like his. The strap of the leather bag she was carrying ran from her left side and over her right shoulder, pressing between her breasts along the way. Damn, she really was attractive, but there was also definitely something no-nonsense about her. He stopped a few feet away—he'd planned on moving in closer, but got the feeling she wouldn't be overly welcoming about too little body space.

"I'm just looking for a bathroom," she said evenly.

He wasn't sure what she was here for, but he could tell it wasn't him. There was just none of that missile-lock vibe he'd gotten from Zatōichi. In fact, she seemed as surprised to see him as he was to see her, and more discomfited besides. It occurred to him that he might probe her story a little. If she was some kind of operator, it would be good to know it. And if she wasn't . . . well, she sure was pretty. More than pretty. And alluring for some other reason he couldn't quite put his finger on.

"I just used one myself," he said. "Strangest decor I think I've ever seen—heavy on form and light on function, in my opinion. But then again, any port in a storm, I always say."

She looked at him like she was trying to figure out what his deal was. It was okay. He was feeling the same way about her, though hopefully hiding it better.

"Right," she said. "Thanks for the restroom wisdom. I'm just going to go use it now. You have a good day."

"I'll tell you what could make my day better."

She looked at him, and he sensed she was losing patience—whether because he was interfering in some kind of op or because she got hit on a lot, he wasn't sure. Weirdly, he hoped it was the first one. It was more intriguing, and honestly, more of a turn-on.

He waited a moment for a response, and when none was forthcoming, he went on. "A drink with you. Not here at fabulous Club

Les Nuits, of course, they were obviously unprepared for our arrival, and their loss, too. But maybe some other place in the neighborhood. What do you say?"

"I say it's very nice of you to ask. But no, I'm going to meet some friends."

"You could bring me along. People say I'm personable."

"I can tell you are. And maybe we'll run into each other again somewhere in Pattaya. But not today, okay?" She gave him a moment's cool stare, then walked on past him.

"And then she left," he called out after her. "And broke my heart."

She headed into the women's restroom without even a backward glance.

He stood for a moment, uncertain. He couldn't help thinking about the hiking sandals. Or the bag, which was big enough to conceal a gun or who knew what else. Was it possible she was here to emplace something, just like he was? If so, she was going to hate that bathroom.

Maybe he ought to stick around for another minute. See what happened when she came out. If she did have a gun—or, hell, a sword, for that matter—and she'd been intending to use it on him, it would already have happened; she could have dropped him clean as he was walking toward her, and he would have had nothing to do in response but die. Yeah, he could stick around. Get a better sense of what he was dealing with. Maybe even get to deal with it. After all, if no security guards had shown up yet, it seemed unlikely he had anything to—

The club doors swung open again and two uniformed hotel guards strode in. Dox shook off the surprise and immediately headed toward them, giving them a big wave as he moved.

"Well, thank God," he called out, loudly enough for the woman to hear from the bathroom. "What does a man need to do to get a drink around here?"

The guards looked at each other, then at him. "Sir," the one on the left said, "you not supposed to be here."

"Not supposed to be here? Ain't you the bartenders?"

They looked at each other again, and again the one on the left spoke. "No. Club closed. Open at nine. How you get in?"

Maybe the one on the right didn't speak English. It didn't matter. "I just walked in. Are you telling me I'm too early? No wonder nobody's here."

"Yes, club closed. Doors locked."

"Locked? I don't believe so. I just pulled and the door opened easy as pie."

They looked at each other again. This time, the talkative one said something in Thai to his partner, which began a lively exchange. Then the English speaker looked at Dox again. "These doors supposed to be locked. Club closed. You no should be here. Please, sir. You have to go."

"Wait a minute, are you telling me these doors were left unlocked by accident? Now that concerns me. You see, if the doors are supposed to be locked and they're left unlocked, that's a problem, I've been in establishments like that and I promise you, sir, it is never good, there is a danger of pilfering and lord knows what else. I'd like to offer my services in assisting you in lodging a formal written complaint, to your ombudsman or some other appropriate authority, detailing the deficiencies in hotel security."

"Please, go. Go. Club not open."

"Well, sir, if you're satisfied that the club is secure, all right, then—I don't want to create a problem, but I would advise you—"

"Please, sir. Please. It's okay. Club closed. Just go. All okay."

"All right, if you're really certain everything is okay. I'm just glad we managed to identify the problem with the doors. Even though I was initially hoping you were bartenders and disappointed to learn I was mistaken, I salute you gentlemen for your courtesy and professionalism."

"Thank you, sir. Please go now."

He gave them each a crisp salute and headed out. He hoped they weren't fixing to search the club now—if they did, they might find that pretty lady, whoever she was. And the presence of another intruder would only reignite their suspicions about him.

He doubted they'd bother too much, though. If they were the careful type, they wouldn't have let him go so easily in the first place. He got the sense they were more concerned about covering their own asses and not having to fill out paperwork than they were about securing the club. Besides, as Kanezaki had pointed out, it wasn't like the place was a bank or military installation. This Sorm guy would probably have his own bodyguards, who could be expected to provide stiffer opposition than a couple of hotel rent-a-cops. But for now, he had a feeling he was okay.

Back in the lobby, he considered lingering, but decided on balance the safer move was to just go. Though he wished he could have had a chance to figure out what that pretty lady was up to. And maybe get to know her a little better.

Well, it was a small world, and a smaller town. It seemed like a crazy coincidence, but who could say, she might even have been a professional, here for Sorm, like he was. There was definitely something about her, he just couldn't articulate what. He supposed he'd keep an eye out later, just in case.

Probably he was wrong, though. Probably it was just a dumb coincidence and he'd never see her again. The thought actually made him sad. He laughed at his own foolishness and headed back out into the Pattaya day.

19

Livia squatted atop one of the stall toilets in the women's restroom, listening. The big guy with the Texan accent she'd run into on the way in was talking loudly again—to a security guard, or guards, it sounded like. Had something gone wrong? Little had told her there was an anomaly in the camera feed when his people tried to cut it—some kind of interference. So maybe someone had seen her, or the guy? Or come to investigate just because of the anomaly?

She wondered for a moment whether the guy himself could be here on some kind of op, but then thought no. He was good-looking, and she supposed his crazy confidence and talkativeness were somewhat endearing, but it was hard to imagine he was anything other than a tourist party animal who'd gotten lost and just happened to try the club doors the moment Little's people had unlocked them. Maybe it was an act, but the criminals she dealt with were all skilled at acting, and she had a nose for that kind of bullshit. She didn't smell it on the Texas guy.

Still, he was talking so loudly out there, he might almost have been trying to warn her. But why? For all he knew, she was just looking for a bathroom, as she'd said. Even if he were some kind of pro, and even if he thought she was, too, why would he warn her?

Because if they find you, they get more suspicious of him.

Well, that was fair. But still, he seemed like nothing more than a hick with a nice smile.

The corridor conversation ended and she heard the entrance doors open and close. It seemed like Texas had left. But she could still hear the guards, talking to each other in Thai. Probably trying to figure out what to do.

She realized maybe she shouldn't have turned on the bathroom lights—they might notice that. On the other hand, sitting in here in the dark would be impossible to explain. It was a tradeoff.

She stepped off the toilet, eased down her shorts and panties a bit, and sat. If they came in, they'd see her feet now, but she needed to look the part in case she had to support her "I was just in here to pee" story. She imagined them coming in, and decided she might be able to turn things to her advantage. She pulled open the stall door. The club was empty, right? So she wouldn't have been expecting anyone, wouldn't have bothered closing the stall door. This way, the sight of her partially exposed on the toilet would shock and fluster the guards if they came in. The idea was to turn around the dynamics—they'd be expecting an apology and a story, and would suddenly feel apologetic for intruding on her instead.

A little bit like Texas was doing, with that bullshit about lodging a complaint with an ombudsman?

Yeah, a little. Maybe. But still.

After a few minutes, the talking in the corridor stopped. The entrance doors opened and closed. There was a loud metallic *clack* as the lock engaged. She waited, and when a few more minutes had gone by marked by nothing but silence, she stood, pulled up her panties and shorts, and looked around.

She'd been hoping for a standard toilet, with a tank inside of which she could hide the gear. But these were just steel bowls, riveted to the wall. She supposed it was meant to look like minimalist chic. To her, it looked like prison plumbing.

Texas had said something about the bathroom decor. Was it possible he'd been trying to hide something himself? But no, more likely he was just riffing on whatever she said. She got the feeling that was a thing for him. A lot of improvisation when he was hitting on someone.

She considered. Unless there was a panel on the other side of the wall, which would have been odd in a nightclub, there had to be a way to access the innards of each unit in case there was any kind of malfunction or required maintenance.

The wall was covered in small steel circles, each about the size of a silver dollar, the edges almost touching each other against a black background. She didn't see anything, but . . .

She brushed her fingertips along the spaces between the circles. In a few seconds, she felt an indentation running in a straight vertical line just above and to the right of the toilet. It was nicely done—you couldn't see it, but you could feel it.

She pushed in and felt a click. She pulled her hand back, and a two-foot-square façade opened toward her, its magnetic lock disengaged.

She smiled, took out the SureFire, and looked inside. *Perfect.* The innards of a standard toilet tank, concealed behind the wall. And the floor the tank sat on was close enough to reach.

She pulled the Glock and the goggles from her bag, reached into the access area, and placed them on the floor. Then she clicked the façade closed again. *Perfect.*

She texted Little. *Need you to unlock club doors again ASAP. And kill camera feed. For 30 seconds.*

A moment later came a reply. *Done. Go.*

She went. This time, she took the stairs. She still wasn't sure about Texas. But even if he was just a tourist, he was obviously persistent. She wouldn't have been shocked to find him in the lobby, waiting for her with that big smile and a line of patter about bathrooms or broken hearts or whatever.

His looks and his confidence had definitely been . . . appealing. But this just wasn't the time or place. For a moment, she felt oddly disappointed. Then she let it go and went down to the parking garage. She'd leave the hotel that way.

And be back again that night.

20

Dox slept for the rest of the afternoon and evening at a trekker hotel, waking at eleven at night. He'd never needed an alarm clock, even on those happy occasions when he'd spent the whole night making love to some pretty lady, or those less happy ones where he woke with a monster hangover. Tonight, he wanted to be refreshed by a few hours' sleep and get to Les Nuits when it was maximally hopping, which would likely be anytime after midnight. So he'd set his internal alarm for eleven and gotten in a restorative snooze. Now it was showtime. He went to the bathroom and took a long leak and a longer shower, then sat on the bed naked for a few minutes, letting the air dry him, his eyes closed, going through the plan, gearing up for what was coming.

He checked in with Kanezaki, who confirmed that the contractors were in position and everything was good to go. Then he pulled on his skivvies, fixed the bellyband holster in place, and dressed in a pair of designer jeans, a loose-fitting, short-sleeved black silk shirt that would nicely conceal the bulge of the Supergrade etcetera, and some fancy-looking but comfortable shoes he'd picked up for the occasion. He checked himself in the mirror and decided he looked tonight's part.

Then he went out, fired up the Kawasaki, and rode back to Bali Hai Pier.

He found a big dirt lot crowded with scooters and motorcycles and parked the bike, passing the chain through the helmet, and then walked the area for a bit as he had earlier that day, getting familiar with its night rhythms. The famous, or infamous, Walking Street had come fully to life, with neon everywhere, electronic dance music pouring out of the go-go clubs, girls in skimpy uniforms lined up along the entrances shimmying to the beat and calling out to customers. The pushcart vendors were out, too, selling all manner of street food, and the air was redolent with the smells of pork dumplings and fried rice and fish sauce. Rivers of tourists, mostly young Western men, cruised up and down and back and forth in their sleeveless shirts and flip-flops, ogling the girls, sometimes succumbing to their flirtations, other times moving on like dogs who couldn't make up their minds about which morsels they most wanted to eat.

It seemed like not very long ago he'd enjoyed this kind of scene, all its promise and possibilities. All those pretty girls flirting with him had always felt like harmless fun. But now . . . he just wasn't seeing it the same way. Some of the girls calling out and flirting from the bar entrances seemed to be enjoying themselves okay. But most of them looked bored. And sad, really. That's what it was. It all felt sad. This wasn't a life anyone would choose for herself, was it? Not if she had any better prospects in the world. He'd never given that sort of thing much thought before, but since meeting Chantrea after arriving in Phnom Penh for the whole Gant-Sorm-Vann imbroglio, he was starting to see things differently. Chantrea was a nice girl from a good family, living on the edge of poverty, trying to get a psychology degree and earning a little money on the side working the bar scene. Was that really by choice? And had he been helping her, or taking advantage?

And how many of these girls had no choice at all but were actually being coerced? Coerced by people like Sorm?

And trapped by people like you?

Was that true? Was he like, what, someone selling a fix to an addict? That seemed oversimplified. Or was he just telling himself it seemed that way because denial was more comfortable?

What is with you, man?

He didn't know. Maybe this whole experience in Cambodia, and now Thailand, would evolve him. He supposed he hoped it would. But he wasn't going to have much chance to evolve if he was dead. And if he didn't get his head straight before going into the hotel and taking care of business, he wouldn't exactly be improving his odds of living.

You're okay, amigo. Shake it off. You just need to focus.

Right. He blew out a long breath and texted Kanezaki.

About to head over to the meeting. Is our friend there?

Yes. Say the word and I'll make sure the door is unlocked.

Roger that. Expect to hear from me within the hour.

He purged the messages, shut down the phone and put it in its case, and headed over to Hotel Ruby.

It was past midnight when he got there, and if the place had seemed lively during the day, that was nothing—the lobby was twice as crowded now, cacophonous with echoed conversation, and when he stepped off the elevator onto the club level, there was actually a line of people waiting to get in, everybody looking ghostly under black lights. Music was pulsing from inside the entrance doors, and three no-bullshit-looking guards sporting sidearms were wanding everyone before letting them pass—the former Royal Thai marines Kanezaki had warned him of. Yeah, they looked like tough hombres, too. Fit, unsmiling, and businesslike. The kind of men who did their job and did it well, whether the job in question was running a metal detector or shooting you dead.

While he waited in line, he glanced around, foolishly hoping he might see the pretty lady. He didn't, of course. Though maybe she'd be inside.

As he got closer, he started grinning and grooving a little to the dance music. When he reached the guards, he placed his cell phone on a plastic tray and said, "How y'all doing tonight?"

One of them gave him a curt nod that suggested this guy had seen it all before and found none of it interesting. He moved the wand methodically from Dox's scalp to the soles of his feet. Then he examined the cell phone, handed it back to Dox, and nodded again.

Dox put his palms together in a *wai*. "Thank you, sir, for the vote of confidence and for the important work you do here." Then he moved inside, into a roiling sea of laser lights and lithe bodies dancing to throbbing house music, the air heavy with the smells of aftershave and dance sweat and fruit cocktails. There were fog machines at work, too, or haze machines, or who could say what, but the dance floor was filled with billowing clouds cut by roving overhead colored lights. He threaded his way through the crowds, circumambulating the place, trying not to get distracted because *My God, if some of these women aren't straight-up tens, then a ten just doesn't exist.* Of course, the lady he was really hoping to see was that intriguing one from earlier, but he saw no sign of her. He told himself that was good—if she was back, it could only mean she was a pro, and things might get complicated. But even so, he would have liked to see her. Well, just ships that had passed in the night, he supposed, and probably for the best.

He made sure to stay screened by a healthy number of people as he moved past Sorm's VIP room. Okay, three black-clad dudes flanked in a semicircle in front of a big, solid-looking door, a red velvet rope line just behind them keeping the crowds back. The men were scanning the club, and looked at least as badass as the Thai marines by the entrance. Earpieces, combat boots, and armored vests. No sidearms he could see, but if these guys weren't packing heat in small-of-the-back holsters, he was Fred Flintstone.

He rolled on by, flowing with the crowd, and came to the karaoke room where he'd emplaced his gear. He'd been hoping it would be unoccupied, but knew by virtue of Murphy's law he wouldn't be that lucky. And indeed, when he peeked through the door window, he saw a group of a half dozen young Americans—college boys and girls, from the look of them—happy and prosperous, with their drinks and their feet resting on the ottoman, one of the boys belting out something into a microphone, his expression suggesting that whatever it was, he was really feeling it.

It would have been easier if he'd had some kind of hotel uniform. On the other hand, in his experience the main thing in these matters was "Act as if," and he'd never met anyone who could act as if quite the way he could. *Okay,* he thought. *Here we go.*

He pushed open the door and strode in with great purpose. The guy with the microphone was singing "Don't Let the Sun Go Down on Me," and not doing a half-bad job of it, either. He was so intent on his musical stylings that he didn't even hear Dox come in. But the others looked up.

"Excuse me," Dox said loudly. "I apologize on behalf of hotel management for the interruption, but we have a report of unsafe furniture in this room." The door swung shut behind him, cutting off the worst of the dance music from outside.

They all looked at him with more-or-less identical *What the hell?* expressions, with the exception of the kid with the mic, who also looked crestfallen. Dox understood—he'd been singing the part about how his cuts need love to help them heal, and that was about the best moment in the whole song. The singer lowered the mic, and for a moment the room was filled with nothing but the wordless orchestra.

One of the girls, a pretty little blonde number in a silver cocktail dress so formfitting that if it wasn't painted on, Dox didn't know what was enabling her to draw air, said, "What?"

"Thank you, ma'am, if I could trouble you to just pause the music. I need to check that ottoman."

They all looked at each other.

The blonde shook her head as though to clear it. "What?" she said again.

"Please, ma'am, this really should take no more than a minute. We've received a report that the ottoman in this room is structurally unsound, whether from a defect in its manufacture or because of misuse, we have not yet determined. The hotel takes very seriously its responsibility to ensure the safety of all its guests and club patrons. So please, although it is a lovely song and sir, you were doing a very fine job of singing it, if you could please pause the Elton John."

The girl looked dumbfounded and shook her head again, but she did pick up the remote and, after searching for a moment, pressed a button. Beyond the bass notes of dance music from the surrounding club, the room was suddenly quiet.

"Thank you, ma'am, that is very helpful. I need to check that ottoman, and it has been my experience in over thirty years of furniture inspections that music and safety do not mix. Now, if I could have those of you with your feet up on the ottoman slowly lift them—slowly, sir, please, I don't want to take a chance on anyone injuring themselves— and place them on the floor. And now your drinks—feel free to enjoy them, but we need the glassware off that unsafe ottoman for just a moment."

They all moved their feet and lifted their drinks, staring at him as though trying to decide whether he really was an authority figure or whether he was crazy, or maybe both. He'd been lucky so far—alcohol was unpredictable, sometimes making people more susceptible to a little social engineering, other times less so.

He stepped close to the ottoman, reached under the edge, and popped it up on its side so it was between him and the college kids.

"My God," he said. "This is terrible. Even worse than I feared. Someone could have been badly injured."

He reached into the hole he'd created, felt the butt of the Supergrade, and quickly extracted it, slipping it into the bellyband under his shirt. Then he did the same with the spare mags, the Emerson, and the flashbang.

When he was done, he returned the ottoman to its normal position, then stood and held up the broken pieces of plywood. "You would be amazed at the number of injuries caused each year by defective otto-mans," he said, looking at each of them in turn. "I'm relieved no one has been harmed tonight. Please go back to your socializing, and ma'am, I have to add, that is an absolutely stunning dress; silver becomes you. Enjoy the party, and you don't need to worry about this piece of fur-niture any longer, but I would advise for safety's sake that you refrain from placing your feet on it until such time as we have completed more comprehensive repair operations."

The singer shook his head. "What the . . . You're saying we were in danger from the ottoman?"

"In these matters, sir, it's hard to say how much. But it's certainly better not to take chances. The main thing is, you're perfectly safe now and the ottoman has been defused. Thank you again for your coopera-tion, and again, please enjoy Club Les Nuits."

He walked out without a backward glance, cutting through the fog and lasers and gyrating crowds on the dance floor to the other side of the club, and then heading to the restroom closest to Sorm's VIP room. The guards were still flanking the VIP-room door and scanning their surroundings, but he was in ghost mode now and they took no notice of him.

The bathroom was crowded—most of the urinals occupied, and a dozen young Thais and Westerners adjusting their gelled hair and smoothing their plucked eyebrows in front of the mirrors. The music was loud, too, almost as loud as it was out on the dance floor. He tossed the plywood scraps into a trashcan propped at the apex of a spiraling steel base, and went into a stall, where he double checked the Supergrade—full magazine, cartridge in the chamber, good to go. He eased the weapon back into the bellyband and let his shirt drape over it.

Okay. Showtime.

He stepped out of the stall, pausing to wash his hands for form's sake. He dried them under a jet-loud blower and turned to the door to go.

One of the drunken Americans—the singer—rolled in, saw him, and just stood there. *Ah, shit.* Shame on him for not having checked his back. He hadn't been expecting any trouble from a bunch of college kids. Or it might have been just a coincidence. Either way, he could tell from how the kid's mouth was thinning out into a determined line he was going to have to deal with it.

"Bro," the kid said. "What was that? You're not really hotel maintenance."

"Ingratitude is one of the indignities of my profession, son," he said, rubbing his cleaned hands together. "I save people from potential peril, and they thank me by questioning my credentials."

"Speaking of credentials, I'd like to see some."

"You are more than welcome to lodge a complaint with my supervisor, if doing so will make you feel better. But I have duties to perform."

He started to move past the kid, and the idiot actually grabbed him by the arm. Dox took hold of the kid's wrist in his free hand, broke the grip, and squeezed hard enough to make it hurt, at the same time communicating to the kid with the quickness and ease of the move that the pain he was feeling was nothing but a coming attraction if the kid was dumb enough to want the full movie.

He stared into the kid's eyes. "Son," he growled, "if you don't get your dumb ass back to Elton John right fucking now, I will reach down your throat, pull out your liver, and beat you to death with it. *Comprendes?*"

The kid didn't even try to break loose—he just lost some color and gave two quick nods.

Dox saw some people looking. *Shit.*

He let the kid go. "And be sure to wash your hands when you're done in here. I can't abide improper restroom hygiene."

He headed out, circling wide of Sorm's VIP room and pausing far enough from the bathroom and with enough people in the way to ensure the kid wouldn't see him when he exited. He relaxed and retracted his energy, the way he did when he was in a sniper hide, just going away and making himself invisible in plain sight. After a minute, the kid came out and headed in the direction of the karaoke room, still looking a little pale.

Okay, Sorm, he thought. *Here we fucking go.*

He took a deep breath and shifted back into character, heading obliquely across the dance floor toward the VIP room, the gyrating people parting before him, their movements weirdly robotic under the pulsating lights. He boogied to the music like someone who'd had way too much to drink, pausing to dance here and there with some of the ladies he passed, sometimes to their apparent annoyance, sometimes to their apparent delight. He'd dated a dancer years back, and she'd insisted on teaching him the basics, cha-cha and rumba and the tango, which was the only one he really liked. He hadn't minded, he was always up for something he thought might be foreplay, but he'd never expected any of it to be operationally useful. And yet look at him now.

He cleared the floor but kept on dancing. The guards were only twenty feet away now, and there was nothing between him and them but a handful of people and some fog from the machines.

Fifteen feet.

He swayed his hips and shoulders and rolled his arms and threw in a pirouette for good measure.

The guards weren't scanning now. They were looking right at him. And their looks weren't the least bit friendly.

Ten feet.

"Hey," he called out, doing a little box step. "That's the VIP room, ain't it? What's it cost to dance in there?"

21

Livia was on a stool at the far end of the bar closest to Sorm's VIP room, sipping a cosmopolitan from a martini glass. She'd retrieved the Glock from where she'd hidden it, and now it was immediately accessible via a cross-draw in the bag she was wearing on her left side, the strap over her right shoulder. The purse was a little large for the skimpy black cocktail dress she was wearing, but there were plenty of women in the club with outsized bags. Some of them were pros, carrying the tools of their trade; others were just party animals packing a change of clothes for the morning after a hoped-for hookup. Her own excuse, of course, in addition to the Glock, was the night-vision gear.

The only other thing that might have looked slightly out of place was her choice of flats as footwear. Heels would have been more the look for clubbing, but on the other hand, for a night of dancing, sometimes the priority had to be comfort. Or, in her case, speed and mobility. But none of it really mattered. If the dress was short and tight enough, men didn't notice the accessories. The platinum wig and oversized horn-rimmed glasses weren't standard fashion choices either, she supposed, but they'd be better than nothing against any video recordings.

She'd been chatting briefly with an Australian guy who'd come over to hit on her, their heads inclined just a few inches apart so they could hear each other over the club music. But when she'd refused his offer to buy her a drink and told him she was meeting a friend, he'd moved on. That was fine. She'd wanted a few minutes to scan the club from this position and get a feel for the guards outside Sorm's VIP room. Those few minutes were done now. She was ready.

She wiped the stem of the martini glass with a napkin and took out her phone. Her heart started hammering, and she breathed slowly and deeply for a minute until she felt calmer. Then she called Little.

"Can you hear me?" she said, turning her head away from the people next to her so she could shout.

"Barely. Sounds like quite a party over there."

She glanced around. "It is. Are you ready?"

"Say the word and I kill the lights. And open the locks."

She got up, unzipped the purse, and circled the edge of the dance floor in the direction of the VIP room, her heart hammering hard again. "Ten seconds," she said.

"I'm with you."

She kept moving. She was forty feet away now. The music was loud. Pulsing. Laser lights crisscrossed the floor in front of her. The dance floor was packed with undulating bodies, arms in the air, everybody moving, fog from hidden machines rolling and rising around them.

She pulled the goggles from the bag and fired them up. "Eight seconds."

"Still with you. On your mark."

Thirty feet. There were maybe fifty people between her and the guards now. Her concealment was getting thin.

She dangled the goggles low, holding them by the head strap so she could pull them on instantly.

Twenty feet. Just a little closer. She wanted it to go down fast. No time for anyone to react.

"Five," she said. "Four. Three—"

A big guy emerged from the crowds of the dance floor to her left and called out to the guards. "Hey, that's the VIP room, ain't it? What's it cost to dance in there?"

Even if she hadn't seen him, she would have known from the voice alone. Texas.

What the hell?

"Wait," she said. "Not yet."

"Standing by."

What the hell? she thought again.

The guards were looking at Texas. Looking at him hard. Whatever he was trying to pull off, she thought he had maybe three seconds before he got preempted.

"Is that rope line behind you Corinthian velour?" Texas called out, still moving in. "Rich Corinthian velour, just like in my ancestral home in Abilene."

Then he did a weird little jig and spun in a circle. And as his back turned to the guards, a gun came out from under his shirt like a magic trick—

One of the guards saw the move, or at least recognized that Texas was way too close and that his hands had momentarily disappeared. The guard's hand swept behind his back—

Texas finished his spin, the gun coming up en route, and—

The guard started to shout something in Thai—maybe "Gun!" But Texas stopped him with a round right to his forehead. An instant later he put another round into the head of the guard next to him, and another into the third, the shooting so fast and certain that all three were shot before the first had even hit the ground.

The shots were loud and unmistakable even over the pulsating music. She heard shouts from the dance floor, the sounds of confused conversation.

Texas stepped over the bodies, straight through the velour rope line, spun so his back was to the door, and blasted it right under the handle with a donkey kick. The door flew open—

Three men in black uniforms and tactical armor were standing just beyond it, guns drawn. Texas, already bent low from the kick, cried out, "Oh, shit!" and simultaneously dove away and tossed something backward into the room. The men saw it. One of them shouted, "Grenade!" in English.

Without thinking, Livia spun away and yelled into the phone, "Cut the lights!"

The club instantly went dark. There was a gigantic *Boom!* and a flash of light from inside the room. And then another *Boom!* and flash, and another. And more. Not a grenade, she realized. A flashbang.

She pulled on the goggles and got out the Glock. There was pandemonium behind her. People shouting, stampeding away. The lights in Sorm's VIP room were still on. It must have been on a separate system, as part of some sort of safe room. The room was empty now. The three soldiers or whatever they were had spilled out into the club, and they must have managed to move before the flashbang went off, because it looked as though they could still see, their guns up in two-handed grips as they tried to acquire a target.

One of them got off two shots. The rounds hit the floor to the left of Texas. Texas rolled the other way and fired twice from his back, hitting the soldier in the chest. The soldier spun away. He might have been hurt, but with the body armor, he definitely wasn't out of the fight.

Another of the soldiers circled right. They were going to flank Texas. Their vision might have been okay, but she could see that the concussive effect of the flashbang had messed up some of their coordination. Still, even if Texas could get off headshots and obviate the body armor, three on one, he wasn't going to make it.

Texas rolled and shot twice again. The guy who was flanking him jerked from the impact of the bullets. But again they were chest shots.

In the dim light from the VIP room, Texas probably couldn't see the armor. Or rolling around on the floor, center mass was the best he could manage. Or both.

The third guy moved the other way, hugging the wall. The first guy leveled his pistol, and Texas shot at him again. The round went past the guy's face. Texas had figured out the problem, but there was too much going on and his position was too poor—

Texas shot again. This time, the round caught the guy in the face and he went down. But while Texas had been engaging him, the third guy had moved stealthily along the wall and was bringing up his gun—

Livia took aim and fired. The first round caught the guy just below the throat. She moved in and kept shooting, walking up the barrel a notch as she closed. Her second and third rounds were both headshots. The guy went down.

Texas whipped his head in her direction and simultaneously started to bring his pistol around, but then whipped his head and the pistol forward again. Even in all the craziness, he must have sensed that wherever the shots had come from, they hadn't been intended for him. "What the fuck?" he cried out.

And then he rolled again, and just in time, too, because the second guy fired and put two rounds in the carpet where Texas's body had been just an instant earlier. Seeing he'd missed Texas, the second guy swung his gun around to try to acquire Livia. He was too far to risk a headshot, so she sighted center mass and eased back the trigger, moving in as she fired. Once. Twice. A third shot. He twitched from the rounds. She brought up the muzzle and took aim at—

There was a boom to her right and blood erupted from the side of the guy's head. While he'd been engaging her, Texas had sighted in the finishing shot.

Livia looked around wildly. People were running in all directions, screaming and shouting. The house lasers were still crisscrossing through the darkness, the music still thumping. She didn't see any more opposition.

She glanced at Texas. He was still on his back, his head raised off the floor and swiveling left and right, his gun up and extended in a two-handed grip.

"What the fuck?" he cried out again, without even looking at her.

"Where's Sorm?" she yelled. "He wasn't in that room!"

"Sorm ain't here! Can't you tell? This was a setup! We gotta git!"

He brought his legs in and popped to his feet. For a big guy, he moved fast.

"Where is he?" she yelled, scanning left and right.

"I don't know! For all I know, he wasn't ever even here! Come on, we gotta vamoose!"

He moved alongside her and turned so they were facing in opposite directions, with a 360-degree view of the room between them.

"How do you know he wasn't here?" she shouted.

"I don't know! All I know is who was here—three professional badasses in body armor who'd likely have punched my ticket if you hadn't been here to stop them. Do you get it? Sorm knew we were coming. Or I was coming, or you were coming, or whatever, lord have mercy, can we please discuss our theories of whatever the fuck just happened once we're safely away?"

"What if he went out through the room? It has a back door!"

"I know it does, but—"

"If he was here, that's the way he went. I'm going after him."

From the direction of the entrance, she saw three men fighting their way through the crowd. "Shit," she said. "The security guys. From the entrance."

"Don't kill them," Texas said. "They're just doing their jobs. They've got nothing to do with Sorm."

She knew it was true. But she was so close, and if these men tried to stop her—

"Just let me handle it," Texas said. "All right? Lose the goggles and put away the gun. Trust me. Otherwise we're going to have another gunfight, and I swear two in a day is my absolute limit."

Still she hesitated.

"I'll get them to go the other way, all right? Just do what I say!"

Certain she was making a fatal mistake, she pulled the goggles and dropped them in the purse, followed by the Glock.

Texas didn't say another word. He just slipped the gun back under his shirt, squeezed one of her hands in his, and started waving frantically at the approaching guards with the other.

"Thank God!" he shouted. "Thank God you're here! Oh my lord, they're shooting people over there in that karaoke room! And singing Elton John!" He pointed in a direction away from both the entrance and Sorm's VIP room. "There, over there, do you hear me? For the love of God, hurry! I'm scared! I'm scared!"

The security guys took off. Livia shook her head, amazed it had worked. People really fell for this guy's hick routine. Without another word, she pulled the Glock and took off straight into Sorm's safe room.

"Damn it, don't!" Texas said from behind her, but she didn't care—if there was any chance Sorm had been here, she was going to kill him.

She leaped over the bodies of Sorm's Thai guards and into a room filled with acrid smoke. The back door was open, a riser of fire-escape stairs lit up in cold fluorescent light behind it. She bolted straight through.

"Wait!" she heard Texas call from behind her, but she didn't even slow, she hit the stairwell and tore downward four steps at a time. She could hear Texas's footfalls echoing just behind her.

"They might be expecting this, damn it!" she heard him shout. She didn't care. She couldn't let Sorm get away. She couldn't.

She heard Texas close behind her, and then somehow he was past her, moving so fast he was pinwheeling his arms for balance. He nearly fell, but managed to grab a banister at the riser below them and stabilize himself. He threw an arm around her waist and caught her. She wanted to sweep his legs and keep running down the stairs, but for some reason held back.

"Listen to me!" he said. "Just listen. The guy who arranged all this for me. The intel. Hacking the door locks. Everything. He's supposed to have contractors waiting on the ground floor behind the fire exit. If this thing is on the up-and-up and Sorm went that way, the contractors already have him. And if it ain't on the up-and-up, then the guy those contractors are waiting for is me. We can't go out that way. There's no upside, only danger. Please, just listen to me. We'll get Sorm another way."

She recognized on some level that what he was saying made sense. But still, she couldn't. She just couldn't.

"No!" she said. "He was here. He was—"

"Damn it, we can't go out that way. More bad guys could be expecting us, don't you see? Please. You seem like a nice lady and I don't want you running straight into a damn ambush. I can tell you mean business with Sorm. So do I. Trust me, okay? We'll get him."

He was right. She hated it, but he was right. She shook loose from his arm. "The guest-room floors are all locked," she said. "We can only get out on the lobby level. Or the parking lot, through the fire exit."

"I can get my guy to pop the locks."

"The same guy you're worried set you up?"

"I see your point. But if I just keep things general, we ought to be all right. Hold on."

He pulled out a cell phone and called someone. "No," he said. "No, I didn't get him. I don't even think he was here. There were three operators, though, who I just barely survived, no thanks to you, I might add." There was a pause. "We'll talk about that later. Right now, I just need to git. Can your geek squad pop the locks on every floor in the fire-escape stairwell?" Another pause. "Don't you worry about which floor, you just have your guys pop all of them." Pause. "When? Five minutes ago would be nice, but I'll settle for right fucking now, thank you very much."

A second later, there was a loud metallic clack from the door behind them. Livia pulled it. It opened.

"Good to go," Texas said into the phone. "I'll check in again when I'm settled. And you best look into why this thing went so damn sideways. 'Cause somebody knew I was coming, that is for damn sure."

He clicked off and powered down the phone, then slipped it into the shielded case.

"Let's put yours in, too," he said. "Better not to take chances."

She realized it was a Faraday case. And that her phone was still on. With everything that had happened, she had forgotten to turn it off.

She didn't like handing over her phone, but under the circumstances, a Faraday bag made sense. In fact, she should have been carrying one herself. Seattle PD couldn't track a powered-down phone. But she didn't know what Homeland Security was capable of. She turned off the unit and handed it to Texas, who enclosed it in the case and then, to her surprise, handed the case to her.

"Here," he said. "Keep it in your bag. With two phones, it's a little thick for the bellyband, and I don't want anything in the way of my gun, besides."

That also made sense. She put the case in her bag, then pulled off the wig and glasses and stuffed them in, too. She wanted to look different from what witnesses might be describing. She arranged everything to make sure the Glock was on top, easily accessible.

They went through the door, then moved quickly down a long, wide corridor, passing guest-room doors, the plush carpet and high ceiling creating a hush that felt bizarre after the club's viscera-grinding electronic music.

"Hey," Texas said. "Hey. Slow it down. We're just hotel guests now, remember? Maybe heading back to our room for an amorous nightcap."

She looked at him, still enraged at having been so close to Sorm and being forced to abort.

"I'm not saying that's actually happening," he went on. "But you gotta act as if."

"I know how to act as if."

"Well, I expect you do, I can see that. But right now, you're acting as if we're having some kind of tiff. So that's what anyone who encounters us is going to see. And I can work with that if you like, of course. But I think it would be less unusual and therefore less noticeable if we could pretend to get along for a little while. At least until we're out of the hotel."

"We're getting along fine."

"You see, that's what I'm talking about. When you say it like that, it just doesn't sound like your heart's in it."

She heard the elevator chimes from down the corridor, about fifty feet away. "Shit," Texas said. "Take it easy, now. We ain't gonna shoot anyone till we see the whites of their eyes, okay?"

"Stop telling me what to do."

"I meant it more as a suggestion. And here's another one. Get your arm around me now. Act as if." He put a hand on her waist and pulled her close. She stiffened, again wanting to sweep his legs and leave him there while she went on alone.

"Here on Earth," he said, "it's customary to relax and enjoy this kind of human contact. And if you don't, people will notice."

She heard the elevator doors open. A second later, two uniformed hotel rent-a-cops turned into the corridor and started heading toward them. Their pace and posture were relaxed—a routine patrol, not an emergency. But still she stiffened.

Texas squeezed her close. "Easy, darlin'," he whispered into her ear. "Easy. Just two strolling lovers, lost in the rapture of their mutual desire . . ."

He waved to the guards, and she saw him give one of them a wink as they passed.

She didn't like any of it. But it seemed to work. And she understood the purpose was operational. Or at least part of the purpose. With this guy, she realized she just wasn't sure.

They took the elevator to the parking level and went out through a side exit, each of them scanning for trouble as they moved. There were a dozen police cars parked around the hotel, and approaching sirens from more. And a lot of gawkers lined up, trying to figure out what was going on. But the two of them just kept walking arm in arm through the warm Pattaya night until they were clear of the hotel grounds, and no one paid any attention.

"I parked my bike at the pier," Texas said. "Let's head that way. Don't you worry. We'll get Sorm. Just not tonight."

When Little pulled that shit, it felt like forced teaming. But with Texas, somehow it didn't. And besides, he was obviously no friend of Sorm. They'd do better together than at cross purposes.

But that didn't mean she trusted him. She didn't trust anybody.

22

In just a few minutes, they had nearly reached the pier. Dox couldn't figure this lady out. She was obviously a pro, though what kind he couldn't quite say. And any pro would know they'd do better walking arm in arm like lovers than like two strangers who didn't like or trust each other. She had to know it wasn't real for him, he was just acting as if. Or, okay, maybe it was a little bit real, she sure was pretty and there was definitely something about her, and besides, after a gunfight didn't everyone want to be held at least a little?

He saw the bike in the lot—easy to spot because of its size—and instantly realized something he should have thought of earlier. "Hang on," he said. "My helmet's chained to the bike, but we need to get you one, too. They don't enforce helmet laws out here so strictly, but we don't want to take a chance on some cop looking for a bribe. Plus it'll prevent anyone from seeing our faces."

It took only a moment to find a guy pulling off his helmet after parking. "Hey," Dox said, whipping out a Benjamin and pointing to the helmet. "A hundred US for that helmet there. Deal?"

The guy looked at him like he didn't understand. Which he probably didn't.

Well, it was always dumb to just talk louder when someone didn't speak your language, but maybe money was different. He pulled out another Benjamin and extended the bills with one hand while pointing at the helmet with the other. "Two hundred, sir. And that's my last offer. Take it, or live with regret for the rest of your life."

The guy gave him a big *wai* and a bigger smile. He took the money, handed Dox the helmet, then headed off, probably to buy new headgear and spend the excess on various forms of Pattaya bacchanalia. Dox handed the helmet to the woman and they kept moving.

They came to the bike. Dox unlocked and shouldered the chain, grabbed the helmet, and started to swing a leg over the seat.

The woman put a firm hand on his shoulder, stopping him. "I'm in front," she said.

She might as well have told him she would fly them to the moon. "Look," he said, feeling flummoxed, "this is a Kawasaki Z800, a touch big for a little lady like—"

"Maybe I'm not as little as you think. Or you're not as big."

"Well, that stings, I won't lie."

"Get on in back."

"Look, it's customary here and throughout the civilized world for the man to ride in front. Doing it the other way is just going to get us noticed." He might have added, *or killed in a crash,* but thought that might be a tad incendiary under the circumstances.

"You're wasting time."

He wanted to argue, but she seemed so determined. Plus he couldn't think of anything else.

"Fine," he said. "I hope you know how to ride." He also hoped no one, and especially not Rain, would ever learn about this.

She pulled on the helmet and held out her hand for the key. He scowled, but that only made him feel more helpless. "Fine," he said again. He handed her the key. She swung a leg over the seat. He pulled on his helmet and got on behind her.

She fired the ignition, revved the engine, and turned her head toward him. "Hold on tight," she said.

"Fine," he said yet again, feeling like an idiot. He put his hands on her hips.

"Tighter," she said.

"Well, all right, then." He clasped his hands around her belly. Damn, her stomach was hard and flat. Whoever she was, she was in some shape.

And damn, it was a good thing he'd listened when she told him to hang on, because she hit it suddenly and hard, the back of the bike fishtailing in the dirt as she accelerated, but she compensated instantly with her body weight one way and then the other, and never seemed other than completely in charge. At the street at the edge of the lot she accelerated more, leaning into the turn and showing great throttle control, then rocketed ahead to the intersection and turned again, carrying a ton of speed through the corner. Dox clung to her, bug eyed under the helmet, wondering what the hell he'd gotten himself into.

In under three minutes, they were heading northeast on Route 7, the main road back to Bangkok. "Wait," Dox shouted over the whine of the engine. "We don't want to go to Bangkok. Make a right on 36 up there ahead."

She didn't even slow. "I have another lead on Sorm in Bangkok."

"Look, generally in my life when strange men show up unexpectedly and try to kill me, for at least the next day I try to avoid doing anything that might be predictable. So please indulge me—we can always go back to Bangkok, I just don't want to go there right now. Go southeast on 36—it'll take us to Rayong and Saeng Chan Beach. We'll spend the night there and use another route into Bangkok tomorrow."

He knew his advice was sound—as sound as advice ever got. And she was obviously a pro, so she must have already known what he was saying made sense. But even so, he could tell she was struggling.

"I know you want Sorm bad," he said. "But you gotta also want him smart."

Even as he said it, he realized he was getting himself into a potential jam. He wasn't supposed to kill Sorm, after all. He'd even promised Vann and Kanezaki he wouldn't. But he was certain this woman sure as shit *was* going to kill Sorm or die trying, and now he was practically offering to help her. Well, he'd have to figure all that out later. For now, they just needed to get safe.

He didn't know what he would do if she ignored him and tried to stay on Route 7. It wasn't as though he could grab the handlebars. But luckily it didn't come to that. She slowed as they approached the sign for 36 and turned smoothly onto it.

An hour later, they were in Rayong. Dox hadn't been here in probably a decade, but even at near three in the morning, he could tell it hadn't changed much. Palm trees, low-slung buildings, and not a Walking Street all-night party scene in sight. Apparently, being an hour farther south from Bangkok than Pattaya, it had been spared the overdevelopment suffered by its more famous coastal cousin.

They drove slowly east on the beach road, everything sleepy and still under a low crescent moon, the waves of the Gulf of Thailand to their right breaking white along the sand.

"See how they've done the beach in all those semicircles of sand and stone?" he said. "Like half moons. That's where the name comes from. *Saeng chan* means *moonlight*."

She turned her head slightly. "Where are we going?"

"All right, I can see my attempts at playing tourist guide have come to naught. Just keep heading up the beach road. There's a little place where I used to stay, back in the day. I'll bet you it's still here."

And it was. Paradise Cottages and Spa was the name—a collection of thatch-roofed bungalows strung out along the south side of the road, directly across from the semicircles of the beach.

The woman parked the Kawasaki, and Dox dismounted. He was glad the gravel lot was dark and empty so no one could witness his shame as he got off the back of the bike. Still, he had to admit she could ride and then some. He pulled off his helmet. There was a breeze coming off the water, and the night air was pleasantly cool. He could smell the ocean—a clean, salty smell Pattaya had buried under diesel and concrete.

And another smell—durian fruit. There must have been a tree nearby. Most Westerners hated the smell, but for him, it was one of the delights of being in Southeast Asia.

The woman cut the engine and pulled off her helmet. He was quick to extend a hand. "Key, please." He half expected her to argue, but she didn't. It was his bike, after all. She handed him the key.

"What are we doing now?" she asked.

He was grateful to be back on familiar ground, at least somewhat in charge. "What we do now is get a room. Just one room, 'cause we have a lot to talk about. Not to mention—"

"You want us to act as if."

"Just act is all. I'm not trying to take advantage of you."

He thought she was going to argue, but she just said, "I know."

That threw him. He couldn't get a fix on what made her cooperative and what turned her obstreperous.

"Oh," he said. "Well, good. And you know I might put on a little show for whatever tired clerk we encounter, right?"

She swung a leg off the bike and dismounted. "Yeah, I'm starting to pick up on that."

"Well, it's just a show. I got two ways of hiding—one is to be invisible, and the other is to make a spectacle of myself. Each has its advantages and disadvantages."

She laughed. It was only a little, but it was the first time he'd seen her do it. He liked it. It made him strangely happy to know it was even possible, and to think maybe he was the cause.

"You, invisible?" she said. "That I'd like to see."

He smiled. "Well, that's the thing—you wouldn't see it. That's the whole point."

"Okay, then, you just let me know when it happens."

"Deal. But for now, it's going to be more spectacle. So when we go into that guest-reception bungalow over yonder, I'm going to put my arm around you. 'Cause we're a couple of semi-randy homo sapiens whose pheromones mixed at a bar a while back, and who are now planning on acting on their mutual attraction here at Paradise Cottages and Spa."

He'd been trying to make her laugh again with that. But instead she frowned. "You don't have to talk to me like that," she said. "I'm not an alien."

That threw him again. "Well, hell, I know that. I'm sorry. I was actually just trying to make you laugh. I liked when you did it a minute ago. You have a nice laugh, and that was the first I'd heard it."

For a moment, she didn't respond. Then she nodded and said, "Let's just go in. I'm tired."

He couldn't figure her out. All he knew for sure was she was carrying an almighty weight and couldn't find a way to set it down.

They went in. He put his arm around her as promised, or as warned, anyway, and without being prompted she did the same. Under any other circumstances, he would have been glad—that she was listening, that she trusted him, hell, maybe even that she was starting to like him. But the way she did it seemed so reluctant. And somehow sad. He wanted to prompt her again about acting as if, but decided it just wasn't worth it. It was three in the morning in Rayong. Nobody was going to notice an incongruity as minor as an Asian woman seeming reluctant about a big white guy having his arm around her.

Hell, he thought. *It's probably not even a damn incongruity. It's probably more the damn norm.*

Either way, the clerk, a teenager who'd been out cold with his head on the desk when they came in, didn't seem to give a shit. He wiped his eyes, took Dox's cash, and handed him a key. Dox thanked him, and he and the woman went back out and walked along a gravel path lit by dim footlights until they found their bungalow.

It was a nice place, and just as he remembered it: spare but cozy, with polished wood floors, white sheets, and French doors that opened right onto the beach. The lights were on a dimmer, and he kept them low so as not to attract insects. He opened the doors—Rain would have considered it an unpardonable breach of security, but for God's sake, Dox himself hadn't known until ten minutes earlier that this was where they were going—and the room was immediately filled with the sound of the ocean, not fifty feet away.

He smelled the durian fruit again. "Mmm," he said. "I love that smell."

"Durian?" she said from behind him.

He stood there for a moment, his eyes closed, just enjoying the smell of the fruit and the sound of the waves. "You bet. Call me strange if you like, but it's one of my favorites."

She didn't answer. He glanced back at her, and she was staring at him with the oddest expression.

They'd stopped at a convenience store on the ride in and picked up some sandwiches, chips, and bottled water, and after a moment the woman got up, tore the bag open, and started devouring one of the sandwiches. He walked over and did the same. Being in a gunfight made a person ravenous. It increased all the appetites, in fact. He'd have to watch himself. She was pretty and he liked her, and he was definitely suffused with that incredibly *alive* feeling you could have only when you've survived someone trying to kill you and you got to kill him instead. But she sure didn't seem a fan of human contact.

They stood and ate wordlessly, and the sandwiches and half the water were gone in minutes. "Whew," he said, holding back a belch. "I needed that."

She nodded.

"I think we've got some notes we ought to compare," he said. "But I could use a shower. If you'd like, you're welcome to go first."

She shook her head. "I'm fine."

"You sure?"

She nodded again.

"Hey, when I come out of that bathroom, you're still going to be here, right?"

She looked at him. "Why do you say that?"

"I don't know. I just can't figure you out."

"I'll be here. Just give me a minute first."

She went to the bathroom and came out a little while later, looking different. She'd been wearing makeup, he realized, and had washed it off. He liked her better this way. He almost said so, but then decided it wouldn't sound right.

The shower was heaven—roomy, clean, and with great water pressure—and he would have loved to linger and unwind in the steam and the heat. But they did have a lot to cover. And though he believed her when she said she'd still be around when he got out, he didn't think it would be a good idea to give her too much time to reconsider, either.

He dried off, then brushed with the hotel-provided toothbrush and toothpaste. There was a whole complement of toiletries, in fact—comb, brush, cotton swabs, even earplugs, though who would ever need earplugs in a sleepy place like this? Well, maybe reprobates who didn't like the sound of waves on the beach. Or who suffered the misfortune of a snoring partner. Earplug fetishists, maybe. About the only thing the hotel didn't provide, it seemed, was a condom. Which was unusual, as, in his experience with such establishments—and, in fact, back in the day with this very establishment in particular—the hotel-provided condom was considered both chic and de rigueur.

He looked at his duds, which he'd left in a pile on the floor. The thought of getting back into clothes so sweat soaked and road grimed after a good shower wasn't appealing, so he pulled on one of the hotel robes instead and hung the clothes on the shower rod to air them. He'd buy some new ones tomorrow.

She was sitting on the couch when he came out, her gun on the coffee table within easy reach. The Glock 21, he saw. Kind of a big gun for someone her size. On the other hand, she'd driven the Kawasaki like a pro.

She still looked tense, and he wished she'd taken a shower. It might have relaxed her some. It sure had him.

"There's another robe," he said, taking the other end of the couch and turning so he was facing her. He placed the Supergrade on the coffee table alongside the Glock. "Might be more comfortable than that little cocktail dress. Though you do look fabulous, I won't deny, especially after surviving a gunfight and fleeing by motorbike through the dead of the sultry Thailand night."

She smiled again. She had such a nice smile. It made him sad that it took so much to coax it out of hiding.

"Hey," she said. "Before, in the hotel stairwell. You said your guy had contractors waiting for Sorm at the fire exit, and that if Sorm went that way the contractors would 'have him.'"

Damn, she had zeroed right in on the very contradiction he knew he was going to have to grapple with.

"That's right," he said.

"What did you mean by that? Why contractors? Why 'have him'? You dropped those guards. Why wouldn't you just kill Sorm yourself? After the flashbang, he would have been helpless."

"Well, this is the part where I have to say it's complicated. And I hope maybe you can help me figure it out." He cleared his throat. "All right, here it is. Some people hired me, ostensibly to have a frank conversation with Sorm, but it turned out to be a setup and they were trying to get me to converse with Sorm's enemy. So now, I find myself embroiled in all that skullduggery, and my best way out of it is to finish the conversation, if you know what I mean. But at the same time, I'm hemmed in by circumstances."

Omitting some names and being general about the details, he told her about Gant, and Vann, and the indictment in New York, and Kanezaki, and Sorm being a CIA and DIA asset, and Zatōichi, and how he'd promised to bring Sorm in, not kill him. Rain would have had a fit that he told her so much. But come on, she was obviously no friend of Sorm. Though in fairness, he knew his inclination to trust her wasn't only that.

"I had a feeling he was on the run," she said when he told her about the indictment. "One of my leads told me he'd switched to a burner and needed fast cash."

That tracked with what he'd learned from Vann. "Yeah, because of the UN guy. Vann. Vann told me Sorm must have gotten wind of what was coming and hightailed it."

He told her more, about how the guy he worked with had tracked Sorm to Pattaya, about the plan to capture him.

"So even if Sorm was there," she said, "and even if he went out the back door of his safe room, you didn't know for sure that he'd take the stairs all the way to the ground level and go out the fire exit, where the contractors were supposedly waiting."

Man, she really had a nose for potential inconsistencies in a story. "That's true," he said. "Like I said, the plan was for me to be hot on his heels to that level, or more likely to drag him by the scruff of the neck. But without that, then yeah, even if he was there, which I seriously doubt he was, and even if he went out the back door of his little VIP room, if he had a hotel room key, he could have gotten out of the stairs at any level he liked."

That seemed to satisfy her. Or at least she didn't ask about any other inconsistencies.

When he was finished, he thought she was going to argue about how capturing Sorm was bullshit, and how they had to kill him. Which, now that he'd talked it through, he figured was an easy compromise—he wouldn't kill Sorm, he'd just help her do it. It wasn't like he'd promised to protect Sorm, after all. Only not to kill him. So this lady could do the actual coup de grace. That way, Dox's promise would be intact and the world would be a better place, too.

But instead she said, "Why are you telling me so much?"

"Am I oversharing?"

She gave him that small laugh again, which he liked.

"It's more than I would have told you."

"It's more than you have told me."

"What do you want to know?"

"You're a cop, aren't you? Or at least you were one."

She didn't flinch. She didn't show anything at all. But . . . something snuck through. In her face, or her eyes. It was too subtle to describe. But it was enough.

"Why do you say that?" she said.

"You're a hell of an interrogator, for one thing. You stay on inconsistencies like a bloodhound on a scent. Meaning okay, could be a cop, but could be a 'gator—an interrogator, maybe air force, I guess I could see that. But you said you had a 'lead' on Sorm. And that one of your 'leads' told you Sorm had switched to a burner. That sounds cop to me, not military."

She didn't answer.

"And besides," he went on, "no 'gator I've ever known could shoot for beans. Maybe at target practice, but not when the bullets are flying the other way. Where'd you learn to shoot like that?"

"My uncle."

"Who's your uncle, Wyatt Earp?"

"Where did you learn?"

"The US Marine Corps. Though I'm a sniper by temperament and training, and prefer to avoid gunfights up close. Okay, your turn."

She didn't answer.

"The thing is," he said, "even if I'm barking up the wrong tree, and I don't think I am, I'm in the right neck of the woods. You're a pro, I can see that, but at the same time I can tell this isn't professional for you, the way it is for me."

"It's just professional for you?"

He thought for a moment. "Well, it's funny you would ask. When I came out here it was. But then I met this nice lady in Phnom Penh, Chantrea, and got to know her, and saw a few things, and . . . I don't know. I guess it has gotten personal, and not just because I tend to find myself irritated when people hire me under false pretenses and then try to kill me on top of it."

"How is it personal for you?"

He was starting to see that it wasn't just that she didn't talk much. She was good at keeping the other person talking, too. Well, he didn't mind. He liked to talk. And maybe he was being played, but he thought if he kept talking it might coax her into reciprocating.

"Where I come from we have a saying. Actually, we have a lot of sayings, including 'A turtle doesn't get up on a bookshelf by itself,' which is one of my favorites, but the one I'm referring to is 'Some people just need killing.' And I think this guy Sorm is one of the people the expression was invented for. How about you?"

There was a pause. She said, "I've known a lot of people like that."

He looked at her and felt the oddest mix of emotions. Understanding. Admiration. Compassion.

And gratitude, because he realized all at once she wasn't playing him. He knew what it must have cost her, to say even that much. And to a stranger, no less.

"I'm sorry," he said. "I've known a few myself. But . . . not the way I think maybe you have. And I'm sorry. For what it's worth, I'm glad to know you. And not just because you saved my ass back at Les Nuits."

She looked at him. She seemed more wound up than ever, like she was fighting something inside herself. At the same time, he thought he saw something new in her eyes. He wasn't sure what—fear or vulnerability or something. It was like he'd hurt her just by saying he was glad to know her.

"Then why?" she said.

He thought for a moment. "Because among other reasons, we've killed people together. A lot of folks might find that an unusual means of establishing a bond between people, but in my experience, it's actually surprisingly effective."

She gave him that reluctant smile, but the look in her eyes didn't change. He realized how much pain that periodic smile masked. He wondered why he hadn't seen it before.

"What's your name, anyway?" he asked.

"What's yours?"

"Oh, right, I forgot. I always have to go first, and you don't go at all. But okay. People call me Dox. Short for *unorthodox*. But my name, which pretty much nobody but my folks calls me, is Carl."

There was a long pause. She said, "I'm . . . Labee."

"That's a pretty name."

She looked away.

Damn it, he'd meant it, too. "What, do you think I say that to all the girls?"

But it was as though she didn't hear him. "Nobody calls me that, either," she said quietly.

"Well, I could, if you like." He held out his hand. "Labee, it's nice to meet you. I'm Carl."

She looked at his hand but didn't take it. She shook her head and balled her fists. She glanced at him, and for a second, it looked almost like she wanted to hurt him. All at once he didn't like how close that Glock was. Didn't like it at all.

But she didn't go for the gun. She took his hand, but rather than shaking it, she used it to tug him toward her. Not suddenly or hard, but firmly, with a lot more grounding and power than he would have expected from her size alone.

He was confused, and wondered distantly whether she had some kind of martial-arts background—Rain could move people like that, making it seem effortless. But before he'd had a second to consider further, she'd somehow twisted and spun him so his back was on the couch, and she was straddling him, reared up with one hand tight around his throat and the other retracted in a fist like she was fixing to punch him. He was so startled he actually froze, though maybe that was a luxury he allowed himself because her hands were empty, and while the grip on his throat was no joke, it wasn't quite like she was trying to kill him with it, either.

She kept still and just stared into his eyes like that for a moment, like she was enraged or desperate or he didn't know what. And then she moved a little, rubbing against him. His eyes widened and he thought, *What the hell?*

Well, his brain might have been asking *What the hell,* but Nessie had no questions at all, responding instantly and dramatically to the friction and pressure. The woman felt it—how could she not, it was Nessie, after all, and besides, her little dress had ridden up when she flipped him so that there must have been nothing between them but his robe and her panties. The thought aroused him more, and she started moving against him harder, riding right up and down and making the terrycloth of the robe feel good enough to drive him crazy.

He put his hands on her hips, but she shook him off angrily and squeezed his throat tighter. Again he thought, *What the hell?* But he realized that with whatever this woman had been through, this must be how she liked it. Or maybe it was even the only way she could do it. So though he couldn't help feeling tense from the grip on his larynx and the nearness of the Glock, he let his arms settle to his sides and just went with it. She seemed to like that, maybe feeling she was achieving compliance or whatever, and relaxed her grip enough so he could breathe a little better.

And then, without his even noticing where she'd pulled it from, he saw she was holding a condom. The one from the bathroom, he realized, she must have taken it while she was in there in case this happened, or because she planned on it happening. He was so bewildered by now that he didn't even move as she tore the wrapping open and eased forward onto his belly, then reached back with both hands and opened the robe. Panting now, she got the condom on over him, and then she brought her knees in and slid off the panties, and moved back into position and eased herself right down onto him. The feeling was so good and so intimate that again without meaning to he reached for her, and again she squeezed his throat until he remembered himself and dropped his arms back to his sides. He stayed stiff and motionless after that, just watching her as she rode him harder and harder, her panting getting louder, more intense, and then her face twisted and she cried out, but she never closed her eyes, she just kept staring down at him, even as she came. And then he saw she was crying.

He was weirdly turned on by the whole thing, but also too freaked out to come himself. Which was all right—not that he would have minded, but the main thing for him was always that the lady got to come. But then it was like she *wanted* him to, and she let go of his neck and put her hands on the couch past his head and looked at him and began to ride him even more violently, her expression pained, her cheeks streaked with tears, and it was strange not to kiss her or be able to touch her with his hands, and to connect with her only by looking in her eyes, and she rode him harder, hard enough for it to hurt, and oh thank you lord that was it, that was what he needed, and he groaned as the pleasure intensified and then he was coming as she had, his arms at his sides and her eyes boring into his.

When it was over, and the two of them were breathing a little more normally, she reached back, gripped the condom, and slid herself off him. She moved over to the other end of the couch, looking down, saying nothing.

A moment went by. He felt a little delirious.

"Thank you," he said. "That was nice."

She nodded but still didn't look at him.

"I'd even do it again, if you promised not to squeeze my throat so hard this time."

She glanced at him and gave him that reluctant laugh. Damn, he could get used to making her laugh. He really could.

"You know," he said, easing off the condom and securing the robe so he could talk to her without a big deflating dick distracting anyone, "I usually like to hold the person I just made love to. But I can see it's not that way for you, and I don't want my advances to be unwelcome, even though that concept strikes me as somewhat paradoxical at the moment."

She looked down again. "I'm sorry."

"Sorry? For what?"

"For not . . . For the way I am."

"Don't you dare apologize for that. I wouldn't change one thing about you."

She wiped her eyes. He thought she looked exhausted. Probably he did, too.

"So, look," he said. "I get that you prefer not to be touched. But what about my needs? I like to be held after lovemaking."

She shook her head and laughed.

Damn, but he liked that laugh. "Okay, how about this—you just hold me and I won't hold you back."

He'd really only been trying to get her to laugh again, but she got up, walked over, and sat next to him. Then, with the air of someone about to do something not only dangerous but also maybe distasteful, she reached out and touched his cheek.

The gesture moved him so much that he covered her hand with his own.

She pulled her hand back. "Don't push it."

He laughed, not sure if she was serious or joking, and held up his palms like someone surrendering to a gunman. "My bad, my bad."

She nodded. "Maybe I'll . . . shower now."

"Sure. And when you're done, why don't you take the bed."

"No, the couch is fine. You take the bed."

"The only way I'm getting in that bed is if you do, too."

"Looks like you'll be sleeping on the couch."

"That's fine. I've slept on plenty worse. Gonna miss you, though."

She got up and started to head to the bathroom, then turned back. She looked at him. "Was that really . . . nice for you?"

"Hell yes, it was. Couldn't you tell?"

"I guess."

"I mean, it was a little unusual from my perspective. But I meant it when I said I'd do it again."

She nodded, but her face turned sad. "I'm glad. I think . . ."

But she didn't finish the thought. She just shook her head, picked up the Glock, and walked off. He watched her go, wondering what she'd been about to say, and wishing she'd said it.

23

Livia turned the shower temperature as hot as she could stand. She used a washcloth to scrub herself with soap, then stood under the scalding water, letting it wash everything off her.

She felt confused, and she wasn't sure why. She'd had boyfriends, and though she'd tried to accommodate them by being more normal, the only way she could get off other than by herself was the way she'd just done it with Carl. She was good at trolling for the kind of man who wanted to get rough with her and who she could turn the tables on. But Carl wasn't rough. He was accommodating. And kind. But still, it had worked. That was what was confusing her.

There were things she couldn't do—what the men had made her do on the deck of the boat from Bangkok to Portland, for one. And because, as she'd learned in college psych courses, negative reinforcement tends to generalize, there were other things she couldn't do, as well. And still others she could do but that weren't comfortable.

She could kiss, but didn't really like to. Except for Sean, who had been her first, all the way back in high school, standing by the snowy swings in an empty playground on her last night in Llewellyn. She supposed she could have kissed Carl. He had obviously wanted to. But she hadn't. What she wanted was exactly what they did.

She was glad he'd come. Sometimes it didn't happen, because the guy didn't like what she insisted on. That always made her feel crappy afterward, like there was something wrong with her. Or sometimes it was the opposite problem—the guy would come too fast, because he liked it too much. Which wasn't exactly helpful, either.

She thought of Goldilocks and the three bears, and laughed a little. Yeah, Carl was just right. Freaked out, but still turned on.

She looked at the floor and let the hot water run down her neck and back. She could tell he would again if she wanted, and the way she liked, too. But it wouldn't be the same. It would feel artificial. It would *be* artificial. She'd have to try to provoke him, make him angry, to make it real again, and the thought of that made her sad.

She'd said so little. And yet . . . he'd understood. Without knowing the details, he'd understood completely, in exactly the way she would have wanted him to understand, if she could have imagined what that might be like.

The hot water was good. She felt herself starting to relax.

She was glad for what happened. After the last few days, she'd needed it. But she didn't want it to happen again. She just wanted . . . to try to trust him. She'd almost told him that, right before heading to the bathroom, but then couldn't say it.

When she was done showering, she put on a robe and went back to the room. He was sitting on the couch, and though his head was up and his eyes open, she had the sense he'd been dozing.

"Better?" he said.

She nodded. "I needed that."

He smiled. "I'm tempted to ask whether you're referring to the shower or what came before it, but I believe a woman is entitled to her mysteries."

She shook her head, liking how irrepressible he was but not wanting to admit it.

"You were right," she said. "I'm not a professional. Not like you. Nobody's paying me."

She sat at the opposite end of the couch and looked away from him. "I was Thai, when I was a little girl. Well, Lahu, but from Thailand. And I was kidnapped, and taken to America. With my sister. Nason. She died."

"I'm sorry, Labee."

Even all these years later, it was hard to talk about Nason without tears, especially to someone who seemed to understand. And worse, in this case, who was calling her by a name she hadn't heard since she and Nason had been little girls. So she just nodded and hurried on.

"And Sorm . . . I'm pretty sure he was behind it. Not the kidnapping itself—that was someone else, and I took care of him. And the people who helped him, or at least most of them. But the logistics. The network. That's all Sorm. What happened to Nason and me wouldn't have been possible without Sorm. And what's happened to God knows how many other children would never have happened without him."

They were quiet for a moment. Then he said, "You know better than I do, but yeah. And my guy at CIA, whose intel has always been solid before, he told me Sorm's not just a trafficker. In his Khmer Rouge salad days, his specialty was sexual humiliation and rape. Even children, in front of their parents. Like I said, some people just need killing."

She knew nothing more true than that. "Yes."

"But how'd you get so close? I mean, night vision and the Glock . . . how'd you get all that into the club?"

She told him about Little and the joint federal-local-law-enforcement task force, leaving out the specifics.

"My lord," he said when she was done. "These state-of-the-art networked security systems are like a wet dream for nation-state actors. I hate to think of where things are going with electronic voting. But what about Sorm? I gather from my guy he's a hard man to find. And apparently, my guy was more right than he knew. Where'd you get the intel?"

"I developed some leads."

He laughed. "One of those leads lend you his Glock?"

She didn't like the question. "What do you mean?"

"Don't get me wrong, you can ride a Z800 like a pro, so maybe you like big guns, too. But I had a feeling the Glock was something you borrowed from someone. And that you didn't ask nicely."

She realized that despite everything, she was still partly buying the hick routine, and underestimating him as a result. "And you say I'm a good interrogator."

"You are. But I suppose I have my moments."

"Anyway, yes. I got Sorm's burner number from someone in his network and tracked it to the club. But you're right, now that I've had a chance to think about it, I realize he wasn't even there. Why would he be? It was obviously a setup. I just couldn't accept it right away. Because—"

"Because you wanted so much to kill him. I get it."

She nodded. The feeling of being that close . . . She realized now she'd gotten carried away. If Carl hadn't been there to talk sense to her, she might have gone tearing down the hotel stairs and straight into another ambush. She had to keep a tighter grip on herself.

"So a setup," he said. "But for which of us?"

"It's hard to say. I never told my contact where I'd be going in the club. But from what you've told me, your guy knew you were going to hit the VIP safe room."

"Yeah, that's true. I hate to think it, though. A lot of water under the bridge with my guy."

"But there are other possibilities. Everyone has been tracking Sorm by what we believed was a burner he was using."

"That's right."

"So whoever was behind the setup, if they knew about the burner, they also knew exactly where one of us was going to try to hit Sorm."

"You're right," he said. "And there's another possibility. I told you, these days, Sorm is a DIA asset. It was DIA who hired me to take out Sorm's UN nemesis by getting me to believe the UN guy was Sorm himself. So if DIA . . ."

He got up, walked over to the French doors, and stood for a moment, looking out onto the dark beach. Then he turned to her. "If DIA knows about my CIA guy, they'd know I'd have called him after surviving their Phnom Penh double cross. They'd especially know because my guy made some inquiries throughout the intelligence 'community' once I'd contacted him. Shit, I bet you I know what happened."

He walked back to the couch and started pacing in front of it.

"These 'intel community' types spend as much time spying on each other as they do on America's ostensible adversaries. So shit, DIA probably knows about my CIA connection. My guy's used me for enough work, after all. So when my guy starts asking questions, someone at DIA feeds him false intel. 'Oh yeah, we know the mobile number of a known Sorm associate.' My guy cross references, and creates a map of a telephone network that leads him to the burner Sorm is supposed to be using. Yeah, in fact, he even told me, 'Sorm doesn't know all our capabilities' to explain why Sorm would have gotten sloppy with his communication security. Well, yeah, Sorm might not know, but DIA does. And then DIA makes sure 'Sorm's' burner is located at Les Nuits, night after night, right in the club VIP safe room. My CIA guy laps it all up and thinks, 'Bingo, we found Sorm.' And I thought the same. But instead of Sorm, it was a damn ambush."

"When you tossed in that flashbang, one of the men yelled, 'Grenade.' In English."

"He did?"

She nodded. "It doesn't narrow the list of suspects that much, but it's at least consistent with your theory."

"Damn, I didn't even hear. Too busy trying not to piss myself, I guess. I don't think I'd have made it out of that club if you hadn't been there."

"I'm glad I was, then."

"That's pretty sentimental for you."

She laughed. It was weird how comfortable he made her.

"Anyway," she said, "I have another lead."

"Yeah?"

"Udom Leekpai. Another Sorm associate. Who sells children out of a shipping container at the Srinakarin Rot Fai Night Market."

"Well, it sounds like we ought to get back to Bangkok and pay old Udom a visit."

A warm ripple of adrenaline spread through her gut. Leekpai was her best lead to that little girl. And to Sorm. She was glad to have someone with her to go after him, and a little bewildered by both the notion and the feeling.

"Say," he said. "Can I ask you something off topic?"

She nodded.

"You have some kind of martial-arts background? Tai chi, or aikido, or something like that?"

The question made her tense, the way his comment about the Glock had. "Why?"

"The way you moved me on the couch. I don't even know how you did it, exactly. It didn't feel like you were pulling hard, but away I went. I have a friend who can do things like that, and he's got a big-time judo background."

That was way too close for comfort. "I've dabbled in this and that," she said, remembering how Little had said something along those lines when she'd put a similar question to him.

He laughed. "Yeah, 'dabbled.' But okay. Like I said, I believe a woman is entitled to her mysteries. Can I ask you one other thing off topic?"

"I get the feeling nothing is really off topic with you."

"Well, I guess it comes down to how you define 'topic.' But anyway, before, when I said I loved the smell of durian fruit. You looked at me strangely. I know most people dislike the smell, but that look seemed like something else."

He really did notice a lot. He would have made a great cop.

"Durian was Nason's favorite."

There was a long pause. Then he said, "I'm glad you told me."

She nodded. And, to keep herself from crying, said, "If you're right. About DIA feeding false information to your CIA contact. It means—"

"Right, it means my contact ought to be able to tell us who at DIA is protecting Sorm. And if he won't—"

"Then the one protecting Sorm is your contact."

"That's right, even though I hate to think it. But I can't call him now. I don't want to power up the phone until we're ready to vamoose in the morning. But I'll tell you what, one way or the other, he's going to have himself some explaining to do."

24

Dox slept fitfully. It wasn't the couch—he'd meant it when he said he'd slept, and slept well, on plenty worse. It wasn't even any kind of adrenaline aftermath from the whole crazy night. It was the worry that Kanezaki might have sold him out.

He didn't want to think it could be. Which meant he had to make sure he wasn't discounting the possibility just because it was uncomfortable.

If Kanezaki had turned on him, there would've had to be a hell of a good reason. Because the man would know that if anything went wrong, he'd be taking on not just Dox, but Rain, as well, and with all due immodesty, there weren't many pairs on earth you'd less want looking to punch your ticket.

Still, Kanezaki himself would make for some formidable opposition. And while that was a sobering notion, it was also such a sad one.

Rain didn't trust anyone. Well, maybe he trusted Dox. And his lady—or sometime lady, who knew what was up with them anyway, Rain didn't like to talk about it—Delilah. Rain trusted her.

But Dox wasn't built like that. He needed to have people he could believe in. Rain was one, of course. And Delilah, too—hell, she'd earned it after all they'd been through, though it was also true he could tell with her right away. And the Dalai Lama—well, Vannak Vann, the UN guy, but he just thought of him as the Dalai Lama. He was on the up-and-up, no doubt. And Labee, who, okay, he hadn't known for very long, but with whom a hell of a lot had happened in the short time they'd been acquainted. He trusted her.

And Kanezaki. Kanezaki was another. He hadn't even realized how much he'd come to trust the man over the years until just now, lying sleepless on a wee-hours couch at the Paradise Cottages and Spa in Rayong Province, Thailand, when he was forced by circumstance to ask himself whether his trust might have been misplaced.

At well past dawn, Labee stirred in the bed and sat up.

"Hey," Dox said. "How'd you sleep?"

She rubbed her eyes. "Pretty well, actually. How about you?"

"Okay at first. But I've been awake for a spell, trying to decide whether my guy could have sold me out."

There was a pause, then she said, "Even if Sorm wasn't there last night, he was there recently. My lead was solid."

"I'm glad to hear it, but that doesn't exactly get my guy off the hook, either."

"Well, we'll know soon enough, right?"

"Yeah. Speaking of which, we should git. I don't want to call him until we're east of Bangkok and past the choke point of the coastal road. Just in case."

There was a pause. She said, "You've been calling him your 'guy.' But it sounds like he's more your friend."

"Yeah, I guess you could say that. Known him a long time."

"I don't think it was him."

"I don't, either, but . . . it could have been. I can't afford to be sentimental about it."

"I get that. But I also think . . . you have good instincts."

He looked at her. She was so pretty in the faint light from outside, and naked beneath the bedsheets. He wished he could have walked over and made love to her right then and there. But he could tell she didn't want that. And it wasn't just a question of it being her way, or more gentle, which he would have favored right that minute. He sensed the night before had been just a crazy one-off. But not a bad one. Not a bad one at all. With luck, what came after it might be even better.

He laughed. "I think that's just self-flattery. You're saying you think I have good instincts because I decided to trust you, is that it?"

"Just because it's self-flattering doesn't mean it isn't true."

"Well, let's hope it is. Like you said, we'll know soon enough."

They took turns in the bathroom and headed out. Back at the bike, he didn't argue, he just held out the key.

She almost took it, but then hesitated. "It's okay," she said. "I'll ride in back."

It was such a small thing, but at the same time he could tell what a concession it was for her. And that she was doing it for his sake, and maybe so she'd seem more normal to him, whatever the hell *normal* might mean.

He shook his head and pressed the key into her hand. "No, I know you like to be the one with your hand on the throttle. So to speak. Plus I like the way you ride. Damn, these double entendres are a big effort and you're not even smiling. Anyway, no shit, you ride as well as I do, or actually better, if my honesty overcomes my pride. I really don't mind. For today, anyway. Maybe I could just reserve the right for another occasion."

She touched his cheek, like she had the night before. This time he didn't make the mistake of trying to touch her back.

Along the way they stopped to buy new clothes—tee shirts and cargo shorts and hiking sandals—and at an incongruously American-diner-looking place, where they fueled up on eggs, toast, bacon, and coffee. Their conversation was comfortable, almost banal, considering the events of the night before and what they were facing now. Mostly they talked about motorcycles, and how stupid it was to ride without leathers, but when in Rome and trying to be inconspicuous and all that. She had a passion for Ducatis, and a Streetfighter was her most cherished possession. He was a Harley man and planned one day to own a V-Rod Muscle, though where he lived, a little Honda Rebel was the more practical choice.

About a half hour east of Bangkok, they found an Internet café. Dox went in and paid cash for access, then came back out to the dusty parking area in front. The late-morning sun was high in the sky and Labee was standing next to the Kawasaki in the shade of a lonely palm tree, alongside a mongrel dog sheltering from the heat. Dox joined her. She already had his phone out of the case and handed it to him. Then she walked off, no doubt recognizing that he wouldn't want her listening to his call. He almost told her to stay, but then thought of how Rain would castigate him for being too trusting and decided to just let her go.

He looked at the dog, which was watching him. "Hey, pooch," he said absently. He was surprised at how nervous he was. He didn't believe Kanezaki could have turned on him. But . . . what if he was wrong?

He fired up the unit and saw that the Wi-Fi connection was strong enough to reach the lot from inside. Good to go. He brought up Signal and made the call.

Kanezaki picked up instantly, even though it was the middle of the night over there. "Hey," he said. "I've been waiting to hear from you."

"Yeah, well, I'm sure you understand that, first with Zatōichi and then after the Pattaya debacle, I needed to make sure I was secure."

"I get that."

"I hope you do. Now at the outset of this whole thing, you told me you had a hunch Sorm was DIA, a hunch you confirmed. I want to know how you confirmed it. Specifically, *who* confirmed it. And how you dialed into what you thought was that Sorm associate's mobile phone, the one that was proof positive Sorm was sheltering in Les Nuits, right in the damn safe room that for me turned out to be anything but."

"Damn it, Dox, you know I can't—"

"Shut the fuck up, son, because you are not getting it. Last time you gave me this whole song and dance about how Sorm's a DIA asset and you couldn't have me kill a DIA asset, but this time you're not going to be giving up a DIA asset, you're going to be giving up a DIA officer, and if you won't do that, then my problem isn't with DIA, partner, my problem is with you."

A motorcycle buzzed by, a couple of kids riding tandem. Then it was gone, a long dust cloud in its wake, and everything was quiet again.

Kanezaki said, "I was afraid you were going to say that."

"Tom? I like you. You know I do. But right now? You should be afraid. Either you got played, or you're playing me. There's no other possibility here. I'll tell you the truth, I am really hoping it's door number one. But you need to prove that to me. If you won't, it's your choice. And your consequences."

The dog that had been sheltering looked at him warily, then came to its feet and moved off.

"All right," Kanezaki said. "My DIA contact is Frank Dillon. The deputy director."

Dox felt a huge surge of relief. Yeah, he'd felt nervous, but he hadn't realized just how afraid he'd really been that Kanezaki might stonewall. Still, the specific information made him wary.

"Franklin X. Dillon? The Delta sniper, from the Battle of Mogadishu?"

"Yes. That Dillon."

"Well, he's a genuine badass. And outspoken, too, especially for a Delta guy, who in my experience like to shoot more than talk. Isn't he the one who did that *New York Times* interview after the battle, blaming the damn secretary of defense himself for the deaths of his comrades, for not having provided the requested tanks and armored personnel carriers?"

"Yes," Kanezaki said, "he's famous for that interview—or infamous, depending on who you talk to. It was one of the things that led to Aspin's resignation."

"If I'm remembering correctly, he's also famous for inventing some kind of new approach to tank-and-APC downtime, some modular thing that doubled the ratio of deployment hours to maintenance hours."

"Yes. So effectively doubling the number of deployed armored units. He said he'd never forgive himself for not having thought of it before Mogadishu. If he had, our guys might have had the armor they needed, and they wouldn't have been at the mercy of ignorant DC brass. Do you know him? Or just by reputation?"

"Back in the day, I did some training with Delta. But our paths never crossed. What about you?"

"He's been with DIA for a decade now, and I know him from various joint ops over the years. He's a kind of frenemy. Very smart guy. Though I can't say I find him as agreeable as you."

"Well, who is?"

"Anyway. He's the one who confirmed for me, off the record, obviously, that Gant was a DIA case officer and Dillon's subordinate. And who gave me the initial intel I used to place Sorm at Les Nuits."

All right. He wasn't a hundred percent on Kanezaki, but they at least seemed to be heading in the right direction. "That's a good start," Dox said. "Now here's something you can follow up on. There are three dead guys in that club. Well, six, actually, but three of them were locals—Sorm's men, I'd guess, pawns someone set up outside the VIP room to be sacrificed. But the other three were different. When I tossed the flashbang into the room, one of them yelled 'Grenade' in English. Maybe you can find out who they were affiliated with."

"Okay. But either way . . . you're right. It was a setup. It had to be. I just . . . I'm sorry. I think I've been trying to convince myself it was something else."

"Don't you get it, though? It wasn't just me Dillon was setting up. He had to know that if anything went wrong and I walked away, I'd suspect you. On which topic, pardon me, but we're not quite out of the woods yet."

"Yeah. I don't know whether the next thing I tell you is going to get us out of the woods or deeper into them. But I wanted you to hear it from me regardless, not see it on the news."

Shit. "Don't think about it, then. Just tell me."

"Vannak Vann. He was killed yesterday."

Dox felt sick. "Oh, no."

"It was an IED. On the corner, not fifty meters from his office in Phnom Penh."

"Who did it? You better tell me who did it. Was it Dillon?"

"Specifically? I don't know. But a safe bet it was DIA. Their man Gant was the one who hired you to eliminate Vann in the first place. That didn't work out. This feels like a Plan B."

Dox realized he was clenching his teeth. And the phone, too. He blew out two long breaths and tried to calm himself so he could think clearly. He looked up and saw Labee watching him from the entrance of the café. She looked concerned. He was too far to be overheard, but his body language must have been clear enough.

"Maybe a Plan B," Dox said. "Or maybe . . . something improvised. It took some doing to bring me in. Initial contact, meeting with Gant, acquisition of the equipment I requested . . . and they had to hire local muscle, the ones who were supposed to knife me in the dark after I'd shot Vann. It wasn't exactly Operation Overlord, but there were a fair number of moving parts."

"Yes. All designed to deploy you as a cutout."

"And then to cut out the cutout as soon as the deed was done. It's been only a few days. Either these guys build in safety redundancies better than NASA and had a meticulous Plan B already in place—"

"No. That wouldn't make sense. Because every element of the plan is also a vulnerability—someone who knows too much, an element they might not be able to control."

Dox could still feel the rage trying to push through. But focusing on the tactical aspects was helping. For the moment, anyway.

"All right," he said. "What we're saying is that they got to Vann by improvisation. No time for cutouts and all the rest. Direct action, because after things went sideways in Phnom Penh, they were desperate. Which brings us back to the question I asked a minute ago. Who. Fucking. Killed. Vann. That's what you're going to tell me. What you are not going to tell me is how I will or will not handle it."

"I'll try to find out. Just give me a little time."

Now that the conversation was done, Dox could feel the rage building again. "I'm going to turn off this phone now. I'll check in with you later."

"Please. And don't wait so long this time."

"Tom? You're in a difficult position and I appreciate that. But there comes a moment where a man has to choose sides. You can't have it both ways here. You can be a loyal player in your 'intelligence community,' or you can give me what I need to kill Dillon dead. And Sorm with him."

"Look—"

"Remember when I told you the only way to make sense of this crazy world is to know who your real friends are? Well, you need to make a decision about that, right now. The organization, or your friends. Them or me. That's your choice now. With everything that flows from it."

He clicked off, powered down the phone and put it back in the shielded case, and paced the parking lot, his sandals kicking up small clouds of dust into the still, hot air. He squeezed his eyes shut and balled his fists and clenched his arms and stomach. He wanted to hurt someone, kill someone.

You're going to. You are going to kill some people who need *killing.*

He blew out a few more breaths. When he felt a little more in control, he walked over to Labee.

"What is it?" she said.

"They killed the Dalai Lama. Blew him up. Not the actual Dalai Lama. The UN guy I told you about who looked like him. A good man, a really good man."

"I'm sorry, Carl."

He realized he was close to tears. "I told him, 'Vary your routes and times, get rid of your cell phone.' I told him he was in danger. And he said, 'In the scope of the universe, and the arc of justice, my life is of little consequence.' Well, goddamnit, I hope he's happy now."

"I'm sorry," she said again.

"I should have known he wouldn't listen. But I should have made him. I should have made him."

"You tried. You did everything you could."

He looked out at the narrow road running in front of the café, gray and rutted and baking under the sun. "You don't know that. And neither do I."

He started to move past her so he could get on the bike. But she held up a hand and pressed her palm to his cheek, stopping him. He stood there for a moment, looking at her, then put his hand over hers. This time she didn't pull back.

"I am going to kill them," he said. "Every last fucking one."

She nodded, looking into his eyes. "We both are."

25

Livia took them farther north, stopping at a gas stand in the middle of nowhere east of Bangkok's Suvarnabhumi Airport. They were less than an hour from the Central Business District, but it was quiet out here, the land flat and dotted with shacks and irrigation ditches and small plots of farmland. Livia gassed up the Kawasaki. When she was done, Carl walked over to an old woman perched on a sagging couch on the shady side of the small cinderblock building—the owner, it seemed. He pulled two bottled waters from an ice bucket and handed the woman some baht, holding up his hand and refusing when she tried to make change.

They took turns in the outhouse, then sat in a pair of plastic chairs under a faded red-and-white Coca-Cola umbrella set up in the dirt alongside the building. While they drank, Carl told her about the rest of his conversation with his guy. "He said he's going to find out who killed Vann," he told her. "Most likely, that means a former Delta guy named Franklin Dillon, the deputy director of the Defense Intelligence Agency. That's some heavy opposition and maybe heavy blowback. If you don't want to be part of it, I'll miss you, but I'll understand."

She looked at him. "You couldn't stop me."

He laughed softly. "Yeah, I'm getting that feeling. Not that I'd want to try."

"I should check in myself. I would have earlier, but you made a good point about the coastal road being a choke point. I didn't want to turn my phone on until we were close to Bangkok."

She fired up the phone. The moment the call went through, Little picked up. "Livia," he said. "Are you all right?"

"I'm fine."

"Why didn't you check in? I have to learn about what happened at the club on CNN, and hear nothing from you?"

"I'm sorry. I was all ready to go when I saw what looked like some kind of confrontation outside a room with three guards in front of it. That's when I asked you to stand by. And then the guards started shooting, and I told you to kill the lights. It was pandemonium after that, and I got out. Do you know anything about what happened?"

"Not one damn thing," he said. "In fact, I have the oddest feeling you know more than you're telling me."

"Really? I walked into what turned out to be a shooting gallery, and the only person who knew I was going to be there was you."

"What? You think I had something to do with that?"

"I don't know what to think."

"Why in God's name would I want to set you up?"

She didn't have an answer to that, and in fact didn't believe Little had anything to do with it. But that hadn't been the point, either. The point was to change the trajectory of the conversation from his accusation to her counteraccusation.

"I don't know," she said. "But on the other hand, I know very little about you other than that you have resources to waste."

"You know what I meant by that. Come on, this is insane."

"What can you tell me about the people who died at the club?"

"You don't think I've been trying to find out?"

"I don't know what you've been doing. But I can give you the information I have. And you can follow up on it."

"That would be great and I'd love to. I only wish you'd done it earlier."

She smiled, glad to have him playing defense. "The guards were Thai. And then, after the shooting started, a door opened and three men in what looked like black combat or SWAT uniforms and body armor came swarming out. One of them yelled 'Grenade' in English, and then there was a series of explosions from a flashbang. Then more shooting. After that, I don't know."

"Yes, there were six bodies total. From what you're saying, three Thai guards, and three foreign operators. It's not much, but I'll see what I can do with it."

"Good."

"Damn it, Livia, you need to stop looking at me as the enemy. We're a team."

"Don't tell me what I need to do. And don't tell me we're a team. Prove it."

"You asked me to get you into the club, and I did. What the hell more do you want?"

"I want to know what happened there."

"Well, so far I haven't been able to find out. But maybe what you just belatedly told me will turn out to be useful."

She didn't mind the dig. In fact, if that was the best he could come up with, she knew she'd won. She hadn't wanted to answer his questions, and by leveling accusations of her own, she'd gotten him to forget he even had any.

"I hope it will be," she said. "I'm going to turn off my phone, but I'll check in again later."

"What, you think I'm tracking your phone?"

"What I think is that my phone is trackable. Are you telling me it isn't?"

"Why does everything have to be an argument with you?"

"Why are you always arguing?"

"Look, I don't have time for a Monty Python sketch. Turn off the phone if you want. If I have anything important to tell you, it'll just wait until you get around to calling me."

She smiled. "Like I said. I'll check in later."

She powered down the phone and put it back in the Faraday case. Carl said, "Why are handlers always such a pain in the ass?"

She shrugged. "Just comes with the territory, I guess."

"You learn anything?"

"I think he's up to something. My supervisor sure thinks so. But I don't think he was behind what happened at the club. On that, I think he's as mystified as we are."

"What do you think he's up to, then?"

She considered that. "He sent me over here to decide whether I wanted to be part of a task force. Something between Thai and local US law enforcement. But . . . since I got here, he hasn't seemed very concerned about any of that. He seems glad I'm here, though. I'm just not sure why."

They were both quiet for a moment. She said, "Anyway, the main thing is, what looks most likely right now is that your theory is correct. DIA was behind Pattaya. Your friend didn't set you up. They did."

"I hope you're right. We'll see what he has to say for himself when I call him later. But let's get out of here now. Don't want to linger anywhere we've been using the phones. For all I know, these guys will lock in on the signal and send in a damn drone. Those things are scary. I shot one out of the sky once, but it was a near thing and I was a lot better armed than I am at the moment."

26

They kept heading north and northwest, sticking to back roads. Dox was surprised, though not unpleasantly, at how quickly he'd gotten used to riding in back. It was actually kind of relaxing. Of course, it would have been a different story if Labee hadn't been such a competent rider. But she was. And he had to admit, insisting on being in front even in the face of her obvious skill would have been childish. If anyone ever gave him a hard time about it, he'd tell them to take it up with Labee, who, if she was in the wrong mood at the time, would probably kick their ass. He'd enjoy a backseat view of that, too.

They found a business hotel at the outskirts of the airport district. Dox got a room and they both napped on the king bed. Their clothes were on and there was no snuggling or anything like it, but still he felt glad that she was letting him into her space a little. The feeling was paradoxical, because hell, the night before, she'd let him into her body. But that was the point, she hadn't so much let him in as *taken* him in. Now she was letting him. And it was different.

When they were awake, he checked in with Kanezaki again. "What have you got for me?" he said, afraid again despite himself that the answer wouldn't be satisfactory.

But maybe he was wrong, because Kanezaki said, "A lot."

"Go."

"Less than twelve hours after you shot Gant, Dillon was on a plane. Guess where he was going."

"I don't want to play guessing games. Just tell me."

"Phnom Penh."

"And you think he blew up Vann while he was there?"

"I can't prove it. But it's not hard to imagine the sequence. Sorm learns through various contacts, maybe through DIA, in fact, about Vann and the sealed indictment. He goes to his case officer, Gant, and says, 'You better take care of this.' Gant spends days, maybe weeks, putting everything together for you to hit Vann. But you hit Gant instead. Now Sorm is having a shit fit. SOP is to have a backup contact if for any reason you lose touch with your case officer. Figure the backup here is Dillon, Gant's superior. Sorm calls Dillon and now he is really agitated, because the clock is ticking, they've lost time, they've lost Gant, Vann is still out there, and worst of all, so is a probably-pissed-off former marine sniper who might just know too much. Dillon says, 'Relax, I'm coming to deal with it personally.' Which he does."

Dox considered. It fit with his general impression that blowing up Vann was less a Plan B than it was hasty improvisation. Which was his sense about Zatōichi, too.

Something else occurred to him. "Hey, you said it was an IED. You sure about that?"

"Yes. The blast site and surrounding damage is nothing like what you'd expect from any kind of missile. This was a bomb, already in place. Why, though?"

"Well, if it's DIA, why not just make it a drone strike? Why send Dillon, and presumably a team, all the way to Phnom Penh?"

"I think you're looking at it backward. Anybody with even rudimentary training can build and emplace an IED. You can even find recipes on the Internet, though the wrong ones will get you blown up. But if you wanted to send in a drone, the logistical tail would be formidable. That's changing fast—the next generation of drones will be the size of dragonflies, with a practically microscopic camera called an optical phased-array receiver, and embedded microexplosives, and everything will be decentralized. But right now, if you wanted to deploy a Reaper or whatever to loiter over a target until you could ID him and launch a Hellfire to blow him up, the whole thing would have to be coordinated through Ramstein Air Base in Germany and other locations, too. You'd have a paper trail visible from outer space."

That made sense. "So not the kind of thing you could use against a UN official."

"Exactly."

Something was nagging at him. About Vann and Zatōichi both. Then it hit him.

"I told Vann to vary his routes and times. Maybe he listened, maybe he didn't. But Dillon couldn't be sure regardless, and if he was going to emplace an IED, he'd have to know which way and at least around what time Vann would be going past it."

"That's true, but they might have put, say, two in place, to make sure they were covering all the possible routes."

"I reconned that area. If I were the one emplacing the device, I would have wanted four separate locations, depending on what entrance or exit the target might use. So now we're talking about not just multiple devices, but multiple spotters, too. And that doesn't feel quite right. They're in a hurry. Improvising. And there are cameras on the UN perimeter, too, so even if you emplaced the device far enough away, you'd still be taking chances on having all these spotters conducting initial recon."

"What are you thinking, then?"

"They had to have some kind of eyes on Vann. But from what you just told me about these microdrones . . . I mean, how far along are they operationally? Maybe not dragonflies, and forget about the explosives, because that seems not to have been what happened here, but what about the size of a small bird? Like a hummingbird, something that could persistently circle at fifty or a hundred feet, where no one would ever even see it?"

"That kind of drone is . . . very far along."

"I'll be damned. That's how they worked it with Zatōichi. I couldn't figure out how he could be coming from the opposite direction. But if they knew my location and direction, he could come from anywhere. And, of course, they did know. They knew I'd try to see Vann. So it's not as though they had to search for me throughout the entirety of Phnom Penh. They could just fly one of their tiny drones in circles all day long around Vann's office. And once I showed up, they could sic Zatōichi on me from any direction they liked."

"And the direction they wanted would have been something other than coming up behind you."

"Right—if I saw him coming up behind me, I might have reacted. Coming from somewhere I hadn't even been seemed like nothing. He might have had me, too, if I hadn't noticed a few anomalies telling me this Zatōichi was a fake."

"I'd say your instinct about this all being improvised after you killed Gant was on the money."

Dox wondered whether he'd been saying too much. Maybe he should have let Kanezaki do more of the talking, and kept his own speculation to himself. On the other hand, he doubted he was giving away that much by thinking out loud. On the *other* other hand, he supposed it was possible that mostly he was trying to act as if Kanezaki was definitely trustworthy, because he wanted so much to believe it.

He decided he didn't care. "Still, to send Dillon out to do this personally, or, more likely, to supervise a team . . . What the hell is DIA getting from Sorm that would make them take these risks?"

"Or as you put it, what does Sorm have on them?"

"Right, or both."

"I don't know the answer. But I'll tell you who does."

"Dillon, I get it. Well, if I can ask him, I will. But then again, I'm not really in the mood to talk anymore."

"I know. And I'm not arguing."

"Good."

There was a pause. Kanezaki said, "Speaking of which, I have one more bit of intel. It's ambiguous, but maybe you can make sense of it."

"Tell me."

"Dillon is meeting Sorm. Tonight."

Dox felt a little adrenaline hit move out through him. "Where?"

"That's the ambiguous part. At 'the tents.' Does that mean anything to you?"

Dox considered. *Tents* in Bangkok could mean one of the night markets, bazaars characterized by hundreds of stalls, each sheltered under a colorful tent. It sounded like Kanezaki's intel tracked Labee's lead about Rot Fai in Srinakarin. It was such welcome news that for an instant, Dox wholeheartedly believed it. But then he forced himself to slow down.

"How do you know that?"

"Come on, sources and meth—"

"Bullshit, sources and methods!" Dox erupted. "I do not have time for your sources and methods. You tell me sources and methods, I'm going to think you're playing me. Now, I've been trying, really trying, to give you the benefit of the doubt. But the last so-called intel you gave me was bullshit and almost got me killed. And maybe you don't realize it, but you are this close—I mean this fucking close—to having a major problem with me. So you tell me right fucking now how you came by this new 'intel.'"

There was a long pause. It felt like capitulation. Dox waited.

"All right," Kanezaki said. "Okay."

There was another pause. Finally, Kanezaki said, "I'm into the cable traffic of the DIA director himself."

Dox shook his head, half-pleased, half-disgusted. "My lord, if you spent half the time spying on the Chinese and Russians as you do on each other, who knows what you might uncover?"

"Whatever. Now you know."

"Now I know what? How do you know this intel is reliable?"

"Are you joking? The DIA director's own cable traffic?"

"Hang on a minute. When was the last time you got anything really useful to you, or compromising to them, from this channel?"

No response.

"Okay, how long have you been doing this? Six months? Six years? How long?"

Kanezaki sighed. "It's been a little under a year."

"Okay, in that year, what have you gotten that's truly to your advantage or their detriment?"

"Well, it's been a little while, but—"

"Oh, wait, don't tell me, the only real nugget you got was right at the beginning, am I seeing it clearly now?"

There was a pause. "Not exactly. I mean, at the outset, there were some difficult negotiations under way between CIA and DIA. About a sensitive, far-reaching op and who would run it. What I learned from the cable hack was invaluable to our winning the contract, so to speak."

"You see? That's exactly what I'm talking about. You cleaned their clock in your sensitive-op-negotiation pissing contest or whatever it was and they said, 'Hell, how did old Kanezaki figure out our exact negotiating position and how to end-run us?' And they examined all their vulnerabilities, and maybe found some sign your hackers had left behind. 'Well, Kanezaki, that wily son of a bitch,' they said, 'he cracked the director's cable traffic!' And what did they do next? You tell me, what did they do?"

Silence. He realized he'd used Kanezaki's name in front of Labee. And said a whole lot of other shit he probably shouldn't have, on top of it.

The hell with it.

"I mean, tell me," he went on. "Tell me, have you ever gotten anything valuable after that? Anything earthshaking? Anything DIA really and truly wouldn't want you to have?"

"Well, no, but the general background itself is—"

"Bullshit, general background! After the first intrusion, you didn't get shit! Now they knew you were in there, they knew, so you tell me, why didn't they close that channel down? Would you have expected them to shut down a compromised channel? Would a shutdown be standard practice for you intel-community types? Or might you do something else? Tell me, goddamnit, I want to hear you say it!"

"Damn it. They wouldn't shut it down. They'd keep using it—"

"Exactly! Bingo! Go to the head of the line! They'd keep it—and play you with it. They'd feed you false intel you'd think was real, just like they did about Pattaya and Les Nuits, where I almost got fucking killed as a result!"

There was a long pause. Kanezaki said, "Damn it. You're right. I'm sorry. Shit."

Dox was still hopping mad, but all at once he felt bad, too. He hadn't meant to browbeat the man like that. Not exactly. It was just . . . he realized he'd been so afraid Kanezaki wouldn't be able to persuade him he was still trustworthy.

"All right, all right. I'm sorry for getting so disagreeable."

"You have nothing to apologize for. They've been playing me. I should have seen it, and I didn't. And I almost got you killed as a result."

"Well, on the one hand, that's all true. But on the other hand, no harm, no foul, right? Life's full of lessons, and this one came fairly cheap compared to the alternatives."

"I guess."

Damn, he sounded so morose. "Anyway," Dox said, looking for a way to get him back in the game, "this is actually good news, isn't it? Because—"

"I know. I get it. Because when I knew but they didn't know I knew, that was good. But when they knew that I knew but I didn't know they knew, that was bad. But now that I know they know that I know, and they don't know it, it's good again."

That was actually a little hard to follow, but it sounded about right. "Something like that, yeah. The thing is, DIA is playing you again. And they think they're getting away with it. But now you know better. And that gives us the advantage. He who laughs last, laughs best, isn't that true?"

"I'm sorry, Dox. I . . . don't know how I missed this."

"Well, that's a conversation for another time. For now, I'll just say maybe you placed too much residual faith in your 'community.' For you, these intel squabbles are a contact sport. But for the other guys, it's no game. You're a good man, and you projected your values onto some people who weren't worthy of it. Now you know better. And I know it hurts to have the scales fall from your eyes, but at least now you can see clearly, right?"

"I'm not crazy about the view, but . . . yeah."

"The view is the view, son. You have to see it clearly if you don't want to start bumping into things."

"All right, I think we've beaten this metaphor to death."

Dox laughed, glad the man seemed to be rallying. "Now tell me exactly what that cable said. And this was, what, Dillon briefing the director?"

"Yes. It said, 'I'm meeting Red tonight at the tents to review the trade.'"

"'Red'?"

"Yes, probably a reference to Sorm's Khmer Rouge past. We're not always as clever with pseudonyms as we should be."

"And what's 'the trade'?"

"I'm not sure. Maybe some aspect of what they get from Sorm, and what they give him in return. Or it's just bullshit, because as you've persuasively argued, they know I'm into that channel of cable traffic."

"Anything else in the cable?"

"Yes. Dillon says he told Red to get a new phone and under no circumstances to use any unit he'd ever used before or that could otherwise be associated with him. He told him to leave the new unit off until he was at the tents. Then he should use it to call Dillon and tell Dillon where they should meet."

"If that's true, it means Sorm has Dillon's number, and we can expect him to use it. Maybe something you can key on. But do you think he really told Sorm all that?"

"Hard to say. He might have. Or it might have been entirely for our benefit. Or some combination."

"Judging from the way old Gant played me, I think it's safe to say these guys hide their lies in as much truth as possible. My guess is it's both true . . . and for our benefit."

"Meaning?"

"I don't know yet. I need to think about it. This 'You know that I know that you know' stuff gets confusing."

Kanezaki chuckled. "Now what do you make of 'the tents'? You must have some idea, because it's the one thing you haven't asked about."

Dox hesitated. He still hadn't fully decided on whether Kanezaki was playing him. He didn't think so, but . . .

And then he decided that for the moment, he had to at least act as if he trusted him. He could always abort later if he changed his mind.

"I have reason to believe 'the tents' is a reference to the Srinakarin Rot Fai Night Market."

"What reason?"

"Sources and methods, son. Sources and methods."

"That's cold. But I guess I deserve it."

Dox chuckled. "Anyway. Let me do a little thinking on all we just talked about, and I'll call you later."

"I'll be standing by."

Dox ended the call and returned the phone to the Faraday case. He briefed Labee on the conversation. She'd heard most of it anyway.

"His information tracks with mine," she said when he was through.

He nodded. "Maybe."

"But you don't like it."

He tried to piece together what was bothering him. Some of it felt obvious. But some of it . . . less so. He decided to start with the first, hoping doing so would shed some light on the second.

"Yeah, the thing about the Night Market sounds good and it tracks with your lead. But still, it's coming from . . . well, you already heard me say his name."

"You were upset."

"Yeah, I sure was."

"Why don't we just call him K. 'My guy' was always a little awkward anyway."

He laughed. "Okay, fair enough."

"And by the way. My guy is Special Agent B. D. Little. Homeland Security Investigations."

He looked at her. "You didn't have to tell me that."

She shrugged. "I know he's using me, though I still don't know exactly how. And besides, I like what you said to K. about how the only way to make sense of things is to know who your real friends are. I haven't had many friends. But . . ."

Her voice trailed off and she looked away.

He wanted to reach for her hand, but thought maybe it would be too much.

"Hey," he said. "You know I feel the same."

She nodded.

To save her further discomfort, he went on. "Anyway. If K. set me up before, he could be doing the same thing again. When I first asked him for help, he claimed to be twitchy about killing a DIA asset, but maybe that was all bullshit. Maybe he was protecting Sorm for his own reasons. I can't shake this feeling we're going to show up at the Night Market and it'll be just like Pattaya all over again."

She looked at him, seemingly back in control of herself. "What do your instincts tell you?"

He considered. "He wouldn't do it. Couldn't. It's not who he is."

"And haven't your instincts always been reliable before?"

For a moment, he thought of Tiara. "Well, maybe there was this one time, but that's not really relevant to what we're talking about here."

"So the answer is yes. Your instincts have always been reliable before."

He nodded. "Yeah. That's true."

"Then that's your answer. K. isn't lying. Your instincts are right. You should trust them. The way you always have."

He chewed on that. He knew she was right. He didn't think Kanezaki was setting him up. But something was still bugging him. He just couldn't figure out what it was.

"Let's git," he said. "All this talk of drone strikes makes me twitchy. Plus I think it's past time you and I had a little conversation with the Night Market's most reprehensible denizen, Mr. Udom Leekpai."

27

Two hours later, Carl and Livia were sitting in the shade of a corrugated awning at a place called Best Friend Bar 10, each with an ice-cold bottle of Chang in front of them.

Carl had told her about a guy in Bangkok he had met through Kanezaki—a guy named Fallon who Carl said was "all right." She wasn't entirely sure what that meant, but was learning to trust his occasional understatements and the judgment behind them. Carl had texted the guy, *If you're available, I'd be grateful to meet you again ASAP at the same place as last time. Semper fi.* The guy had immediately texted back that he would be there in two hours.

They'd barely had time to sip their beers when a solid-looking white guy of maybe sixty in aviator shades came around the corner. He nodded when he saw them, then glanced left and right, perhaps a little surprised that Carl wasn't alone.

Carl waved, then said to the bartender, "A Singha for my friend, sir, thank you."

Fallon stopped at the stool alongside Carl, which put Carl in the middle. Livia moved her stool back and Carl spun around. Now they could all see each other.

Fallon took off his shades and set them on the bar. He looked at Livia, then at Dox. "Well," he said. "I'm glad not all your stories are sad ones."

Carl laughed and they shook. The bartender put a Singha on the bar in front of Fallon, who took a big swallow.

"Fallon," Carl said, "meet Labee. Labee, Fallon."

They shook. He had a good grip.

"Labee and I have found ourselves in a bit of a pickle. And to resolve it, we were planning to have a private conversation with a certain Thai gentleman who may not speak English. We would thus like to avail ourselves of your translation services, and possibly some of the other services I'm hoping might fall under the general heading of Tips, Tours, and Trips."

Fallon sipped his beer. "Does this have anything to do with our mutual friend?"

"Indirectly, yes."

"Because I would have expected him to get in touch himself."

"Well, I could have done it that way. But it would have taken more time. Of which we don't have a lot. Plus, there again, you were kind enough to give me your card."

Fallon didn't respond.

"Let me put it this way," Carl went on. "Had I shared Labee's and my plans with Kanezaki, whose name Labee is at this point familiar with, I have no doubt he would have approved. But nor did I see any need to burden him."

Fallon nodded, seemingly unfazed about Livia knowing Kanezaki's name. Maybe he figured if there was a problem, it was on Carl. "That's fair. If I'm going to get involved, though, I have to ask why you think Kanezaki would have approved."

"Because Kanezaki, as I'm sure you know, is one of the good guys. And the Thai gentleman we aim to speak with is most assuredly not."

Livia was getting tired of all the circumlocutions. "His name is Leekpai," she said. "He sells children to rapists. If that's something you'd like to stop, then you should help us. If you don't care, then we don't need your help. Or want it."

She had a feeling her interjection must have exasperated Carl, but to his credit, he showed nothing.

Fallon looked at her. Finally, he said, "Sells children, you say?"

"Yes."

"To rapists."

"Yes."

He nodded, and his expression hardened in a way she liked.

He looked at Carl. "We don't know each other well. But I don't think you're a bullshitter. And Kanezaki certainly doesn't think so."

Carl sipped his beer. "You're both right."

Fallon nodded. "All right. What do you need from me? And if the answer is just translation services, I'm going to be disappointed."

An hour later, the three of them were sitting in a twelve-person passenger van in a parking area at Bangkok Port in Khlong Toei, a long, baking asphalt scar wedged between the opaque green Chao Phraya River and the labyrinthine metal tubes of some sort of refinery. Livia had used the Gossamer to track Leekpai here. He was somewhere inside the port, beyond a security fence, so there was nothing to do but hope his vehicle was parked somewhere in the enormous lot, and that he would soon return for it. The thought that she might finally be on the verge of learning where she could find that little girl, who Dirty Beard said he had acquired from Leekpai, was maddening. She kept trying to push it out of her mind, but it kept forcing its way back.

Apparently, Fallon owned several vans—two of them with the doors stenciled *TIPS TOURS & TRIPS*; the third, the one they were in, unmarked. And on this occasion, sporting stolen plates, as well. Just in case. Fallon was in the driver's seat, Carl in the passenger's seat, and Livia in back, sheet plastic spread out across the seats and footwells.

She was monitoring the Gossamer carefully, not just because she didn't want to miss Leekpai, but because it was the only way she could distract herself from her surroundings. The smell of polluted water and bird shit and diesel, and the sight of the massive container-moving machines that she had first seen at night and thought were monsters when the men drove her and Nason and the other children to the port . . . it was reanimating that early overwhelming, primal terror. It was making her feel like that little girl again, so panicked, so helpless, so unable even to understand what was happening or to do anything at all to stop it.

Carl and Fallon had been talking about life in Southeast Asia, but Carl must have sensed her distress because he looked back and said, "Everything all right?"

She nodded, not looking up from the Gossamer.

"You sure?"

She nodded again. She was so anxious she thought she might throw up.

Easy, girl. Just breathe. Like before a judo match. Like that. Just breathe.

"Hey," Carl said, "we don't have to do anything. When Leekpai shows himself, old Fallon here is going to bring him right in. All you and I need to do is wait."

She nodded again.

For a gruff guy, Fallon must have had a sensitive side, too, because he said, "I know you'd do it yourself if you could, Labee, but we've already discussed this. Too big a chance this guy has been briefed on one or both of you. So just relax and leave it to me."

Ten minutes later, and about one minute before she thought she would have to step out of the van and throw up, Leekpai's phone started moving. "Here we go," she said.

She kept her eyes trained on the Gossamer. In a few seconds, she had confirmed Leekpai's direction. "Coming toward us," she said. "The parking lot."

Fallon said, "Murphy's law."

She looked up. And saw what he meant. The parking area was crowded with cars, but had been mostly devoid of people while they were waiting. But now waves of them were approaching from the river. A ferry must have come in, maybe more than one.

"Hell," Carl said. "Which one is Leekpai?"

"Call him," Livia said. "He's . . . fifty yards away. Call him now."

Fallon pulled out a phone. Livia read Leekpai's number aloud. Fallon input it, then opened the driver's door and got out. Carl exited, opened the rear sliding passengers' door, and got in next to Livia. He was holding the Supergrade in his lap. In case Fallon ran into any opposition.

"Everybody take it easy," Fallon said. "I'll be right back." He pressed the "Send" button on his phone, dropped the unit in his pocket, and started walking toward the river.

Livia and Carl scanned the crowds coming toward them. A lot of the people were talking on mobile phones. But twenty yards away, a middle-aged Thai guy with long, greasy hair and a face as round as a full moon reached into his pants pocket, then held a phone to his ear. He spoke into it, waited, and spoke again. Then he looked at the phone as though confused, and dropped it back into his pocket. Leekpai.

There were two other Thai men, younger- and fitter-looking than Leekpai, just ahead of him and to each side. They both looked back when his phone rang, then faced forward again, scanning the crowds. Bodyguards.

Carl saw it, too. "Shit," he said. "You get the wheel and bring the van around. This doesn't look like it's going to be as subtle as we'd hoped."

He jumped out the sliding door and jammed the Supergrade into the back of his shorts. Ten yards away, the two bodyguards were looking at Fallon. Looking at him hard.

Barry Eisler

Carl started waving frantically in their direction. "Dr. Rosen!" he called out, as loudly as though he was using a bullhorn, pointing at Fallon as he moved. "Dr. Rosen! Is that really you? All the way here in Bangkok? My God, what are the chances? Everybody, look, that is Dr. Evan Rosen, right here in the flesh, a world-famous Harvard physician and healer and very handsome man, too, and he is right here in Bangkok, gracing us with his exalted presence!"

Probably no one could even understand him, but the spectacle was enough to get everyone—even the bodyguards—to look first at Carl and then at Fallon, who without missing a beat but with a distinctly irritated expression called back to Carl, "Bob, is that really you?"

"You bet it is," Carl said, and then the Supergrade was coming around, and the bodyguards' eyes bulged, and they reached behind them, and Carl dropped the near one with a headshot and Fallon hit the other the same way. Livia popped the clutch, burned rubber backward from between the cars to either side, yanked the hand brake hard and did a J-turn 180, threw it into first, and rocketed forward, then a second later jammed on the brakes and screeched to a stop right next to them, scattering the people nearby. Carl and Fallon already had Leekpai by the arms and threw him in back, landing on top of him an instant later. Carl flung the sliding door closed and yelled, "Go!" And nearly fell backward, because before the word was even out of his mouth, Livia had hit it again and they were accelerating out of the parking lot.

In two minutes, they passed under the expressway, headed briefly north, and made a squealing right onto Rama IV Road. Livia immediately slowed down and merged with local traffic.

"Holy shit, can you drive!" Fallon called from in back.

Carl laughed. "That ain't nothing, you should see her shoot!"

Five minutes later, they were on secondary roads. Livia immediately pulled over, opened the door, leaned out, and puked onto the gravel shoulder. She remained that way for a moment, gasping, afraid there was more. When she was sure it had passed, she pulled the door closed, wiped her mouth, and drove off.

"Sorry," she said. "The port . . . isn't a good place for me."

"Sorry for what?" Fallon said. "Anyone who can drive like you is welcome to puke right inside the van."

They stopped a little while later, in the shadows under the elevated toll road. Carl and Fallon had duct-taped Leekpai's ankles together and his wrists behind his back. He lay prone in the footwell, his body arched across the center hump, his face pale and plainly terrified. Livia moved the front seats forward and joined them in back.

She glanced at Fallon. "Look at his phone. Let's be sure it's him."

"I already checked his license while you were driving."

"Good. But I also want to see who he's been calling."

Fallon reached into his own pocket, pulled out a mobile phone, and pressed the power button. "Passcode protected," he said.

"Tell him we need the passcode."

Fallon told him. Leekpai shook his head.

"Ask him if he knows who I am," Livia said.

Fallon did. Leekpai shook his head again. But a dark stain began to spread out at his crotch and the interior of the van suddenly reeked of urine.

"Glad we put plastic down," Carl said. "Even sanguine as you are about good drivers puking in your vehicles."

"You're lying," Livia said to Leekpai, with Fallon translating in real time. "You do know who I am. Vivavapit. Sakda. Juntasa. That's who I am."

Even before Fallon was translating, Leekpai began to blubber.

"Shh," she said softly. "Shh. They were the ones who took my sister and me. Not you. That means you have a chance they never did. Now tell us the passcode. Don't make me ask again."

Fallon translated. Leekpai mumbled a four-digit number. Fallon input it. "Bingo," he said.

Livia nodded. "See if he has an address-book entry for a Rithisak Sorm."

"He's got nothing in the address book. This phone's a burner."

She kept her eyes on Leekpai. "What about recent calls?"

Fallon worked the keypad. "A half dozen numbers. No names. Most of the calls made today. A few yesterday, too. Yesterday's are all to the same number, and he called that number today, too, just before we grabbed him."

"Tell me the number."

Fallon told her. She input it into the Gossamer. Nothing. The number Leekpai had called belonged to a phone that was currently turned off.

Carl said, "Sorm, you think?"

Leekpai's eyes bulged in terror and despair at Sorm's name.

She looked at him, then nodded to Carl. "Looks like Sorm turned off his phone right after that last conversation. Probably radio silence in advance of the meeting with Dillon. Fallon—ask him."

Fallon did. And said, "Yes. Sorm told him to turn off the phone. Until nine o'clock. He was going to, but we got to him first."

"Why nine o'clock?"

Fallon translated. Leekpai shook his head and said nothing.

She looked at Leekpai. "What's happening tonight at the Srinakarin Night Market? What did Sorm tell you?"

Fallon translated. Leekpai shook his head again.

"We know about the meeting," she said. "If what you tell us now tracks with our information, you can live. If you won't tell us, or if you lie, I'll do to you what I did to the others."

Fallon translated. Leekpai stopped shaking his head and began talking—or babbling, really. Several times Fallon had to stop him, slow him down, ask clarifying questions. But the gist was, Sorm was meeting an important visitor at the Night Market. A visitor who wanted a firsthand look at the trade.

"Are you talking about Dillon?" she asked. But when Fallon translated, Leekpai merely shook his head. Apparently, Sorm hadn't shared the visitor's name. She hadn't really been expecting otherwise.

"Who did you call right before we took you?" she said. Fallon translated. Leekpai began to beg.

"I already know the answer," Livia said. "I want to hear you say it."

Fallon translated. Leekpai said, "Sorm." And immediately began to beg again.

She felt a hunch bubble up. "Are you bringing children from the port to the market tonight? Or is it the other way around?"

Fallon translated. Leekpai spoke rapidly. Fallon listened, then said, "The children are at the market now. They were supposed to be brought to the port two days ago, but Sorm wanted to show them to the visitor. Leekpai was at the port to pay the boat captain for waiting."

Livia tried to control her excitement. And her rage. She looked down at Leekpai. "Two months ago, you provided a little girl to Krit Juntasa. So the American senator could rape her. Who was she? Where is she now?"

Fallon translated and listened to the response. "He says he doesn't know."

She breathed deeply, in and out, trying to control the dragon. "Doesn't know who she was? Or where she is now?"

Fallon translated. "He says neither."

She stared at Leekpai, feeling the dragon slipping loose, trying to hold it back. "Tell him I'll do to him what I did to Sakda if he doesn't stop lying."

Fallon translated. Leekpai began blubbering again and words rushed out of his mouth. Fallon translated simultaneously, "'Sakda came for a girl, but I didn't know who she was or what she was for. Or what happened to her after. Sorm knows those things. Only Sorm.'"

The dragon broke loose. Livia yelled, "You fucking liar!" She grabbed him by the hair, cleared and opened the Infidel—

Instantly, Carl's hand was on her arm, holding it back. "Labee. I don't think he knows."

Cut his face his eyes hurt him make him pay make him pay MAKE THEM ALL FUCKING PAY

Her arm trembled. Carl said, "You're doing a great job with him. We need the information. Keep going. You're doing great."

She breathed hard in and out again. And somehow managed to beat the dragon back. She closed the Infidel. Leekpai watched her, his eyes bulging with fear. She realized they couldn't have done a better good-cop-bad-cop if they'd been trying.

She blew out one more breath and said, "Where are they being held at the Night Market? And that, you better fucking know."

Fallon translated, listened to the response, and said, "He says they're in a shipping container."

Instantly her heart was pounding, her mind flooded with images of the container she and Nason had been held in. The dark. The echo. The smell. She tried to shove it away and couldn't. "In this heat," she said, her voice rising. "You left them in a sealed container in this heat?"

Fallon translated, listened, then looked at Livia. "He says there are air holes. And dry ice."

Yes, she supposed there would be. A farmer doesn't want his produce to rot en route to the market.

But that didn't mean it never happened, regardless.

"Which container?" she said. "Where? Tell him to be specific."

Fallon and Leekpai engaged in more back and forth. Fallon said, "He says Sanam Golf Alley. I don't know what that is."

"Hold on," Carl said. He got out his phone and fired it up. After a minute, he said, "It's not an alley, actually, it's the name of a road. There's a golf course on the east side of the market. Sanam Golf Alley runs along it. In between looks like . . . parking for the golf course. Maybe deserted at night. And south of that is a gas station and . . .

maybe a junkyard or I don't know what. That might be the place, too. Either way, we know the general location."

Livia looked down at Leekpai. "How long will the children be there?"

Fallon engaged Leekpai for a long time, then said, "If they're not at the port at midnight, the boat will leave without them. The captain is upset and the buyers are furious. Sorm's visitor is supposed to hand over a big bribe both for the captain and for the buyers. Sorm has to deliver it personally to avert some kind of trouble."

"Is the girl with them?" she asked. "The girl you gave Sakda."

In her peripheral vision, she could see Carl looking at her, concern in his expression. She knew the question didn't make sense. Why would that little girl be in this shipment? But maybe she was. She could be. She had to be somewhere.

Fallon translated. "He swears he doesn't know. Sorm knows."

Please, she thought. *Please let that be true.*

"Who are the buyers?"

Fallon translated. Leekpai spoke. Fallon said, "A Ukrainian crime syndicate. He thinks. He says Sorm knows."

"Why does he think it's Ukrainians?"

Another exchange. "He says Sorm is very nervous about the delay. And that only the Ukrainians make Sorm that nervous. Because they're ruthless and crazy."

Livia was familiar with the reputation of Ukrainian trafficking gangs. She looked at Leekpai. "Are you supposed to meet Sorm at the shipping container?"

Fallon translated. Leekpai nodded.

"What time?"

Again Fallon translated. He listened to the reply, asked more questions, then said, "He doesn't know exactly what time. Sorm is supposed to call him."

"But he must have some parameters."

Fallon asked more questions, then said, "He's supposed to be at the Night Market no later than nine. And to turn on his phone when he arrives."

Carl said, "Then Sorm's not expecting Dillon until then, either."

"But it won't be much later," Livia said. "Sorm needs time to get those kids to the port. He can't be late."

Carl nodded. "That gives us a manageable window."

Livia thought for a moment. Sorm was going to call Leekpai. They had Leekpai's phone. But the conversation would be in Thai. Even if they were texting, her language skills wouldn't be even close to adequate.

Fallon must have had some notion, because he said, "How can I help?"

Livia looked at him. "Can you hold on to his phone?"

"Is that really all you're going to let me do?"

"Is that *all*? If you won't do it, we're dead in the water."

Fallon smiled. "Well, if you put it that way."

"Hold it up for a second. I want to take a picture of the recent call history. And then let's turn it off again. Until nine o'clock. Just like Leekpai was supposed to."

Fallon held up Leekpai's phone. Livia snapped a photo using hers. "Say the passcode again," she said. "To make sure we remember."

Fallon said it instantly, then added, "But I don't mind you suggesting it. And it was nice of you to say 'we' instead of 'you.'"

She stared at Leekpai. He glanced at her, then at Fallon, then at Carl, then back to her, seeking some sign of hope.

Livia held his gaze. "Anyone have any other questions?"

No one spoke.

She kept her eyes on Leekpai. "Could you guys give us a minute alone?"

In her peripheral vision, she saw them exchange a look. Then they moved away. She heard the sliding door open, then close.

A moment passed. The interior of the van was silent. Leekpai began to cry.

There was some extra plastic sheeting on the seat. Livia squatted alongside him and gathered it up. Leekpai watched her. He started babbling in Thai, faster and faster.

"Shh," Livia said, feeling the dragon fill her. Suffuse her. *Become* her.

She continued to *shh* him. Finally, the babbling stopped. The only sound was of his terrified breathing.

She clenched her jaw and started to cry. "She was *eleven*," she said in Thai. *"Eleven."*

Leekpai shook his head frantically and screamed, *"Mai! Mai! Maaaaiiiii!"* He kicked and bucked and struggled against the duct tape.

Livia planted a knee into his chest and whipped the sheeting across his face, wrapping it around and around and around his head until he was mummified in plastic and his screams were muted and indistinct. He twisted and thrashed for a while longer. Then the muffled screaming faded. The twisting and thrashing became no more than a periodic twitch. And soon, even that had ended, and Leekpai lay completely still.

The dragon folded its wings, but her lungs still felt hot with its fire.

She looked at him for a moment longer, nodding to herself. It was good that he was dead. For what he had done, and for what he would now never be able to do again. But overall, she felt just . . . tired. And vaguely empty.

Maybe it was because in the end, Leekpai was a nothing. The one she wanted, needed, was Sorm.

And they were so close now.

28

The three of them dumped Leekpai's body in a drainage canal, got rid of the plastic elsewhere, and then stopped at a convenience store, where they bought bleach and paper towels and wiped down the interior of the van. Dox was glad Fallon didn't say anything about Leekpai. It was obviously personal to Labee, and Fallon either respected that, or understood they had to kill a prisoner for the sake of their mission, or more likely both.

When the van was clean, Fallon drove them back to Best Friend Bar 10, where they had parked the Kawasaki. Fallon had Leekpai's phone. Dox had Leekpai's wallet, and would shortly dump it in a sewer. They'd checked him, and there was nothing else by which the body might quickly be identified.

Fallon pulled over to the curb and left the engine idling. "Don't worry," he told them. "I'll keep his phone off until nine, and I'll make sure I'm near the Night Market when I turn it on. In case anyone's monitoring its location." He smiled at Labee. "Not that you were going to remind me."

Labee returned the smile and shook his hand. "Don't forget to keep yours off until then, too. And thank you."

"We owe you, amigo," Dox said.

Fallon shook his head. "Nah. I was getting bored doing odd jobs for Kanezaki anyway. Just buy me a Singha sometime. Semper fi."

They shook. Dox and Labee got out of the van and Fallon pulled away.

The two of them rode east out of the city center until they were on quiet roads. After a while, they came upon a little open-air roadside restaurant. They ordered a late lunch of hot-and-sour soup and chicken stir fried with sliced ginger over rice. They didn't talk about Leekpai. In fact, Dox was barely thinking of him. He was still trying to figure out what was bugging him about their intel.

Labee must have seen something in his face, because she said, "What is it?"

He looked at her. "Do you trust me?"

For a moment, it looked as though she would say something. But then she didn't. She just nodded.

"I want you to tell me about these leads of yours."

Her head retracted as though he'd raised a hand to her. "What do you mean?"

"I'm not doubting you. Or asking for proof. Or anything like that. You know I believe in you, Labee. I told you that."

"Then what?"

"You said my instincts have always been sound before. Well, maybe so. But something is wrong here. My gut is telling me so. But I can't figure out what it is. I thought it was K., but that ain't it, he's on the level, you persuaded me. But something's still off. And I need to see the whole picture to understand what it is. If I don't know what you were up to before we ran into each other—how you got that Glock, how you learned Sorm was supposed to be at Les Nuits, how you learned about the Sorm-Leekpai-Night-Market connection—if I don't know those things, I can't see the battlefield the way the enemy does. Meaning I can't anticipate him. And that means the one who's going to get anticipated is me. Us."

He waited. All he could do was hope she'd come to trust him enough to tell him what he needed to know.

When she finally spoke, she didn't look at him. "There are things about me," she said. "And I don't want you to know them."

Lord, what just those two short sentences seemed to cost her. And how much trust it took to enable her to say so little.

"Hey," he said, but still she wouldn't look at him.

"I know you don't much care to be touched," he said. "But would it be all right if I just put my hand on yours for a minute?"

She didn't answer, but her hand was on the table and she didn't move it, so he decided the answer was yes. He reached out and looped his fingers loosely around hers.

"There is nothing I would ever judge you for," he said. "Nothing. I have some notion of what you've been through in your life. And I don't want to pry into any of it. All I want to do right now is kill anyone who ever hurt you."

Still she didn't look at him. But she tightened her fingers around his.

"I would never ask," he said. "Because, among other reasons, I already know everything about you I need to."

He saw she wasn't looking at him because her eyes had filled up. He wished he could have put his arms around her. But that was his way, not hers.

"But you know why I'm asking you now. Something's off about our intel, and I can't figure out what it is if I don't know how you uncovered the trail that led you to Pattaya."

After a moment, she pulled back her fingers. She turned her head farther away and tilted her face down and he saw she was blinking away tears. Then, still looking away from him, she told him a horrific, harrowing story about how she and her sister were kidnapped at only thirteen and eleven, sold by their parents. How they were taken on a cargo ship from Bangkok to Portland by three of the kidnappers, men she called Skull Face and Square Head and Dirty Beard, obviously the way she had conceived of them as a child. She told him the men had threatened to rape Nason, and that Labee had tried to prevent them by "doing what the men wanted" in Nason's stead. She didn't give details about what that meant. She didn't need to.

She told him that of course the men had been lying, and that when they tired of Labee, they tried to take Nason. Labee had attacked them and sliced open the eye of the leader, Skull Face. The men had retaliated by raping Nason so savagely that her sister was left catatonic. Meaning that Labee's efforts to protect her sister had probably been the very thing that doomed her.

She stared off while she told him all this, crying steadily and silently and without visible emotion beyond the tears themselves.

She told him how she had spent sixteen years not even knowing whether Nason was alive or dead. She was given the name Livia by a man who purported to "rescue" her—a man who was actually behind the sisters' abduction. She killed that man. She escaped his house. She became a cop. She tracked down the men who had taken them. It turned out they were all with the Royal Thai Police. She learned they had killed Nason years earlier. In a Bangkok hotel room, she killed Skull Face and two others who had been part of the conspiracy. A US senator—the brother of the man who had "rescued" her. And the senator's bodyguard/bagman.

She had used Special Agent Little's offer of a joint anti-trafficking task force as an excuse to return to Thailand to finish off the others. She had smothered Square Head with a pillow, but not before getting numbers from his cell-phone address book—numbers that enabled her to track Dirty Beard. Dirty Beard had thought to ambush her, showing up with two other cops, all armed with Glocks and equipped with night vision. She had taken their guns and killed them all. Dirty Beard had told her about Les Nuits. And about the Night Market, a contact there named Leekpai, who sold children.

And she told him one more thing. There was a girl in the senator's hotel room. The one she'd been asking Leekpai about in the van. A little girl of about Nason's age at the time they were taken. The senator had been raping her when Labee showed up and had his man take her away because Labee, a treasure from the past, seemed more interesting. Labee had been at gunpoint, helpless, as they led the sobbing girl away. And the girl had looked at Labee with beseeching, agonized eyes. And Labee didn't help her. She couldn't. She had been helpless herself. And she couldn't stop thinking of that girl. She had to find her. Protect her. She had to. She *had* to.

By the time she was finished, his own eyes were wet. Not just because of what she'd been through. But because of what it had obviously cost her to relate it to him.

They sat silently afterward, Labee looking out into the distance. "I've never talked about any of that with anyone," she said after a while, her tone flat. "Never."

"I'm sorry for making you."

She didn't answer.

"Labee, I'm sorry again, but I need to ask you one more question."

Again she didn't answer.

"You say you took the guns off Dirty Beard and his two partners and killed them all. But . . . it sounds like you interrogated them first. Or at least Dirty Beard."

She turned and looked at him.

"I made you cry," she said, again with that flat tone.

"It's not as hard as you might think, but yes."

There was a pause. She said, "I shot the first two. Dirty Beard I handcuffed and drove to a quarry, along with the bodies of the others. That's where I interrogated him. And then I burned all of them."

Dox couldn't help thinking, *Remind me never to get on your bad side.* But he certainly didn't say it.

"Now you know about me," she said. "What I am."

That nearly made him cry again. "What you are is the bravest person I've ever known. I'm sorry if that sounds condescending, but it's the truth."

She looked away. "I'm tired."

"How could you not be?"

"Can you see the battlefield now?"

"Better than I could. Let me think a minute. The two you shot . . . well, Sorm or DIA or whoever might have thought that was my doing. Using what I got from K. to work my way into Sorm's network and develop the intel that led me to Pattaya. But the third guy, Dirty Beard. Burning him to death . . . I want you to know, if I'd been there, I would have poured the gasoline myself. But that's not what matters. What matters is, in my many years in this business, I think it's safe to say I've become known more for bullets than for burning, so what happened to Dirty Beard isn't going to look like something I would have done. It's too personal. And depending on what else they know, they might decide it looks like you."

"Meaning what?"

"Meaning . . . I'm not sure. But I'll tell you what. I'm getting the sense old Dillon has a real knack for figuring out what other people know. And then feeding them something new that fits with it so they think they're developing their own intel and coming to their own conclusions, when in fact whatever they come up with he's effectively planted in their minds. That's what he did to Kanezaki with the ambush in Pattaya. And I can feel him doing it again now. I mean, he's using a communications channel he knows is compromised to talk about how he's meeting Sorm at the Night Market. Why would he do that? Maybe we'd just buy it and act accordingly, sure. But . . . that doesn't feel like his style. I feel like he fed us the Night Market because he knew we already had something pointing in that direction. And sure, he's being oblique with 'the tents' and all, but that's just theater. He'd know if we were already dialed into the Night Market, we'd put two and two together and congratulate ourselves for being so uncommonly clever. We'd walk away feeling like we'd figured it all out and had corroboration for the new intel. But in fact, all we have is a damn fabrication."

She nodded slowly. She looked exhausted. Shell-shocked. He hated that he'd made her tell him what she did. But he also knew there was no other way.

"I see your point," she said. "But it depends on whether Sorm knows, or believes, the one who killed Square Head, and Dirty Beard and his partners, was me."

"Well, look at it this way. Sorm knows all those guys. Works with them. I mean, you said you used Dirty Beard's phone to track him to Pattaya, where he was delivering cash to Sorm."

"That's right."

"Okay. And according to this guy Square Head, Dirty Beard tried to warn them that you were coming, that it must have been you who killed Skull Face and the others two months ago here in Bangkok. Right?"

She hadn't given him details about how she'd killed Skull Face and the others. But given that she'd burned alive old Dirty Beard, he could imagine. Also, when she'd said those names in Fallon's van by way of introducing herself, Leekpai seemed to know exactly to whom and what she was referring, and it obviously terrified him. Anyway, he guessed it was the extremely personal manner in which Skull Face and company had been killed, as much as anything else, that would have signaled to the rest of the gang the killer was Labee.

"Yes," she said. "That's true."

"And then Dirty Beard gets killed himself, burned to death. Sorm hears about it from his buddies on the force. I mean, how could he not make the connection? And how could he not assume Dirty Beard would have given up a lot before he died? Information about the Night Market. And this guy Leekpai, who sells kids there. Probably that's why Leekpai had bodyguards when we got him. Wish I'd thought of it sooner, but okay, no harm, no foul."

There was a pause. "You're right," she said. "I should have . . . I'm just too close to it. I'm too . . . tired."

"You are close to it. But the real problem is, we haven't been putting our heads together. Not like we've needed to. Now we are."

She nodded. "So Sorm knows I'm here. He warns Leekpai. And he tells Dillon you and I are working together, or at least in parallel. And probably the first, because—"

"Because how the hell else did I walk away from the ambush in Pattaya if I didn't have a partner like you?"

She looked at him. "The night vision," she said.

"Pardon?"

"Dirty Beard and his men were using dual night vision and infrared. State of the art. I wondered at the time where they were getting equipment like that. Even police departments in the States don't have it. As far as I know, it's exclusively US military. And export-license controlled."

"Well, you certainly could get it from DIA. Under the table, anyway."

"Exactly."

"What the hell is Sorm trading for that kind of gear?"

For a while, neither of them spoke, and the only sound was of insects in the surrounding vegetation. Dox finished his soup. Labee stared out into the distance. A couple of motorbikes buzzed past, two and three riders apiece, the girls in back sitting sidesaddle. Dox shook his head and thought, *That far I am not willing to go.*

Labee turned to him. She gave him one of those small, sad smiles. "So we're partners?"

He held out his hand. "Hell yes, we're partners. And friends."

She hesitated, then took his hand. She squeezed it hard and held it for a moment before she let go.

"You're right," she said. "About what Sorm would know. And therefore about what Dillon would know. I see it now. You would have made a hell of a cop."

He shook his head. "Not half as good as you."

He thought for a moment. "Now that we've got some additional insight, I see we might have ourselves something of a conundrum about the Night Market."

"What's that?"

"What if the police figure out Leekpai's been taken? Half of them are on Sorm's payroll. They'll warn him."

"I'm not so worried about that."

"Tell me. I'd prefer not to be worried myself."

"A lot of reasons. The initial hours of an investigation are almost always chaotic. Witness accounts will be confused and contradictory. Whatever happened, it happened at the port, so it could be drugs, it could be anything. Will the cops know to associate the victims with Leekpai? And even if they do figure things out that fast, Sorm's phone is off. They can't warn him. I doubt they would know where to find him, either, because as much as they conspire with him, would he really share the details of his activities? And even if they do figure things out incredibly fast, and even if they do have a way to reach Sorm, and even if they do warn him about Leekpai, our worst case is he aborts."

"But what if he doesn't abort? Then we're back to they know that we know that they know . . . you know what I mean. What kind of Night Market approach could we come up with then?"

"Look, Sorm's not going to abort, because he's not going to hear about Leekpai. Their phones are off, he's expecting no contact until after nine. But if I'm wrong, and he does somehow hear about Leekpai, he won't try to set us up. He'll run. Think about it. Between us, we've killed Gant. Those Khmers. Skull Face. The senator and the senator's man. Square Head. Dirty Beard. The sword guy. The three Pattaya bodyguards. The three DIA contractors. And now Leekpai and his bodyguards."

He smiled. "Well, that is an impressive list. And hell, half of it was before we started working together. Imagine all we can accomplish now."

"That's my point. You really think after all that's happened, Sorm would fight us rather than run? Dillon, maybe. But not Sorm. So our worst case is, Sorm aborts. But at that point, what do we have to lose? Do you want to set up at the port instead? If we miss him there, we're done, he's on a boat to who knows where and we're out of leads. And Dillon is still at large, gunning for us."

He sensed she was right, but still didn't like the uncertainty. And then she said, "Wait. I might be able to confirm."

"How?"

"Little. My handler. His files on the Royal Thai Police are extensive. He might have some insight into what they're thinking about what happened at the port today."

"That would be a comfort, I won't deny."

"But we have to go no matter what. Those kids."

He nodded. "Don't you worry about that. I'm not trying to figure out whether. Just how."

29

They stopped at an electronics store, where Carl bought a big tablet computer. While he was inside, Livia called Little.

"Did you ever find out anything about those three English speakers in Pattaya?" she asked.

"Not a thing," he told her. "No one's even claimed the bodies. Whoever they were, they were beyond deniable. No return address at all."

If they were Dillon's men, as she expected, that made sense.

"Was that all?" he asked.

"No. There's something else."

"Good. Tell me how I can help."

She hesitated, then said, "Your files on the Royal Thai Police are . . . impressive."

"Yes, they are."

"I'm curious. What are your capabilities in real time?"

"I'm not sure what you're asking."

"There was a shooting at the port in Bangkok a few hours ago. I want to know what the police make of it."

"What's going on out there, Livia?"

She knew he was going to ask. "Look, my time here has gone in some unexpected directions. And I've developed some unexpected leads. I'll give you a full report when I'm back. Right now, I just need the information."

"I'm asking why you need it."

She thought of the children in that container. Of how hot it must be, even with air holes and dry ice. "You're always saying we're a team," she said, trying to control her frustration. "Can you just answer my questions? Why does everything have to be a negotiation with you?"

"It's not a negotiation. You asked me a question, now I'm asking you one."

Her patience broke. "Listen, Little. B. D. If you think you're going to stare me down and I'm going to blink, you're wrong. All that's going to happen is I'll remember that when I asked you for help, you fucked me. And I will never forget that. And everything I've learned out here, you can fuck off, you'll never get any of it. And you can find someone else to work with on whatever the hell you're really up to on top of it."

There was a long pause. Little said, "Call me back in thirty minutes."

She clicked off and powered down the phone. Still seething, she briefed Carl when he came out of the store. They rode off, parked again on a quiet street, and waited. At thirty minutes, she called back. Her heart was beating hard.

"The working theory is a drug heist," he said. "The two dead men are known to be involved in narcotics."

She was so relieved she almost felt dizzy. She hadn't believed the police would know so quickly it had been about Leekpai. But if they had, it would have blown everything at the Night Market. She would never find that little girl.

"Thank you," she managed to say.

"You're welcome. I wish you'd believe me when I say we're a team."

"I have to go. I'll check in later."

"Livia—"

She ended the call and powered down the phone.

She briefed Carl again. Then they found another business hotel. Livia could barely keep her eyes open. It wasn't just the port. Or killing Leekpai. Or even worrying about the children in that container. Telling Carl what she had told him . . . She had tried not to feel what she was saying, tried to detach her mind from the memories as the words flowed out of her. She thought maybe she'd been partly successful, because the contours of the conversation were hazy now, fragmenting like remnants from a dream. She had told him, hadn't she? Somehow she had. But the effort had just . . . drained her. All she wanted was sleep. Sleep, hell, she wanted oblivion.

But only for a while. Because what she wanted more than anything was to kill Sorm. Save those kids.

And find that little girl.

When she woke, she had no recollection of having slept. It felt more like she'd been unconscious. She waited for a moment, reconnecting with her limbs, aware of the mattress under her, the sense of being in a room.

She opened her eyes. The lights were off, but the windows were open to the setting sun. Carl was studying the tablet closely. His expression interested her. It was both relaxed to the point of placidity, and also somehow extremely focused. She wondered if this was what he looked like behind a riflescope. If so, she wouldn't want to be on the other end. At any distance.

She must have moved, because he looked up. "Hey there," he said.

"Hey."

"How you feeling?"

"Better."

"Nothing like a nap, I always say. When this bullshit is done, I'm going to take one every day for a month."

She rubbed her eyes, then got up and walked over. "What are you doing?"

"Oh, just learning everything I can through Google Earth and otherwise about the world-famous Rot Fai Night Market."

"Any conclusions?"

"A few. One is, being that old Dillon is a fellow sniper, and a damn proficient one, we will not be using the main entrance no matter what. The overall market doesn't offer any good sniping opportunities—way too crowded, I imagine, and with all those tents, there's no clear field of fire—but the entrance would work. And that Golf Alley parking area, which seems to be our best intel at the moment, could be a possibility. But I don't think even Kanezaki and Fallon could get me a rifle and night-vision scope that fast. Plus, I'd need time to zero it. Wish I could see the actual terrain beforehand, though."

"I've been there."

"You have? Why didn't you say so? It's been killing me that we can't have a firsthand look, but that's how they sicced Zatōichi on me—they knew I'd be doing recon around Vann's office and probably had one of those bird drones deployed in the area. Can't take the chance again."

"I should have thought to mention it. There's just been . . . a lot of other shit."

"Don't worry, nothing lost. Walk me through it now. You be my eyes and ears. And we should look at some photos of Dillon, too. There's plenty online. He got semifamous back in the day, and he's pretty high-profile now as the deputy director of DIA."

They started with photos of Dillon, then moved on to the Night Market. She told him everything she could remember, using various maps and photos and videos they found online as guides. His questions were helpful, all of them obviously geared to means of infiltration, ambush, evasion, and escape.

"What do you think?" she asked when they'd been through all of it.

"Well, avoiding the entrance should be easy enough. The whole place is fenced off, but I don't think it's much. The fences seem more intended to mark off the boundaries of the market and prevent spillover than to provide any kind of security. I mean, who'd want to break into or out of a night market anyway?"

"I had the same thought. It's what happens inside that's tricky. Because—"

"Because we don't know what Dillon and Sorm have in mind, yeah. We're supposed to figure it out, though. That'll make us confident in our conclusions. That's Dillon's game."

She considered. "We know Sorm's likely to have a new burner. Or if he doesn't, we have the number he used with Leekpai."

Carl nodded. "I sure hope it's the second."

"Well, what if it's the first? Can Kanezaki do anything with information like that? A burner that gets turned on at a certain time and certain place?"

He looked at her. "You know what? Let's find out. You and I had a breakthrough when we put our heads together. I think it's time we did the same with Kanezaki You all right with that?"

"I'm all right with it. Will he be?"

He smiled. "Those CIA types have a saying: 'Better to seek forgiveness than ask permission.' So I don't think he could reasonably object."

They sat on the bed. Carl made the call, switched to speakerphone, and tossed the phone on the mattress between them.

One ring, then a voice. "Hey. I've been hoping you would call. It makes me crazy that I can't reach you when—"

"Before we go any further," Carl said, "I've got you on speakerphone so I can introduce you to my partner, who I'll just call L. for Lovely Lady."

There was a pause. Kanezaki said, "What?"

Livia glanced at Carl, then at the phone. "Hi. I understand your name is K."

There was another pause. "What's going on?"

"I'll brief you over a beer sometime," Carl said. "For now, suffice to say that L. wants the same thing we do. And in pursuit of that thing, saved my ass from that ambush in Pattaya. Imagine the guilt you'd be suffering right now if I'd died there. Well, L. is the reason I didn't. I believe she deserves some gratitude."

There was a pause. Kanezaki said, "Half the time I can't tell when he's messing with me. But if he's serious . . . L., thank you."

"You're welcome."

"So . . . you two are working together."

Carl smiled. "And very effectively, too, I might add. We put our heads together, and realized the bad guys knew we'd become a team and would act accordingly. And then we realized—if two heads are good, three ought to be even better. So here we are. I've briefed L. on everything you've told me."

"Everything?"

"I'm sorry, amigo, but this compartmentalization bullshit can go too far. Didn't y'all decide it was information siloing that led to 9/11?"

"That was one thing, yes."

"Well, let's not make that mistake again. Anyway. L. and I have been thinking about your intel. Dillon told Sorm to buy a burner and not turn it on until Sorm was at the Night Market. Is that the kind of thing you could make real-time operational use of?"

"Are you joking? Yes. Of course."

"How?"

"How many phones do you think will be left powered down, maybe even kept in shielded cases, until they get turned on at the Night Market? Maybe . . . one?"

"Damn," Carl said. "I see your point."

"And even if it were more than one, only one is going to call Dillon."

"But what if—"

"My guys can instantly determine if the numbers that are calling each other have ever called any other numbers. If the answer is no, which looks likely here, then we have two pristine burners, being used to carry out something clandestine."

"Meaning, on this particular night, Sorm and Dillon."

"Correct."

"Dillon knows your capabilities," Livia said. "Is that right?"

"He knows them well," Kanezaki said. "I don't like to admit it, but some of the technology we use was invented at DIA."

She looked at Carl. "Then this is what Dillon knows we know. They're meeting at the Night Market. They'll each have a burner we can identify and track. Of course, we have the other number Sorm might use to call Leekpai."

Carl nodded. "Speaking of which, text me that photo you took. K., I'm going to text you a photo of a recent-calls log. We have reason to believe the latest entry is a number Sorm might be using."

"Okay. Good."

They were all quiet for a moment. Carl said, "You ever find out anything about those three English speakers L. and I dropped at Les Nuits?"

"Nothing. Absolute ghosts."

"Right," Carl said, nodding to Livia at the congruence with Little's information. "I figured. Dillon's men for sure. And with his bench cleared, I believe Mr. Dillon is about to take the field himself. From what I know of him, I'll bet he's missed the action. Does that make sense?"

"More than you know," Kanezaki said. "We have a whole psych profile on Dillon."

"Why am I even surprised?"

"I'm too tired to argue about sources and methods," Kanezaki said. "L., I trust this man with my life. He's telling me I should trust you. So I'm going to."

"I'll try to trust you, too," Livia said.

There was a pause, maybe while Kanezaki digested the slight lack of parallelism in their assurances. Then he said, "Anyway, yes, CIA has personality profiles on every significant political, business, and media figure in America. The ostensible rationale is that the Russians are doing the same, and we need to be able to see our people's vulnerabilities the same way our adversaries do. The reality, of course—"

"The reality," Carl said, "is that CIA exploits those vulnerabilities for its own ends."

"Well," Kanezaki said, "you didn't hear it from me."

"I'm sure we'll all forget this conversation ever even happened," Carl said. "For now, I just want your insights about Dillon. I already told you, he's a badass with brains. But what else?"

"Dillon has three key personality elements. One, he's a control freak and hates to delegate. Two, he's constantly looking for a more efficient solution, something elegant, a way to kill two birds with one stone. And three, when things aren't going the way he thinks they should, he's quick to intervene and take matters into his own hands."

"That invention of his," Carl said. "With the APCs."

"Yes, that really was elegant—it doubled the effective number of armored carriers in any given theater."

"Damn," Carl said, "if he's such a control freak and hates to delegate, I can only imagine the psychic price he must have paid to bring in someone like old Zatōichi. I hope your government health insurance is generous when it comes to therapy."

Livia looked at him. "It's not just any one of those personality elements that are in play here. It's all three. Think about what this whole debacle must be costing Dillon. First, Gant screws up and gets killed. And then those Khmers waiting for you in the dark, too. Sorm's freaking out now, and Dillon sends in the sword guy."

"Yeah," Carl said, "But I think he must have known Zatōichi was a long shot."

"Sure, it was a long shot and the only piece Dillon had at that moment on that part of the board, but still, Zatōichi gets killed, too. So this control freak, who hates to delegate anyway, flies out with a picked three-man team. They kill Vann, so okay, things are finally going his way and reinforcing his belief that if you want something done, you have to do it yourself. And then the three picked men ambush you in Pattaya—and yet again, you walk away clean, and Dillon's team is dead."

"Speaking of which," Carl said, "thank you again."

She nodded. "So even if Dillon had more people he could quickly draw on locally—and he probably doesn't, otherwise, again, why would he have turned to someone like the sword guy—would he trust them? Or would this former Delta badass say, 'Fuck it, I'll handle it myself'?"

They were quiet for a moment. Carl said, "Told you we all needed to put our heads together. Still, what's Dillon planning? How do we get to him?"

They were quiet again. Livia could feel that all the pieces were there. She just couldn't quite see it yet. But she knew that feeling, that cop feeling of being on the edge of epiphany.

"What if . . ." She paused again, then said, "I'm just thinking about Vann's indictment. Of course it was terrifying to Sorm. It's why he demanded that Gant kill Vann. And Gant agreed. That's a huge risk for DIA, but they took it."

Carl said, "And carried it out, even after things had gone wrong."

"Which brings us back to the same question," Kanezaki said. "The trade. What is Sorm giving them, or what has he got on them, in exchange for that kind of protection? That kind of risk?"

"That's what I'm getting at," Livia said. "Assume it's both. For DIA—or anyone, for that matter—to get in bed with Sorm, to risk exposure of that relationship, they'd have to be getting a lot. And because of Sorm's own nature, he would inherently have something over them, isn't that right? I mean, you're the intelligence expert. You tell me."

"No, that's right," Kanezaki said. "Which is part of the reason CIA cut him loose. He had some periodic intel on Abu Sayyaf and Jemaah

Islamiyah and other Southeast Asian terrorist and separatist groups, but what we were getting wasn't worth the potential scandal."

Dox smiled. "K. says the Agency has more scruples than other members of the community."

Livia nodded. She was so close . . . but she still couldn't quite see it. "But does it really make sense," she said, more to herself than to them, "to believe that anyone—CIA, DIA, anyone in your 'community'— would risk continued involvement with someone like Sorm just for some marginally interesting intelligence?"

Silence.

And all at once she saw it. Right there in front of them the whole time. So obvious it made her think of that George Orwell line: *To see what is in front of one's nose needs a constant struggle.*

"That's it," she said out loud. "It has to be."

Carl was looking at her expectantly. Kanezaki said, "What?"

"What is Sorm?" she said. "What is he most essentially, most fundamentally?"

Kanezaki said, "I don't follow."

"Sorm traffics people. Slaves. He's been doing it for almost forty years. If you want to get in bed with Sorm, it's not because he can periodically offer you something about Abu Sayyaf or Jemaah Islamiyah or whatever. It's because he's one of the world's worst human traffickers."

"But why would DIA—"

"God, do you guys really need a cop to tell you to follow the money?"

"I don't know," Kanezaki said. "What kind of money are we talking about?"

"Estimates vary, but even the most conservative are staggering. The UN's International Labour Organization believes that worldwide, modern slavery generates a hundred and fifty billion dollars a year."

"One hundred fifty *billion*?"

"Correct. With over twenty million people bought and sold annually. A quarter of them children. If you intelligence-community types ever want to do some real good in the world, you could quit fucking around with people like Sorm and try stopping them, instead."

Silence.

She went on. "I mean, come on, you guys know better than I do about Air America and heroin, the Contras and cocaine, the Mujahideen and opium . . . if your 'community' was willing to help traffic heroin and cocaine and opium, why not something even more lucrative? Something that doesn't even require poppy or coca fields, that just continually renews itself?"

Silence again.

Kanezaki said, "Give me a second. Just . . ."

He paused, then went on. "This is how they've been doing it. You're right. God, you're right."

"Right about what?" Carl said. "Stop killing me with the suspense and just say it."

"Sorry. It's . . . L., you're right, how could I not have seen it? In the last ten years, DIA has swung a half dozen elections in Southeast Asia, Latin America, and Eastern Europe. They've become the go-to players for every kind of influence operation. It's gotten so bad, I have trouble getting people on the National Security Council to even return my calls. They know if they want real juice, no messy budget requests, and results so good that no one dares question how they were achieved or where the money came from . . . that's all DIA now. And this is where that operational money's been coming from. Slavery. My God. I just . . . I couldn't see it. I didn't want to believe anything like this could be true. I'm having trouble right now."

"I don't know," Livia said. "Maybe you CIA types really do have more scruples than your DIA rivals. I doubt it, but whatever. Regardless, you cut Sorm loose because you didn't want to get caught associating with a slavery kingpin. And then you projected—you assumed DIA must be worried about the same type of thing. But what if DIA's worry is a thousand times worse than CIA's was? What if DIA isn't worried about getting caught just associating with a slavery kingpin, but about being in business with one?"

Carl looked down and shook his head. "Damn."

"Tell me, K.," she said. "If I'm right. If it were to get out. How much of a scandal?"

There was a pause. Kanezaki said, "It would be . . . unprecedented. I can't even imagine. Prison time for the principals would be the least of it. The whole organization would be dismantled."

"Ain't it pretty to think so," Carl said. "But yeah, there'd be a shit storm for sure."

"Regardless," she said. "For DIA, Sorm is a two-edged sword. If he ever turns on them, it's really bad. So they have to keep him happy."

"Right," Carl said. "Which is why when Sorm gets wind of Vann's investigation and the sealed indictment, and tells Gant to kill a high UN official for him, Gant clicks his heels."

Livia nodded. "Because DIA cannot possibly take the risk of Sorm being indicted and offering up his relationship with DIA as part of a plea."

"But then why not just kill Sorm?" Kanezaki asked.

"Now we're getting somewhere," Livia said. "First, my understanding is that Sorm is a ghost. Very hard to get to. Is that right?"

"Yes," Kanezaki said. "At least, it was true when we were running him."

Carl laughed. "I think that's a charitable view of who was running whom. 'When you owe the bank a million dollars, it's your problem. When you owe a billion, the problem is the bank's.'"

"Anyway," Livia said, "the point is, Sorm is paranoid. A survivor. Not at all an easy man to get to, even for Dillon and DIA. So even if you decided at some point he'd become more a liability than an asset, you'd have a hard time doing anything about it. And Sorm's no fool. How could he have survived as long as he has other than by putting himself in the shoes of anyone who looks at him as an investment?"

"Meaning?" Kanezaki said.

"Meaning if you're Sorm, and you're paranoid under the best of circumstances that DIA might suddenly look at you and decide to cut their losses, how are you feeling when you learn some federal prosecutor in New York has prepared a sealed grand-jury indictment? What do you think DIA is going to make of that? Of the possibility that if you're arrested, and extradited, and facing the rest of your life in prison, you might try to plead down your sentence with an explosive story about how you and DIA are business partners in modern slavery?"

"You'd be even more paranoid," Kanezaki said. "Even more careful."

Livia nodded. "Correct. We've been assuming Sorm went on the run because of Vann's indictment. Maybe that, too. But more likely—"

"The one he's really running from," Kanezaki said, "is DIA."

"Damn," Carl said. "So Sorm didn't want Vann dead just to eliminate the threat from Vann. He also knew it was the only way to eliminate the threat from DIA. Goddamnit, I told him, the damn Dalai Lama, I told him he had to watch his back. Ah, shit."

"I'm sorry," Livia said. "But . . . it feels right. And I think there's one more thing. I'm not sure, but . . ."

She paused to think it through, then went on. "Put yourself in Dillon's shoes. And we need to, because that's what he's been doing with us. You've had a great run with Sorm. Made God knows how much money. Created a giant slush fund. Bought secret influence with a dozen governments. Sidelined your CIA rivals on every important project. You're like an investor who made a killing in a bull market. But that market's gotten more and more volatile lately. Huge new risks. You feel like you've been riding the market down, and what you're looking for now is a way to get out. Are you going to miss that opportunity?"

Silence.

"I mean, you guys tell me. You know Dillon."

"If Sorm demanded that Dillon kill Vann," Kanezaki said, "he'd be relieved when it was done. Reassured. Because why would Dillon take the risk of killing a high UN official when he could have solved his volatility-in-the-markets problem by just killing Sorm himself?"

Carl said, "You're saying killing Vann was a way for Dillon to prove his bona fides."

"Maybe," Kanezaki said. "In fact, probably Dillon would have preferred not to kill Vann at all—with Sorm dead, Vann wouldn't be a threat, so why take the risk?"

"Yeah," Carl said, shaking his head. "But he decided to kill Vann anyway, to get close to Sorm. Goddamn."

"If so," Kanezaki said, "it means that if Dillon really does want out of this market, now would be a golden chance to do it."

Carl nodded. "Yeah, and he probably tells Sorm something like 'Problem solved, now let's review your operations because you know me, I'm all about efficiency and elegance and killing two birds, and I have some ideas about how we can lower our risks and double our profits. Oh, and make sure to turn off your new burner and all that, because all I want to do is protect you from here on out.' Sorm smells all that money and thinks he can trust this guy now. So he agrees to meet him."

Livia looked at him. "Almost there. One more step."

Carl gave her a wan smile. "Preach it, sister. I could listen to you all day."

"All right. Cops think motive, means, and opportunity."

"Okay."

"You're Dillon. You want out of the market. There's your motive. Sorm suddenly trusts you. There's your opportunity. Now, what are your means? Especially if you're all about killing two birds with one stone."

Carl looked at her. For a second, his expression was what she had seen earlier, what she imagined he would look like behind a riflescope.

"His means," he said, "are you and me."

"Yes. I think so. It would certainly be elegant."

"Hey, L.," Kanezaki said. "Has anyone ever told you you'd make a great intelligence officer?"

"No thanks."

"He meant it as a compliment," Carl said.

Kanezaki laughed. "Forget I said it. The main thing is, it makes sense. Dillon wants out of a market that's come to pose unacceptable risks. He wants to close *all* accounts—not just Sorm, but also the two of you. What better way, what more elegant way, to do that than to let you 'figure out' that Dillon and Sorm will both be at the Night Market, and get you to make a run at them there?"

"Dillon will hang back somehow," Carl said. "He'll give us Sorm. And drop us then. That's the plan, anyway. If he's going for elegance."

"You know how I know you're right?" Kanezaki said.

"Long and fruitful experience with my considered judgment?"

Kanezaki laughed again. "That, too. But also, isn't that exactly what Gant tried to do in Phnom Penh? Get you to kill the target, and then have you killed right after?"

"I knew I'd seen this show before," Carl said. "Now let's just make sure they don't change the ending in the remake."

30

It was just past sunset, with pink fading to red in the western sky, when Dox and Labee arrived at the Night Market.

Dox had badly wanted to at least ride past the Sanam Golf Alley parking lot and that junkyard next to the gas station. But he knew he had to avoid routine recon, like what he had done outside the Dalai Lama's office. Because Dillon knew he knew.

But didn't know he knew Dillon knew.

So they did something different. Labee took them wide of the market, approaching it from the northwest, then headed east along a narrow, rutted road hemmed in by encroaching vegetation. The road grew rougher and increasingly overgrown, and finally dead-ended past the market at the northeast corner of the golf course. The golf course was set back from the remnants of the road and surrounded by a perimeter of tall, thick foliage. Beyond the foliage was a fence topped by netting, about thirty feet high. Which seemed not to be working as well as expected, because all around on the ground were moldering golf balls.

They dismounted and removed their helmets. Dox raised a shirt-tail and wiped the sweat from his face. It smelled like jungle back here, and though the din of the market was audible, the insects around them were much louder.

He pushed the bike deep into the foliage, ran the chain through a wheel and the helmets, and walked back to Labee.

"Good to go?"

She nodded.

He checked his watch. "Eight thirty. Plenty of time."

They pulled on baseball caps—better than nothing against any circling bird drones—and walked west until they'd reached the northeast corner of the market. Dox had been expecting either to have to jump the corrugated fence or to break through it, but they were in luck— beyond the vegetation, he could see a gap in the metal alongside the fence of the golf course.

They pushed through the underbrush, walked right through the gap, and found themselves in a paved lot with lines of bright incandescent lights strung overhead, and dozens of antique cars and trucks displayed beneath them. Scores of people milled around, oohing and aahing at the vehicles, snapping photos, wandering in and out of the long, open-air, brick-and-corrugated-metal buildings to either side, all of which seemed to be set up as some kind of Americana automotive time machine: old gas pumps, vintage signage, and, of course, rows of classic cars and trucks. The area was relatively quiet, but the din—including a drum band, from the sound of it—farther south was unmistakable.

"This is the antiques section," Labee said. "The least crowded."

Dox nodded. "Looks just like it did online. Nice to finally be here in the flesh, though."

They headed south, and the crowds quickly grew denser and noisier. There were food trucks, with tables and chairs set up neatly before them; an old-school barbershop, complete with a revolving striped pole; and every vintage item imaginable, from vinyl records to leather jackets to jukeboxes and gumball machines.

They kept moving, and after a few minutes reached the edge of the main market. Before them were thousands of colorful tents and stalls, countless shoppers and diners and revelers, families with babies in strollers, roving teens, and pensioners probably on the hunt for bargains. The sounds of laughter and conversation were mixed with the throbbing beat of a *taiko* ensemble, and the air was suffused with a dozen delicious smells: grilled seafood of every kind, roasting meat, fried noodles, coconut pancakes and custard and crepes.

It was Dox's kind of place, and on any other night he would have been enjoying it. But tonight, even beyond the ordinary operational edge, he couldn't shake the feeling that they were missing something. A miniature drone overhead. Or Dillon somehow having managed to think one move ahead of them.

Labee looked at him. "What is it?"

"Not sure. But something's bugging me. Let's duck into this store here."

It was one of the brick structures at the perimeter. They went inside and wandered toward the back, surrounded by cluttered collections of retro Japanese anime toys, stuffed animals, Hello Kitty dolls, and Little Bo-Peep dresses that walked a delicate line between adorable and fetishistic.

"Sometimes I can get paranoid about sniper hides," he told her. "Occupational hazard. Once you've been on the right end of a few thousand-yard kills, you start imagining being on the wrong end."

"You think Dillon's got a sniper rifle?"

"No, that ain't it. This isn't sniper terrain. And I don't think it would be favorable for one of his microdrones, either—the lighting sucks, the crowds are too dense, and the overall area's too big. But . . . I don't know. We're not making it any harder for him by sticking together, for one thing."

"You think we should split up?"

"Well, I hate to. Especially because the phones are off. At least for"—he checked his watch—"another fifteen minutes."

He paused and thought. The phones. The way Kanezaki was going to zero in on Sorm's and Dillon's. And he realized what had been nagging at him.

"Hey," he said. "You think old Dillon might have access to the kind of real-time cell-phone monitoring we're about to get from Kanezaki? I mean, he would, wouldn't he?"

She nodded. "Seems like a safe bet."

"Well, when we turn on our phones, then even if he hasn't managed to track them yet, won't some DIA geek-squad guy immediately focus on the phones that just came on in the middle of the Night Market?"

She nodded. "You're right."

"I mean, maybe I'm wrong. But if there's one thing I'm sure of about Dillon, it's that he is one smooth son of a bitch."

"But if we can't use the phones, how will Fallon tell us when Sorm tries to call Leekpai?"

Dox looked at his watch again. "Well, we'd need to get new ones. But I haven't seen any for sale here. And even if there were, it wouldn't solve our problem—a brand-new phone getting switched on in the middle of the market. Besides, we don't have time to activate a new phone."

A half dozen young girls wandered in, high-school or maybe college age. Dox watched them for a moment and was struck by inspiration. "Hang on," he said. "I believe I have identified a solution to our conundrum. It's not perfect. But it won't be what the bad guys are looking for, I'm sure of that."

He walked over to the girls. "Pardon me," he said. "I apologize for the intrusion. Do any of you speak English?"

One of the girls nodded and said in a heavy Thai accent, "I speak English."

"Wonderful! Young lady, I would like to buy two of your mobile phones."

"I'm sorry?"

He wondered whether she spoke as well as she had claimed. Or maybe it was just the nature of what he'd said that had thrown her.

"I understand my request is unusual. But I badly need two phones tonight, and I'm happy to pay for the opportunity." He pulled out a roll of bills. "How about five hundred dollars per phone?" He counted out ten Benjamins. "Or, hell, make it six hundred. I don't have time to haggle." He counted out two more.

The girl looked at her friends, then back to him. "You're serious?"

"Very serious, yes. And here's another two hundred to prove it. Seven hundred per phone." He pulled out another two bills.

The girl consulted with her friends again. They spoke among themselves, increasingly excitedly. Then several of them frantically dug into their purses. One pulled out a phone, followed a moment later by her friend.

"I'm sorry, ladies, I believe we have two winners." He took the phones and handed the girls seven hundred apiece. He looked at the units—both older-model iPhones. A good bargain for everyone.

"Say, these aren't passcode protected, are they?" Before the translator could interpret, the girls had taken back the phones, unlocked them, and turned off the passcode protection. He looked and saw they were deleting all their texts, which he could understand they might not want a stranger to read. Not that he'd have any interest, or could decipher the Thai anyway. They handed the phones back and he switched the language on each unit to English.

He offered them each a *wai*, the phones sandwiched between his palms. "Thank you, ladies. And I hope you won't think I'm exaggerating when I say you might just have saved my life."

The two girls both exclaimed "Thank you!" in English. Then they all ran off, probably to buy all sorts of Night Market goodies they hadn't thought they could afford.

Barry Eisler

"That was nicely done," Labee said. "I once bought a truck the same way."

He handed her one of the units. They checked the phone numbers, called each other to confirm, and headed back to the entrance. Dox looked out at the sky again. He still didn't like it.

"You know what? Let's stay put for the moment. I have an idea."

He downloaded Signal to the girl's phone, then used it to call Kanezaki. After the exchange of IDs, he said, "How we doing over there?"

"Nothing yet."

"Well, here's the deal. I have a new phone I'll be using. Obviously Signal's working fine now, but let me give you the number in case I'm out of Wi-Fi range and you need to call me directly." He read Kanezaki the number.

Kanezaki said, "What's this about?"

"Just being careful, that's all. You won't be able to use the old number anymore. Reach me at this one."

He clicked off again. "Come on," he said. They headed out, and within a minute had found a pushcart vendor selling fried insects. He took out the burner he'd been using and powered it up. Labee obviously knew what he had in mind. Without saying a word, she did the same, handed him the phone, and started ordering various fried insects from the old woman pushing the cart. While the two of them were engaged, Dox knelt as though to adjust his hiking sandals and slipped the old phones into a box on a shelf at the bottom of the cart. When he stood, Labee was holding two bags of fried insects. The old woman gave them each a *wai* and moved off.

Dox watched her go. "You don't think Dillon would hurt her, do you?"

Labee shook her head. "Even if someone tracks the phones, they'll see her and instantly realize what we did."

270

"I hope you're right. I've got enough things I'm going to burn in hell for." He upended the bag and poured a bunch of whatever was inside it into his mouth. "Dang, them's good eating."

Labee handed her his.

"You don't like insects?" he said.

There was a pause. "When I was a girl, sometimes . . . that's all I could find to eat."

He suddenly felt like shit. "I'm sorry, Labee. I didn't—"

"It's fine. Just not a good association." She gave him a small smile. "Not as bad as the port, though. So you don't have to worry about my throwing up."

He liked that she was joking with him. He wasn't sure if it was a sign of increasing comfort, or dealing with the stress of an op. Probably both.

He checked his watch. "Nine o'clock. Time to let Fallon know we've got new phones." He took out Fallon's card, input the number, and waited while the call went through.

"Hello?" came the familiar gravelly voice.

"It's me. Got a new phone."

"Good timing, too. Guess who just called."

He looked at Labee and nodded. "Sorm?"

"You bet. I didn't pick up. I texted back that I couldn't talk, and asked him, 'What time?' It was oblique for communication-security purposes, and also exactly what he would have expected Leekpai to ask, given that they'd already agreed on the place. He texted back right away. Ten o'clock sharp."

Dox felt a nice little hit of adrenaline snake out through his gut. "Outstanding. Sir, when this is done, I am buying you that Singha beer. Though I myself, you'll be unsurprised to learn, will again be drinking Chang."

"Well, you won't be the only friend of mine who's also a philistine. I'm going to stay in the area in case you need me. Just south of where the meeting is supposed to go down."

271

"Appreciate that. Hopefully everything will go smoothly, but it's good to know there's backup if we need it."

He clicked off. "You heard, right?"

Labee nodded. "Ten o'clock. Now all we need is—"

Dox's phone buzzed. Signal. He answered.

"I got him," Kanezaki said.

Dox nodded to Labee. "Tell me."

"First, that number you told me might be Sorm's—it came on five minutes ago. The parking lot west of the market. It made a call and received a text back."

"I know about that one. Anything else?"

"Yes. As predicted, two brand-new burners, both activated at virtually the same time. The first from the same position as the call from the parking lot."

"Sorm."

"Yes. The second from right in the middle of the market."

"Dillon."

"Yes."

Damn, that wasn't much more than fifty yards from where they were standing. They were lucky they hadn't just run into the guy. Or unlucky.

"Are they moving?"

"I don't know. The phones are already off. But I was able to get a machine-text translation of the call."

Dox grinned. "I meant it that time I called you a miracle worker."

"Dillon wanted to know where Sorm was. Sorm was being cagey. He told Dillon to go to a place called Soul Garage in the northwest corner of the market. Do you know what that is?"

Dox had practically memorized everything he'd seen and learned online. "I know exactly what it is. A custom and vintage motor-scooter place in one of the market's quieter sections."

"Dillon was clearly trying to draw Sorm out, asking Sorm if he was already there. Sorm said not yet. 'Just wait for me in front.' I don't think Dillon was happy. He was expecting Sorm to be in position. Then you could drop Sorm, and he could drop you. Now he's the one who's going to be a sitting duck."

"I doubt Dillon would let that happen. But yes, most likely he'll be heading in that direction. Call me if anything changes. I'm going after him."

He clicked off, his blood up now at the prospect of how close Dillon was, and how close he was to killing the man. "Dillon's likely heading toward Soul Garage from south of us. Sorm, I don't know. He might be heading there from the parking lot on the west side of the market. But he wants Dillon to be there first, so it's possible he's going to check on the truck beforehand."

"We should go for Dillon first. He's—"

"Listen. You go to the truck. Sorm might be heading there now. That'll give you a shot at Sorm while I go after Dillon. From the timing of their conversation, I expect I'm already behind him. But if I hurry, I can pick him up."

"I don't want to—"

"No, Labee. You can ride in front anytime you like. But tonight, I'm taking on Dillon. He killed the Dalai Lama. You can have Sorm. That's the deal. Take it or leave it."

He hadn't meant to be so harsh. But this was not the time to fuck around.

She looked at him. "I thought we were partners."

Damn it, she looked so hurt it might have killed him. But he couldn't afford the distraction. "We are partners. With two separate jobs to do. Go to the damn truck. If Sorm shows up, he's yours. If he doesn't, make your way to Soul Garage and that'll be your second chance. Now go on, git. There's no time."

He turned before her expression could change his mind and headed northwest across the market, his head swiveling as he moved. With all the people and tents and activity, it was about as bad a countersurveillance environment as imaginable, so Dillon would be having a hard time watching his back. The problem was, the same factors that would make it hard for Dillon to spot him were making it hard for him to find Dillon.

He cleared the tents and walked quickly up an avenue with long, low-slung brick buildings to either side, each with a half dozen stores selling anything anyone had ever invented that was vintage and kitsch. Unlike the antiques section on the opposite side of the market, it was shadowy over here, the only illumination coming from a few incandescent bulbs strung overhead and from inside the stores. And though both sides of the thoroughfare were lined with antique trucks and microbuses, the finer specimens—and the crowds they attracted—were all on the other side.

The street grew darker. There were no people here at all. He didn't like it.

He hugged the line of vehicles to his right, his eyes scanning the long, low rooftops, his hand around the grip of the Supergrade under his shirt.

Where are you, you son of a bitch. Where—

A soft voice came from eight feet behind him. "Don't move, Dox."

Dox froze. A huge hit of adrenaline mushroomed through his torso. Bastard had ghosted right up on him from between the parked trucks.

He didn't move his head but swept the area in front of him with his eyes. He saw nothing threatening. Or, unfortunately, useful.

"How you doing, Dillon?" He was surprised, and not displeased, that his voice sounded so calm.

"I'm fine. I want you to very slowly take your hand out from under your shirt. Your empty hand."

Dox complied.

"Good. Now where's the woman?"

"Ah, *'Cherchez la femme.'* A cliché maybe, but still, words to live by, if you ask me."

A second went by. Then there was a shock and an explosion of white behind his eyes. He staggered. For a second, he thought he'd been shot. But then he realized—Dillon had pistol-whipped him in the head.

"That's funny," Dillon said, from a distance again but not as far as the first time. Maybe six feet now, or five. "You want to hear something serious? There's lots more where that came from. Those three men in Pattaya were my best."

Dox felt blood trickling down his neck from what must have been a gash in his scalp. It didn't bother him. On the contrary, it was nice to have proof he was still alive. And besides, he'd been hit in the head more times than he could count, with fists, chairs, and on one memorable occasion with a rubber mallet, usually without much effect. He was hardheaded, figuratively, of course, but literally, too.

But Dillon didn't know that. He'd think the blow from the gun butt had caused more damage than it had. Plus the man was obviously taking Pattaya very personally. If Dox could enrage him further—and hell, Dox had enraged experts in his time, he knew no one who could do it better—he might be able to get Dillon to momentarily forget the rule that if you could touch it, you could take it, and get closer than he ought to for the satisfaction of inflicting more punishment.

A long shot, no doubt, but actually a pretty sunny alternative compared to the overall current range of options.

"I feel your pain," Dox said, putting a little grogginess into his tone and making sure to wobble as though the pistol-whipping had messed up his balance and coordination. "That sad moment when you realize your best just weren't good enough."

"I fought with those men, asshole," Dillon said. Closer now. Four feet at most. "Bled with them."

"Well, I don't mean to sound Pollyannaish here, but the good news I guess is that they're not bleeding anymore."

"Okay," Dillon said. At most three feet away now. "I'm going to ask you one more time. If you give me anything other than a straight answer, I'll put a bullet in your head. Now. Where. Is. The woman."

Damn, not as close as Dox had been hoping, but maybe close enough, and anyway he sensed this was the end of the line.

He relaxed—tension would slow him down and telegraph the move. He would just say whatever incongruous thing popped into his mind, hope it provided a second's distraction, and spin and go for the disarm. Probably it wouldn't work, but there was nothing complicated to consider. There just weren't any other options.

"Here's the thing about women—" he started to say.

Labee's voice cut him off. "If you even think about pulling that trigger, it'll be the second-to-last thing that goes through your brain."

Without an instant's worth of thought, Dox spun clockwise, bringing his right arm up and out, and snatched the gun straight out of Dillon's hand. Labee took a long step away, keeping her gun pointed at Dillon's back.

"Damn," Dox said. "Those disarms really work. Or can work, anyway. I'd always hoped never to have to try one." He glanced at the gun in wonder and saw a sweet little SIG P229.

Then he was flooded with a surge of relief so strong it actually made his knees buckle. "Hoo-boy," he said. "I'll tell you the truth. If you'd asked me a few seconds ago, I wouldn't have predicted I'd be standing here right now. Oh, Labee. Don't you ever again let me try to tell you what to do. In fact, I want you to start telling me."

Dillon looked at him. "I'm not here for the two of you, you dumb hick. I'm here for Sorm."

Dox laughed grimly. "Well, I expect that's half-true. The wrong half."

Labee stayed silent and steady. She knew Dillon was his. As Sorm was hers.

"What happened to you?" Dox said, keeping the SIG on Dillon. "Back in the day, you were a damn hero."

Dillon sighed, apparently realizing his last ruse was done. "The higher you go . . . the more different it looks."

"Yeah?" Labee said, apparently unable to contain herself. "How does selling children into sex slavery look from your exalted position? Because I could tell you a lot about how it looks from mine."

Dillon looked at Dox. "I don't suppose there's any way we might start over?"

He sounded more amused by the absurdity of the notion than hopeful about its possibility. Dox had to admire the man's cool.

"If there was," he said, "you blew it when you killed the Dalai Lama."

"The Dalai La—"

Dox stepped to the right so Labee would be off line in case the bullet went all the way through. And shot Dillon in the forehead.

Dillon's head jerked and a spasm went through his arms. His legs folded and he collapsed backward, hitting the pavement with a dull *thud*.

"Yeah," Dox said. "The Dalai Lama. That was for him, you son of a bitch. And I think he'd even have approved."

"Take his phone," Labee said. "Sorm."

Dox knelt and started going through Dillon's pockets. Dillon had been wearing cargo shorts like any good tourist, and it was a wonder Dox hadn't heard the man clanking when he'd snuck up from behind, because he was carrying two cell phones, one satellite phone, and one cell-phone tracker. Not to mention the SIG, two spare magazines, and a nice little Emerson CQC-10 folder that Dox immediately took as a trophy, a habit he had once tried to explain to Rain but that the man would never understand.

"You shouldn't have followed me," he said as he stripped Dillon of the gear. "Not that I'm ungrateful, lord knows, but your best shot at Sorm might have been at the truck. We better hope he's coming this way."

It was a good thing the bellyband had extra compartments and was expandable, because at this point he had enough gear to fill a damn backpack. He got out of his shirt, pulled off the bellyband, and started filling it. He glanced at Labee, who was scanning the area, her gun at low ready. "Hey, did you hear me?"

She paused her scanning and looked at him. "We stick together."

It was such a simple statement, and more a conclusion than an argument. But he found he had no response. So he just nodded and said, "All right, then."

Among Dillon's phones, only one of the mobiles was turned on, so that must have been the unit he was using to talk to Sorm. Dox kept that one out. By the time he was done filling the bellyband, he could tell it would be too much to run with. So he fixed it around his back and across a shoulder, then pulled the shirt on again, leaving it unbuttoned. A bit of a wild look, but the main thing was access to the Supergrade.

Wherever Sorm might be coming from, it seemed a safe bet he was still planning on meeting Dillon at Soul Garage, so they hurried in that direction. The avenue grew lighter again, but visitors were still sparse. At the far end was an open garage with black-and-white tiled flooring in front and a sign overhead reading *Soul Garage*. A half dozen vintage scooters were lined up in the street before it. In between, on the sidewalk, were a few tables and chairs occupied by a handful of people, drinking coffee and smoking cigarettes. It looked like Soul Garage was as much a club as it was a shop.

They slowed and ducked between a pair of antique fire trucks parked fifty feet down the avenue. Labee started scanning behind them. Dox put his back to hers and scanned the other way.

"See anything?" he asked.

"No."

Dillon's phone buzzed. Dox glanced at Labee. She nodded. He clicked the answer button and raised the phone to his head. "Yeah," he said, trying to imitate Dillon's smooth voice and Yankee accent and keeping his voice low as though trying not to be heard.

"Where are you?" The accent was weird—Southeast Asian, French, he couldn't tell.

"At Soul Garage. Where are you?"

"I'm looking at Soul Garage . . . who is this?"

Dead phone.

"Damn it," Dox said. "He made us. But he's close."

They looked around wildly. They saw nothing.

"He must have been across from it," Labee said. "If he's heading south toward the container, he's on the other side of those buildings. Come on!"

She pulled the Glock and took off running. Dox followed close behind, gripping the Supergrade. At the first break in the long buildings, she cut left, then right again. Thirty yards ahead were the tents and lights and crowds.

"Slow down," Dox said. "Slow down. This is how Dillon got me, I was moving too fast and didn't spot where he'd set up."

But she didn't listen. Damn, she was fast. He was having trouble keeping up.

At the edge of the tents and heading south was a short man in beige slacks and a white button-down shirt. The kind of outfit designed not to be noticed. The man had gray hair, was holding a cell phone to his head, and was moving about as quickly as possible without his speed becoming obvious.

"Slow down, damn it," Dox said, managing to catch up and grabbing Labee's arm. "I think that's him."

The man must have been psychic. Or just very lucky. Because at that instant, he glanced back. His eyes widened in recognition when he saw them and his mouth dropped open in fear. Then he turned and took off into the market.

Dox and Labee sprinted after him, Labee slightly ahead. Immediately Sorm was swallowed up by the crowds. But the course of his passage was clear: there were shouts, and people being shoved aside and knocked down. Someone screamed, and a food cart with several fryers on it went over, coating the sidewalk with boiling oil. Labee leaped over it but there were more obstructions ahead—Sorm was obviously throwing everything he could grab as he ran and it was working, dozens of people were on the ground or milling angrily in his wake and it was slowing them down a lot. An angry Thai man yelled something at Dox and tried to grab him as he passed. Someone else shoved him. He kept running, Labee pulling ahead, faster and more nimble than he was.

A thought blossomed in his mind, crystal clear amid all the confusion: *Why would this human-trafficking kingpin be alone?*

They'd been dumb not to consider it before. And now Labee was totally intent on Sorm. Tunnel vision.

Dox slowed and scanned. And saw a Thai man emerge from behind a stall, a gun coming up—

"Labee! Down!"

She crouched instantly. Dox put three rounds in the man's chest. The man staggered back. Labee hit him twice more. The man fell.

People screamed and scattered. Sorm kept running. Labee leaped after him. Dox followed—*Well, there go our well-intentioned attempts at subtlety, I guess*—keeping the Supergrade up in a two-handed grip at chin level, moving as quickly as he could while trying not to overlook another—

A second man popped out from behind a stall as Labee went past. He took aim at her back—

Dox put a round in the man's spine and kept galloping straight in, firing as he moved, hitting the man with multiple rounds. The man fell and Dox leaped right over him. He heard more shots and screams ahead and thought, *Oh no. Please no.*

He ran harder, not caring anymore if he missed someone, but he needn't have worried, the shots must have been Labee's because another man was lying crumpled on the pavement, the screaming people around him scattering.

Then they were through the crowds. He saw Sorm again, forty yards ahead, with Labee twenty yards behind him. A semi with a container attached was pulling out of the lot south of the golf course and already moving fast. Sorm ran past the front end to the other side and then disappeared as it overtook his position.

The truck accelerated more. Labee dashed out ahead of it. She took aim at the driver—

The driver must have panicked, because he hauled the wheel left. Labee fired. The truck went off the road. There was a drainage ditch alongside, and the left wheels went in. The truck shuddered, tilted—

The driver hauled the wheel right and kept the truck from going over. But he overcorrected, swerving toward the gas station now. The right wheels went into the ditch on the other side, this one deeper than the first, and the driver tried to correct again, but the left wheels were up in the air now, and the truck was tilting, falling, heading straight toward the gas pumps—

Dox saw Sorm again—running across the junkyard alongside the gas station. He must have gotten onto one of the running boards and then leaped clear as the truck started to go over.

The truck fell to its side, sheared straight through the pumps, and shuddered to a stop. The station lights all blew. For an instant, every-thing was pitch-dark. Then the ground beneath the container erupted in orange flame.

"Get the kids out!" Dox yelled. "I'm going after Sorm!"

31

Livia had been so intent on Sorm that for a second she ignored Carl and started taking off after the fleeing man. Then she remembered herself. And that little girl.

She sprinted to the truck. Burning gasoline was spreading fast, on the ground and along the exposed sides of the trailer. From inside, she could hear high, terrified screams.

She raced around to the back. It was already scorchingly hot. The only light was from the dancing flames, and amid all the moving shadows she couldn't see clearly. She looked for the handle—

And saw it was secured with a chain and padlock.

The screams from inside were louder now, even more terrified. She heard palms banging on the metal sides within. She whimpered in panic, fighting back a memory of having banged on the inside wall of the container as a child, trying to get someone, anyone, to hear and help, help her and Nason—

The flames had crept closer to the back of the truck. She looked around wildly. Ten yards behind her, on the other side of another drainage ditch, was the junkyard Carl had described in the van with Fallon and Leekpai. She raced over and looked for something, anything. She saw a long steel rod—maybe a disused locking mechanism from a container. She grabbed it, thankful for its heft and solidity, and tore back to the truck. The flames were all over the trailer now. The children were keening inside.

The driver pulled himself out one of the cab windows and leaped to the ground. He saw her, pulled a blade from under his shirt, and charged, screaming.

No time to access the Glock. She screamed back and stabbed the end of the bar straight at his face. He managed to weave past, but she snapped the end in with a flick of both wrists and caught him in the neck. It staggered him. She repeated the move, snapping the bar in harder, using more arm and hip action and catching him in the jaw this time. He fell to a knee. Before he could come up, she reversed her grip and swung the bar like a baseball bat, catching him above the ear and blasting him onto his side.

Keys. Where are the keys?

She took a step toward the driver, then balked. Maybe the keys were in one of his pockets. Maybe in a compartment inside the truck. Maybe they'd been thrown clear in the crash. Wherever they were, if her first guess wasn't right, it would be too late to try anything else.

She dashed to the back of the truck again and jammed one end of the bar into the chain, spun it to take up slack, and put all her weight on the other end. There was a groan of metal straining against metal. But then the end of the bar hit the ground and she was out of leverage.

She screamed in frustration, thinking *Keys, you should have tried to find the keys.* But it didn't matter—even if she'd chosen wrong, the bar was her only hope now. She went back to the door. The heat was becoming unbearable. She got the bar through the chain again, leaving more room this time, refusing to think about how hot the interior of the container must be now, or how much gas was right under the ground. The metal groaned and she thought it would break, but it didn't. Her weight wasn't enough.

She screamed again. The flames were everywhere now. It was hotter, so much hotter. She planted her feet in the door hinges and used the bar to walk herself up the side, like a slow-motion pole vaulter. The chain creaked and groaned but didn't give. Finally she was at the very top, upside down, her heels jammed in the side of the door, all the slack in the chain gone, all her weight on the bar and every strand of muscle in her thighs straining to shove the bar one more inch, just one more inch—

She was sobbing now. It wasn't going to work. Her skin was burning, she could smell her own singeing hair—

The chain snapped and flew free. She plummeted. The end of the bar caught her in the midsection and there was an explosion of nausea and pain. Then she slammed into the ground, the breath driven out of her.

She realized with horror that her shirt was on fire. She rolled, remembering the drainage ditch, somewhere close—

She went over the edge and splashed into the water. The shock cleared her mind. She leaped out and raced back to the truck. She grabbed the lever, barely even feeling the metal searing her palms, and pushed it high. The locking bars cleared their fasteners. She wrenched open the door and dozens of shrieking, crying children began stumbling out, practically trampling over each other in the extremity of their panic and streaming past her into the night. She tried to help them, dragging the fallen to their feet and pushing them along, searching face after terrified face by the light of the flames for that girl, that little girl, but not seeing her anywhere.

In seconds, the children were gone. Scattered. The container was empty.

She staggered back from the heat, holding her throbbing side, crying. She heard Carl's voice from her right: "Labee!"

She looked up and saw the big sniper coming toward her, dragging a struggling, staggering Sorm by the hair.

She moved back farther. Carl reached her and threw Sorm at her feet. Sorm looked at the fire and shrank back from the heat.

"You got the kids out?" Carl said.

She nodded, looking at Sorm, feeling the dragon unfold, the hate inside her hotter than the fire.

"I told you," Carl said. "He's yours. But those pumps could blow. And the cops will be here. Finish him and let's git."

She pulled the Glock from her shorts pocket and pointed it at Sorm's face. "Where is she?" she said.

He shook his head, obviously petrified. His eyes darted from the fire to the gun and back again.

"Where is she?" she screamed, flecks of spittle hitting him in the face. She put the muzzle of the Glock against his forehead. "Where is she? Where did you take her? Tell me! Tell me! Tell me where she is!"

Sorm trembled, his head shaking, mute with terror.

Carl put a hand on her arm. "She's not here, Labee. And he doesn't know. They're all the same to him. They're all the same."

She screamed again, this time incoherently, no words, just a cry of grief and rage and despair. She grabbed Sorm's hair and dragged him toward the truck. The heat was like a tangible thing, a throbbing, crawling force wrapping itself around her.

"Labee, no!" Carl shouted. "The pumps!"

She didn't listen. She barely heard him. She got to the back doors, picked up the chain, and wrapped it around Sorm's neck. His hands flew to his throat but she had already slipped the other end through one of the locking bars and hauled it hard, jerking him back against the truck. She wrapped the excess in a kind of hangman's noose, then around and around and around his neck again. Sorm's eyes bulged and he clawed uselessly at the links. His feet did a weird little tap dance on the ground.

A fresh rush of burning gasoline surged from under the pumps and raced toward them over the ground. She didn't care. She didn't care if she burned. As long as Sorm did.

And then a strong arm encircled her stomach and dragged her back. She screamed in pain—the pole had done something to her—and struggled. But the arm and the man behind it were implacable. Carl.

He kept moving her back. "Where is she?" she screamed again.

But Sorm was past hearing. The flames were all over his legs now, moving up his sides. The burning puddle was a pond now, a river, a lake, and Sorm was screaming at the center of it, his shirt on fire, his hair smoking, his skin melting, his mouth stretched wide in a rictus of perfect agony.

"Where is she?" Livia screamed again, but Carl kept moving, away from the truck, from the flames, from—

One of the pumps erupted. The truck was engulfed in a fireball, Sorm along with it. Carl threw her down and landed on top of her, covering her with his body. Pain erupted inside her. She shrieked.

There was another explosion. A third. Burning debris rained down around them. They were fifty feet away, but the air was hot as an oven.

Carl dragged her to her feet again. She staggered and he threw an arm around her waist and kept her going. She was distantly aware of him fumbling in a pocket. He took out a phone. "We're going to need that pickup after all," he was saying, his voice almost supernaturally calm as he half walked, half carried her. "And beaucoup quick."

Fallon. But the thought felt faraway, disconnected.

"Right, the explosions and smoke and fire, afraid so. Just follow the big orange flames and you'll run right into us."

A minute later, the white van screeched to a stop alongside them. Carl threw open the door, pulled her in, and slammed it shut behind them. Fallon was moving before the door was even closed.

"We need a doctor," she heard Carl say. He laid her down across the plank seat. "She's burned, and I think hurt inside, too." He looked in her eyes. "Labee, stay with me now. We're with old Fallon. I'll bet he can drive as well as you, or at least he'll try to. You're going to be all right."

She barely heard him. She couldn't stop crying. "Where is she?" she said again. "Where?"

Carl knelt alongside her and touched her cheek. "I don't know, darlin'. I don't know."

"I couldn't save her," she said, and her body convulsed with a sob. "I couldn't. Oh, God, I couldn't save her."

He stroked her singed hair. "You saved the others, darlin'. All of them. Every one." His voice cracked, then he went on. "And you're going to save more. I told you, I know everything about you I need to, and I know that."

The sobs took her then, pain and grief obliterating everything and carrying her away to the blackest, bleakest shores. She gripped his hand and pulled him in, and he put his arms around her, and she clutched him and sunk her face into his shoulder, and her body shook with the force of her tears, and he held her close and whispered her name, Labee, Labee, Labee, again and again and again.

And then the world went dark, and she was gone.

32

One week later, Livia was back in Seattle. People were horrified at her sunburn. Stupid, she acknowledged. She'd gotten carried away. The tropical sun was no joke. And a stupid tuk-tuk accident had left her with cracked ribs and a bruised liver. Nothing life-threatening. Just embarrassing, after all the shit she had survived as a cop.

Little came in from wherever to debrief her. They sat in the cafeteria again, Livia with her mineral water, Little with his coffee. He told her a war had erupted between Thai and Ukrainian trafficking gangs. She told him that was fine with her and she hoped they all killed each other.

"You know what?" he said. "So do I."

They sat for a moment, the silence weirdly comfortable. "Well?" he said. "Now that you've had a firsthand look and a chance to consider, what do you think of my offer?"

She sipped her mineral water. "I'll tell you, B. D. After ten days out there, I don't think there's that much for me to do."

"Yeah. It's almost like the job's already done."

She looked at him. Did he know? Or was he fishing?

He nodded. "Oh, yes," he said, and for a weird second it was as though he had read her mind and was responding to her thoughts. "I know."

She waited, unnerved.

"Vivavapit," he said. "Sakda. Sorm. And Juntasa and the senator before that. I know what you did, Livia."

She tried to keep a poker face, but could feel herself paling in fear and surprise.

He put a fist over his chest. "And from this father's heart—thank you."

She looked at him, still worried, but confused, too.

"I get it," he said. "You thought I was working some kind of angle. Well, I was. And I am. Just not what you think."

He took his wallet from inside a pants pocket and pulled a photo from it. Little, maybe ten years younger. With a beaming teenaged girl alongside him, her arms wrapped around his neck, the side of her face pressed against his. The Little in the photo couldn't have looked more happy. Or proud. She wondered absently why not a photo on his phone. And realized: he wanted something tangible.

"Presley," he said. "Because her mom was a fan. She's fifteen in the photo. Now, she's twenty-four. Or . . ." He shrugged helplessly, stopped, and looked away.

"Just a walk to the grocery store on a summer evening," he said. "Wanted to get some popcorn for a movie we were going to watch. *Ratatouille*. She liked animation. I still haven't watched it. I keep hoping"—his voice caught—"maybe we'll still see it together. You think we might?"

Livia looked at him, remembering that odd expression she'd noticed when they'd first talked about her women's self-defense class, suddenly understanding what it had meant. She felt a strange mixture of wariness . . . and empathy. "I don't know."

He shook his head. "No, of course not. No one knows. That's the worst part. Not knowing. Can you imagine what it's like to have the kind of resources I do . . . and still to not know? To find nothing? Not one. Single. Answer? It's like the phantom pain from an amputated soul."

She wished she didn't, but she knew that pain acutely. Right down to the metaphor.

"I'd end myself if I knew for sure she was gone," he went on. "That's the truth. I've wanted to for a long time." He looked at her, his eyes brimming. "But you can't. Because maybe that little girl is out there. And maybe she needs you. And you have to be here for her. You have to stay. You have to. No matter what."

Livia felt her own eyes filling up.

He took off his glasses and pinched the bridge of his nose. "Her mother found a way around that. Heroin. When she finally overdid it, I'm sure she told herself it was an accident. Maybe it even was. So now the vigil is mine alone. Mine, and maybe people like me. Because how many people, Livia, how many people could look you in the eye like I am right now and say, 'I know what you've been through'? 'What you're going through'? Well, I can. And I do."

They sat in silence after that. A couple of cops Livia knew came in but steered clear, probably sensing something in the atmosphere at the table.

Little told her more. He'd been looking for someone like Livia, someone motivated the way he was but younger, more capable, someone who knew the streets. Two months earlier, he had read about Senator Ezra Lone's death from a heart attack in a Bangkok hotel. Little had connections in Bangkok and dug deeper. The heart attack story began to sound like bullshit. He learned Ezra Lone was the brother of Fred Lone, which led him to Livia. He checked ICE records, and learned Livia happened to be in Thailand when Ezra Lone expired.

"The FBI flew a team out there to investigate, did you know that?" he asked.

She was suddenly wary again. She said nothing.

"Oh, yes. A lot of people know it wasn't a heart attack. What they don't know, and never will, is who did it. Because a certain federal law-enforcement expert on Thai crime groups and police corruption fed them false information that led them in unhelpful directions."

She looked at him. "And now I'm going to owe you for that?"

"You don't owe me anything. I owe you."

"Owe me? You used me."

"If I used you, it was by giving you everything you wanted most in the world."

"You could have —"

"No, Livia. You wouldn't have believed me. This was the only way. And if you hadn't wanted it, you would have walked away. Just like you can walk away now. I'll keep your secrets either way. I told you. I owe you."

She wondered if *owe you* meant *own you*. But somehow, it didn't feel that way.

"All I'm asking," he said, "is that you think about it. What we could do together. My intel. Your street smarts. Think of the people we could punish. And the children we could save."

"It's a lot."

"I know."

"I want to be left alone for a while. And however long 'a while' is, I need you to respect it."

He gave her the big, sunny smile, the one she'd sensed at that first meeting he used to lull people. "Tough to the end. And yes, I will respect it. And I'll always be hoping you'll call."

On her way back to her desk, Livia stopped by Strangeland's office. The lieutenant would have known Little was in the building, as she seemed to know about everything that mattered. Better to initiate that conversation than make Strangeland come to her.

Livia tapped on the door window and, when Strangeland looked up from the paperwork in front of her and nodded, went in. She closed the door behind her and stood.

"What did he want?" Strangeland asked.

Livia smiled, not remotely surprised. "He's still pitching me to be on his task force."

"What did you tell him?"

"I told him . . . it wasn't for me." But the truth was, she wasn't sure what she had told Little. Or what she wanted.

Strangeland nodded. "It's good you faced your demons, then."

"Yeah."

"Did you exorcise them?"

For a moment, she remembered her last days in Bangkok. Waking up in Fallon's apartment, Carl by her side, an IV in her arm. It turned out Fallon was a former marine corpsman, and a hell of a prepper. While she'd been out, he and Carl had thrown the Kawasaki in the back of the van, gotten her safe, and tended to her injuries.

She'd spent two days in bed. She slept a lot but wasn't idle. Between Little's files and new intel from Kanezaki, it was easy to track down the last two men who had been involved in her and Nason's kidnapping—the one who had been in the van, and the one who had whipped that little boy, Kai, in the field. And as much as she hated to ask for help, in her condition she knew she couldn't do it herself. So she asked Carl. He told her he'd see what might be done.

The next morning, he brought a canvas duffel to the bed and unzipped it. Inside was a sniper rifle. "Nothing better than having a man like Kanezaki in your debt," he said. "Who else could deliver something like an RPA Rangemaster .50 cal with a Schmidt & Bender PMII tactical scope, practically wrapped in a red bow? The man's a miracle worker, I've always said so."

Like the others, the men were both cops. They worked in the countryside, in Chang Rai. Carl had driven her out in one of Fallon's vans. He shot one from the top of an abandoned construction site. The other was from a slight rise in a rice paddy. Both were thousand-yard shots. It was a little bittersweet to let someone else pull the trigger. But she was glad she got to see his expression when he was behind a scope—relaxed and yet focused, as she had expected. And watching the men's heads explode through a pair of binoculars had offered some satisfaction, too.

She shook Fallon's hand when they said goodbye and thanked him. He waved it off. "I told you," he said. "I was getting bored. I should thank you. Come back sometime. We'll make some more trouble."

Carl drove her to the airport. They parked and both stood at the curb. A traffic cop waved that Carl should move on, and Carl waved back and yelled, "Yes, sir. On my way right now, and thank you."

He looked at the bag she'd placed on the ground. "You going to be all right with that?" he asked.

She looked at him and frowned. What she was carrying wasn't much more than a purse. With her ribs and the bruised liver Fallon had diagnosed, she couldn't handle a lot of weight. But still. "I think I'll manage," she said.

"Because if you're looking for a porter, you know I'm available."

She smiled at that. "You're a lot more than a porter."

"Well, I try."

She wanted to get the goodbye over with. But there was something she wanted to ask.

"Hey," she said. "What were you about to say, when Dillon had the drop on you? 'Here's the thing about women' . . . ?"

He laughed. "I was so scared I barely remember. But I think it was probably something like 'If I ever find the right one, I'm never going to let her go.'"

She was surprised at how much that hurt. "You'll find her, Carl."

He looked at her as though struggling for the right words. Then he said, "Labee? I think you are just beautiful. In every way."

He hugged her then. And she hugged him back.

"Livia?"

She shook her head. Strangeland was looking at her.

"LT?"

"Your demons. Did you exorcise them?"

"Sorry. Yeah. I think so."

Strangeland nodded slowly, presumably a little thrown by the way Livia had faded out for a second. "That's good. We need you here, Livia. Seattle needs you. A lot of scumbags to put away."

Livia nodded.

"Anyway. Glad you're back."

"Thanks, LT." She turned and left.

It was good to be back, she had to admit. She was tired, but that was to be expected. The main thing was, she'd faced her demons, as she'd told Strangeland. And killed them. They were all dead now.

33

Dox flew to New York. Kanezaki had told him about a memorial service at the UN. For Vann.

It was a lot of important-looking people, and a few of them even made some okay speeches. But Dox got the feeling none of them had really known the man, or adequately appreciated him. They talked about his compassion, but he doubted they understood it. When the speeches were done, they'd go back to whatever they'd been doing and go on doing it just the same way.

Like you?

Well, that was fair. He'd have to think about it. He sure didn't want to wind up like those burnouts in Pattaya. He wished old Vann were around so they could talk about it. He'd really been hoping for that philosophical conversation.

After the service, he and Kanezaki took a stroll. The day was humid and gray and drizzling.

"I like walking with you under these umbrellas in New York," Dox said. "It satisfies my latent urge for more cloak and dagger in my life."

Kanezaki laughed. "I think you might get a little break from all that. If you like."

"How do you mean?"

"Dillon's death is being dealt with quietly. And with Sorm and his network wiped out, you don't have anyone else coming after you. At least not from that direction."

"Well, that's good to hear."

"On top of which, DIA is out of the human-trafficking business."

"For now, anyway."

Kanezaki nodded. "For now. With that much money in play, they'll try to get back in. And others, too."

"Maybe you can make that a little more difficult, what with the scales gone from your eyes and all."

Kanezaki gave him an enigmatic smile.

Dox frowned. "What?"

"Vann. He really was a good man."

"He was. How'd you know him, anyway?"

"He was a friend of my father's."

"Sounds like there's a story there."

"Maybe for another time."

"You knew him well, then."

This time, Kanezaki's smile was more knowing than enigmatic. "Yes."

Dox stopped. "Hey, man, what are you not telling me that's making you look so smug?"

Kanezaki didn't answer. He just kept smiling, though there was some sadness in his eyes, as well.

All at once, Dox realized. "You were working with him. That's why you wouldn't let me kill Sorm at first. Not because he was a DIA asset. You could give a shit about that. You wouldn't let me because Vann wanted him alive and behind bars."

Kanezaki nodded. "I actually thought you were going to figure it out sooner."

"Now you're just being mean."

"Maybe a little. But in fairness, there was a hell of a lot going on. I guess you could use that as an excuse."

Dox laughed. "Thanks. I appreciate that. I'm glad to know you were helping him, even if I should've seen it sooner. Really glad. But how?"

"Where do you think Vann was getting the intel on Sorm that led to the indictment in the first place?"

Dox grinned and clapped him on the shoulder. "Well, Kanezaki, you wily bastard, you. I really should have known."

"I'm glad you didn't. If you could have spotted it, it would mean others might have, also. And actually, I almost wish they had. It might have drawn some of the heat from Vann. Maybe they wouldn't have gone after him. Or I could have—"

"That wasn't your fault, son. I tried to warn him myself."

Kanezaki nodded. "Well, we'll never really know. And we'll always have to live with the doubt. But yeah. I gave Vann everything the CIA ever had on Sorm. It was a lot. Do me a favor—don't tell L. the specifics. Though maybe you could just mention to her that not all of us in the community get in bed with the Sorms of the world. Some of us are trying to stop them. Even if we have to break a few community rules along the way to do it."

It was polite of Kanezaki to still call her L. Labee had told Dox who she really was, and he knew Kanezaki must have tracked down Seattle PD sex-crimes detective Livia Lone. But only Dox would know her as Labee.

"I'll tell you, son, this is a dirty business we're in and that's never going to change. But I'm damn proud to know one of the few truly good guys."

"Back at you."

They started strolling again. "I really am sorry for doubting you after the late unpleasantness in Pattaya," Dox said.

"I'm sorry for being so gullible about Dillon's bullshit that I almost got you killed."

"It was an honest mistake. And it all worked out in the end. I shouldn't have been so hard on you."

Kanezaki stopped. "You want to make it up to me?"

"I knew I shouldn't have said anything."

"I have something new for you."

Dox laughed. "Partner, I am taking a vacation. Don't call me, I'll call you."

"Don't make me wait too long. I don't know that many people I trust."

Dox smiled and held out his hand. "Now that you mention it, I only know a few myself."

34

There was so much to catch up on at headquarters that Livia didn't get back to her loft until after dark. She took her shower, but cool this time rather than scalding. Her skin was still too raw.

She sat at her desk and caught up on paperwork while eating some rice-and-vegetable takeout she'd brought in. Between the shower, the meal, and the jet lag, she was suddenly exhausted.

She walked over to the shrine, knelt, and lit the candle and the incense. She remained still for a while. Then she said in Lahu, "I met a good man, Nason. A really good man. He helped me. He's . . . a friend."

Her eyes filled and she paused, then added, "I tried to save you, little bird. I tried so, so hard."

She sobbed for a long time after that, just letting it pass through her, knowing eventually it would.

When it was done, she caught her breath and said, "I killed them, little bird. All of them. Square Head. Dirty Beard. The two other men who helped them. And a man called Sorm, who was behind the whole thing and so many others like it. They're all gone now. Dead. All the men who hurt us. They're dead. They'll never hurt anyone again. It's done. It's over."

She was so exhausted. Empty. She had to sleep. Yes, just sleep. Sleep.

She wiped her eyes and blew out the candle.

And in that darkness, knew the truth.

It wasn't over. It wasn't.

And no matter what she did, it never would be.

AUTHOR'S NOTE

I made a few changes in the surroundings of the Srinakarin Rot Fai Night Market, chiefly placing a gas station and junkyard in the empty lot south of Sanam Golf Alley. Otherwise, the locations in this book are depicted, as always, as I found them.

NOTES

CHAPTER 1

Livia's thoughts on how if you walk up and say a person's full name three times, that person can't help but smile are, if I remember correctly, from Dale Carnegie's *How to Win Friends and Influence People*. In my experience, Carnegie was right.

CHAPTER 3

For more on the concept of "forced teaming," I recommend Gavin de Becker's *The Gift of Fear*.
    https://en.wikipedia.org/wiki/The_Gift_of_Fear

"The answer is always no if you don't ask" is wisdom courtesy of Madeline Duva.

CHAPTER 9

"Work is love made visible" is from a poem by Kahlil Gibran.
    http://www.katsandogz.com/onwork.html

It's possible Livia's use of a cell-phone tracking device in Thailand wouldn't be technically feasible. It's hard to know, because Harris Corporation insists on draconian confidentiality agreements with the law-enforcement agencies that purchase its cell-phone monitoring products. Regardless, if it's not feasible today, it will be tomorrow.

https://theintercept.com/2016/03/31/maryland-appellate-court-rebukes-police-for-concealing-use-of-stingrays/

http://arstechnica.com/tech-policy/2013/09/meet-the-machines-that-steal-your-phones-data/1/

CHAPTER 11

Livia is right to be concerned about Agent Little monitoring her cell phone:

"Cellphone Data Spying: It's Not Just the NSA" https://www.usatoday.com/story/news/nation/2013/12/08/cellphone-data-spying-nsa-police/3902809/

"This Is How Often Your Phone Company Hands Data Over to Law Enforcement" https://www.forbes.com/sites/kashmirhill/2013/12/10/this-is-how-often-your-phone-company-hands-data-over-to-law-enforcement

"The Problem with Mobile Phones" https://ssd.eff.org/en/module/problem-mobile-phones

CHAPTER 12

I stumbled across the airplane graveyard on a wonderful website called Renegade Travels. The Penis Shrine and Chinese Cemetery were also tempting locations, but in the end the airplanes won out.

https://www.renegadetravels.com/abandoned-747-airplane-bangkok-suburb/

CHAPTER 13

Beating thermal imaging is hard but not impossible, and I'm grateful to two former marines, David Rosa and Luisito Sugatan, for showing Livia how (though I won't deny, a bit of luck was with her, as well).

http://www.askaprepper.com/how-to-hide-from-thermal-vision/

https://www.oathkeepers.org/defeating-drones-how-to-build-a-thermal-evasion-suit/

CHAPTER 14

Integrated image intensification and infrared isn't widespread, but it's coming.

http://www.foxnews.com/tech/2015/05/05/high-tech-military-goggles-combine-night-vision-thermal-imaging.html

CHAPTER 16

A bit about the Naval Special Warfare Cold Weather Detachment training on Kodiak Island, Alaska, that Dox mentions. You can see why he was so fond of it.

https://gizmodo.com/how-the-navy-seals-prepare-for-extreme-cold-weather-sur-1737644998

CHAPTER 26

Everything you wanted to know but were afraid to ask about optical phased-array receivers and the coming micro-miniaturization of cameras.

https://www.economist.com/news/science-and-technology/21724796-future-photography-flat-cameras-are-about-get-lot-smaller

CHAPTER 29

If you think CIA complicity in drug trafficking is a conspiracy theory, this History Channel documentary will be eye opening.

https://theintercept.com/2017/06/18/the-history-channel-is-finally-telling-the-stunning-secret-story-of-the-war-on-drugs/

And don't miss this Jeremy Scahill interview with historian Alfred McCoy, author of *The Politics of Heroin: CIA Complicity in the Global Drug Trade*.

https://theintercept.com/2017/07/22/donald-trump-and-the-coming-fall-of-american-empire/

The UN's International Labour Organization estimates that human trafficking generates $150 billion a year globally.

http://www.ilo.org/global/about-the-ilo/newsroom/news/WCMS_243201/lang--en/index.htm

306

ACKNOWLEDGMENTS

Thanks to Bill Moore, a.k.a. Bmaz, of Emptywheel, for background on grand juries and related matters.

Thanks to Randy Sutton for always answering my cop questions.

Thanks to Richard Lee and Christian Montiel of J&M Motorsports for taking the time to answer my embarrassingly remedial questions about how you can tell when someone is competent on a motorcycle.

To the extent I get violence right in my fiction, I have many great instructors to thank, including Massad Ayoob, Tony Blauer, Wim Demeere, Dave Grossman, Tim Larkin, Marc MacYoung, Rory Miller, and Peyton Quinn. I highly recommend their superb books and courses for anyone who wants to be safer in the world, or just to create more realistic violence on the page:

> http://www.massadayoobgroup.com
> https://blauerspear.com
> http://www.wimsblog.com

http://www.killology.com
http://www.targetfocustraining.com
https://www.nononsenseselfdefense.com
http://www.chirontraining.com
http://moderncombatandsurvival.com/author/
peyton-quinn/

Thanks as always to the extraordinarily eclectic group of "foodies with a violence problem" who hang out at Marc "Animal" MacYoung and Dianna Gordon MacYoung's No Nonsense Self-Defense, for good humor, good fellowship, and a ton of insights, particularly regarding the real costs of violence.

Thanks to Naomi Andrews, Jacque Ben-Zekry, Wim Demeere, Gracie Doyle, Alan Eisler, Emma Eisler, Meredith Jacobson, Mike Killman, Phyllis DeBlanche, Lori Kupfer, Dan Levin, Maya Levin, Genevieve Nine, Laura Rennert, and Ted Schlein for helpful comments on the manuscript. Special thanks to Mike Killman for never letting me get lazy about creating action scenes that are both dramatic and tactically correct, and for his fascinating, discursive editorial comments generally.

Most of all, thanks to my wife and literary agent, Laura Rennert, for being such an amazing daily collaborator and otherwise doing so much to make these books better in every way. For anyone else grateful about how much faster I've been able to write the last four books (with *The Night Trade* completed just six months after *Zero Sum*!), Laura's the one we owe it to. Thanks, babe, for everything.

ABOUT THE AUTHOR

Photo © 2007 Naomi Brookner

Barry Eisler spent three years in a covert position with the CIA's Directorate of Operations, then worked as a technology lawyer and startup executive in Silicon Valley and Japan, earning his black belt at the Kodokan Judo Institute along the way. Eisler's bestselling thrillers have won the Barry Award and the Gumshoe Award for Best Thriller, have been included in numerous "Best of" lists, have been translated into nearly twenty languages, and include the #1 bestseller *The Detachment*. Eisler lives in the San Francisco Bay Area and, when he's not writing novels, blogs about torture, civil liberties, and the rule of law. Learn more at www.barryeisler.com.